TOO LATE

Cassidy and Goose Pony formed a team on one side of the back door while Sergeant Bodine and Commo Sergeant Edwards had the other side of the door. Lying next to the outer walls, as close as they could get to them, a team could not be seen by terrorists unless a tango came outside to look, which none had seemed inclined to do so far.

Now it was time to wait for the signal. Major Russell had chosen to strike at dawn. To Cassidy Kragle on the ground hugging the back outer wall with Goose Pony, it seemed daylight would never come. The longer they maintained a position, the greater chance they had of being discovered.

Daylight gradually seeped over the Tindouf Airport. Buzzards appeared and slowly circled the decaying corpses on the tarmac. Cassidy fingered the trigger and safety of his MP-5 submachine gun. It was almost time.

Then, suddenly, a burst of gunfire erupted—from inside the terminal. Goose Pony gasped.

"God Almighty" he hissed. "They're killing the hostages."

Books by Charles W. Sasser

DETACHMENT DELTA: OPERATION ACES WILD
DETACHMENT DELTA: OPERATION DEEP STEEL
DETACHMENT DELTA: OPERATION IRON WEED
DETACHMENT DELTA: PUNITIVE STRIKE

DETACHMENT DELTA

OPERATION ACES WILD

CHARLES W. SASSER

AVON BOOKS

An Imprint of HarperCollins*Publishers*

AVON BOOKS
An Imprint of HarperCollins*Publishers*
10 East 53rd Street
New York, New York 10022-5299

Copyright © 2005 by Bill Fawcett & Associates
ISBN 0-06-059220-6
www.avonbooks.com

First Avon Books paperback printing: January 2005

Avon Trademark Reg. U.S. Pat. Off. and in Other Countries, Marca Registrada, Hecho en U.S.A.
HarperCollins® is a registered trademark of HarperCollins Publishers Inc.

Printed in the U.S.A.

10 9 8 7 6 5 4 3 2 1

This book is for my son
David Charles–Hemingway Sasser

CHAPTER 1

Fort Bragg, North Carolina

Major Brandon Kragle, tall and broad-shouldered, a striking example of health and Army Special Forces conditioning, stood spread-legged in the center of what appeared to be an ordinary living room—a new sofa, television set, lamps, end tables, coffee table, clean carpet, framed photos on the wall. Appearances weren't always reality. The living room was actually one of four such rooms at the Shooting House, also called the House of Horrors, on the U.S. Army Delta Force compound at Fort Bragg, North Carolina.

Five sergeants preparing to enter the CQB (close quarter battle) phase of Delta Force training were positioned about the dimly lighted room among life-sized paper human targets and real-looking mannequins in natural "terrorist" poses. One mannequin crouched behind a student, its hand on the soldier's neck, the other hand pointing a pistol at the door. A second "tango," as terrorists were called, stood on his other side brandishing a stubby Uzi submachine gun.

"We're not peacekeepers or nation builders," Major Kragle barked. "We're the only unit in the military that remains on a constant war footing. We don't take prisoners in this business. It's serious business, and you have to kill and be damned good at it."

The major's tough, determined demeanor, indeed

everything about him, suggested a thorough professional. Thick mustache, cropped dark hair, and weathered skin gave him a craggy outdoors look. In a previous incarnation he might have been an Indian fighter or mountain man. Striking gray eyes swept a hard gaze over the five sergeant trainees. If they passed this final shooting phase, they became full probationary members of the U.S. Army's 1st Special Forces Operational Detachment-Delta. Delta Force: the nation's crack counterterrorist unit.

The door crashed open and three other fit-looking armed troopers in jeans and T-shirts or sports shirts burst into the room. One of the students flinched. Major Kragle introduced the three as members of Troop One, of which he was commanding officer.

Staff Sergeant "Ice Man" Thompson, Troop One's weapons expert, was an average-looking man in his thirties with prominent scars on his left cheek, souvenirs obtained on clandestine missions into Afghanistan and the Philippines. In addition to being a master of both foreign and domestic weapons, he was a gourmet cook and former world title middleweight kickboxing champion. He was the kind of guy no one laughed at if he were caught in the kitchen wearing an apron. He carried an Uzi submachine gun.

Sergeant "Mad Dog" Carson was a communications guru. Outward appearances marked him as a real knuckle dragger, not exceptionally tall but with shoulders so broad he almost had to turn sideways to get through a door, arms as thick and as long as fence posts, upon whose ends were attached hands the size of a gorilla's. Long, dark hair curled up around his neck from out of a slogan T-shirt that read *KILL 'EM ALL, LET GOD SORT 'EM OUT*. Dark eyes filled with surprising intelligence and cunning glared at the new meat.

"Fu-uck," he said, forming two syllables out of the word and thus amplifying its obscenity. "They look like a bunch of pussies to me."

None of the five dared contradict him. He wore a holstered 9mm pistol.

Sergeant First Class "Gloomy" Davis's most striking feature was his pale blue eyes, as cold and sharp as glacier ice. He was a wiry little man with great drooping blond mustaches and a web of laugh lines at the outer corners of his eyes that softened his appearance, if only a little. Underneath his black T-shirt inscribed with *LOVE A HOOKER HOGETTE* he wore a single bullet on a chain. The "hog's tooth" identified him as a trained sniper. He carried a stubby MP-40 submachine gun.

One of the students tried to be funny and ease the tension. "Doesn't anyone in Delta have *real* first names?" he asked.

Major Kragle shot him a look that would have withered poison ivy, then ignored him.

"We're not cops," he continued. "We don't capture tangos and send them to prison so their asshole buddies can take more hostages to negotiate for their release. But if they want to be martyrs and go see Allah and his virgins, we're here to send them on their way. We drop them where they stand."

He paused to let his words sink in.

"In this scenario," he said, "*you* five men are hostages held by terrorists in this room. You are women and old men and five-year-old kids. In a few minutes you are going to be rescued and these tangos are going to be dead."

The sound of increased breathing filled the room. Major Kragle rewarded the trainees with an icy grin.

"Don't worry," he added, "we haven't shot a student all

week. It would ruin my whole day if I had to explain to Colonel Buck, my boss, how we busted in and shot up a bunch of people we're supposed to be rescuing."

A cautious hand went up. "Sir? Are you using live ammunition?"

"You betch-um, Red Ryder."

He placed a handheld radio on the coffee table.

"Listen carefully when the radio comes on," he directed. "Watch closely."

He and the three enlisted men abruptly left, closing the door behind them. The trainees remained still and eerily intent, not knowing what to expect.

After a moment, the radio crackled to sudden life. *"Stand   by . . . Five . . . four . . . three . . . two . . . Execute! Execute! Execute!"*

An immediate blast blew the door open and filled the room with smoke. The four-man assault team, which had stood so calmly in this room only minutes before, exploded into action, hurling themselves through the door on the run, intent and deadly.

Major Kragle was the first man inside. He hurled a flash-bang grenade that detonated near the ceiling, inevitably drawing all eyes to it and away from the doorway. He turned right to the heavy side of the room where there were more people and therefore increased danger. He scuttled swiftly along the right wall, keeping his back to it, blasting away at targets with a 9mm Glock pistol. One of the bullets snapped past less than two inches from a trainee's cheek to knock the head off a mannequin crouching at his shoulder.

He turned at the corner and slid rapidly along that wall, knocking out even more targets scattered about the room among the five stunned students. He halted at the far corner and turned to face back into the room.

In the meantime, Gloomy Davis had also entered the room with his MP-40 and turned left, working that side of the room. He engaged targets on the far wall opposite the door. He turned at the first corner and halted to watch the left wall and the center.

While the terrorists' attention was distracted away from the door by the first two operators, the next two men—Ice Man and Mad Dog—burst in virtually unnoticed to opposite sides of the door. Ice Man took the heavy side of the room and engaged targets to assist Major Kragle, the number-one man. Mad Dog took the other side to aid the number-two man, Gloomy Davis.

Trainees found it impossible to keep an eye on so much movement in opposite directions, or even to discern who was who in the flurry of violent motion. The assault team dominated the room, owning everything and everyone in it. Not a square inch escaped observation and fire. It was all speed, surprise, and ferocity.

Fire splashed from muzzles of pistols and submachine guns. The slap of overpressure caused by bullets flying past heads and faces made the students want to disappear into the wallpaper or underneath the carpet. Yet, they couldn't move. They were stunned motionless, shocked into immobility as complete as that of the paper targets and mannequins. Their minds focused on one thing only—survival.

The crackle of gunfire ended as suddenly as it began. The team of shooters immediately returned to a calm, controlled state. Most men would have been visibly excited. Not these.

Smoke eddied. Every target had at least one bullet hole in its head. Some had two or three. No trainee was so much as scratched.

Someone finally found his voice. "Oh, Jesus!"

Major Kragle looked amused. "Did all of you see what happened?" he asked.

A student let out a pent-up breath. "Major, sir. What we saw was the door fly open and that damned grenade go off. After that, all we saw was a blur. You guys were on us like stink on hog shit."

"Not all over *you*, sergeant." Brandon waved his pistol at the terrorist targets. "All over *them*. That's the way it's supposed to happen. That's the way it's *got* to happen."

He holstered his pistol.

"In six weeks' time," he said, "your final exam will be to conduct a hostage takedown just like the one you've seen demonstrated. You will have live hostages, just like today. They will be your fellow students. Pass the test and you can consider it just another day of training. Fuck it up, shoot and kill a buddy—and you fail."

Sweat broke out on foreheads. Faces paled. Major Kragle gave them his dry smile.

"Welcome to the War on Terror," he said.

CHAPTER 2

Refugee Camp Smara, Algeria

Zorgon's wife Swelma and her sister Gebele prepared the evening meal. Soft colored scarves covered their dark hair, but the scarves were transparent enough not to mask lovely brown faces below eyes that reminded Chaplain Cameron Kragle of fierce deer. Their long flowing Arab robes, called *myflas*, seemed as ephemeral as the twilight they let into the room whenever they pushed aside the door curtains, coming and going barefooted and silent from the separate kitchen, producing platters of broiled camel and goat, vegetable plates, dates, and jugs of home-made fruit juices, and soup with rice to the delight of four Western guests who sat on pillows around the dinner rug.

Chaplain Cameron thought Sahrawi women seemed less subservient than most Muslim women. In fact, the women he had observed since arriving in the camps as escort for three female American missionaries often appeared to hold the real power. Perhaps it had something to do with the war that had left a shortage of men in the refugee camps of Algeria's Western Sahara.

Swelma glanced shyly at the visitors as she bent at the waist and whispered something in Arabic to her husband, interrupting him as he was about to tell a story about the Green March.

"Everything looks absolutely delicious," Rhoda Hoffstetter gushed. "I can hardly wait to try everything. Zorgon, ask your wife if she's sure we can't help."

Zorgon translated the request. Swelma smiled, shook her head, and floated out again on bare feet.

"She thank you for your generosity," Zorgon said in quite passable English, one of three tongues the little Sahrawi spoke. West Sahara, homeland of the Sahrawi, had been a Spanish colony before Spain left and Morocco invaded, sending thousands of the surviving Sahrawi fleeing to Algeria. "But she say dinner is almost serve. It is delay because there are strangers in the desert for two days now. She tell me now that more are seen. There is much gossip when strangers come."

"*We* are strangers," Rhoda pointed out, concerned.

Rhoda Hoffstetter, president of Reach the Children Inc., a nondenominational Christian charity mission that collected and distributed shipping containers of clothing, school supplies, and other provender for children and their families all over the Middle East and North Africa, was a small, plump woman in her late fifties, with yellow cropped hair and a round earnest face. She had a disconcerting habit of diddle-doodling her head, bobbing it eagerly up and down like a bobble head in the back window of an SUV filled with kids.

"There are others as well," Zorgon said as he continued his tea brewing ritual. "We think they must be Algerians. Sometimes they come and bring others to inspect the camps, but not often. Sahrawi are not too much liked in Algeria. If not for the United Nations and our other friends, we would be cast to wander in wilderness. Like Moses."

He prepared boiling green tea in the faltering yellow light of an oil lamp. His face was dark and sharp and gaunt from a hard desert life, but his black eyes twinkled merrily, and he was prone to break into chuckles at the least provocation. He had lost one arm during the war and exodus from West Sahara, it having been blown off at the shoulder. As a replacement, he wore a makeshift arm consisting of an old bicycle inner tube stuffed with rags and sawdust, to the end of which he had appended a hard-molded rubber novelty hand with its middle digit extended in a gesture known universally as "the bird." The arm swung freely when he walked. It dragged on the carpet behind him as he scooted on his haunches nearer the teapot on its little brazier of coals.

In Spanish, he asked his son to bring in additional briquettes. The boy of about ten wore soiled khaki trousers that matched his father's, both pairs apparently gifts from benevolent Christian missionaries. He jumped up obediently and trotted out.

Zorgon resumed his tale about how, in 1975, when he was ten years old and Morocco invaded West Sahara, refugees fled east into the desert with what few treasures they could carry in packs, in donkey carts, on the backs of camels, or—for the more fortunate—in vehicles. Zorgon's family walked for two months with the Green March. His grandmother starved to death on the way.

"One day I see Morocco airplanes bomb refugees as they walk through a pass. It seems very far away. But soon a truck comes by and there are many people in the back. They scream and cry and blood pours from the back of the truck and leaves a trail on the road which the flies swarm. I am terrified and we run and we run, but to what? The airplanes come and they bomb us too, my mother and my sister and all the others. That is when I lose my arm. It is only through God's grace that I survive. My mother carry me across the Algerian border to here, where refugees are building a camp. Then she dies from heartbreak, and I am left to live with an uncle."

He glanced up at his four guests—two older women, a tall, younger woman, and the even-taller military-looking chaplain with the buzz-cut blond hair and striking blue eyes.

"Rhoda, do not worry," he said. "I have talk to Malud on the telephone at Protocol."

Chadli Malud was the elected governor of the Sahrawi camps, as well as their delegate to the United States and the UN.

"I thought Malud was gone from the camps and could do nothing to help," Rhoda said.

"He was in Washington, but he return today. He will meet with us tomorrow. He will discover why the containers for the children have not been deliver."

"Thank God, Zorgon. If they've been lost or . . . worse yet, *stolen* . . . Everything is for the children."

"Malud will take care of it, Rhoda," Zorgon reassured her.

Cameron Kragle had met Rhoda and her two companions only a week before after General Ray Holloman, commander of the Air Force Special Operations Command (AFSOC), called in a marker by asking Cameron's father, General Darren Kragle, for help in escorting a group of missionary women to Algeria, one of whom was his twenty-five-year-old niece. The Kragles owed Holloman too much to turn him down. He had put his neck and his career on the block more than once for them.

Cameron was the logical son to send. First of all, he was a chaplain, a man of God with Delta Force's support element at Fort Bragg. Second, older brother Brandon's

Troop One had recently extracted from Iraq to instruct new D-boys while it rested and refitted. Major Dare Russell's Troop Two, of which Cassidy Kragle, the younger brother, was an engineer sergeant and demolitions expert, was still in Baghdad. Most of Delta was receiving no leaves, no authorized absences, and was stuck at Fort Bragg until it was needed again—which in the present climate wouldn't be long.

That left Cameron. *Then I heard the voice of the Lord saying, Whom shall I send? And who will go for us? And I said, Here I am. Send me.*

Algeria, along with most of North Africa and the Middle East, was a terrorist hot spot. In addition to terrorist activity, the semi-dormant civil war in Algeria threatened to bust out again in response to the U.S. presence in Iraq. The U.S. State Department had issued travel warnings. Traveling just about anywhere in the world since the start of the War on Terror was risky business for Americans.

"That whole region is a kettle about to boil over," the General warned. Even his three sons called General Darren E. Kragle "the General." "Missionaries on a quest in God's name are indomitable and don't look at things rationally. They think it's God's will that they deliver the Word along with food and clothing to every misbegotten child in the world, even if they have to wade through their own blood to get there. Cameron, General Holloman trusts you to get his niece and her friends to Algeria and back safely. Let me warn you in advance. This girl's something of a cracker and a bit of an embarrassment to her uncle. Keep her out of trouble."

Cameron had liked Rhoda the instant they met. He was attracted to her earnestness and that inner glow of goodness and willingness to sacrifice her own needs and comforts to serve the Lord and God's little children.

Jean Marrs was a tougher, jollier version of Rhoda. Her short-cropped graying hair and broad, weather-beaten face made her appear to be about sixty. She was wide and tall with big rough hands acquired from decades spent in India and Sudan on medical missions. Her long plain dresses and lack of makeup reminded Cameron of the fundamentalist churches to which Gloria sometimes dragged the Kragle sons when they were boys.

Cameron hadn't known what to expect of Kelli Rule. About all he knew of her when he took the assignment was that she was a born-again Christian and a self-professed pacifist and peacenik. Twice she had been arrested while participating in Washington peace demonstrations protesting the Iraqi War. She had even shown up briefly in Baghdad prior to the war with a bunch of Give Peace a Chance idealists to offer herself as a "human shield" against American invaders.

He had half expected a shrill, humorless zealot from the self-righteous political Left who hated about everything American, and lined up, as the General put it, with a bunch of socialists and communists from the Ivy League colleges. He had been taken aback when this strapping, attractive young woman first sauntered up to him with her impish grin and a toss of her long brown hair. She had a firm grip.

"What else could any red-blooded chaplain ask for?" she said in the most charming Old South corn pone and sugar molasses voice. "Going to the desert with three wicked women of God. You're not Catholic, are you, bless your little pea-picking heart?"

She was almost six feet tall, he supposed, since the top of her head reached just past his cheekbone whenever they stood side by side. She was lanky and loose-jointed, well curved, with long brown hair left carelessly wild. He noticed immediately the brown eyes sparked with flecks of cat-green and the wide mouth that twisted up impishly at the corners. Her wonderful accent was pure antebellum South, Scarlett O'Hara South. As a Southerner, she had learned to get away with the most awful insults as long as they were accompanied by the words "Bless your heart."

"She's so bucktoothed she could eat an apple through a picket fence, bless her heart."

Or, "It's amazing that even though she had that baby only six months after they got married, bless her heart, it still weighed ten pounds."

Cameron still hadn't quite figured her out. Her ability to surprise and delight made the trip a pleasure so far, instead of a chore undertaken for an old family friend. Not that he expected anything romantic between them. It wasn't that he deliberately excluded women from his life. It was just that the hollow left in his heart by Gypsy Iryani's death in Afghanistan was so huge he didn't think any other woman could fill it. Sometimes he feared even God fell short of the task.

"Lawdy, Lawdy," Gloria often tsked-tsked. "One o' these days, honey-chile, you is going to run on some little girl and the whistles and the bells is gonna ring and chime and you is gonna *fall in love*."

Gloria, whom almost everyone called "Brown Sugar Doll" or "Brown Sugar Mama"—although her skin was far too dark to be termed brown—had taken over the Kragle household—no, she had dominated it—as housekeeper and surrogate mother for the General's three rambunctious boys after the boys' mother died giving birth to Cassidy. She had raised them more or less single-handedly, with generous mixtures of love from a heart bigger and warmer than Texas and scoldings from a finger that got to wagging the instant someone crossed her unsparing standards of right and wrong. She had stayed with the General long after "her sons" were grown and gone, until last year, when she had married Raymond.

"Did the whistles and bells chime for you and Raymond?" Cameron had teased, hugging the ample black woman, whose dyed-red hair wrapped inside an even redder kerchief lent her a remarkable and perhaps intended resemblance to Aunt Jemima. Growing up, the Kragle sons had thought her majestic, magnificent, beautiful, almost divine. She lived by her own rules, did as she wanted—which was always the *right* thing to do—and the world treated her with the awe and respect she deserved.

Gloria had chuckled—a rich, warm, motherly sound that had comforted Cameron since he was four years old. "Lawdy, chile. I be too old to hear bells and whistles. Well, maybe they was a whistle or two. But no bells a'chiming." She pushed him to arm's length and regarded him with a solemnity she alone possessed. "Baby, you is gonna have to let her go someday."

"I don't know what you're talking about, Sugar Doll."

"Hogwash! Gypsy is gone, chile, and no matter how much you grieves and misses her you ain't ever gonna see her again until we all get to heaven. In the meantime, we got to keep on living."

Cameron didn't want to go there again. He looked away. "I serve God and His church. It is enough."

"It *ain't* enough, honey-chile. Not when a man is thirty years old and all by hisself. I always figured Brandon for the bachelor of the fambly, not you. But here you is, still on the open range while Brandon done got hitched to the sweetest little girl from Texas you ever seen."

"Summer was born in Israel, Brown Sugar."

"That don't matter none. She grew up in Texas and that little baby of hers is gonna be half Texas—"

Her hand flew to her mouth and her eyes popped wide. Cameron looked sharply at her.

"Brown Sugar, you don't mean it—? Summer Marie?"

"Lawdy, me and my big mouf. Now don't you go talking none. Ain't nobody but me and her knows about it yet. She ain't even told Brandon."

Cameron shook his head. "Brandon's not going to like it. He's always said men in the military should never have kids. They grow up without a father at home."

"Don't you go ragging on the General now. He did the best he could and y'all turned out pretty good, even if I do take some credit for it."

She wagged her deadly scolding finger in his face. The boys always knew she meant business when the finger came out.

"When is she going to tell him, Sugar Mama? It's not something she can hide forever."

"That's up to her, chile, not you and me. So keep your mouf shut, hear?"

She chuckled.

"In two, three months, that little blond Summer is gonna be springing out all over and the whole world is gonna know."

Cameron now took another look at Kelli sitting crosslegged in the soft light on the other side of the Sahrawi dinner rug. It was hard to look at her and imagine whistles and bells ringing and chiming, even harder imagining her expecting a baby. Not that she wasn't attractive. She was pretty enough for any man, although she might be somewhat daunting to many, what with her stature, her forwardness, and her activism in the name of Almighty God.

She was trying to break into his reveries. He lifted his brows in a question mark. She grinned brightly and, using her eyes, directed his attention to a framed picture on the wall, a magazine cutout of a common recliner chair, the type in which American men liked to relax while they watched a game on TV and had a beer. Chairs were not normally a part of the Arab culture.

Kelli got up and moved around the rug with her pillow to sit between him and Jean.

"What do you suppose is with the chair?" she whispered.

He shrugged. She watched Zorgon making tea. "God bless his little camel-riding heart," she said.

Zorgon poured tea from glass to glass with his one remaining hand in a ritual that was almost religious among desert peoples and tribes. Dragging his inner-tube arm, he handed out tiny glasses of the sweet potent brew, passing them one by one to Rhoda, who distributed them around the dinner rug. Kelli wrinkled her nose.

"I thought it was green tea. It's *black*."

Jean laughed softly. "You'll get used to it, honey."

Kelli closed her eyes and muttered, "Thank you, Lord, for what we are about to partake." One eye opened to regard the fare on the rug. She added, "Whatever it is. Amen."

Zorgon sipped his tea. He used his one good hand to place his self-constructed prosthesis on his lap. It rested with the finger pointing lewdly at the others. Kelli giggled. Zorgon absently rearranged it to divert the finger.

His son reentered with more briquettes for the brazier. The boy seemed afraid. He bent and whispered into his father's ear. Zorgon motioned for him to be seated.

"Such is the fate of we Sahrawi that a small boy is frightened by lights he sees in the desert," Zorgon explained. "We cannot return to our homeland because Morocco is still there and our Polisario, our freedom fighters, have lost the war. Algeria does not want us. We are not allowed to leave the camps to work or travel. We are here now for almost thirty years without a homeland, unknown and unwanted by the rest of the world. We exist only through international charity."

He looked up from his tea, his thin face grim in the pale light. His black eyes no longer twinkled. He reached down and massaged a bare brown foot.

"One of our generation is now disappeared," he said, "and women run the camps because so many of our men die in fighting the Moroccans. Many of us are Christians because missionaries from the West come with food. We hang on by our thumbnails. If Islamics take control of the government in Algeria, which they keep try to do over and over, they will murder the Sahrawi. But what makes the difference whether we are slaughter by terrorists or merely die out with time?"

He sighed. "For a people without a home," he said, "there is nowhere to go."

His eyes wandered and stopped at the framed photo on the wall, latching onto it with the desperation and hope of a drowning man for something floating in the water.

"One day," he promised from his sadness, "I will own a chair."

CHAPTER 3

Washington, D.C.

A Marine officer of the guard escorted General Darren E.
Kragle, commander of the United States Special Opera-
tions Command (USSOCOM), and Director Claude
Thornton of the FBI's National Domestic Preparedness
Office to the War Situation Room in the basement of the
White House for a top secret meeting, the subject of
which had not been disclosed. The two men recognized
and acknowledged other officers and members of the
State and Defense departments, CIA, FBI, Homeland Security, and the military—Defense Secretary Donald Keating; General Abraham Morrison, chairman of the Joint
Chiefs of Staff; CENTCOM's General Paul Etheridge;
CIA Deputy Director Tom Hinds; National Security Director Condoleezza Rice; Director MacArthur Thornbrew
of the National Homeland Security Agency . . . Everyone
present, the General noted, was involved in either the War
on Terror, the Iraqi war, or both.

Hushed murmuring filled the room of sturdy
mahogany-paneled walls and a great polished table laden
with coffeepots and breakfast pastries, none of which
were French. Thornton poured two coffees and sat down
next to the General.

The FBI agent, now director of National Domestic Preparedness and the FBI's chief counterterrorist expert, was
a big, black, solidly-built man in his late forties, with a

shaved head the color and texture of a bowling ball. General Kragle and he had been close friends ever since the terrorist bombing attack against the USS *Randolph* in Aden harbor. Thornton at the time was the FBI's senior resident agent in Cairo, a man General Kragle grew to trust without question.

Thornton stirred cream into his coffee and leaned toward the General.

"During the Napoleonic wars," he said, "the French captured an English officer and took him to their headquarters for Napoleon to question. 'Why do you all wear red coats when they make easier targets for us to shoot at?' Napoleon asked him. The English officer explained that blood didn't show on the red coats and therefore wouldn't lead to panic."

General Kragle waited for him to go on. The General was an exceptionally tall and rugged-looking man in his late fifties with rows of service ribbons on his dress greens stretching all the way to the top of his shoulder. His lean face with its thick brush of a mustache looked permanently weathered, as though carved out of oak. Hair in a more-salt-than-pepper buzz cut looked as stiff as nails hammered into his skull. His was the face of a professional soldier in whom close brutal combat had put so many layers of callous that his soul stayed tightly bound within those layers, unable or unwilling to venture far outside its protective cover. Wars in the trenches and political wars in the capital had turned his gray eyes cynical and wary. Patience was never one of his virtues.

"Is that it, Claude?" he finally growled. "What's your point?"

Deadpan, Thornton said, "I was just explaining why the French have worn brown trousers ever since."

"Uh."

The agent shrugged. "That's what they teach my son at the Naval Academy."

"Have you considered homeschooling?"

It wasn't that the president of the United States was late for the meeting; everyone else was respectfully early. President Woodrow Tyler was always punctual, not the only way in which he was opposite his predecessor, John Stanton. In General Kragle's opinion, which he was never loathe to render, Stanton had been a man whose personal corruption rotted out the core of everything he touched, who trailed a plume of dishonesty like a skunk trailed odor. John Stanton was a soft man for a soft age, a man too weak, too self-absorbed and too ideological to recognize the terrorist alliance forming in the Muslim world and strike back. America's enemies concluded from Somalia, from the USS *Randolph*, from the first WTC bombing, from the African bombings of American embassies, from a steady decade-long campaign of terrorism against the United States that America would not fight back. And it hadn't, as long as John Stanton occupied the White House.

To both General Kragle and Claude Thornton, former president Stanton's kidnapping and death in the Philippines at the hands of the same terrorists he had tolerated for so long represented a form of poetic justice.

General Kragle's experiences with politicians had been largely negative; his confrontations with John Stanton had made him even more cynical. Government, he observed, was made up of many people with different and sometimes venal agendas. People who held high office wielded enormous power, often simply to further their own selfish ends. It was surprising how many would willingly sell their own souls in order to acquire power over others and to retain it.

Woodrow Tyler was the only president since Ronald Reagan called the Soviet Union "the Evil Empire" that the General felt comfortable in supporting as near unconditionally as his nature allowed him to. Tyler was not the ordinary run-of-the-mill pol. He was a real human being, a blunt, homespun Texan with a propensity for dry humor, wearing cowboy boots with his suits, and malapropisms—"It's time for the human race to enter the solar system"—but who seemed to have a firm, commonsense grasp on his leadership and upon himself. He assumed office at a period in history when the West needed a cowboy willing to shoot it out at high noon, kill the enemy and pursue the nation's interests, even when opposed by the "international community."

Although warning that defeating the terrorist enemy could take years, President Tyler recognized the short attention spans of his countrymen and how it would be used by his political enemies. He had called a similar meeting to today's before the commencement of hostilities against Iraq.

"Win this action," he admonished. "Win it quickly. The American people have short tolerance for war—a condition that the 'loyal opposition' will exploit."

Few trouble spots in the world were improving even now, when terrorists faced their first sustained and systematic global response. In fact, things seemed to be getting worse. The Middle East crackled with its everlasting problems. Kidnappings of Westerners were commonplace. Aircraft hijackings and suicide bombs were almost competitive sport. India and Pakistan hovered at a state of low-level conflict. Most of Asia from Korea out to the Rim careened from one problem to another, ranging from nuclear threat to terrorism by suicide. A new anti-Americanism and anti-Semitism was rising out of

Malaysia like a flute-entranced cobra. Africa remained a continent in torrid perpetual genocide. Battle lines zig-zagged around the world.

United States Special Operations Forces, especially Delta, were busier than ever hopping from one crisis to another to apply their special brand of counterterrorism. General Kragle was firmly convinced that the day the United States lost or abandoned the War on Terror was the day New York, Los Angeles, Houston, Chicago, and other American cities turned into Jerusalem, Jakarta, and Baghdad, under constant threat of terrorist bombings and attacks. To give up now would reward terrorists with exactly what they wanted, and would cost America dearly for years to come. It could even be the beginning of America's downfall.

Fallout from the war—paranoia, propaganda, and plotting—had eaten into the heart of American politics. It was a presidential election year in America, and President Tyler's political enemies were out on the trail in full cry attempting to bring down the administration any way they could. Constant carping and political cheap shots and dirty tricks abounded in a way that would have been unthinkable in earlier times, especially during wartime.

President Tyler was being portrayed as a warmonger and as a drooling idiot. Websites like *Tylerbodycount.com*, *Presidentmoron.com*, and *Toostupidtobepresident.com* depicted him in full Nazi regalia while wearing a little toothbrush mustache. Senator Lowell Rutherford Harris, who had emerged from the primaries as the Party of the People's presidential candidate, called for Tyler's impeachment and for all involved in planning the Iraqi War and the War on Terror to be brought up on criminal charges.

"In my first five seconds as the newly inaugurated president," he vowed, "I will fire MacArthur Thornbrew as director of the National Homeland Security Agency, I will fire CENTCOM's General Paul Etheridge, I will fire US-SOCOM's General Darren Kragle. I consider all these, along with the Joint Chiefs of Staff and the secretary of defense and secretary of state, to be criminally negligent in their conduct. This president is the greatest threat to the freedom and security of this globe that the world has ever known. It is up to peace-loving peoples everywhere to *bring him down*."

None of this went unnoticed by the nation's enemies. North Korea, one of the countries along with Iran and Iraq that President Tyler dubbed the "Axis of Evil," was producing nuclear weapons and selling them to international terrorist networks, daring to defy overwhelming American strength only because of U.S. internal divisions and because it knew that if Tyler was knocked out of office his successors, desiring peace at any costs, would go back to the way things were before 9/11—go back to being an easy mark, a talonless eagle.

Such was politics being played for keeps in a modern America splitting at the seams. General Kragle couldn't help wondering at times whether President Tyler had the balls to stand up to such fierce opposition when it seemed prepared to do anything, literally *anything*, to destroy him and everyone around him.

A Marine officer in dress blues marched into the Situation Room and snapped the General's attention back to immediate business.

"Gentlemen, the President of the United States!" he bellowed.

The assemblage shot to its feet. President Tyler never merely entered a room, he stormed it. A lean, fit man with a rugged face and an almost military haircut. Blue suit. Red tie. General Kragle shot a look at Tyler's feet. Sure enough, polished cowboy boots. Ready to ride tall in the saddle.

"Folks, I really don't mind people picking on me," he began promptly with that cocky half-smile touching the corners of his mouth. "I've never held myself out to be any great genius, but I'm plenty smart. I know what I can do. And I've got good common sense and good instincts."

He paused and let his focus slip around the room. No one uttered a word. They simply looked curious, and perhaps a bit cautious.

"One of my jobs as president," he said, "is to make sure nobody gets complacent. One of my jobs is to remind folks of the stark realities that we face in the War on Terror. Each morning I go into that great Oval Office and read threats to our country. We have to take every one of them seriously. It's the new reality.

"But there is a greater enemy than terrorism facing the U.S. and the West, and that is lack of resolve, which has little to do with money and weapons and everything to do with motivation and focus. Our enemy in Iraq and around the world believes America will run. We've run before. The performances to date of the candidates who oppose my reelection speak of an 'exit strategy' that might indeed save American lives in the short run but cost us our freedom and our way of life. They would like to cut and run, no matter the consequences. They've managed to vulcanize America"—he meant *Balkanize*—"and convince a majority of their fellow party members that running away is the best thing to do. Polls suggest they are succeeding in persuading a growing number of Americans that the war is not worth winning. It's a dangerous game—and we could all end up losers."

The longer he spoke, the more set and determined the lines in his face became.

"We don't need an 'exit strategy.' We need a commitment to win this war. If we quit and do nothing, I promise you we will face it at some point down the road. We can either wage this war against terror in Baghdad or Kabul, or we'll end up waging it in Baltimore and in Kansas."

He took a sip of water.

"America will never run again," he declared with great force, squaring his shoulders. "That's why I called you here today. You are the leaders in the War on Terror, you people in this room. I wanted you to see my face when I promise you that America will not run, that I have a commitment to the security of this nation, that I will not yield, no matter what.

"And I wanted to see your faces when you make the same commitment. At stake is nothing less than the moral leadership of the free world. At stake is nothing less than the freedom of the world itself. We are all going to be savaged by our opponents who cry for peace but who really mean surrender. Our opponents are prepared to use everything at their disposal to defeat us. Evidence suggests they will stop at nothing. I want you to be prepared for it, for you will be targeted as well as I. They will destroy each of you if they can."

One at a time, he looked each person in the eye.

"If you don't have that commitment for America and don't believe I have the same commitment," he said, "now is the time to say so. You can walk out of this room now and I will replace you, no questions asked. But if you stay, be prepared. Folks, things are going to get mean."

CHAPTER 4

TERRORISM MAY DISRUPT ELECTIONS

Washington (CPI)—Director MacArthur Thornbrew of Homeland Security is warning law enforcement officers that al-Qaeda and other terrorist groups may be plotting to disrupt this year's presidential elections. Particularly vulnerable, he said, were such aerial targets in the United States as nuclear plants, bridges, dams, national historical sites, and electrical plants. Presidential candidates may also be targeted.

In the first video image from al-Qaeda in a year, Osama bin Laden's chief deputy Ayman al-Zawahri threatens more attacks on America and calls on Iraqi guerrillas to "bury" U.S. troops. The tape was broadcast on Al-Jazeera TV.

"What you saw until now are only the first skirmishes," al-Zawahri warns in the eight-minute tape. "The true epic has not yet begun."

Al-Zawahri singled out President Tyler and promised that he would not live out a second term in the White House if he were to win the election.

"Your evil President Tyler with his hard-booted, hard-hearted gang is a huge evil on all humanity," he continued. "American people, it turns out that most of you are riffraff who have no share of great ethics. You elect the evildoers among you who tell many lies and are impolite. Praise be to Allah, you are in a critical situation. Today,

America has started to cry out and crumble before the entire world. We will chop off the hands which reach to inflict harm on us, Allah willing. We will chop off President Tyler's head if he is elected again, Allah willing. Any nation that interferes to help the United States will also be targeted . . ."

History suggests that terrorist strikes during major elections are an effective tool. At a minimum, a campaign of suicide bombings is expected to accompany the fall elections. Thornbrew warns that a major new terrorist attack within the U.S., especially if it employs weapons of mass destruction, would not only disrupt elections but could cripple the government . . .

CHAPTER 5

Washington, D.C.

General Kragle was not a man prone to nostalgia, recriminations, loneliness, or melancholia. He was a "direct action" man who lived his life hard, charging ahead through every day. However, home in Tampa, such as it was, hadn't been the same since Brown Sugar Mama married Raymond and moved off to South Carolina. Rita was dead these many years. The sons were gone from home. Now that Gloria had left, little remained for him wherever "home" happened to be, except shadows and echoes and memories. He often found some pretext or another to stay gone as much as he could.

After the rather curious solidarity meeting with the President of the United States, the General had spent a pleasant evening with his friend Claude Thornton hashing it over and catching up on old times. Claude's son from the Naval Academy took them out for dinner and a couple of drinks. It was rather late when they called it a night and the General caught a taxi to his hotel.

The phone rang almost the instant he opened his room door. Puzzled, he answered it. He hadn't told anyone except Claude that he was staying at the Washingtonian. Everyone else had his cell phone number.

"Jerry Hurst," said a voice. A statement, not a question. The name stunned the General into a catch-breath pause.

"No," he finally managed, deciding this had to be a wrong number.

A mirthless laugh on the other end, followed by the singsong paraphrasing of the tag line from the old horror movie *Poltergeist*, "Captain Kragle, we're ba-a-a-ack."

The voice sounded cracked, almost like its owner had laryngitis or something. The undertone was whiny, irritating.

"Who is this?" the General demanded, his voice suddenly cold and deadly. Hurst's was a name he hadn't heard in over thirty-five years, a name he had tried hard to forget.

"Think about it, Captain." *Captain?* "We'll get back to you."

Another burst of mocking laughter. The line went dead.

The timing of the call was almost like someone must have been watching and waiting for him to return. He dialed the desk clerk and confirmed it. As he expected, there had been no previous calls throughout the evening. He rushed to the window and scanned Pennsylvania Avenue. A cop down the street manned a barricade that directed traffic around the White House because of all the terrorist threats. A young couple, arms wrapped around each other, strolled in the balmy summer night. There was no one else about.

The General tossed and turned most of the rest of the night in his solitary rented bed. Why was this surfacing now, after all these years? He felt as though he had been mugged; he could almost hear the click of the switchblade as an unknown mugger prepared to leave him gutted and twisting in the wind.

He finally got up, dressed in jeans and a summer shirt, and, instead of having breakfast in the hotel restaurant, took an introspective walk along Pennsylvania Avenue.

He ended up at the Vietnam War Memorial, remembering events in his past that were better to have remained buried. Which he thought *were* buried.

He stood with uncharacteristically slumped shoulders before "the wall," staring deep into its eternal black depths. He ran a thick finger down a row of names, touching the marble gently, as though feeling the pain and sorrow of the deaths the names represented. His finger stopped.

Gerald R. Hurst.

He sighed deeply and took a seat on a nearby bench where the wall, and the name on it—*Gerald R. Hurst*—remained in view. A weariness settled over him that was more than physical, was instead a deep down exhaustion of the soul.

It was still so early in the morning that few visitors were about. Feeling safe and anonymous, just another old soldier visiting lost memories and dead comrades, he slumped on the bench and raked heavy hands through the stubble of his cropped military haircut.

Who would understand and forgive events that had occurred in the foreign jungles and prison camps of Vietnam nearly a lifetime ago, when he wasn't sure now, with the revived memory, that *he* understood or had forgiven himself?

CHAPTER 6

Vietnam, 1968

It had been a cold Landing Zone. Huey choppers swept down as swiftly as attacking hawks and deposited the Montagnard "Mike Force" Ready Reaction platoon and its two American advisors. The LZ was a clearing overgrown with elephant grass less than two klicks from the VC village of Vinh Tho. Darren Kragle was a freshly promoted Special Forces captain. Although for all practical purposes he commanded the Mike Force, U.S. Green Berets were still known as advisors.

Lieutenant Jerry Hurst was new in-country and was Kragle's second-in-command—a stocky officer with a baby face masked in a perpetual expression of surprise and foreboding. Captain Kragle wondered how the lieutenant had ever made it through SF Qualifications.

He consulted his map, called out the azimuth to Ching Hi, who was good and alert on point, and got the platoon lined out for fast movement. Hurst radio-checked with Lieutenant Colonel Bruton, overall commander in charge of the operation.

"Dalton Salton says the other platoons have inserted," Hurst reported. "No contact either. It looks like we've either landed in a dry hole or caught them with their pants down."

He sounded relieved that nothing had happened so far.

Bruton, radio call sign Dalton Salton, commanded a 9th

Infantry battalion. Captain Kragle's tribesmen had been assigned by the SF "C" Team at Vung Tau to assist the battalion in an operation to envelope and destroy a suspected Viet Cong headquarters and operations center in IV Corps.

"Advise Dalton our ETA at Phase Line Green in twenty minutes," Kragle directed Hurst.

Hurst radioed it in, then looked up. He seemed uncertain. Kragle slapped him on the back.

"Just follow my example, Lieutenant, and do as I do. It'll be all right. The first time is always roughest."

"Captain Kragle?"

"Yeah, kid?"

Hurst's eyes darted. "Captain . . . I mean, uh . . . Is it normal to be scared? I mean, *really* scared?"

"Hells bells, kid! You don't think I'm scared? Get your act together. You got a job to do. If you don't do it, you won't have to worry about Charlie. *I'll* kick your ass instead. Understood?"

That seemed to bolster the young second lieutenant. He even attempted a wavering smile.

"Loud and clear, Captain."

"Saddle up. Move out."

Caterpillar style, the Montagnard platoon crept off the LZ toward Vinh Tho. It moved through banana groves and into fields of twisted scrub brush where dead trees stood with bare arms upraised like gray skeletons. Reeds and bamboo grew tall enough to conceal movement as the Special Forces element neared the VC hamlet. Clothing sodden with sweat chafed the men's skin. Odors of stagnant pools and rotted vegetation hovered in the heavy air.

Vegetation thinned out. Ahead appeared the edge of a wide rice field diked into square plots. Captain Kragle gave a hand signal to fan the column out on either flank for the final approach. On-line, the platoon faced the village on the far side of the field. Petrus Thuong, the radio operator, followed in Captain Kragle's footsteps. Hurst wanted to stick with the commander also, but Captain Kragle ordered him to control the right flank. The lieutenant's hands shook so hard he had trouble releasing the safety on his M-16. If he weren't careful, the poor bastard would end up shooting himself or one of the 'Yards. He was so scared by now that he couldn't even talk on the radio.

"Snap out of it, Lieutenant. You sonofabitch, you hear me?"

Captain Kragle himself ran the final radio check with Dalton Salton and received orders to begin movement to contact. So far, so good, even though he still held serious misgivings about how the raid was being conducted. He had argued with Bruton about it, but the colonel was an arrogant, know-it-all fuckhead.

Rifles snapped to on-guard position. Squads dressed up their lines for the assault, leaving plenty of distance between soldiers. The little fighters from the Northern Highlands walked out of the sparse weeds and into the rice. Vinh Tho's thatched roofs rose above split bamboo fences on the other side of the field. Thin streamers of smoke wafted upward from breakfast fires. Captain Kragle took off his bush cap, dipped it full of warm rice water and put it back on his head.

Crack! Bang!

Two shots rang out from the village. Then two more. A sentry had spotted them and sounded the alarm. Tiny black-clad figures tumbled out of huts to take a look. They ducked back inside for their weapons. Kragle pumped his arm.

Go! Go! Go!

Montagnards broke into a water-sloshing run toward

Vinh Tho. Terrifying howls rose from straining lungs. The charge sounded like a pack of attacking wolves. Rifles began popping. Lieutenant Hurst lagged behind. Captain Kragle heard him sobbing as he stumbled along with his head down so he wouldn't have to see where they were going. He wondered if the man's eyes might not even be closed.

CHAPTER 7

Refugee Camp Smara

Zorgon seemed to dismiss strangers and lights on the desert as common if rather unsettling occurrences. It was only when gunfire interrupted dinner that Chaplain Cameron Kragle realized that something extraordinary was descending upon the Sahrawi refugee camp.

Shooting, a hard echoing obscenity ringing through the warm desert night, began with a single burst of automatic rifle fire from out around the edge of town where square mud houses and rounded nomadic tents gave way to the Sahara. Zorgon startled so abruptly that his homemade arm swung around and slapped him in the face.

Cameron bolted to his feet, quickly reverting to the habit of a man trained in counterterrorism and guerrilla warfare before taking up his ministry. The night was a fighter's friend. He hustled to blow out the oil lamps and cast the room into darkness. The three missionary women—Rhoda, Jean, and Kelli—huddled together in breathless silence while the men found out what was going on.

The lull after the first volley lasted perhaps thirty seconds at most. Cameron and Zorgon pushed aside a corner of the door curtain and peered out into a starlit desert night where the sod houses and tents of Zorgon's neighbors stood out in scattered clumps of black shadow. A hush descended upon the camp as people took a deep breath and tried to decide if this were an anomaly or if it was a harbinger of something far more threatening.

The one breath was all they got.

An explosion strobed against the sky for a single blink. The hard, ringing echo and chatter of rifle fire, the ominous double booms of rocket-propelled grenades brought the camp to frantic life. People in confused singles and small terrified bunches suddenly scurried about in all directions. A baby camel galloped past, the misshapen silhouette of its head swinging in terror, pursued, it seemed, by a group of frightened women clutching babies and children.

Swelma and her sister Gebele dashed across the little courtyard from the separate kitchen, calling out questions in Arabic to passersby and receiving a few panicked shouts in reply. They bowled Zorgon out of the doorway, chattering excitedly as Swelma collected her son and ushered him to a neutral corner.

"They are slaughter us in our homes!" Zorgon cried.

"Who is slaughtering us?" Cameron demanded.

"Them!"

The camp was definitely under attack, and by a large force, from the sound of it. Armed security elements, the *Polisario*, were starting to fight back. There was a badass fight going on out there, a real slug fest, but it seemed one sided. Bursts of AK fire rolled together like a thunderstorm, raging ever nearer. Tracer rounds inscribed brilliant green etchings into the darkness. Strobelike flashes winked on and off only a few houses away.

The camp was being overrun.

"Let us kneel and pray," Rhoda Hoffstetter suggested from the interior darkness.

Kelli had moved soundlessly up to stand beside Cameron at the door. She grasped his arm, startling him.

"I think God will understand if we postpone kneeling at this precise moment," she said calmly. "So, okay, Chaplain Delta Force, what *are* we going to do?"

"Do you have weapons?" Cameron asked Zorgon.

"The United Nations does not permit it. Only the Polisario are armed."

"We're not going to *kill* people, no way!" Kelli cried in dismay.

A jolt of anxiety shot through Cameron's system. Hadn't he accompanied these women to Algeria to keep them safe from terrorists and assorted other villains? Then why wasn't he keeping them safe? He felt constricted breathing warm and rapid on his neck as the older women, Jean and Rhoda, also clustered with him at the doorway.

Zorgon came up with the only logical course of action. "Run to the desert," he suggested, pointing. "Hide in a wadi until they go or you can safely escape. Go toward Protocol and Tindouf where there is places to hide."

"What about you?"

"I take care of family, Chaplain Cam'ron. You take care of your ladies. Westerners will be executed, of course."

Kelli gripped Cameron's arm tighter. "He's right," she said. "We stick out like cockroaches in a fruit salad."

There wasn't much time. Fighting drew near. It seemed everyone in the camp had the same idea at the same time—flee to the desert. Smara was metamorphosed into a scene out of Dante's *Inferno*. Gunfire climaxed in a feverish pitch. Explosions filled the air with dust and smoke and hammered at eardrums. Mobs of frightened women running for their lives contributed their screams to the hellish din.

"Join hands and hold tight," Cameron directed the missionaries. "We'll be moving fast."

Zorgon swept the door curtain aside for them to pass. Cameron made out the outline of his thin brown face as he shouted something to his family back inside the room.

"Allah go with you," Zorgon said softly.

Cameron nodded. "And God with you, Zorgon." He never expected to see the one-armed little man again.

They joined the wild exodus, the four of them linked together like a daisy chain. Holding Kelli's hand, Cameron stuck to the shadows of walls and buildings as he led the way toward the camel and goat kraals that ringed the outskirts of the settlement. They sprinted in an odd conjoined gait across a children's primitive playground with a bunch of other people. They barely reached cover on the other side before two silhouettes armed with rifles ran after them. Cameron had no idea if they were friend or foe. He shoved the women around the corner of the house and looked about for a weapon. Anything.

One of the riflemen paused, looked back, and fired a shot. Rifle flame stabbed at the darkness. Then he and the other man bolted toward the desert. Even the Polisario were fleeing.

Cameron grabbed Rhoda and buried her face against his chest to stifle the start of a scream. She trembled violently, dangerously close to hyperventilating.

"Oh, Lord, what's happening?" she sobbed. "They're killing the children!"

Cameron shook her gently by the shoulders. "Rhoda! We can't stop here. Take deep breaths. Go on. Breath in. Slowly."

He would hate to have to carry her if she passed out.

"But . . . But the children! What about the children?"

"There's nothing we can do at the moment."

Jean next to him panted more from exertion than raw fright. She was a big woman unaccustomed to aerobics stimulated by gunfire in the night. "I'm okay, Chaplain," she assured him. "Rhoda'll make it too. She's tougher than she appears."

"Okay, I'm ready," Rhoda acknowledged after a couple of wavering breaths.

Kelli squeezed his hand.

"Let's go!" he said.

They rejoined the shrieking mass of terrified humanity as it poured out of the refugee camp from all sides and began scattering into the surrounding desert. Cameron feared they were dangerously near the tail end of the evacuation because of their slow shuffling pace dictated by the older women. Camels in their tiny makeshift kraals blared long belches of protest. Goats bleated in alarm and threw themselves against their fences in an effort to join the mass exodus.

A machine gun opened fire at so close a range that Cameron imagined the muzzle flames scorching the back of his neck. He heard the throaty, measured *Thud! Thud! Thud!* of a .51. He looked back and saw the flickering blossom of its muzzle flash. Heavy rounds banged through the night, seeming to suck away all breathable air, chewing at the running, screaming masses of people. Bright, evil webs of green tracers dropped human silhouettes all over the place, filling the air with the rich, slightly coppery odor of newly-spilled blood. Bullets impacted with sick meaty sounds. Cameron stumbled over a small body fallen in his path. Rhoda screamed.

"Run! Run! *Run!*" Cameron urged, tugging on the daisy chain.

He heard a round strike Jean. The solid-core bullet, a

two-inch-long projectile of steel and lead, lifted Jean off her feet and deposited her on the sand. Joined at the hands, the entire party ended up sprawled in a bloody heap.

The machine gun gnawed over and through and around them, then kept going to seek out fresh targets.

CHAPTER 8

GOVERNMENT IN ALGERIA TOPPLING

Algeria (CPI)—Fierce fighting in this capital city on the Mediterranean erupted before dawn today as rebels battled it out with the government troops of President Ahmed Ali Benflis. By mid-morning, insurgents were pressing toward the capital building itself, where Benflis is said to be under siege.

Amari Saichi, a former army paratrooper who goes by the nom de guerre "Abderrazak the Paratrooper," is the leader of a radical Islamic sect known as Salafia Jihadia. He came over a captured television station this morning to urge Algerians to either support his efforts to capture the government or, at the least, stay out of the way. He promised that resisters would be executed without mercy.

"Algeria is for Algerian Muslims selected by Allah," he said. "All foreigners and non-Muslims will be killed or driven out."

For the past fifteen years Algeria has been wracked by a ferocious civil war that has killed as many people so far as did the colonial war against France from 1954 to 1962. Over 120,000 Algerians and 150 foreigners have died. Gaining independence in 1962 did not bring peace and prosperity to the country. Instead, the bloodbath continued when Islamic fundamentalists took to the hills and streets. Throat slitting, dubbed the "Kabylie Smile,"

has long been an Algerian specialty employed against police officers, regional administrators, and other government representatives.

Salafia Jihadia and its leader Abderrazak are known
to be affiliated with the terrorist organization al-Qaeda,
which was responsible for the September 2001 attack on
the United States. Abderrazak was reported to have had
at least one telephone conversation with Osama bin
Laden a few days prior to 9/11. He, like Islamic extremists worldwide, views the 9/11 attack on the United
States as the beginning of a worldwide Islamic revolt that
will restore Muslim fundamentalists to power around the
globe and launch a new era for Allah.

Reuters and Consolidated Press International (CPI) report that Salafist guerrillas have seized a number of Saharan towns and villages, including Chenachane, Aoulef,
and Tindouf. Tindouf is the location of the only major airport in southwestern Algeria. Abderrazak has promised
to kill or drive out all infidels should he come to power—
which includes all Christians, foreign refugees, and other
"enemies" or opponents.

A survivor who escaped to Tindouf and managed to
find shelter long enough to telephone relatives in Algiers
said genocide may already be occurring in the Sahrawi
refugee camps near Tindouf. The Sahrawi, former citizens of West Sahara, were forced to flee their homeland
in 1975–76, when the Spanish deserted their last colony
in Africa and Morocco invaded. Over 300,000 of them
live in three refugee camps inside Algeria near what was
once the border with West Sahara.

The Sahrawi are particularly despised by Islamic extremists, not only because they are foreigners planted on
Algerian soil but also because many of them have converted to Christianity in recent years. The witness said

attackers swept through the refugee camps shortly after nightfall killing everyone and destroying everything in their path. He said hundreds have been killed, while survivors fled on foot into the desert. The status or whereabouts of Sahrawi governor-in-exile Chadli Malud is unknown . . .

CHAPTER 9

Yuma, Arizona

The county hospital in Yuma was low, red-brown mud in color, and baking underneath a scorched-red sun. That seemed to describe the entire state in the summertime, Claude Thornton thought. Two uniformed Border Patrol officers met him in the hospital parking lot when he arrived in an airport rental. One was tall and lean, the other short and stocky. Both had mustaches and sunburned faces. Thornton initially thought of them as Mutt and Jeff, until they said their names were Appleton and Pear, a combination even more improbable.

"We get that look all the time when we tell people our names," Appleton said with a wry grin.

"The other guys call us the Fruits," Pear innocently volunteered.

Thornton felt tempted to ask, *Are you?* He let it pass.

He had been high in the skies over Arizona on his way to San Diego for an Operation Ice Storm meeting with Border Patrol, INS, and other immigration and domestic terrorism officials when Della Street buzzed him with what she said was a matter that might require his personal attention. That was the convenient thing about flying private Homeland Security aircraft. He didn't have to wait in lines at airports to get his shoes checked and he could always divert. Mobility was the name of the game when it came to the War on Terror, whether the skirmishes were fought internationally or within the borders of the United States.

"Why don't you give me the rundown on what you got here?" Thornton requested of the two uniformed officers as they escorted him across the parking lot to the hospital. "My assistant only gave me the Reader's Digest version."

"Do you want it annotated or unannotated?" Appleton, the taller, asked. He wore lieutenant bars and did most of the talking.

"Let's go for unannotated. I'll read your reports later."

They went inside to the nurses' station. A plump Apache woman in white with a blue collar gruffly told them they'd have to wait, the emergency room doctor was working on a code blue. Thornton wasn't much on waiting, but Appleton filled in the time.

"I don't know if we can tell you a bunch more than we told your secretary—"

"Assistant. She's my *assistant*, Della Street."

"Is that for a fact really her name? I know an Elvis Presley works at the Quik Trip down the street. Anyways, like I told Miss Street, last night we latched onto this truckload of coyotes—that's Mexican wetbacks, illegals—crammed into an old step van hauling butt across the flats near the border southwest of Sheep Mountain. The inside of that van must have been two hundred degrees and smelled like an outdoor Navajo shit house in July. We hauled in twenty-three Mexes, along with these two other guys who looked like ragheads. You know—Arabs, Middle Easterners. We ain't profiling. That's against the law, but *these* two were ragheads. Them two hombres was so sick they were puking all over the others."

"They were hallucinating," Pear interjected. "They were out of their ever-loving minds, talking funny in raghead language and all. Appleton and me both speak Spanish. They wasn't speaking no Tex-Mex like I ever heard."

"It wasn't Spanish," Appleton confirmed. "We had got this bulletin a coupla weeks or so ago about Operation Ice Storm. Is somebody up there in Washington, D.C., finally getting smart enough to get off their fat asses and do something about illegal immigration?"

Operation Ice Storm, which fell under Thornton's Domestic Preparedness jurisdiction, was a new program aimed at dismantling illegal alien smuggling through Mexico. Smugglers bringing Mexican illegals across the border into the United States also provided an open pipeline for terrorists bent on mischief. Thornton had argued for years that the southern border must be sealed, with troops if necessary.

"What about those two sick guys . . . ?" Thornton prompted.

"All the Mexes was sick and dehydrated. It's fierce out there in the summer," Appleton said. "They're here in the hospital now. But them two ragheads, they were *really* sick. One of 'em's hair looks like it's falling out. Both of 'em was vomiting blood. They got funny-looking splotches all over their scrawny little camel-humping carcasses. The Ice Storm bulletin said we should notify the FBI if we come across anything peculiar. Well, this sure looked peculiar to us."

It looked peculiar to Thornton as well. That was why he directed his pilot to land at Yuma instead of proceeding the rest of the way to San Diego.

"That's about it," Appleton concluded.

"Thanks. You did the right thing."

It wasn't often Islamics were picked up in the company of wetbacks along the Mexican border. Pardon, they were "undocumented citizens" these politically correct days. But when some Pedro or Carlos started dealing with Salim and Ahmed, that set off alarms all the way to Washington. The War on Terror was being fought on various fronts around the world. With elections approaching, everyone expected terrorists to open a new front along the Mexican border as they attempted to infiltrate the United States with *Jihadia*.

Thornton and the Fruits waited in the lobby for the doctor another half hour. Thornton cell phoned the airport to let his pilot know of the delay. He thumbed through an old *Field & Stream*. Pear expressed curiosity about how a black man got himself elevated to the head of an important agency like the FBI Domestic Preparedness Office.

"Affirmative action," Thornton told him, blank-faced.

"No shit? I think I read in the papers about you last year when some ragheads tried to nuke New Orleans and you stopped them. Ain't the President's national security advisor a black lady too?"

"She's a black lady."

"She's a *pretty* black lady."

The doctor was in a hurry when he came out. He quickly shook hands. "Doctor Gonzalez," he introduced himself.

Thornton flashed his FBI credentials. "Claude Thornton. What can you tell me about these two men?"

"I can start with telling you there's no longer two. One just died."

"I need to speak to the other one."

"You can speak to him all you want, Agent Thornton, but he's not likely to respond. He's in a coma."

"Heat stroke?"

"I don't think so. It's the same thing that killed his friend. We need to take a few more tests, but I'm at least 95 percent certain."

"And—?"

"They have radiation poisoning. They've been around something hot, like nuclear materials."

CHAPTER 10

Algeria

Rhoda seemed to lose all control when the mysterious marauders shot Jean and, joined together by their hands, the missionaries crashed to the ground. By some miracle known only to God, the machine gun that raked fire across the huddled group failed to score a second hit. Rhoda nonetheless continued to shriek herself into spasms of horror, threatening to attract further attention even though others were screaming and crying all over the camp and the desert. The invaders were shooting anything that moved, including goats, camels, dogs, and children.

Kelli clasped a hand over Rhoda's mouth to shut her up. "Rhoda, God is with us," she whispered urgently. "The Lord stands with us. He's with Jean."

Cameron checked Jean's pulse. It was timid and reedy. He ripped off the T-shirt he wore underneath his regular shirt and made a pressure bandage to stop the flow of blood from the ugly wound in her chest. He tied it in place with his belt and Kelli's sweater. Then, crouching over the women, he looked around for an escape route.

The massacre moved rapidly from place to place, its progress and location marked by screams and the flickering splashes of muzzle fire. The immediate vicinity quieted somewhat. Shadows flitted past them like furtive ghosts.

"Rhoda, Kelli's going to let go of your mouth,"

Cameron whispered, his voice harsh in order to get through to her. "Don't scream. Nod if you understand."

Her head diddle-doodled spastically. Kelli released her mouth but held her hand ready.

"Rhoda?"

"Yes! Yes! The children . . . !"

"You'll have to walk on your own, Rhoda," Cameron snapped. "I need Kelli to help me with Jean."

Rhoda appeared to have gone into a trance. She muttered over and over, "The children . . . Lord, the children . . ."

Cameron gave up. "We have to get out of here. Kelli, drag her with you if you have to. First, help me lift Jean."

They hoisted the unconscious missionary into Cameron's arms. Dead weight. He placed his ear next to her lips. She was still breathing.

"She's heavy," Kelli warned, hovering near. "Can you do it?"

"With God's help. Grab Rhoda's hand."

Cameron was in excellent physical shape, a large man himself, but Jean's weight soon had him gasping for breath. They were already free of the camp and out past the kraals, but they needed to put distance between themselves and the raiders. Most of the gunfire came from their right and rear, but it seemed to be moving back toward them.

A revving engine punctuated by gunshots and excited shouting headed their way. Kelli grabbed Cameron's arm to alert him.

"I hear it," he said. "It looks like we have some brush up ahead."

It was too dark to make out anything other than what appeared to be darker clumps of shadow. Cameron, carrying Jean in his arms, crashed into the brush. Thorns ripped at his arms and clothing. He kept going, pushing through to make a pathway for Kelli and Rhoda.

He stepped off the bank of a dry streambed, landing on his back with Jean's body on top. They slid to the bottom in a small avalanche of dirt and gravel. Kelli and Rhoda followed. They all ended up in a scrambled heap at the bottom of the wadi.

"Don't move!" Cameron hissed.

They held their collective breath as the Land Rover roared on by. It had to be jammed with gunmen, judging from the chatter of its occupants and the volume of rifle fire. Fortunately, Rhoda remained huddled inside herself, fervently praying, but silently.

"Don't give up, Rhoda," Kelli whispered. "Remember that Moses was once a basket case."

General Holloman's niece was impressing Cameron tonight. Whatever else she might be, she was also proving to be one cool customer. *If you can keep your head while all about you are losing theirs . . .* Kelli was keeping hers.

Cameron leaned his back against the wadi bank, his shoulder pressing against Kelli's. He lowered his voice to prevent Rhoda's overhearing, providing she was that cognizant of her surroundings. Kelli had a right to contribute to any plan. Besides, he was fresh out of ideas of his own. It was a cinch he and Kelli weren't going much farther carrying Jean and leading Rhoda by the hand. About all they could hope to accomplish was invite the killers to a return engagement.

"We can't carry Jean out across the desert without knowing where we're going," he summarized, gazing into the blackness. "And in Rhoda's condition, she's an alarm waiting to go off at the wrong time."

"That leaves us where?" Kelli wondered, her corn pone voice, even at a whisper, still sweet as sorghum molasses.

She sounded oddly out of place in such foreign circumstances. "Where do we go and what do we do when we get there?"

"I was hoping you might have a thought."

"Praying won't hurt anything."

"They're shooting everybody they come across. We can't simply sit here and pray and wait to be next. On the other hand—"

"—we have nowhere else to go," she finished for him. "What kind of people are these savages to . . . to pillage and murder in the night? And why are they doing it?"

"Aren't you the one who's always saying give peace a chance and can't we all just get along and reason together? You were a human shield in Baghdad."

Once uttered, it sounded harsher than he intended. Kelli remained silent for a moment.

"I'm not as scatterbrained as you seem to think," she said.

She was already proving that. He took a deep calming breath. "I apologize, Kelli. That was unfair."

"Accepted. It was unfair. But you had to blame somebody and I'm here."

A submachine gun chattered nearby.

"My granny, bless her heart, used to tell me worry was interest paid on trouble before it was here," Kelli said. "But I think it's perhaps time we started paying more interest."

What would Brandon do under these circumstances, Cameron asked himself? Big brother always seemed to come up with a solution to every challenge. He and the General were alike—resourceful, imaginative, violent when necessary, and a weapon down to their bare hands. He sometimes envied them. Still, wracking his brain, he could think of nothing even they could do. Brandon had his limitations.

This seemed as good a place as any to hide out and pray they weren't found. Cameron made Jean as comfortable as he could. Kelli cradled Jean's head in her lap.

The night horizon took on an angry red cast off in the direction of Protocol and the city of Tindouf. They—whoever *they* were—must be burning the city and thus cutting off the only possible route of escape. Kelli and Cameron didn't discuss it, but he could tell she was looking and knew what it meant. Between the red and them lay nothing but blackness filled with terror, from which there was no deliverance.

The Sahara had two seasons, one of extreme heat and one of extreme cold. It was often said that both seasons could be experienced within a single twenty-four-hour period. The night became as though God had squeezed all the heat from the rock and sand, leaving a frigid wasteland of undulating sand, stony ridges, and shallow wadis. Ice buried itself inside Cameron's gut and refused to melt. Jean whimpered occasionally when gunfire, sometimes distant, sometimes near, intruded into the trapped darkness of her mind.

Kelli pressed against Cameron, warm and soft and vulnerable and afraid, even though she was doing a good job of keeping the upper lip stiff. Something deep inside him stirred, something primitive that ancient men huddled deep inside caves with their females must have felt when the saber-toothed tigers roared in the nearby night. A protective instinct.

What kind of man was he to huddle here, frightened and helpless, until their executioners arrived with the ax? But yet, what could he do except lie in the sand, trapped like a desert lizard, and hope they weren't found? He hadn't a weapon, not even a pocket knife, with which to defend himself and his women.

Cameron's warrior blood boiled with anger and frustration.

Gunfire slackened to occasional shots as assailants hunted down evaders and executed them. Once, Kelli emitted a little cry of terror as a patrol of men galloped past the thorn bushes. A few minutes later, not far away, they heard the voices of a man and woman obviously pleading for their lives. Two gunshots followed. Kelli flinched and squeezed the feeling from Cameron's hand. The pleading had stopped. Someone, a man, laughed.

Cameron felt around for a large stone, a stick to use as a club, *anything* that might serve as a weapon in the event they were discovered. He was sure God wouldn't have them passively turn the other cheek and take a bullet through it. His hand closed on a jagged hunk of sandstone. Kelli correctly deduced his intentions.

"Thou shalt not kill," she quoted, "and whosoever shall kill shall be in danger of the judgment."

"For I will defend this city to save it," Cameron quoted back, "for mine own sake and for my servant . . ."

In the original Greek, he sermoned to his Special Ops troops deploying to Iraq and other trouble spots around the world, the commandment "Thou shalt not kill" actually read "Thou Shalt Not Commit Murder." After all, David slew Goliath and won favor in God's eyes.

Cameron had also killed during the 1991 Iraqi war, when he was nineteen years old, and he had killed later in Afghanistan because it was necessary in the rescue of his brother Cassidy from al-Qaeda terrorists. All that happened before he became a born-again Christian and an ordained chaplain. He had since sworn to live the Christly life as prescribed by the Ten Commandments.

But what would the Lord have him do now? Die on his knees with a whimper?

"Lord, if I be wrong in this," he quietly prayed, "please forgive me of my sins."

Their only chance lay in his wresting a rifle or, better yet, a machine gun from one of the invaders. At least he had to try.

"Stay here," he told Kelli. "I'm going out to get a weapon."

"Cameron . . ." Her voice trailed off, choked.

He squeezed her hand. "I won't be long."

"Promise?"

"God willing."

She let him go. He rose to his feet, crouching, the sandstone in hand. Before he could disappear into the night, however, lights suddenly flashed on nearby and they seemed to be surrounded by movement and voices shouting in Arabic. Running footsteps thudded against the hard sand floor of the wadi. Flashlight beams crisscrossed against a young Sahrawi fleeing for his life. Bursts from an AK-47 dropped him skidding in the sand.

Cameron froze. Maybe they wouldn't be seen.

Flashlight beams shot back and forth, searching. One of them flickered across Cameron's face, then returned, blinding him. A shout brought more people running. Suddenly, harsh light exposed the tiny band of missionaries: Rhoda diddle-doodling and praying louder and louder; Jean's bloody form lying motionless; Kelli on her knees in the sand, taut as though ready to spring, long brown hair blowing across her face; the chaplain coiled and defiant on his feet, tall with short-cropped blond hair and angry blue eyes that marked him as anything but Sahrawi or Arab, the sandstone ready in his fist.

They weren't going to kill Kelli without a fight. He would die protecting her, protecting his charges.

Within the shadows and among the dangerous silhouettes behind the shadows, within the excited jabbering, Cameron picked out one word repeated again and again with a kind of savage glee: *"Americain! Americain!"*

A dumpy, dark-skinned little man wearing a dirty robe and an even dirtier keffiyeh launched into the light and jabbed the muzzle of an AK-47 against Kelli's temple, knocking her to the ground.

Cameron sprang at him, stone raised to smash the man's head before he pulled the trigger. The little man shouted something in Arabic and splayed a warning hand at Cameron. He stood spread-legged above Kelli, the rifle in one hand pointed at her terrified face.

Cameron hesitated, realizing that the reason they hadn't already been shot was because their captors had something else in mind. Americans made good hostages.

The guy motioned for Cameron to drop the rock. But before Cameron had a chance to comply or not, he heard something whistling through the air behind him. He wheeled to meet the new threat. The butt of a swung rifle almost took off his head. Poleaxed, he dropped to the ground.

The last thing he remembered before he lost consciousness was somebody dragging Jean away by her legs. He heard a gunshot, loud and ringing and authoritative. He heard Rhoda praying louder than ever.

CHAPTER 11

Fort Bragg

Major Brandon Kragle had another sit-down with Troop
One's new operations sergeant. Master Sergeant Alik
Sculdiron, a square chunk of a man as hard as woodpecker's lips with a skull to match, had replaced Winnie
Brown after sharks got Sergeant Brown during the Philippine operation. The Polack was one hell of an operator.
Brandon had to admit that. He proved it in Iraq when a
Troop One detachment working with the CIA tracked
down Saddam Hussein's murderous sons Odai and Qusai.
Sculdiron had functioned like the old pro he was during
the final fight, such as it was. Brandon had relayed a single
terse message to his father at USSOCOM after it was
over.

Odai and Qusai are dead-a.

The thing about Sculdiron was that military customs
and traditions sometimes proved difficult for old soldiers
to give up, even after they attended Delta training and in-
doctrination. Sculdiron wanted the troops to *look* military,
damn it. That meant haircuts and faces shaved. Pressed
uniforms with insignia while in compound.

The sit-down occurred in the "ready room," where
troops kept their packed ruck sacks and other go-to-war
gear.

"I don't give a damned what you did in the Seventh SF,"
Brandon told his team sergeant. "You could have worn

dress blues and pink panties every day for all I care. It doesn't apply in Delta. It's not what these men *look* like. It's how they perform that counts."

Sculdiron's eyes narrowed to slits. His face reflected the Tartar blood deposited in his Slavic gene pool by the armies of Genghis Khan—broad brow, high cheekbones, wide-set eyes that disappeared into slits whenever he was either deadly serious or highly amused. An almost neckless head sat squarely on shoulders nearly as broad as Mad Dog's. A Polish Jew, he had fought with the Russian army in Afghanistan, where he was wounded three times and collected a shit pot full of medals. With the help of the CIA, he fled the Russians ten years ago to come to the United States and enlist in Army Special Operations. Gloomy Davis, always quick with a quip, noted that the move lowered the average IQ of both services.

"Sir," Sculdiron argued in that booming, accented voice of his, "relaxed grooming standards don't mean they have to go around looking like Joe Shit the Rag Picker."

He couldn't seem to accept the fact that by all practical measures a man ceased to exist in the regular army once he was assigned to Delta, an organization so secret that a special branch known as the Department of Army Security Roster managed its records. Even the name of the unit and its phone numbers changed every few years. All operations were conducted on a strictly need-to-know basis. OPSEC—operational security—dictated that the men talk to no one outside the unit about what they did. Not even to their wives. And especially not to their girlfriends.

Most of all, it was necessary that Delta operators not look military. They lived on a civilian clothing allowance and infrequently wore uniforms. That meant relaxed grooming standards, which Sculdiron condemned—

beards, longer hair than the average GI's, a few handlebar mustaches such as Gloomy's. The men had to be able to blend in. They often operated like guerrillas or, more precisely, like terrorists. They first had to become terrorists in order to become experts in counterterrorism.

Troop One's top sergeant understood all that. Brandon and he had gone over it before. Except for Sculdiron's one "military" quirk, the other Deltas liked, admired, and respected the tough NCO. Especially after the last mission to Iraq.

"Give the Polack a chance, Boss," Gloomy had urged.

"Every man in this outfit gets a chance."

The last two ops sergeants assigned to Major Kragle had been killed in action. Word went around Wally World, the Delta compound, that you had better keep your survivor packages up to date if you were assigned to Troop One. Losses were hard on a commander; KIAs were friends as well as team members.

"I could reassign you to the Intel Section, Brandon," Colonel Buck Thompson, Delta Force commander, had offered after the losses of Operation Deep Steel.

"A desk job?" Brandon shot back, disbelievingly.

"Just for a while. You deserve the rest."

"Is that what my father thinks?"

"Major, your father may be USSOCOM, but *I* command Delta."

"Sorry, sir. I meant no disrespect."

Colonel Buck stood up behind his desk, a tall rugged man who had recently resorted to eyeglasses for reading, and lighted one of the few cigars he allowed himself. He squinted through the blue smoke.

"You've served more than your time in the trenches,

Brandon," he said. "You have a brand-new beautiful wife. Soon, there'll be kids—"

"There won't be kids," Brandon promptly retorted. "Sir, Delta is where I want to be, where I was *meant* to be. I want to be with Delta as a operator, not as a desk jockey—"

Colonel Buck raised one eyebrow. "All old soldiers—if we survive—end up behind desks. Ask your father."

"Sorry, Colonel. I didn't mean anything by that. What I meant to say is that at this point of my career I may as well be out selling used cars if I'm not doing what I was born and bred to do. The War on Terror won't be won without guys who are willing, who won't quit . . ."

Buck chuckled and sat down behind his desk. "Spoken just like your father," he said. "Your old man won't retire and you won't quit. All you Kragles are cut out of the same bolt of cloth. Crazy, stubborn Irishmen."

Delta required men who were willing to go anywhere in the world, at any time, and literally do any damned thing. Who *could* do any damned thing.

Now, Brandon was more abrupt with Sergeant Sculdiron than he intended. He had been edgy, tense since hell broke loose in Algeria. His brother Cameron and the three women missionaries with him hadn't been heard from since attacks began on the Sahrawi refugee camps.

"Damn it, Sculdiron," Brandon exploded, rising to his feet. "You are damned good at this business. I've never questioned that. So let's make a deal. You help me see to the men's training and performance. I'll look after their appearance. Clear?"

"Airborne, sir! All the way!"

"Cut it out, Sculdiron. Just cut it out."

Frustrated, he paused outside the ready room and looked toward the two-story nondescript military building that housed headquarters and Delta's other shops. Part of his frustration, he admitted, came from forced inactivity, from waiting around for something to happen.

Major Dare Russell's Troop Two had moved into Iraq to continue the Delta mission while Brandon's Troop One was jerked back and placed on "Bowstring." The Delta Force squadron designated Bowstring had to be ready to deploy at a moment's notice to anywhere in the world in response to terrorism directed against American interests. It had to stay close to home, training itself and training students, rucksacks packed, while other D-teams either pulled missions or were assigned "Singleton" duties training with the Secret Service, the CIA, FBI, and other military or civilian counterterrorism units.

While Brandon and his men hung around cooling their heels at Bragg, Dare Russell's detachment, which included Brandon's little brother Cassidy, was busy getting in on the capture of Saddam Hussein, caught hiding like a rat in a spider hole near Tikrit. Not a man in Delta failed to envy the operators on *that* mission. Major Russell's message to USSOCOM topped Brandon's.

Sons are gone. Now we've bagged dad.

Gloomy Davis had explained the play on words to Sergeant Sculdiron. "Bagged dad—Baghdad. Get it?"

"Uh," the team sergeant snorted. "Trim that mustache."

As Brandon left the ready room, he thought about checking in once more with the commo shop before he took off for lunch. Delta communications maintained satellite linkups all around the globe and would be the first to hear any news regarding Algeria. Gloria had been burning up the telephone lines to the General and Brandon all morning. The General in turn had tried every means possible to get a call through to Tindouf or Protocol out at the Sahrawi camps. All communications seemed to have been cut.

Brandon emitted a deep sigh. Kragles weren't much on waiting. He had been in and out of commo so much this morning that the commo chief threatened to throw him out on his butt.

"As soon as we have news," he said, long-suffering, "you'll be the first to know, sir."

Brandon's beeper buzzed against his skin underneath his loose sports shirt. A number appeared on the instrument's tiny readout face, a number he had expected, hoped for, since he first learned of events rapidly unfolding in Algeria.

He rushed back to the ready room and stuck his head inside. "Sergeant Sculdiron, assemble the troop. We've got an alert."

CHAPTER 12

Fayetteville, North Carolina

Summer Marie Kragle surveyed herself in the full-length bedroom mirror of the off-base apartment she shared with her warrior husband. She turned sideways to get a look at herself in profile, smoothing the front of her faded blue shirt over her belly. She wore jeans, and her tiny, hard body was just as taut and curvy as it had always been. Perhaps there was a slight bulge to her tummy, but only slight, and so negligible that Brandon hadn't noticed so far when they were naked and in bed together making love.

Wide-set emerald eyes looked back at her from the mirror. The ashen-blond hair was longer, lighter and more stylish than it had been when Brandon and she first met in Israel. A rueful smile touched her lips.

Little Miss Suzie Homemaker.

Time had a way of changing things and people. It was quite a stretch from this modern young woman in the mirror back to the former Summer Marie Rhodeman, one of only a handful of CIA field agents who spoke Hebrew, Arabic, and several Afghan dialects, and who was bold enough to use her facility in languages and her chameleon-like talents to infiltrate terrorist bands and root out the most insidious of their associates. Brandon dubbed her "the Ice Maiden" during the two Delta operations in which they had worked together.

Sometimes Summer missed the action of the old days. But, she scolded herself, she had had her time in the sun. Now, at nearly thirty years old, she was ready to settle down and . . . well, *be* Miss Suzie Homemaker.

Perhaps, as with most women, the maternal had always been in her, dormant but present and waiting. The biological clock and all that. If there was a defining moment when her mind, her emotions, her soul, spirit, and life switched from the fast track to more domestic concerns, it had to have been during her last mission, when, disguised as Ismael the deck hand, she found herself on the Saudi freighter *Ibn Haldoon* with North Korean SCUD missiles in its hold and three stowaway Korean children hiding in a rope locker.

The three children had stolen aboard the freighter while it ported in North Korea to take aboard clandestine missiles for transfer to terrorists in the Philippines. This desperate attempt to escape their home country offered a stark example of how terror was more than suicidal fanatics running about blowing up people and buildings. There were places in the world where states and their leaders officially sanctioned terror against the weakest and most humble of their own people.

Summer smuggled food from the galley to eight-year-old Lee Soon, her little brother Gil Su, and Jang, who was about thirteen, while she made up her mind what to do about them. Lee Soon crawled up on the hawser next to Summer and lay her little head against her protector's arm. After a moment's hesitation, Summer encircled the child with her arm and drew the little girl close.

"We are going to America," Jang the teenager said. "America will not send us away."

Summer choked back tears. She could hardly remember the last time she cried.

"Yes—" The knot in her throat choked off whatever else she intended to say.

The children ended up in Virginia with a large foster family that loved them. Summer wanted to adopt them after Brandon and she married.

"It wouldn't be fair to them," Brandon objected. "They have what we could never give them—a stable home with a dad who comes home from work every night."

He was right. Of course he was right.

The army was no life for a kid. Especially if the prospective father was a Special Operations soldier married as much to the service of his country as to his wife. Gone from home all the time. Long periods of separation. Assignments to distant and unattractive places. The constant tension of an uncertain future. Forget about birthdays, anniversaries, Christmas, and a child who might need a reassuring hug in the middle of the night. The needs of family took second place to the needs of his country and the men who fought for it. And the danger, the constant possibility that he might leave one day and never return. The Delta Memorial already listed a disconcerting number of names.

Whenever the beeper went off or he received a telephone call, he walked out the door and couldn't say where he was going or when he would be back. She had been CIA and *knew* how to keep a secret, but he couldn't even tell her. He wouldn't be able to call home or make any other contact. When he returned, tanner than before and maybe with a few more fresh scars, the wife could still expect little enlightenment.

"So, uh, where were you?"

"Honey . . ."

"Brandon!"

"Southwest Asia."

"So, uh, how was it?"

"Sucked. Wanna go to bed?"

Delta warriors were strange men. When one of Delta's founders died—Command Sergeant Major Walt Shumate—his fellow soldiers discovered with much hilarity and appreciation that he had willed his famous mustache to Delta. The mustache was now proudly displayed under glass in a place of honor in the Hall of Heroes out at Wally World. *That* was strange.

Summer turned pensively from the mirror and walked to Brandon's study. She always felt near him there when he was gone. Brandon's chaplain brother Cameron referred to it as the Shrine. The small room contained his desk, spare army gear, and a clutter of photos, awards, and mementos dating all the way back to when Colonel Charlie Beckwith and then Major Darren Kragle, now "the General," activated U.S. Army 1st Special Forces Operational Detachment-Delta as the world's premier counterterrorist force.

Mixed in with books on shelves were old worn combat boots; Brandon's first beret, bronzed; combat knives; handguns; Army FM's, field manuals; small bronzes of Green Beret soldiers; autographed books written by Uncle Mike Kragle, now senior correspondent, managing editor and major shareholder in Consolidated Press International (CPI) . . . On the walls were photos of John Wayne from the Vietnam-War-era movie *The Green Berets*; other photos of Wayne with the General and with Colonel Beckwith; a large picture of Brandon, Cameron, and Cassidy together in berets and BDU uniforms; a photo of CSM Shumate and the General when Shumate and his mustache were still connected; numerous pictures of Brandon's Delta teammates—Gloomy Davis, Thumbs Jones, Ice Man Thompson, Mad Dog Carson, Sergeant

Winnie Brown and Mother Norman . . . There was also a photo of Brandon and Summer together in Afghanistan with Bek's Northern Alliance guerrilla band. Summer at the time was disguised as black-haired Ismael.

She could almost hear him in all the pictures saying, "The army life is no life for a kid. I know. I was an army brat."

She dabbed at the tears that squeezed onto her cheeks. *My God, look at me. The Ice Maiden is crying.* She who had killed men and faced ruthless terrorists was afraid to tell her own husband that she was almost three months pregnant.

So far, she had told only Gloria—dear sweet Brown Sugar Mama. Gloria and she talked almost every day on the phone. There was a sharp inhale and a long silence when Summer sprang the news on her.

"Has you told Brandon, honey-chile?" Gloria finally asked.

"Oh, Mama. I don't know how to do it. You know how he is."

"Lawdy, I knows that for a fact. He and his daddy be just alike."

Father and sons shared a complicated relationship that excluded overtly emotional displays and dealing directly with deep personal issues. They got up and walked out of a room whenever *Oprah* came on TV.

"All of them, they stubborn like mules," Gloria went on. Summer could almost see her wagging her finger. "But they the best men outside of my Raymond I has ever knowed in my entire life. Chile, what I saying is you got to know *how* they is and *why* they is. That boy—all three of them—done grow up without no daddy 'cause he's off gallivanting from one war to the next."

"This is different though, Mama. Our child will have a mother at home for him or her."

"Oh? What do you think I be, darling—limburger cheese? They might not have no flesh-and-blood *white* mama, but they got me. I was a mama to them boys."

"Mama, I know that. Oh, you know what I mean . . ."

"I be just teasing, lamb chop. I know what you talking 'bout. I done chew on the General his whole life 'bout it. They need they father, and they father was never there. But the General is who he is and Brandon is who he is. Honey, Brandon ain't gonna quit the army. And he ain't gonna be real happy either 'bout you being in the fambly way."

"He'll change his mind."

"Is we talking 'bout the same Brandon Lee Kragle?"

"Oh, Mama . . ."

Summer now left Brandon's study and returned to the bedroom. Brandon and she were going out tonight for what might be the most telling night of their marriage so far. She thought soaking in a long hot bath might make her feel better. She wanted to look rested and her prettiest when she told her husband he was going to be a father.

She stripped out of her jeans and shirt and took another look at herself in the mirror. She *was* beginning to show. She laid out the sheer low-cut black dress that even she had to admit made her look delectable. They would have a drink, a good dinner, dim lights that brought out the copper highlights in her hair, and . . . *Guess what, I'm pregnant.*

More tears squeezed from between her eyelashes.

She turned on the water and was waiting for the tub to fill when the phone rang.

"Summer . . . ?"

Colonel Buck Thompson's wife Mollie, president of the Wally World Wives Club, always telephoned whenever the men were alerted for a mission and couldn't call themselves. It was part of her duties. Summer knew the drill. The tone of Mollie's voice said everything.

"Do we have any idea where they're going this time?" Summer asked, resigned to it.

"They don't tell me either, Summer. But if you've been watching the news, there's some trouble in Algeria involving Americans."

Summer caught her breath. "Brandon's brother is in Algeria—"

"We'll have the deployment meeting Thursday. Ten o'clock at my home, okay?"

Summer hung up. She stood in front of the mirror. Water running in the tub sounded as loud as a waterfall. She stood there, pregnant, and her husband didn't know. There was always a chance that he might never know. Tears crept down her cheeks.

CHAPTER 13

Yuma

FBI Domestic Preparedness Director Claude Thornton sorted through the belongings of the dead Middle Easterner and his comatose comrade. The most interesting thing he found was a wad of U.S. currency thick enough, as Border Patrol Lieutenant Appleton put it, to choke a horse.

"Most of the coyotes we see out here don't have a pot full of pee even if they had a window," Appleton mused. "Wonder what these guys did to get so much."

"It may be what they were *going* to do," Thornton said.

"It must be good work if you can get it."

Other than the money and filthy clothing, there were a few coins and a key to the Cactus Motel.

"The Cactus is a cockroach trap out east on U.S. 10," Appleton said. "It's run by another raghead. We've always thought he was up to something, but could never prove it. Maybe this is our lucky day, eh, Pear?"

"Show me how to get there?" Thornton requested. "Let me make a few phone calls first."

He telephoned the FBI regional office in Phoenix and asked for a crime-scene team to fingerprint the illegals, extract DNA samples, and run the results through the crime lab for identification. He also notified the CTC—Counterterrorism Center—in Washington, D.C., and made a verbal on what he had discovered so far. Finally, he contacted NEST West. Two nuclear emergency search teams covered the nation, one the western half and the other the east, their job to track down and secure nuclear materials or devices smuggled into the United States. He figured he ought to spread the alarm, get some people working on it—considering that one man was already dead and another dying from suspected radiation poisoning. Obviously, they had recently handled something hot. And whatever it was, it was still missing.

"As soon as that sick Arab can talk, I want to know about it. This is my cell-phone number," Thornton advised Dr. Gonzalez, the ER doctor, and then drove out to the Cactus Motel with the Fruits, Appleton and Pear, in their Border Patrol station wagon.

A blazing sun beat down on the dry outskirts of Yuma. The station wagon's air-conditioning went out on the way and they had to roll down the windows to keep from suffocating.

"The government cut our budget in order to put more money into welfare and public health care for illegal immigrants," Appleton said, only half joking.

On the surface at least, Thornton thought, this thing had the makings of something huge. With elections approaching, the government was considering raising the national threat level to Orange, greater than it had been at any point since 9/11. Al-Qaeda or its many affiliates were striving to launch devastating new attacks involving nonconventional weapons such as chemical, biological, and nuclear agents. The bastards could strike *anywhere*, *anytime*. That was what made Thornton's job so frustrating.

Had these guys succeeded in smuggling something into the United States that would make the World Trade Center look like a firecracker by comparison? If so, they and their internal sleepers had to be identified and stopped before mass homicide could be implemented. The clock was always ticking.

The Cactus Motel, a low green-painted stucco building of about ten rooms, sat on the desert sand next to the highway on the outskirts of Yuma. A lone saguaro grew in a pitiful cactus garden in front. Woodpeckers had drilled holes in it, colonies of ants marched up and down its ancient trunk, and a lizard watched suspiciously as the station wagon stopped in front of the designated *officina*. Business seemed to be poor. An old black Nissan pickup was the only vehicle on the lot.

The desk clerk finally answered the bell. He hesitated at the inner door as though paused for flight when he spotted the *Migre* uniforms.

"Get in here," Pear ordered in Spanish. "Let me see your green card."

"*Si, si. Absolutemente. Lo tengo.*"

He fished the document from a drawer and handed it to Pear.

"*Como se llama, hombre?*" Appleton asked.

"*Soy Carlos.*"

"*Habla Inglis, Carlos?*"

"*Pues si. Pero no muy bien.*"

"*Bueno. Entonces . . .*" He indicated Thornton and nodded at the agent to go ahead.

"Who rented Room Six, Carlos?" Thornton asked, showing the key.

"They are not there still," the clerk said.

"I didn't ask that."

"*Lo siento, senor.* They did not leave her name."

"You rented a room without obtaining a name?"

The skinny Mexican stood with his arms hanging along his sides, wearing a sheepish grin.

"Are you the owner?" Thornton asked him.

The clerk played deaf and dumb.

"An Arab named Youseff Balaghi owns it," Appleton said.

"*Estoy trabajondo solemente*," Carlos put in. "I work here only."

"Let's go at this another way," Thornton said. "Can you describe who rented Room Six? Was it a pair of Arabs?"

The clerk brightened. "No, no, senor. She was a gringo. An American, I think. She is not from around here, and she must be very rich. She drives him car, is, how you say . . . ? A Beemie?"

"A Beamer? A BMW?"

"*Si*. A Beamer. Blue. The gringo she is man with gray and brown hair and gray and brown short beard, but she is still look young. Younger than you, I think, senor. That was all I knowing. I am called and told to rent she a room and ask no question."

"Who told you to rent her . . . him—was it a woman?"

"*Si*. She. She was an *hombre* with beard." He made gestures indicating a beard.

"Little mixup of pronouns," Appleton said.

"Okay, fine," Thornton said, impatient. "Who told you to rent the room?"

"But of course it was Senor Youseff. That is two days past. She pay for a week."

"Okay, Carlos. Let's see that room."

"I do not have the key."

"We do."

The room appeared not to have been occupied. The bed was still made and the ashtray clean. A sterile paper strip was still around the toilet seat and the end of the toilet paper roll folded.

"Did this *hombre* stay here?" Thornton asked Carlos.

Carlos shrugged. "She tell me not to let maiden clean him room."

Obviously, the bearded man must have rented the room for the two Arabs, who nuked themselves instead and ended up in the hospital.

Thornton asked the Fruits to seal everything off and direct FBI Crime Lab experts to search the room when they arrived in Yuma. He gave the room a quick preliminary look for anything obvious. A notepad next to the telephone caught his eye. Something written on the removed previous page had left an impression on the pad. He held it at an angle against the sunlight streaming in through the open curtains, shifting the pad until light cast faint shadows across the indentations. It was enough for him to discern a name, probably a last name, and a partial telephone number.

"Two-oh-two," he read aloud. "Isn't that a Washington, D.C., area code? The next digits look like seven or nine . . . three or eight . . . one . . . I can't read the rest of it. Maybe Crime Lab can decipher it. But the name, looks like L—O—U—G—H. Lough. Ring a bell with anybody?"

Appleton shrugged. Pear gestured with open hands. Carlos looked blank. Thornton replaced the pad where he found it.

"Let's go ahead and close down the room for the crime lab," he said.

They walked outside into the burning sun. Thornton's cell phone chimed *Dock Of the Bay* by Otis Redding.

"This is Thornton."

"Doctor Gonzalez. You wanted me to call about the sick man. He just died."

"I wonder what they did with them bombs," Appleton said.

CHAPTER 14

Fort Bragg

1st SFOD-D, Delta Force, was not a Special Forces unit in the traditional Green Beret sense, although most of its operators were SF qualified. A national asset, its sole purpose was to perform counterterrorist and other special operations as directed by the National Command Authority. Once the President of the United States issued a "finding" for Delta deployment, he expected a select strike force to be immediately delivered anywhere in the world to, as Delta operators were fond of putting it, "do any damned thing."

Three hours after Major Brandon Kragle's troops received alert at Wally World, a Blackhawk helicopter sat down on a helo pad about fifty miles northwest of Fort Bragg in an eruption of rugged terrain called the Uwharrie Mountains National Forest, the depths of which offered a secure REMAB (remote marshaling base) used by teams in a hurry to get into isolation, briefed, and on their way. The REMAB consisted of a cluster of World War II era plain wooden buildings that included a rustic barracks and orderly room, a mess hall, a warehouse and armor room, a small motor pool, staff offices, and a range for zeroing in and testing weapons.

The sun was already low in its nest and beginning to look like a cracked dragon's egg spilling red across the horizon when Major Kragle's eight-man detachment dis-

embarked. Eight was the most common size for a deploying unit. The tough men walked purposefully across the
tarmac toward the mess hall, where the operations briefing would take place. All wore black assault suits originally designed for Delta but that had since become the
uniform of choice for SWAT teams around the world.
They carried fully loaded rucksacks, weapons, radios, and
other gear sufficient to handle any mission assigned them.
Extraneous equipment could be weeded out and other
gear added after the mission briefing informed them of
what they were to do and where they were going.

"Fu-uck," Mad Dog Carson rumbled from his cav-
ernous chest. "Why can't we go to Tahiti or Japan or
someplace where the motherfuckers don't wear dirty dia-
pers on their heads? I ain't lost nothing I want to go back
for in Baghdad."

"Maybe we're going to Miami Beach," Doc TB Blackburn offered, although it was a foregone conclusion that
Delta missions these days were almost always headed for
that portion of the globe in the Middle East known as Terror Alley.

"Fu-uck!" And Mad Dog had nothing further to say. He
felt obligated to bitch on every call-out, although he
would have bitched even harder if ordered to stay behind.
It was said the hulking commo man was so good with radios that he could take two tin cans and a ball of twine and
talk to Moscow.

Master Sergeant Gloomy Davis, the dour little sniper
with the handlebar mustache and deadpan expression, was
in the middle of telling one of his stories about his home-
town of Hooker, Oklahoma, the Hooker Hogette cheer-
leaders and his old girlfriend Arachna Phoebe. His clear
blue eyes twinkled with suppressed humor as long as he
wasn't looking through a telescopic rifle sight. He related

his tales with such gravity and conviction that new men on the team like Diverse Dade and Perverse Sanchez were never sure if he were serious or not.

According to his tale, Mad Dog had gone on leave with Gloomy to Hooker to meet sweet Arachna. "With his characteristic finesse," said Gloomy, "the Dog looks her over and says, 'I do like those tight jeans you're wearing. I sure would like to get in your pants—' "

Sergeant Sculdiron interrupted with, "Ground your gear outside the mess hall. That don't mean in a pile, hear? Dress it up. Then go on in. They're waiting for us."

"This drama will be continued—" Gloomy apologized.

The only lights on the entire REMAB shone through the mess hall windows. That meant the detachment probably wasn't going to be here long enough to eat and sleep much.

Sergeant First Class Mozee Dade, whom Mad Dog had promptly labeled "Diverse" in reference to his representing African-Americans in Troop One, shrugged out of his ruck and other gear and started a dress-right-dress line of equipment on the cracked sidewalk. Diverse had taken Thumbs Jones's slot as demolitions/engineer after Thumbs bought the farm on Mindanao. Handsome and expressionless, Diverse was tall and long all over with the finely chiseled midnight-black face of a Zulu warrior and the startling amber eyes of a lion. A bit of an oddity in the soldier's rough-and-tumble world, he enjoyed culture, the arts, good cuisine, and a refined life whenever he wasn't on mission. He and the team's weapons expert, Ice Man Thompson, had hit it off immediately; Ice Man was also a gourmet cook who liked Mozart, Chopin, and Russian literature.

"So," Diverse nudged Gloomy, "did Sergeant Carson get in Arachna's jeans or not?"

Mad Dog grunted. Gloomy grounded his gear.

"Arachna has been around some," Gloomy understated, "and the girl's not exactly a pushover for every smooth-talking galoot that comes along—"

"Chew call that *smooth*?" Staff Sergeant Corky Sanchez said in explosive Chicano. He was short and muscular with a shock of black hair, a wide forehead, piercing deep-set eyes protected by prominent cheek-bones, a nose like a raptor's beak, and a jaw line shaped by an ax. Diverse Dade had given the Mexican immigrant his team name the day Sanchez reported to the Troop as a new heavy-weapons man, one of the best with an 81mm mortar to ever complete the SF weapons course.

"Equal opportunity employment demands that if I'm Diverse, he's Perverse," Sergeant Dade said. And "Perverse," Corky Sanchez became.

"*Chew*?" asked Sergeant First Class "Doc TB" Black-burn, amused. The team's medic, a huggable teddy-bear giant with a broad, open face, was one of the youngest men in Delta. "I thought *chews* was something wetbacks wore on their feet."

"Chew know what I mean, Doc."

Doc had a ready laugh. "Hoo-ya!" he said. "So, Gloomy, did the Dog score or what?"

"As I was saying, the lady's no pushover," Gloomy went on. "She gives ol' Dog a scorching look that would have had a poodle pissing on the floor. 'Sorry about that, dude,' she says to Mad Dog, 'but one ass in my pants is enough.'"

"She ain't no lady," Mad Dog corrected him. "That bitch oughta have a bounty on her head."

A man of extremes who lived with, commanded, and held the respect of men of extremes, Major Kragle led the way into the lighted mess hall, followed by Gloomy

Davis, the sniper only two steps behind and carrying his encased .300 Winchester, Mr. Blunderbuss. Perverse Sanchez held the door open for Diverse Dade and Mad Dog, who flipped him a quarter tip. Team Sergeant Alik Sculdiron was the last of the eight to enter, coming in behind Ice Man and Doc TB.

There were only four long tables in the mess hall. The one up front had eight places set with red file folders, each stamped with the designation TOP SECRET and each with the title *Operation Aces Wild*. In front of the table, facing it, between it and the stainless steel serving line, sat a half-circle of army officers in uniform and one civilian, whom Brandon recognized as Thomas Hinds, a deputy director of the CIA, a man built like a college halfback thirty years after he had tossed his last football. He smoked a cigarette as the detachment filed in and stood at relaxed military attention behind their chairs.

The only *really* high-ranking officers in the collection were General Carl Spencer, who headed the Joint Special Operations Command (JSOC), and CENTCOM's General Paul Etheridge, reinforcing Brandon's hunch that this was a hurry-up-and-go mission. Colonel Buck Thompson, Delta Force commander, sat at the lower-ranking end of the line, along with a few ops, intel, commo, and logistics officers attached like Siamese twins to their briefcases. Even Brandon's father, USSOCOM's General Darren Kragle, was absent, and Brandon wondered about it; the General never missed an ops briefing.

With the exception of Diverse and Perverse, the men of newly designated Detachment 2-Charlie had been through these things before, many times in the cases of the old-timers like Brandon, Ice Man, Gloomy Davis, and Mad Dog.

Delta's feisty Command Sergeant Major Gene Adcock

entered from the kitchen beyond. "Take . . . seats!" he commanded.

"At ease," confirmed General Spencer. "Smoke 'em if you got 'em."

It was his dry way of poking fun at army policy prohibiting smoking at any official function. The CIA director looked around, shrugged, snuffed out his cigarette butt with two fingers and stuffed the remains in his pocket, a maneuver attesting to his status as a military vet.

General Spencer's was the only levity, such as it was, allowed in the entire procedure. The priority and urgency of the operation—Aces Wild—became apparent by the promptness with which the briefing began. CENTCOM's General Etheridge stood and assumed the podium while a captain unveiled a map of Algeria and northwest Africa.

"General Kragle sends his regrets for not being here today, but he is occupied in Washington," General Etheridge said, and immediately moved on. "We'll be brief tonight, because time is of the utmost essence. You may have gathered by now that the destination of Aces Wild is Algeria. Within the past few years, militant Algerian Islamics have expanded their rebellion to include a jihad against the non-Muslim world and especially against Israel and the 'Great Satan' America. The details are in your folders—plane hijackings, suicide bombers, kidnappings, and executions, the usual wacked-out tango stuff.

"Yesterday and last night local African time, Salafia Jihadia, led by a character known as Abderrazak the Paratrooper, besieged the capital at Algiers and captured a number of cities and towns, most of them in isolated southern and western Algeria. One of these towns is Tindouf, on the Algerian border with the former Spanish colony of West Sahara, now occupied by Morocco. Here."

He walked to the map and pointed.

"We have reports of what amounts to genocide against refugee camps near Tindouf, where the West Saharans have lived since the late 1970s. Your folders include a brief history of the Sahrawi. Thousands of them, certainly hundreds, may already have been massacred. More than two hundred thousand have fled into the desert, most of them across the border into Moroccan-held territory. The Sahrawi through their military wing, the Polisario, have been at war with Morocco off and on for more than twenty years. Morocco is afraid if she doesn't respond to this 'invasion,' terrorists will target *them*. Therefore, Morocco has sent troops to the border to capture the Sahrawi or run them back. In the meantime, Salafia Jihadia fighters are chasing the Sahrawi into West Sahara to wipe them out once and for all. In a word, gentlemen, this is one fucked-up mess. And now the President wants us to un-fuck it. Mr. Hinds, do you want to take over from here?"

CENTCOM sat down. The CIA deputy director stood up. His voice had a cigarette rasp to it.

"The primary concern of Aces Wild, at least this portion of it," he said, "is the Sahrawi governor-in-exile, Chadli Malud. As far as we know, he is not among the dead, nor has he been captured. Without Malud's leadership, what we have with the Sahrawi is the possibility of another Palestine, a homeless people resorting to terror. So far, Malud has managed to control and minimize the radical Islamics in the refugee camps and negotiate a cease fire with Morocco, which is now apparently over. Malud has been working with the UN and with the United States and other nations to seek a solution to the Sahrawi problem.

"Gentlemen, Malud is vital to peace in the region, now more so than ever. If the Polisario assumes leadership of the Sahrawi, what the world has is another Hamas or

PLO. Strange as it may seem, the Islamic branch of the Polisario, long at odds with Malud's peace process, advocates joining cause with Salafia Jihadia and al-Qaeda. The West doesn't need another ten or twenty thousand terrorists with bombs running around blaming the United States for what happened to them."

He started to sit down, but then stood back up and said, looking directly at Brandon Kragle, "We do hear reports of three American missionaries that may have been seized by the terrorists."

"Sir, *three*?" Brandon asked.

"That's all we know at this point, Major. We only know that because of a wounded survivor who overheard the terrorists talking about one American killed and three others apparently taken hostage. I'm sorry, Major Kragle—"

Brandon held up a hand to indicate the CIA agent should continue the briefing. The expression on his face remained set. Mission came first with a Delta soldier, duty above all else. Gloomy Davis rested a hand on Brandon's arm.

JSOC's General Carl Spencer, in his fifties with an iron-gray buzz cut and an angular build, stood up and said, "I'll give you the mission portion of the briefing. Operation Aces Wild is a three-pronged operation. The Tenth Mountain Division will be inserted along the Algerian-West Saharan border to stop the continuing massacre. A second Delta unit in Baghdad has been tasked to take care of the hostage situation as it develops."

That, Brandon acknowledged, would be Dare Russell's outfit, with whom younger brother Cassidy was an engineer sergeant. Dare was a good man and a commander who knew his stuff.

"I don't have to explain the political situation to you men," JSOC went on. "Algerian president Ahmed Ali

Benflis has called for UN intervention, but hell will freeze over and the Sahrawi will all be dead by the time that sorry bunch acts. President Tyler is also in a difficult position. In an election year, he can get away with sending in rescue for our people held hostage. He can probably even justify inserting the Tenth for humanitarian purpose, although his opponents raised hell when he sent Marines into Monrovia last year to stop bloodletting there. That brings me to Delta-2 Charlie, *your* mission. The President will be literally crucified if it becomes public. Therefore, men, this is a sheep dip: All knowledge of your existence will be denied if you are compromised."

He paused and thumbed through a sheaf of papers.

"You can open your folders now," he resumed. "They contain area studies, target data, communications codes, weather and other EEI, essential elements of information."

He waited until the rustle of opening folders ceased.

"You men are versatile and resourceful," he said. "You have to be, on this one. Your mission, gentlemen, is to insert clandestinely into Moroccan sovereign territory, if necessary, and do whatever you have to do—let me emphasize that, *whatever you have to do*—to bring Chadli Malud out safely. I don't have to tell you how politically sensitive this is.

"Okay, timetable is as follows: Prepare to depart at Oh-six hundred hours via C-141 enroute to Madrid, Spain, where you will stand by until we receive intelligence on Malud's whereabouts. A CENTCOM and Delta command center will be set up secretly in Madrid to coordinate the action. Helicopters from AFSOC's First Special Operations Wing, the Night Stalkers, are already being transported via C-5 to Madrid to provide you transportation and air support once Malud is pinpointed. Questions as to detail will be addressed either in your folders or during

the 'execution,' 'service support,' and 'command and signal' portions of the op order. Good luck out there—and
may God speed you, one and all."

Under total OPSEC blackout, the men of Delta-2 Charlie broke up into ones and twos with support staff officers
for more detailed specialization preparations. Brandon
tried not to think about the fate of his brother Cameron
and the female missionaries he had escorted to the
refugee camps. That was Dare Russell's business.

Aces Wild? Sounded like every card in this deck was
wild. Nothing could be counted on except that things were
going to be changing rapidly for the next several days.
And Murphy's Law. You could always count on Murphy's
Law, which stated simply that anything that could go
wrong *would*.

CHAPTER 15

Algeria

Chaplain Cameron Kragle slowly regained consciousness. He felt as though he had slept for days, only to wake groggy and with a splitting headache. He was being roughly jounced about. His face banged against metal. At first, he couldn't open his eyes. They felt sticky and matted together with dirt and perhaps blood. When he attempted to wipe them, he found his hands tied painfully behind his back and his feet drawn up and attached to his wrists.

He soon realized that he lay in the back of an open pickup truck with a loud muffler. It hit a bump that bounced him into the air. He came down with such a jolt that for a moment he thought he was going to black out again. Whoever lay next to him groaned aloud from the rough ride. He coughed from the dust clouding into the pickup bed and finally opened his eyes. It was still dark, but not as dark as before. Daylight must be coming. He moved his head to alleviate some of the discomfort.

It all came back to him in a nauseating rush—the wadi and the dumpy bearded little man in the dirty robe with his AK-47 pressed against Kelli's temple, the banging rifle shot . . .

"*Kelli!*"

"I'm here next to you," came her familiar Deep South

drawl. "You've had me worried. You've been out for so long."

She grunted in pain as the truck jounced over more rocky ground.

"Rhoda?" Cameron inquired.

"That's her on your other side. I think she's fainted. They've kept us tied in the back of this truck so long. Most of the night, it seems. Now that it looks like we're going somewhere, I think the man driving this thing, bless his heart, must have got his driver's license out of a Cracker Jack box."

A gut-wrenching sigh on Cameron's other side confirmed Rhoda's presence.

"Jean . . . ?" he asked. "There was a shot."

Kelli sighed deeply, waveringly. "Oh, God, Cameron. You don't realize how . . . how cruel and Godless! They dragged Jean away and they . . . They just shot her for no reason. I don't think she even knew it. I guess they didn't want to be bothered. And you. You were so brave, bless your heart. But foolish, going up against those poor infidels armed with nothing but a stone."

"They're more than infidels. They're cold-blooded murderers."

"My old granny always admonished me to live every day as though it were my last, because one day it would be. I'm starting to see what she meant."

Comforting thought.

Reach The Children Inc. had brought Cameron along to ensure the safety of its missionaries. So far, one was dead and the other two were in the back of a pickup tied up like goats on their way to the slaughterhouse.

Lord, I really messed this one up for You.

The rough road, the choking dust, the loud muffler on

the little pickup ultimately made conversation more difficult and distressing than rewarding. The missionaries fell
quiet and merely endured the ride until they came to
paved streets. Cameron glimpsed brown plaster-and-mud
buildings. All electricity seemed to have been cut off, as
there were no lights. He assumed they were in Tindouf.

"Where do you suppose they're taking us?" Kelli
asked, now that talking was easier and travel not quite as
punishing as before.

"Terrorists consider Americans highly negotiable
hostages," Cameron said.

"Even though the U.S. government does not negotiate
with terrorists? Then why keep us?"

"Politics, Islamic style," Cameron said. "First of all,
there's world opinion. Second, it divides American public
opinion and brings out the antiwar and pacifist crowds.
You should know that, Kelli."

She let it pass; he said it merely as fact, not as an accu-
sation. During the pause wedged between them, Rhoda
spoke up for the first time in a very bleak but calm voice,
"I think we should pray for our souls and for the souls released this terrible night."

"Will you lead us, Rhoda?" Kelli wisely suggested.
Prayer helped restore Rhoda's confidence and sense of
value.

As they prayed, the truck passed through town and into
the desert again. Presently, it arrived at the single-strip
airport on the outskirts. Cameron recognized the tower attached to the baked-plaster terminal; they had landed here
via Air Algiers on their way in. Lights burned inside, although the sky was rapidly losing ink and turning pale
with the approach of the sun.

The truck drove around to the business side of the terminal that fronted the runway. The engine died but contin-

ued to ping. Someone dropped the tailgate and men pulled the trussed prisoners out of the pickup bed and let them drop to the ground with their hands bound behind their backs. Rhoda cried out in shock and pain as her head bounced off the tarmac and blood oozed from it.

"Rhoda!" Kelli exclaimed. "Are you okay?"

"No talk, no talk!" their captors bellowed angrily.

"*Lord, they know not what they do . . .*" Rhoda prayed.

"They know what they're doing," Cameron disagreed. A pair of sandals kicked him viciously in the side.

"You! No talk."

Bearded men in robes and either black keffiyeh or red headbands like those worn by the 9/11 hijackers freed their feet, not out of compassion but only so their legs could be used as handles for dragging them up the concrete steps and into the terminal. They left skin and hair and blood on the steps.

They were pulled up another long flight of stairs inside the terminal and presently deposited, battered and bleeding, inside a rather large but windowless room. Cameron noticed a number of other silent people sitting against the walls with their knees drawn up to their chins before the door slammed, plunging the prison back into total darkness.

Cameron rolled over now that he had the use of his legs and sat up. "Kelli? Rhoda?"

They promptly answered him and moved as close for comfort as they could get. Someone else scooted across the floor toward them.

"Chaplain Cam'ron. It is me."

"Zorgon!"

"I am untie your hands." He fumbled one-handed with Cameron's bindings. "There. You are untie. Shall you help me untie your lady friends?"

Cameron freed Kelli while Zorgon took a little longer in releasing Rhoda's wrists.

"What about Swelma and Gebele?" Rhoda asked. "And your son?"

Zorgon's inner-tube arm dragged on the floor with the dry slither of a snake. His breathing sounded loud and tortured in the confines.

"We become separate in such confusion," he explained at last. "I have not see them since. I am caught and brought here."

Rhoda murmured, "Zorgon, I am so sorry."

Cameron searched the darkness with his hand until he found Zorgon's good arm. He squeezed in commiseration.

"Who are all these other people in here, bless their hearts?" Kelli asked. "Are they Sahrawi?"

"*Christian* Sahrawi," Zorgon replied. "I hear our jailers talk. We are prisoners of Salafia Jihadia."

"Who are they?" Kelli wanted to know.

"Terrorists," Cameron said.

"Bloody, bloody mens," Zorgon added. "I have heard much about them and their ways. They will make demands and if their demands are not satisfy, they will start to shoot Christians in their heads one by one."

He paused for a ragged breath.

"One by one until we all are dead."

CHAPTER 16

AMERICAN TROOPS IN ALGERIA

Africa (CPI)—President Woodrow Tyler ordered U.S. Marines and elements from the crack 10th Mountain Division into Algeria this morning (Algerian time) in response to what the administration is calling genocide against Sahrawi refugee camps . . .

At dawn, U.S. warships off the Atlantic coast of West Sahara launched several flights of helicopters loaded with combat troops. They are inserting along the Algerian border to form a buffer zone between Salafist fighters waging war against the Algerian government and Sahrawi fleeing into the desert.

First reports indicate that the refugee camps are strewn with corpses decomposing in the desert sun.

"Men, women, children, babies . . . goats, camels, dogs . . . It's a charnel ground," a battalion commander radioed back to the ships. "Everywhere you look are bodies. The stench is nauseating. There are no signs of life anywhere. The residents have fled, and those responsible for the murders have either withdrawn to Tindouf or have chased refugees into Moroccan-occupied West Sahara."

Morocco has refused to grant U.S. troops access to West Sahara to protect Sahrawi refugees.

With U.S. forces already committed to Afghanistan and Iraq, the President's decision to send troops to this latest hot spot, even for humanitarian purposes, has drawn strong criticism from the antiwar movement. Senator Lowell Rutherford Harris, Party of the People presidential candidate, fired an immediate broadside against President Tyler.

"[Tyler's] is the most arrogant, inept, reckless, and ideological foreign policy in modern history," he said. "The more we throw our weight around, the more we encourage other nations to join with each other as a counterweight."

Tyler stressed that U.S. deployment to Algeria will be small and will end as soon as stability is restored and the Sahrawi are safe . . .

CHAPTER 17

Washington, D.C.

General Kragle had intended to depart Washington first
thing this morning in order to accompany Aces Wild into
isolation and mission briefing at Bragg. Although his
presence wasn't necessary, he made it a point to see off
most missions. He wanted the troops of Special Operations, including his sons, to know they had USSOCOM's
full backing. Instead, he had barely returned from his
early walk to the Vietnam War Memorial and his rumina-
tions over the "Jerry Hurst" telephone call of last evening
when he received a second call. He contemplated not answering the ring.

He picked up the receiver and glared at it. "Hello?"

"General Kragle?"

"Look, if this is some kind of—"

"General, you need to hear me out. I have something
you need to know."

This voice was different from the previous one. It was
deep and steady, without the whine and the crackle.

"How did you know I was staying at this hotel?"

"A number of people know that."

"All right. I'm listening."

"We can't talk like this." He suddenly sounded hurried,
like a husband whose wife was about to catch him on the
telephone with his mistress. "I'll call back later."

"When?"

"Tonight."

Click.

What the hell, *what the hell*, was going on?

He was tempted to go about his business and forget the entire matter. But the implied threat in the "Jerry Hurst" call, the past it dredged up, and now this second, even more mysterious contact kept him in place. He took his room for another night and killed time walking the streets, thinking, deep and troubling issues on his mind. He had a war to fight, his sons were out fighting it, while here he was stuck in Washington because of nut jobs on the telephone.

He had a feeling, although nothing had yet been confirmed, that his chaplain son Cameron had been caught up in Algeria's nasty little mess; eldest son Brandon would be skying up for Madrid shortly; youngest son Cassidy remained in Baghdad but had been alerted to handle a hostage takedown should a situation develop with Cameron's missionaries in the Sahrawi camps. Having three sons follow him in SpecOps sometimes posed a problem; all could find themselves in jeopardy at the same time. Sometimes the General wondered why, after the upbringing he had provided, his sons would even *want* to follow in his footsteps.

He blamed it on the Kragle genes, a peculiar mixture of Celt and Norsemen blended with American Indian that traditionally bred an anarchic, warlike people who were often difficult if not downright impossible to govern. Early generations of Kragles had fled as far from government control as possible to become the original backwoodsmen of American history. Kragles helped Daniel Boone and Davy Crockett settle Kentucky and Tennessee; the old homestead near present-day Collierville, Tennessee, remained in the family, passed down from generation to generation. A Kragle had fought in every American war since at least the French and Indian Wars—and they were still fighting.

It was in the genes.

"I ain't gonna blame it on the genes if something bad happen to my boys," Gloria had cautioned the General on numerous occasions, the warnings usually accompanied by her scolding finger. "I blame it on *you*, Darren, and Lawd ain't never seen no wrath like gonna come down on you with both feet."

Earlier, the General had tried to telephone Claude Thornton, but Della Street said he had departed for California and wasn't expected to return for at least two or three days. There was always Claude's cell number, but on second thought what was he going to tell Claude? That some voice out of the past called him and dropped the name of a dead man? That was no crime. Besides, he wasn't sure he was ready to deal with what the name dug up. Certainly he wasn't ready to talk to someone else about it.

He had dinner at a deli—sandwich and Coke—and returned to his hotel room to await the second mystery man's telephone call. He showered and changed into fresh khaki trousers, soft-soled hiking boots and a sports shirt. He paced the floor. He checked his watch every few minutes. Darkness settled slowly, kept at bay by city lights.

He swept the window curtain aside and looked out across Pennsylvania Avenue from the Washingtonian Hotel to the White House on the other side and down the block. It glowed a rare and lovely white in the evening lights, a symbol of hope and freedom to the world. General Kragle never looked at the president's mansion without a feeling of pride and patriotism.

But America was now a nation under siege and America's symbol of hope and freedom reflected that change. Guards armed with automatic weapons and high-powered rifles patrolled the grounds and walls. Fighter aircraft prowled the skies overhead. All because of a bunch of fanatics full of hate and resentment and the capability of sowing fear into the hearts of Americans.

Claude Thornton joked that things had gotten so bad that even the *New York Times* didn't have to make it up. Still waiting for the call, the General opened his copy of the "nation's newspaper of record" left at his door that morning and skimmed the front page. The lead story devoted itself to presidential candidate Lowell Rutherford Harris, whom the *Times* had already endorsed. A photo of Harris delivering a campaign speech took up much of the top fold. He was a rather short man with a long face whose lips seemed perpetually stretched into a line of tension and distaste, as though he had just stuck something bitter into his mouth.

"No president of the United States," he carped in a quote, "should employ misguided ideology and distortion of the truth to take the nation to war. In doing so, the president breaks the basic bond of trust between the government and the people. President Tyler has committed one of the worst blunders in more than two centuries of American foreign policy. We should ask Congress to investigate whether this constitutes criminal behavior."

Politicians over the last fifty years had demonstrated a profound ignorance regarding the nature of America's enemies. It seemed some of them never learned, in spite of repeated humiliation and deadly attacks against Americans. Intentionally or otherwise, they became soldiers for the terrorist cause.

"President Tyler is a sad figure," Harris went on. "He's

not too well educated, and he's leading the country toward fascism even though he wouldn't understand the word fascism anyhow."

Arrogant little twerp! The General tossed the paper aside in disgust. He paced the room and fought to keep his mind off Jerry Hurst. That was over. That was in the past. He had done what needed to be done at the time.

The phone rang. He snatched the receiver from its cradle.

"All right, now I want to know what this is all about," he insisted.

"Meet me at Abraham Lincoln in twenty minutes. Come alone or you won't see me."

"How will I—"

The dial tone buzzed in his ear. The General cursed in frustration—but nonetheless followed instructions. He had to hurry to make it. He grabbed a light windbreaker on his way out the door.

The Lincoln Memorial stood on a high terrace at the top of an imposing flight of stairs. The Potomac River, a glimmer of reflected colored light, could be seen from one side while the other side presented a magnificent view of the Mall all the way to the Washington Monument. The General made it with two or three minutes to spare. He waited inside the open center section dominated by the gigantic statue of Ol' Abe. This time of the evening the Mall was almost deserted. There were enough concerts and political events going on elsewhere to draw tourists away.

"He saved the union," a voice suddenly spoke up from the shadows.

The General slowly turned in its direction, unwilling that the contact see he had been startled.

" 'In this temple as in the hearts of the people for whom he saved the union the memory of Abraham Lincoln is enshrined forever,' " the stranger read from the inscription above the statue. "Funny," he went on, "this is the first time I've come here. You?"

The General took a step forward. "I've been here before." The man was a dim silhouette in the shadow of one of the pillars. Medium size and medium height. Nothing else stood out about his appearance.

"General Kragle, we can talk from this distance. I prefer you not be able to identify me."

The General stopped. "I'm tired of games, Mister—?"

"The name doesn't matter." He seemed unoffended. His voice remained soft, even mild. "Like Abraham Lincoln, we are faced with a great responsibility to save the union."

The General wasn't quite sure how to respond. "You said you had something I needed to know. About—?"

"Jerry Hurst."

"What do you know about Jerry Hurst?"

"There's not much time," the stranger said, suddenly in a hurry again. "You'll need to listen closely. Have you heard of The Committed?"

"The committed?"

"I thought so. Few have. Spell it with a capital C—The *Committed*. I'm about to tell you a story you won't want to believe. General, these people have connections, deep connections, and as their name suggests, they are *committed*."

"What are you—a conspiracy nut? Black helicopters, the CFR . . . ?"

"Don't scoff, General, until you hear me out. Jerry Hurst is small potatoes. So am I. So are you, actually. The United States government is at stake. Even now, there is a plot to—"

The pneumatic *Pft! Pft! Pft!* of silenced automatic weapons cut off whatever else he intended to say, followed by the meaty thunking of large-caliber bullets striking flesh. General Kragle had heard silencers before, had even used "Hush Puppies" in Vietnam and then elsewhere during the early days of Delta Force. Instinctively, unarmed as he was, he flung himself to his belly and crawled like a giant fast lizard for the cover of one of the pillars.

The mystery man toppled forward and rolled down the marble steps, spraying blood from ruptured arteries and other wounds. He came to rest with his head down toward the pool and his legs bunched. His assailants made no attempt to finish the job with the General. A car took off at a high rate of speed. Then the only sound, other than the distant hum of traffic, was the trickling sound of spilled blood dripping from step to stone step.

CHAPTER 18

Vietnam, 1968

Strategy for the assault on Vinh Tho called for Captain Kragle's Montagnards and an infantry platoon of Alpha Company, 4/39th, 9th Division, to assault from eight o'clock and eleven o'clock respectively, while three other Alpha platoons set up an anvil on the other side of the village in the three o'clock position against which the attacking elements would smash the fleeing VC.

During pre-mission briefing, 4th Battalion commander Lieutenant Colonel Bruton said the Viet Cong had pulled back out of the hamlet without offering resistance beyond mortaring one of the helicopter landing zones the first time U.S. infantry marched on Vinh Tho. He expected the same thing from the VC again. Only, this time, the anvil would be in place, moving in faster and closer with rings of steel against which to beat hell out of the enemy and prevent his scattering into the Nam Can Forest. *This time*, he vowed, he would make the enemy stand up and fight— and be decimated.

Timing of participating units was critical, surprise essential. Element leaders discussed times, phase lines, armaments, fire support, coordination, actions at the objective . . . Contingencies were constructed to cover weaknesses in the plan.

There *were* weaknesses. Captain Kragle thought the assault had been poorly planned and said so.

"Whose clusterfuck idea was this, sir?" he finally demanded.

Colonel Bruton stiffened. He was a soft-looking, rather pudgy man with a narrow chest and an ego almost as broad as his behind. Overzealous men in combat made deadly mistakes.

"What the hell are you talking about, *Captain*?" the colonel shot back. "*I* made this plan."

"No offense, sir, but you're going to get our asses chopped off."

Captain Kragle got up and stabbed a thick finger at a map stretched on the wall. "Doesn't the army read its own intel reports?" he growled. "NVA and VC regional force units, hard-core types equipped with the latest commie-block weapons, have been moving into the AO for the last month in preparation for TET. Their objective is to control everything this side of the My Tho River from here to Saigon. This operation calls for at least a battalion, not just one rifle company and a Mike Force."

"The rest of my battalion has its own objectives," Colonel Bruton countered, thrusting out a defiant jaw. "Their objectives will tie up enemy forces and draw them away from support of Vinh Tho."

"Second point," Kragle went on. "Platoons are being choppered in and inserted without accompanying eighty-one-millimeter mortars for contiguous fire support—"

"We'd have to waste an infantry platoon providing security for mortars," Colonel Bruton retorted defensively. "We don't have extra platoons available. Besides, we're coordinating fire support from the one fifty-five howitzers at FSB *Savage*. We also have Cobras and a flight of Air Force fast movers on call."

"Yes, sir. But Vinh Tho is on the outer edge of the one

fifty-five range. That means platoons will be operating at least part of the time out from under artillery protection. In fact, my own men are going to be moving throughout VC-controlled areas most of the time without fire-support umbrellas—"

"That's why we have the Air Force and gunships."

"Sir, have you factored weather into the equation?"

"The forecast calls for clearing."

"Weather this time of year is unpredictable," Captain Kragle continued to lecture while Colonel Bruton puffed up like a red-faced balloon. "If we get rain and low ceilings, which is likely, we'll lose all air support, and we lose our means of extraction. If helicopters can't fly and something goes wrong on the ground, we'd have to pull all the way back to the My Tho River for boat pickup. We'd be out of artillery ranges for most of that time."

Colonel Bruton's lips twisted in disdain. "There won't be enough VC left after we're finished with them to cause a Boy Scout troop any problems," he snapped. "My men are shit tired of humping our asses off out there and getting picked off by toe poppers, punji pits, and farmers armed with fifty-caliber Chicom rifles. We're spoiling for a fight. Aren't you overestimating the enemy, Captain Kragle?"

"Sir, all I'm saying is that this thing stinks. There's no telling how many men the enemy has moved in out there. I'm estimating at least a regiment."

"Look, Captain, if the Green Beanies are too chickenshit to go out and fight, maybe we'd better transfer you to the Girl Scouts."

Kragle's gray eyes blazed with fury. Outranked, however, he held his tongue. He had rendered his opinion, and it was rejected. The operation was starting off soured.

Lieutenant Jerry Hurst followed Captain Kragle out of the battalion TOC—tactical operations center. He licked lips so dry they almost crackled.

"We're not making it back, are we, Captain?" he said.

CHAPTER 19

MALL MURDER MYSTERY PUZZLES POLICE

Washington (CPI)—Police have identified the victim of a shooting at the Lincoln Memorial early last evening but have not ascribed a motive to the slaying. Detectives say the victim, identified as Charles Edward Lough, 39, worked as a political lobbyist for Entertainment Media Enterprises. EME and its Hollywood and New York branches are noted for pushing the envelope in producing sexually explicit films for TV and home video consumption.

A witness, whom police decline to name, allegedly met the victim at the Lincoln Memorial at about 9:10 p.m. Shortly afterwards, unknown assailants using silenced weapons gunned Lough down out of the darkness. Police say it has all the marks of a professional assassination. They say they have no suspects . . .

CHAPTER 20

Fort Bragg

Summer knew the routine, having been married to Major Brandon Kragle for the past year. As soon as the men deployed on a new mission, the Delta Force commander's wife and a Delta officer who hadn't deployed called a wives meeting. Pastries and coffee and Kool-Aid were an attempt to lighten the mood and make the nervous women feel that this wasn't the end of the world. After all, most of them had gone through this before—and would likely go through it again.

Wife drills were primarily designed to inform families about what to expect if the worst happened. Inevitably, in a world of low-intensity conflict, mad dictators, and even madder terrorists, men would go on some mission and not return alive. American Special Operations soldiers who volunteered to live precarious lives and work at extraordinarily high operation tempo lost their lives in combat at a rate sixteen times higher than conventional U.S. forces.

The women filled out cards indicating who they would like to come to their homes for support if their men were wounded or killed. At one time or another, nearly every woman at a meeting would be called upon to support a woman recently inducted into the Gold Star Wives Club, all the members of which were widows. Two officers wearing dress greens would appear in the company of the support persons. Thankfully, the days of notification by telegram were long over.

Sergeant Margo Foster telephoned Summer early in the morning after Aces Wild departed Bragg.

"Girlfriend, do you need company for the meeting?" she asked.

"I don't need it, but it'd be welcome."

"Be right over."

Although women soldiers weren't allowed into Delta Force proper, Margo belonged to the Delta intelligence detachment, which *did* admit women now and again. For that reason, the men called it "Funny Platoon." She was not a wife and therefore technically ineligible to attend deployment meetings, but younger Kragle brother Cassidy and she had a "relationship" that allowed her to bypass technicalities. Besides, the wives of Wally World Wives Club liked her.

Summer had been taken with Margo when they met on Summer's wedding day at the Farm in Collierville, Tennessee. She was amused by the comely brunette's candor and sense of humor. Margo in return had been equally impressed by Summer's credentials as a CIA field agent. In no time they were like sisters who, also like sisters, turned to Gloria as a surrogate mother.

It was Gloria who bluntly warned Margo about getting involved with a Kragle man. "Lawdy, that Cassidy ain't never gonna marry you, girl, until you ain't no soldier boy no more. He done lost too much once't, and he ain't willing to take another chance."

Like the other hardheaded men in the Kragle family, Cassidy believed women should not be in dangerous military positions, that no one belonged in combat at all unless he had a pair the size of basketballs. Summer resigned from the Agency not because Brandon insisted on it as a condition of marriage but because she knew he would be happier. So far, Cassidy refused to even discuss marriage with Margo until she left Funny Platoon. It didn't help matters that Cassidy's first wife Kathryn had been kidnapped by al-Qaeda terrorists when *she* was in the military and that she had died from terrorist anthrax poisoning following 9/11.

Margo was still considering her options—Cassidy or her career in the army.

She arrived at Summer's, driving her bright red Mazda and wearing jeans and a ball cap that let her ponytail bounce through an opening in the back. Most of the other wives were already at Mollie Thompson's house, speculating about where the detachment was going, when Summer and Margo arrived.

A uniformed Delta lieutenant confirmed that Algeria was the target, but supplied few other answers. No one knew—or at least wasn't saying—how long the men would be gone, what their exact destination was, or what they would be doing. No, wives wouldn't be allowed to initiate phone calls or receive them. The mission was top secret and under OPSEC blackout. Nothing must be said about it outside this room. Unit representatives would be available to deal with family emergencies.

Meetings such as this were hard on wives. Carole Blackburn, at nineteen the youngest member of the club and roundly pregnant with Doc TB Blackburn's first child, dropped her head on the table and began to weep. The more senior veteran wives crowded around to comfort her.

"Everything will be all right," they said. "Our husbands are very good at their jobs."

Carole sniffled and wiped her eyes. "But . . . But how good are the enemy?"

Summer's heart went out to her. She bent close to

Margo and whispered, "I suppose it's too late to warn you to cease and desist falling in love with Cassidy Kragle?"

"Were you warned about Brandon?" Margo shot back.

Summer lowered her head. "The heart is a lonely, *blind* hunter," she said. "It loves who it will."

Her hormones must be screwed all to hell. Margo noticed her tears.

"Summer . . . ?"

"I'm sorry. I'm . . . uh . . ."

She couldn't seem to restrain her tears. Embarrassed, she rose abruptly and hurried outside into the sunlight. Margo followed.

"It's all right," Margo comforted her. "Women do cry, you know."

"I don't!" She laughed tearfully. "I *am* crying, aren't I?"

"And a good one at that, girlfriend."

Summer found a Kleenex in her jeans pocket and dabbed at her eyes. She had never carried tissues before. She looked at Margo.

"It must be because I'm pregnant," she blurted out, unable to hold it all inside any longer. Pain shared was pain diminished. "I'm going to have a baby and I'm afraid Brandon won't want it."

CHAPTER 21

U.S. MISSIONARIES SEIZED IN ALGERIA

Algeria (CPI)—The U.S. State Department confirmed today that Salafia Jihadia has seized three American missionaries in its ongoing rebellion to take control of the Algerian government and turn it over to fundamentalist Islam. Four Americans from Reach The Children Inc. were known to be in the Sahrawi refugee camps when scores of terrorist rebels armed with assault rifles, mortars and rocket-propelled grenades attacked the camps and torched tents and houses, killing hundreds and wounding many more. The fate of the fourth missionary is still unknown.

The names of the missionaries were not disclosed pending notification of next of kin.

In a letter directed to President Woodrow Tyler, the Islamic Jihad Black Death Squad of Salafia Jihadia admitted it had taken the three missionaries and was holding them with other captives at the Tindouf Airport. The letter read, in part:

"Consider this your three-minute warning before we turn the U.S. into the fires of hell. Let America and Israel cry for their dead from today and the destruction that they will suffer. The prophet Muhammad, peace be on him, said, 'Hit the infidel wherever you find him.'"

The letter was accompanied by a list of names of jailed terrorists who also must be released and the usual demands: the return of "stolen" money in frozen accounts, the immediate pullout of U.S. troops from Iraq and the Middle East, and the withdrawal of U.S. troops protecting Sahrawi in Algeria.

"Until these non-negotiable demands are being met in good faith," the letter went on, "one infidel each morning will be publicly executed for his crimes, beginning tomorrow . . ."

CHAPTER 22

Al Rashid Military Complex, Baghdad

With the possible exception of hot chow, mail call was the single most important event of a combat soldier's day. Staff Sergeant Cassidy Kragle, tall and athletic like the rest of his clan, with blue eyes and dark hair grown longer than the average soldier's, lounged on a fifty-gallon gasoline drum in the Iraqi sunshine outside Delta 1-C's command post, catching up on his mail. He had a goodly collection of it too. The detachment had only returned to Al Rashid last night after a week along Iraq's northern border chasing down Hassan Ghul, a top Jihadi out of Osama bin Laden's terror network. Major Dare Russell, team commander, received an electronic letter of congratulations signed by the President of the United States himself, in which the President said Ghul's capture was strong proof that al-Qaeda had a hand in the murderous terror campaign to prevent Iraq's forming a stable government after Saddam Hussein's downfall.

A Bradley fighting vehicle growled past, kicking up choking swirls of dust. Cassidy flapped a hand at the dust, eliciting a round of cat calls and hoots from 101st troopers hanging all over the Bradley.

"The spooks are back!" one of the GIs shouted. "Hey, Sergeant Spook, you guys win the war yet?"

Cassidy shook his head and grinned. "Winning the war's on next week's agenda," he called back.

Good-natured and sometimes jealous heckling by other servicemen went with the territory of being a Delta Force soldier. Delta found itself an object of curiosity and speculation whenever and wherever it appeared, by virtue of its "shadow warrior" reputation and its need to exist in official anonymity.

Cassidy received a letter from Gloria informing him that Cameron had gone to Algeria with a group of missionaries. Brown Sugar Mama didn't like it—having another of her "sons" going "overseas amidst them Muslims"—but *Lawdy*, she reckoned as how God's works had to be done even among heathens in these "end times."

She thanked him for sending her the requested snapshot of himself standing in front of the Delta CP with Bobby Goose Pony. She said she cried when she got it because, tall, dark and lanky the way Cassidy was, he reminded her of his daddy back when the General was in Vietnam.

Lawdy, she wrote, *it seems how time has a way of just twisting its tail back on itself.*

Gloria wrote every day. So did Sergeant Margo Foster of Delta's Funny Platoon. Cassidy had a bundle of scented letters from her that made Top Sergeant Alan Bodine roll his eyes when he held mail call. Margo tried to keep her letters light and funny—*I can imagine it must have been you when Saddam was captured who came up with the saucy retort "President Tyler sends his regards"*—but there was an undertone in them that both thrilled and unsettled Cassidy.

There had been that same undertone in their relationship for some time now. Margo called it the "next step," but Cassidy refused to discuss it. The romance was moving too fast for him. His deployment to Iraq came at an opportune moment to cool down their ardor. It had been over

two years since Kathryn's death, and Margo was the first
woman since then with whom he had anything going beyond a quick date or one-night stand, but he still told himself it was too soon to move on in the relationship.
Besides, he knew one thing for certain: he wasn't getting
involved in marriage with another military woman.

Maybe it was already too late. He *was* involved. But,
my God! How Margo felt underneath his hands when she
was naked! How she smelled and tasted!

He shook his head to clear it of her image. But it was
there to stay, he suspected, revived by something as seemingly insignificant as the perfume scent on her envelopes.

"Cass, are you proposing to make love to me before you
leave or what?" she had boldly demanded on their last
evening together before his deployment.

"Or what," he selected, teasing.

"You devil!"

She had an apartment off-post in Fayetteville. She ran
giggling into the bedroom, flinging clothing off as she
went. She was already naked, standing barefooted on the
shag carpet with the soft light of the bedside lamp haloed
behind her. Small and curving in all the right places,
ponytail loose to spray brown hair around her face, legs
spread slightly so that light behind shown through between them at the *V* and made the hair there glisten like
spun gold.

"Take your jeans off, soldier," she challenged softly.
"Don't worry. I'm not asking you to marry me or anything
like that."

Making love to her was different from what he had
imagined. He thought when the time came they would be
overcome with passion and would devour each other. Instead, their lovemaking was warm and slow and thorough,

luxurious and incredibly sensual. He lay on his back and she spread her legs over him and let herself down slowly while she drew him inside her, deep but ever so slowly, getting deeper, smiling down at him in that dreamy hooded-eye manner of a woman experiencing extreme pleasure. He reached and cupped both rounded breasts with their hardened nipples and she reached behind and stroked between his legs when he entered her . . .

"Kragle?"

It snapped him back to Iraq. Goose Pony, the stocky half Arapahoe, half Kickapoo, half whatever from New Mexico, stood in the doorway of the command post behind him.

"You had a look on your face, man. What were you thinking about—pussy?"

Cassidy blushed. He and Goose had gone through the SF "Q" Course together, to Engineer and Demolitions School, and then volunteered together for Delta Force. Goose always seemed to read his thoughts.

"It's none of your frigging business, Goose Pony. Go get your own thoughts."

"There ain't enough time, paleface. Major Russell wants to see the detachment inside mosh-skosh. We just got the message for a new operation. Aces Wild."

"Sounds like a poker game."

"Algeria. It's a hostage takedown. Looks like some missionaries got themselves caught and put in the iron pot."

Cassidy stiffened. He immediately thought of Cameron.

CHAPTER 23

San Diego, California

The FBI Crime Lab did fast work on identifying the two dead Arabs. National Domestic Preparedness Director Claude Thornton had their names by the next morning when he prepared to depart Yuma for the delayed Operation Ice Storm meeting in San Diego. He and his pilots had spent the night in Yuma at a motel near the airport.

One of the dead was Salim Boughader, the other Ali-Salem Tamek. Both proved to be so full of radiation that they almost glowed. Neither in himself was much of a catch. They were low-level foot soldiers who had traveled around some among the various terror organizations—al-Qaeda, Salafia Jihadia, Hamas, Hezbollah . . . They were of the caliber who strapped explosives around their waists and detonated themselves next to Israeli school buses full of first graders. Or who hijacked airplanes and flew them into New York City skyscrapers.

Then what were these guys doing handling something as sensitive as nuclear materials? Usually that was left to terrorists further up the food chain. The only thing Claude could figure was that they were merely delivering a package, smuggling it across the border to be used by someone else. But what had happened to it? Had it been shoved out of the step van somewhere in the desert before the Border Patrol nabbed the load of coyotes? The Fruits, Lieutenant Appleton and Agent Pear, had organized a search team to

trace the step van's tracks back to the Mexican border—
and had found nothing.

That left two other options, the way Thornton calculated it: The smugglers had turned the delivery over to
someone on the *other* side of the Mexican border; or,
highly probable, Boughader and Tamek were one of several teams of smugglers with WMDs, a sort of backup system for each other in case one team got caught or screwed
up as these two dummies had and nuked themselves with
radiation. Either way, that left a nuclear explosive device,
a bomb, floating around somewhere in the United States.

Jesus!

Thornton telephoned his assistant director, senior FBI
agent Fred Whiteman.

"Hey, white man."

"Hey, black man. Wassup, bro'?"

Whiteman and Thornton had attended the FBI Academy together more than twenty years ago. In addition to
being totally loyal, Whiteman was a crack investigator
and a man willing to take chances. The banter between
them was part of their friendship.

"Fred, I think I've stumbled onto something in Arizona," Thornton said.

"So I've heard. It seems you're always stepping in doo-
doo and coming out smelling like roses."

"There's no rose smell to this one, Fred. To tell you the
truth, I don't know what kind of a smell it's got. But I've
got a strong hunch we'd better put some resources on it
real quick. I've got NEST on it now, the Border Patrol is
working their asses off, and Quantico and Langley are on
line."

Thornton briefly filled him in on the two dead Arabs
and the missing nuclear materials.

"What do you need from me, Claude?"

"I want you to personally come to Yuma with a team and find that WMD, if that's what it is. Check with Appleton and Pear at the Border Patrol. They'll fill you in. We've got two leads right now—Youseff Balaghi, the owner of the Cactus Motel in Yuma, who's currently out of pocket, but has to be asshole deep in whatever's going on."

"And the other?"

"Lough. L—O—U—G—H. That's all I know. Ramrod the name for me, Fred, and call me back on what you find."

"And you'll be . . . ?"

"In San Diego. You know my cell number."

Thornton had already turned his rental car in, upon the Fruits' insistence that they could all work together out of the station wagon. They dropped the agent off at the airfield where his Homeland Security Learjet waited for takeoff. Things had changed a bit since those days when Thornton had been cast into the Egyptian desert out of sight and out of mind. The Fruits were impressed.

"I'm still pounding a beat," Thornton said, smiling. "I'm just pounding it at a faster pace."

In San Diego, more than twenty men and a handful of women, mostly of Spanish descent, crowded into a small conference room at the INS office for the Operation Ice Storm meeting. Thornton disliked bureaucracies and meetings almost as much as the General did, but his position in federal counterterrorism demanded he make his appearance. From his experience, he concluded bureaucracies were good at stating problems but not so good at finding solutions. Mostly it was talk, talk, talk, with little settled except when the next meeting would be held.

"Mexico's President Fox has met with President Tyler and promised to move against smuggling operations that are most likely to deal in terrorists," said assistant U.S. attorney Bob Skorlos. "Since then, federales have arrested Mexico's Lebanon consul on charges of helping a ring smuggle Arab migrants into the U.S. from Mexico. The concentration of Ice Storm should be on these key enemies, these smugglers who collaborate with corrupt officials like the Mexican consul."

"Whatever we're doing is not working," said INS commissioner Joseph Browne. "Islamic terrorist groups are still using Mexico as a refuge. We've identified at least eighty nationals from Lebanon, Syria, Iraq, Algeria, and Saudi Arabia who were in the process of being smuggled into the U.S. They weren't sneaking in to work at Burger King either."

All agreed that the U.S. border with Mexico was a literal sieve.

"The bottom line is this," Browne concluded. "As a country we have to come to grips with the presence of twelve million illegals in this country, afford them some kind of legal status, decide what our immigration policy is, and then enforce it."

"No, Mr. Commissioner," Thornton disagreed, rising to his feet. He was considered one of the hard liners when it came to immigration policies. "We already have immigration laws. It's your duty to enforce them."

"You think we don't know our job?" Browne challenged, also shooting to his feet. "But how are we supposed to do it when Washington cuts our budget, police departments are ordered not to arrest illegals or even report them to us, and states offer them welfare, free medical care, and school? Damn it, with that kind of incentive I'd be running across the border myself. The Mexican border is a perfect conduit for terrorists. We need to seal it, but do you really think that's going to happen with the

ACLU and all the civil rights groups biting our asses every time we pick up an illegal? It's all nothing but political bullshit."

He sat down, his face red and his cheeks puffing. Thornton remained standing.

"Gentlemen, and ladies," he said, "if arresting a Mexican diplomat for smuggling Arabs can't convince Congress of the need for strict INS enforcement, then maybe a WMD going off in our cities or a series of 9/11s might. The reason I couldn't make this meeting yesterday was because we came across two dead Arabs in Yuma charged with enough radiation to solve Southern California's electric shortage. I'm prepared to state that we have Islamics running around our country right now with a low-level nuclear charge potent enough to wipe out downtown San Diego or any other major city in the U.S. I can't overstate this fact: We are *not* prepared. If we don't clean up our borders, then we had better be prepared to clean up our cities after terrorists finish with them."

How much blunter could he be? It distressed him when powerful politicians and officials failed to see the terrorist threat, refused to act against it on all levels, and simply would not face the reality that the War on Terror was one in which the fate of Western civilization hinged.

"Where do we start?" asked attorney Bob Skorlos.

"My staff and I at the Office of National Domestic Preparedness have prepared a paper that will go to the President this week for his approval." Thornton opened his briefcase and withdrew thick sheaves of paper. "I'll hand out copies. The reports list in logical sequence the steps federal, state, and local governments must take in closing down alien smuggling operations from Mexico. My office and Director Thornbrew of Homeland Security will oversee the implementation of this proposal once it's approved—"

Dock of the Bay from his cell phone interrupted. Someone chuckled. The readout on the instrument's face told him Fred Whiteman was calling back.

"Excuse me, people," he said, starting the report copies around the table. "This is important. Don't let my absence interfere with anything important."

He stepped out into the hallway for privacy. "Yeah, Fred?"

Whiteman got right to the point. "The name is Lough, Charles Edward. He's a porn film maker and lobbyist for Entertainment Media Enterprises. EME is the conglomerate that brings us films such as *Debbie Does Dallas, Chicago and Des Moines* with a gerbil, two German shepherds, a donkey and—"

"I get the picture."

"The dead man spent his last day—"

"*Dead man.*"

"He was gunned down, murdered last night at the Lincoln Memorial."

"I'll be damned."

"Him too. I'll e-mail you a full report. It seems Lough met yesterday afternoon with the Party of the People National Committee Chairman in a D.C. restaurant. Gerald Espy—that's the POP NCC—has clammed up. He's not even admitting he was anywhere near the restaurant. Witnesses say Lough and Espy had a big blowout. Lough left so pissed off he could have chewed through a bundle of edible panties."

"Fred—"

"Right."

"What are the police saying?"

"What can they say? They're working on it. This is about

the ten millioneth murder in Gomorrah on the Potomac this year. Anyhow, the next thing we know, our old buddy now deceased met an old friend of yours at the Lincoln Memorial and was gunned down by unknown assailants."

"What do you mean 'old friend'?"

"General Darren Kragle."

"The General? Are you sure? What was it all about?"

"Dunno, Claude. I haven't been able to get him to answer his phone."

CHAPTER 24

Washington, D.C.

The General had seen men die violently, had killed men, but it shook him each time nonetheless. Death dealt out by other men must never be taken lightly. After he finished with the police last night, he returned to his hotel room and tried to catch a few hours' sleep. He was largely unsuccessful at it. The mysterious callers kept intruding into his thoughts.

One caller brought up a past the General thought long buried with Jerry R. Hurst. The other purported to warn him of . . . of what? *The Committed?* Whoever they were. Of a plot against the U.S. government that he, the General, wouldn't believe? It sounded political, but then almost everything in Washington, D.C., was political. In the nation's capital, you trusted no one and expected not to be trusted. *That* maxim was the only thing you trusted in Washington, D.C.

Didn't Charles Edward Lough's murder prove that?

The police identified Lough quickly from documents in his wallet.

"Do you know him?" detectives asked the General.

"That was the first time I saw him. I didn't really see him then. He called, said he had something I needed to know, then stayed in the shadows. That's really about all I know."

"The name 'Lough' ring any bells?"

"Not really. I knew a Colonel John Lough in Vietnam, a B-52 Air Force pilot. But that was over thirty-five years ago."

The General recounted his brief conversation with Lough, omitting only references to Jerry Hurst. Hurst was his business and he would take care of it his own way. It was something of which he was not proud and which would undoubtedly end his career in disgrace. The army might even file criminal charges against him.

Detectives seemed as puzzled by "the Committed" as the General was. They looked at each other and shrugged.

"You have no idea what he meant by a plot against the government?"

"Should I?"

They handed him business cards. "If you think of something else, give us a call. I'm afraid we'll have to ask you to stay close and available for a few more days."

He got up early to have breakfast in the hotel dining room. He refused to answer two phone calls from Claude Thornton. He didn't feel like speaking with his old FBI friend yet. He had no illusions that the matter of Jerry Hurst would go away if he left it alone, but he didn't want to deal with it right now.

Later, he called Central Command in Florida, provided his code over a secure line and waited for it to be authenticated. The operations officer came on the line. The general asked for a quick update on the two phases of Aces Wild.

Major Dare Russell's Detachment 1-Charlie had just airlifted out of Baghdad on its way to the airport in Tindouf, the ops officer said. Elements of the 10th Mountain Division had surrounded and secured the airport, except for the terminal. Terrorists held it, along with an undetermined number of hostages.

"We have a satellite dedicated to Tindouf," the ops officer explained. "So far nothing much is moving at the airport. Bad guys still hold the city. They're chasing down Sahrawi while the Tenth chases them. If you don't mind my saying so, sir, we've got a real goat fuck going on over there."

In Madrid, Major Brandon Kragle's Det 2-Charlie had scrambled aboard Blackhawk helicopters and was at the present hour enroute to Algeria and West Sahara to rescue Governor Chadli Malud.

"We received a confirmed sighting of the governor some several miles onto West Sahara territory, sir. It should be a quick hop in to get him, then right back out."

"Good. Any other problems?"

"It's going five-by so far, sir. There were some explosions in Madrid before the detachment took off. All we know is that some passenger trains were blown up. They didn't affect the mission."

"Put Paul on the line, will you?"

CENTCOM's commander, General Paul Etheridge, was one of the most powerful military men under the Joint Chiefs of Staff. Central Command conducted much of the War on Terror in the Middle East and Southwest Asia.

"Sir, you haven't heard?" the ops officer asked.

"Did he go to Madrid with Aces Wild?"

"Sorry, sir. General Etheridge is not with us anymore."

"Run that by me again."

"He resigned, sir. This morning. That's all I know."

The General hung up and pondered the news a minute, his unease growing. He tried to call Paul Etheridge's private quarters, but received a recording. He dialed JCS and asked for General Abe Morrison, chairman of the Joint Chiefs.

"Darren, what the hell is going on?" Abe demanded when he came on the line.

"I was about to ask you the same thing."

"First, you're involved in some kind of street shooting," General Morrison said, "and now Paul calls in this morning first thing and says he's resigning. What was the shooting about, mister? We're going to need some reports."

"Can I get back to you on that, Abe? Did Paul say why he was resigning?"

"He said it was personal and I couldn't talk him out of it. I'm hearing rumbles that AFSOC is also talking resignation. You haven't heard that about General Holloman, have you?"

"This is all a surprise to me."

"It seems there's an epidemic going on. You're not having symptoms, Darren?"

"No, sir."

The General locked the door and sat alone in his hotel room, gazing out upon Pennsylvania Avenue and the White House down the street. The room phone's ringing came as no surprise. He half expected it.

"Yeah?"

"General Etheridge has real good sense." The crackling "Jerry Hurst" voice greeted him. "Do you have good sense, Captain Kragle?"

"What is this all about?"

The crackling voice dissipated into crackling laughter. "You have no idea how much I'm enjoying this, Captain. You have seventy-two hours to join General Etheridge— or you can join Mr. Lough."

"Are you threatening—?"

"Of course I am. Isn't that a hoot? Remember, seventy-two hours or Jerry's back in town to stay."

"Hold on a minute."

"Seventy-two hours."

Dead air.

CHAPTER 25

Vietnam, 1968

Captain Darren Kragle's Mike Force went through Vinh Tho like green grass through a goose, scaring up little more than bare-assed chickens, scolding ducks, and a few hogs. Contrary to Colonel Bruton's supposed intelligence, the village was almost abandoned. Initially, intermittent firing from both sides, none of it very effective, punctuated the assault. Then the VC, a few black-clad figures darting among the hooches, faded out the back of the hamlet. Kragle hip shot his Stoner at a small group before it disappeared across the single-log monkey bridge and into dense banana palms that fringed the Nam Can Forest. It was almost as though the VC expected the attack.

Kragle lost sight of Lieutenant Hurst and half expected to find him cowering in the rice paddy. Apparently, however, he found the prospect of being left behind and alone more terrifying than remaining with the assault. He pumped along so close behind Petrus Thuong, the radio operator, that if Petrus had stopped suddenly Hurst would have suffocated from burying his head in the 'Yard's ass. He looked so damned scared that the only thing he had eyes for was Petrus's back. He flinched every time an isolated raindrop struck him.

Captain Kragle grabbed him by his battle harness to pull him up short. Hurst hadn't even *seen* his commander. He screamed in sudden panic.

"Damn it, Hurst. Shut the fuck up. Just stick with me from now on, all right?"

Hurst's head nodded spastically; he was too scared to speak.

The Mike Force linked up with the other rifle platoon, the second assault element, before the two units split up again according to Colonel Bruton's battle plan.

"Piece of cake," the platoon leader commented.

"It's not over yet," Captain Kragle cautioned.

The infantry moved north along the canal to ford further up. Captain Kragle took his force on through the village, crossed the canal at the monkey bridge, fanned out toward the south, and entered the banana groves to drive the enemy into Bruton's waiting anvil. The 'Yards passed through the groves into fields of twisted brush, head-high reeds, and the skeletons of dead trees. They entered an overgrown rice paddy nearly knee-deep with stagnant water. Drops of rain fell a bit more frequently, and the gray ceiling lowered.

Captain Kragle didn't like it. As Van Heflin or Victor Mature might have put it in one of their African movies, things were quiet—yeah, *too* quiet. Darren knew the enemy was out here, and out here in numbers. But *where* was he out here, and what was he up too?

He didn't have to wait long for the answer.

A tattering of distant rifle fire marked the entry of the anvil platoon into the fray as they engaged retreating VC. Then, almost immediately, the tatter became a startling crescendo of rifle and machine-gun fire punctuated by RPG and mortar explosions.

"*Goddamnit!*" Captain Kragle had warned that pin-dicked little fuck Bruton of at least a regiment of hard core in the AO—and now it sounded like the colonel's single reduced-force company had stepped into it with both feet.

Hurst's eyes bulged. He seemed ready to bolt.

"Get me the RTO," Darren ordered to keep the lieutenant focused.

Excited shouts rang out ahead from the lead squad. All eyes snapped to the right, where 'Yards were pointing across the rice paddy. In the brush on the other side, VC were scurrying about in what appeared to be an effort to encircle the Mike Force and cut it off from Bruton's main element.

Another shout from the rear security squad made the VC intentions even more clear. Groups of black-clad figures ran in between the Mike Force and the canal, cutting Darren's unit off from withdrawal in that primary direction. It was all too clear what was happening. American elements had been suckered into a trap because of Colonel Bruton's piss-poor intelligence, piss-poorer planning, and his arrogance. The enemy was maneuvering in a classic divide-and-conquer scenario, isolating each unit in preparation for bringing down his own hammer.

RTO Petrus Thuong, with the radio on his back, dropped to his knees next to Captain Kragle, followed by Hurst. The lieutenant gripped his rifle so tightly his knuckles turned white. Petrus's eyes were riveted on the hordes of VC sprinting just out of effective rifle range on either side.

"*Uy dai!*" he cried. "VC running hard, try to cut us off."

Captain Kragle took the radio handset from the little Asian, who turned his back so Darren could work the controls. Setting the frequency required at least three hands. He cradled the handset between chin and shoulder while he dialed in a freq of 57.1 and listened for a "zero beat" to indicate exact calibration. He finally got it and began transmitting.

"Dalton Salton, this is Rover One, copy? Over."

No response except a static rush of whistling and shrieking. Even more firing and sounds of battle vibrated from Colonel Bruton's position.

"Dalton Salton, do you read? Over."

Again no response. Darren frowned and switched freqs to the 155 howitzer fire-support base Savage.

"Angel Watch, this is Rover One, over."

Still nothing.

"I'm being jammed," he realized. "The little bastards are jamming our radio commo."

Hurst prayed silently. His lips moved but nothing came out. Then everything burst forth in raw horror: "Captain Kragle, they've got us surrounded. They're going to kill Colonel Bruton—and then they're coming for us!"

CHAPTER 26

TERRORISTS ATTACK MADRID

Madrid (CPI)—Ten bombs blew up four trains during morning rush hour in the Spanish capital, killing at least 200 people and injuring 1,200. The deadly train bombings sent nations around the world scrambling to protect transport networks from more potential terror attacks.

Signs indicate that the bombings were carried out by Islamic extremists who operate and have confederates in countries around the globe. FBI agents were dispatched to help Spanish police in using fingerprints and names to seek a full picture. Among the list of suspects are al-Qaeda, Salafia Jihadia, and the Moroccan Islamic Combatant Group. The Spanish newspaper *El Mundo* reported that the Spanish embassy in Egypt received a letter two days ago in which an Islamic militant group threatened that Spain would be the target of terrorism if it did not withdraw from Iraq and Afghanistan and denounce the U.S.-led War on Terror. Spain has been a major U.S. ally . . .

CHAPTER 27

West Sahara

During the quick preparation stages of Operation Aces Wild, Blackhawk attack helicopters, called "Venom," were disassembled in the United States, loaded into cargo C-5As and, along with Night Stalker pilots and crews of the 160th Special Operations Aviation Regiment, shipped to Madrid under total OPSEC blackout to support Major Brandon Kragle's Detachment 2-Charlie. Although, like Delta Force, the existence of the Night Stalkers was officially denied, they existed in a big way and had earned reputations as James Bonds of the aviation community. They flew mostly at night using the latest technology to deliver and extract SpecOps teams behind enemy lines.

Three of the flat-black unmarked birds now raced above the West Sahara desert in the middle of the night toward the objective known as Hill 138. All birds were loaded to the max with fuel, six-barreled 7.62 miniguns, and wing-mounted 2.75-inch rocket pods. Two gunships flanked the third, which carried the eight Deltas of Major Kragle's detachment.

Flying conditions had been marginal at best when the helicopters departed Spain. Major Kragle had the authority to scrub the mission if he felt it at risk. Only the realization that Governor Chadli Malud might not survive the night without intervention, and certainly would not survive the next day, made him designate it a go. Malud and a small band of Sahrawi were surrounded on Hill 138. Salafia Jihadia to the east of him hunted for his head. Moroccans on the west wanted to drive the Sahrawi back into Algeria and thereby avoid confrontation with terrorists. The Moroccan government saw the havoc terrorists raised with other governments who cooperated with the Great Satan, such as Madrid only today, and did not want its cities and citizens to become terrorist targets. Better to kill Sahrawi than risk that.

After in-flight refueling over Algeria, the birds dropped down to NOE (nap of the earth) for entry into West Sahara. Morocco had already refused fly-over permission and lodged a protest with the UN about alleged encroachment of the U.S. 10th Mountain Division onto its soil near the Sahrawi camps. Officially, therefore, this arm of Aces Wild did not exist.

"In other words, we've screwed the pooch if something goes wrong," was how Mad Dog Carson put it.

"Chew an authority on 'screw the pooch'?" Perverse Sanchez asked.

"Fu-uck. Even pooches need love. Chew wetbacks oughta know that."

Up front in the cockpit of the detachment's chopper, aviation crew wearing helmets and NVGs (night vision goggles) reminded Brandon of alien insects. As a pilot himself, he realized the skills it required, and the hazards posed, in the aircraft's racing along at one hundred feet above the deck, low enough to fry chickens in barnyards, over flat desert wastes and the rocky mouths of twisting wadis. A pilot had to stay intensely focused on the ground lest it suddenly rise and bite off his face.

The flight had been mostly quiet and introspective until the weather worsened after entry over West Sahara. Wind picked up. Blowing sand blasted against the aircraft skins.

The ride turned roller-coaster and roused the Deltas from napping. Dressed in black fire-resistant suits, buckled into web seating, they were jostled carelessly about.

Master Sergeant Ice Man Thompson sat quietly, one hand clenching the seating rail between his knees, the other grasping an MP-5 submachine gun, scars on his face earned in previous encounters brought out in relief by the gloomy red glow of the interior night-vision lights. Mad Dog Carson and Doc TB across from him leaned against each other as braces. Mad Dog was expressionless. Doc TB looked pensive, as though thinking of his pregnant wife and their expected child.

The new guys—Diverse Dade, the Zulu demolitions expert with the lion's eyes, and Corky "Perverse" Sanchez—possessed the rare ability to fall asleep almost immediately and to sleep the sleep of the righteous. Perverse opened one eye, blinked at Mad Dog, and closed it again. Diverse Dade yawned and stretched. Gloomy Davis leaned toward him.

"Arachna Phoebe married this dumb Polack one time . . ." he began, lapsing into another of his tales from Hooker, Oklahoma.

"Hold on," Team Sergeant Sculdiron interrupted. "*I'm* Polish."

"Okay, I'll tell it slower. Anyhow, this Polack was old and Arachna only married him for his money. On his deathbed, he asks Arachna if he can make love to her one last time. 'Look,' she told him, 'I gotta get up in the morning. You don't.' "

Perverse opened one eye again. "I really don't like thees bitch," he decided.

"She wouldn't marry a greaser anyhow," Mad Dog said, "even if he had money."

These were good men, all of them good men, Brandon

thought: Gloomy Davis leaning forward with his hands cupped, balancing over the case end of his .300 Winchester rifle, Mr. Blunderbuss, riding out the storm at his commander's side; the Dog and Doc TB; Diverse and Perverse; Ice Man; even Team Sergeant Alik Sculdiron, awake and watchful as always.

Brandon thought of other good men like them who had died on previous missions to Afghanistan, the Philippines, Iraq, and elsewhere. Rock Taylor, Winnie Brown, Mother Norman, Thumbs Jones . . . and there was also Gypsy Iryani. In this business, losses had to be expected and accepted, but they nonetheless rode heavy on Brandon's conscience and his mind. The thought of losing more of his men in combat was almost unbearable.

Word came back via intercom: "Twenty minutes!"

Sergeant Sculdiron got busy checking the men and their equipment. They had rehearsed action on the objective prior to embarking and they were ready. He went over it again.

"Carson?"

"Right security . . ."

"Thompson?"

"Left security . . ."

"Davis . . . ?"

Captain Wilbanks, the aircraft commander, came up on the intercom. "Major, if this shit gets much worse we're going to need a camel. We're pushing the envelope. We shouldn't even be flying now. Visibility is down to a football field and I've reduced speed back to nothing."

"How much longer?" Brandon asked.

"H-minus-one-five-mikes. Fifteen minutes. Everybody awake back there? We'll have to get in and back out fast. We should be able to land or at least hover right on the hill. If there's too many of them, well . . . We'll just have to load what we can take and leave the rest."

Malud was the essential package. That was the way it had to be. Harsh reality.

The ride got even rougher. Rough enough to jar spines and clack teeth together.

"Ten minutes! Get ready!"

The detachment wouldn't be able to unbuckle until the last moment. The men tensed, leaning forward, weapons in hand, watching and waiting for the Blackhawk to pull up and hover and the doors to open.

The pilot's next intercom shot Brandon with a sudden unexpected adrenalin jolt. Time switched to fast forward.

"I see troops on the ground," Captain Wilbanks almost shouted. "I see—*Holy shit!*"

Those were the pilot's last words.

Murphy, you sonofabitch—

CHAPTER 28

Tindouf Airport

Chaplain Cameron Kragle, the two women missionaries from Reach the Children Inc., and Zorgon huddled together in the complete darkness of their captivity at the airport. They had been confined for hours, perhaps a day, maybe even a night. It was difficult to tell how long without some sort of outside reference. It was still dark the one time the door opened and jugs of water were thrust inside before the door slammed again. The stench of human waste filled the room; there were no toilets. Around them, captured Sahrawi formed their own little support groups. A child whimpered. A woman's voice comforted it.

It occurred to Cameron that so many of the Sahrawi had been massacred in the beginning that survivors held little capital as hostages. In the eyes of a world grown callous, what difference did a few more or less of any despised or scorned group make? What it meant was that the American missionaries had to supply the main ammunition for the Salafia Jihadia to expend against the conscience of the world in order to have their demands met.

Cameron kept his concern to himself. No need to further alarm Kelli and Rhoda. His soul was troubled enough for all three of them, considering how he had mucked things up. But what could he have done differently to change the outcome?

Sobbing softly, Rhoda fell asleep in whatever asylum

Cameron's right arm around her afforded. Although seemingly made of sterner stuff, Kelli also sought refuge by nestling up to Cameron on the other side. Zorgon got as close as he could and drifted to more distant places where he didn't have to think about his missing wife and son.

Cameron placed his arm around Kelli and drew her close so that the scent of her hair and skin filled his nostrils. Her curves melted against his body. She felt warm and comfortable and vulnerable and dependent. He experienced a thickening of the throat and a protectiveness that he had not felt since Afghanistan and Gypsy Iryani.

He hadn't been able to save Gypsy either. Neither he nor Brandon.

The thickening in his throat hardened into a knot of anxiety and dread.

Kelli stirred and nuzzled sleepily against the hollow of his neck. "Ummm . . ." she said. "Have you slept, Cameron?"

"I dozed off watching TV."

She laughed softly, a trait she retained even under dire circumstances, and snuggled deeper into his arm so her lips were only inches from his ear and his lips from hers. In a short time they had learned this was the best way to hold conversation without disturbing others or drawing retribution from the guards, who forbade the prisoners to talk at all.

In this manner, whispering, they spoke to each other about their separate lives and families, of back home and events that molded them into the individuals they were. Both were spiritual, religious, and each held strong and sometimes conflicting beliefs and opinions. Kelli, an unabashed pacifist, took from the Bible how Jesus said to turn the other cheek. Cameron on the other hand, being a military man, took from the same Bible how God smote

His people's enemies. He thought Kelli's politics naïve and misplaced; she had voted for John Stanton for president, twice.

"Peaceful ends can only be reached through peaceful means," she argued. "How many children have been killed already in this War on Terror? How many more will be killed? We do have to be concerned about terrorism. Bless his heart, President Tyler believes we are doing the right thing, but we will never end terrorism by terrorizing others."

"Will you go out there and tell our captors that?" Cameron responded, gently but forcefully. "Defending yourself is not terrorizing others. Turn the other cheek, sure, but you don't have to *keep* turning the other cheek. How can you believe God would stand by and do nothing after what we've witnessed—the genocide of men, women, and children?

"Western civilization is at risk. America has faced down three great challenges within the last century. First came the Nazis with their 'perfect race' and World War II. Then came the Marxists, the 'perfect class,' and the cold war. Now come the Islamics to impose the 'perfect faith.' They pose a much more serious threat then either the Nazis or the Marxists because they hate us more than they love life."

"Terrorism exists because there are a lot of people living in abject poverty who have lost hope for better lives," Kelli stubbornly insisted. "We have to find the root causes and eradicate them before there will ever be peace. Yes, I could hate these people for what they did to the Sahrawi and to Jean, but hate destroys the hater and begets only more hate. I don't think God would lead us to hate instead of to love and forgive."

"Evil exists in this world. God would not have us accommodate evil for the sake of peace. 'War is an ugly thing, but not the ugliest of things—' "

Kelli stopped him by placing her fingertips over his lips. "I know, I know. John Stewart Mill."

She finished the quote for him: " 'The person who has nothing for which he is willing to fight, nothing more important than his own personal safety, is a miserable creature and has no chance of being free unless kept so by better men than himself.' "

"Close enough," Cameron approved.

"Chaplain, you might quote scriptures in circles around me, but I went to school too."

They continued their philosophical discussions to pass the hours, Cameron enjoying the opportunity to get to know this unusual, rare, and vivacious young woman. Neither realized their voices had grown louder, attracting someone else to their circle, until a soft voice intruded, "I am overhearing you and admiring such conversation when we confront peril. I would like to contribute."

"The peace conference scheduled for today is about to be canceled anyhow, due to conflicts," Kelli said. "Join the forum, bless your heart. Whose side are you on?"

The newcomer ignored the question and introduced himself instead. "My name is Giemma."

His English was precise and correct but accented. Cameron wondered what he looked like.

"I am North Sudanese," Giemma said, answering the unspoken question. "I am a Christian. I have learned that never must we give the devil a ride, for he will always want to drive."

"Well spoken," Cameron whispered.

"When you speak of evil, I will say that I have witnessed it. In the Christian Bible, Jesus is saying no words that we should kill innocent people. But in the Koran, it says to slay the infidels, slay them all, because the infidels are not truly human. I will tell you a story about that, with your permission?"

Oral history lived on in African cultures. Both Cameron and Kelli gave their immediate assent.

"Ten years ago," the unseen stranger began in the darkness, "when I am a mere child, I am captured by Muslims and taken away to become a slave. I am a Christian before then, as are many Sudanese, but I am warned that I must convert to Islam or I will be killed. So I pretend I am Muslim to save my life, and I am sold to a family to be their servant.

"For ten years I am with the family, from the time I am six years of age until I am sixteen, when I run away and after much hardships come to here where I am again captured by Muslims. For those ten years I am told I am a member of the family. But because I am once a Christian I am considered unclean and therefore cannot eat with the family. I am to sleep in a small shed in the rear of the family house because to live inside would pollute the family. Because I am kafir, I am also not allowed to pray with them, even though they think I am an Islam convert."

He fell silent. After a few moments, the boy cleared his throat and continued.

"Among my Dinka people is the word *Dut*, which is a special nickname for a Dinka boy. I speak English and do not understand the Arab language at first. The family is calling me *Dut*. I soon understand. It is not *Dut* I am called. It is *Jedut*. That is an Arab word for those slimy, crawly things that I see on a dead cow."

"Maggots," Kelli supplied, making a face.

"Yes. For ten years while I serve them I am nothing more to them than maggots. So are all who are not Islam. We are maggots to be conquered, converted, or killed in the name of Muhammad. That is what I see and that is what I believe. It is an evil that confronts us, and we in this room will see evil face to face."

He directed his last statement to Kelli, whom he could not see. He touched her to make sure she was listening. "To this lady who is talking of love and forgiveness," he said, "we shall see what she believes when evil enters this room."

Giemma fell silent after that. He lay down next to Zorgon and went to sleep. With her own thoughtful silence Kelli indicated that Giemma's story, heaped on top of horrors she had already endured, touched her deeply. She didn't feel like talking anymore. Soon, her regular breathing told Cameron that exhaustion had finally claimed her.

Left to himself, Cameron tried to think of some way out of their predicament. Here they were, locked inside a darkened room guarded by fanatics who probably intended to execute them sooner or later—and he couldn't think of anything to prevent it. All he succeeded in doing was giving himself a headache. Fatigue eventually overcame him and he dozed fitfully.

The door opening awoke him. Daylight streaming in hurt his eyes. Others around the room stirred, squinting and blinking against the harsh light. Kelli and Rhoda roused and pressed against Cameron. Zorgon lay asleep on the floor next to Giemma, using his inner-tube arm as a pillow. He sat up and twisted his arm around to his lap. The five of them, including Giemma, formed their own little enclave among the Sahrawi captives.

Cameron and Kelli got their first look at Giemma, their new acquaintance—a slightly built lad of seventeen or eighteen with blue-black skin and an amiable expression, clad only in the tunic-like *araga* that North Sudanese wore over their shirts and trousers. He scooted over as close to Cameron and Kelli as he could get. He was trembling with fear.

Cameron made out a man standing in the doorway in the bright light. He was tall for this part of the globe and wore a full beard, a red-and-white keffiyeh and a dirty, loose white-linen Arab garment that hung to just above his sandals. His nose was enormous, bulbous and scarred as though from acne, giving him a rather clownish appearance. Cameron immediately thought of him as Big Nose. The holster on his gun belt contained an automatic pistol. Two other Arab types stood immediately behind him, brandishing Kalishnikov assault rifles.

There was nothing clownish or funny in the wolfish smile Big Nose cast at Cameron's little group.

"I trust you slept well, praise be to Allah," Big Nose taunted in passable English.

Cameron started to rise in protest. "We are American citizens. Why are you holding us like this?"

The two riflemen snapped their weapons to cover him. Big Nose motioned for him to remain seated.

"I know who you are," he said. "Allah has need of you."

His dark, hard eyes raked over Cameron, the two women and Zorgon before settling on Giemma. He seemed to make up his mind.

"You," he ordered, pointing. "You are friendly with the American infidels. Therefore, you shall be first. Come with me."

Giemma's beseeching eyes cast wildly about looking for deliverance, but he dutifully clambered to his feet. He had been a slave too many years to resist.

"No!" Kelli cried. "He's done nothing. Let him stay."

Big Nose seared her with a predatory look. "Then who shall it be? You?"

"If God wills it."

"*Allah* does not will it yet. Sit, my pretty one. Your time will soon come."

CHAPTER 29

West Sahara

The Stinger missile struck the Blackhawk's main rotor gearbox with a shuddering impact that rendered the chopper virtually uncontrollable. What kind of luck was it that the helicopters should run across bad guys on the darkest night God created earth out of the black hole and that these bad guys could even see the choppers, much less hit one with a shoulder missile? Only Captain Wilbanks' skill at the controls kept the bird from disintegrating in the air and smearing itself in a fiery streak across the desert. It also helped that he had cut speed because of the sandstorm and poor visibility.

Major Brandon Kragle's detachment in the chopper's belly endured one chaotic ride for about five seconds as Captain Wilbanks used his blades' remaining lift to collect the charging helicopter and bring it up short, sort of like reining in a stampeding horse. It threatened to start tumbling through the sky, in which case it would hit the ground in a roll, small blades still churning, and literally beat itself and all passengers to pieces.

Wilbanks managed through physical strength and experience to keep the bird upright. He nosed it straight into the air to bleed off excess speed and let it drop almost straight down.

It fell out of the black sky onto the black desert with a resounding crunch. It skidded on its belly across the sand a short distance, wildly slinging chunks of blade and other parts in all directions, before it slammed nose down into a wadi and came to rest in a smothering cloud of dust and sand.

Perverse Sanchez had unbuckled moments before the crash to use the piss tube. The impact threw him against the forward cabin wall. He bounced off and landed on Ice Man's lap. The others were still buckled in. Doc TB received a gash on his chin, but otherwise the coughing and shouting indicated that most of the detachment survived in good shape.

Even the red night-vision lights went out when all systems shut down. The cabin was totally dark. Major Kragle quickly called roster in the sudden stillness.

"Sculdiron . . . ?"

"Okay."

"Gloomy Davis . . . ?"

"Right here, Boss."

"Dog . . . ?"

"Fu-uck."

"Doc . . . ?"

"Yes, sir."

"Mozee Dade . . . ?"

"Hoo-ya."

"Ice Man . . . ?"

"Yeah. I got Perverse on my lap. You okay, Sanchez?"

"What chew mean, okay? I done broke my fooking arm."

"All accounted for," Brandon said. "Doc, you and Ice get Perverse out of here before this thing catches fire and goes up."

"Yes, sir. I'm on my way."

Brandon produced a red-lensed flashlight from his battle harness. Others were doing the same thing. Muted beams of red light played about the cabin and provided enough illumination for Doc TB to reach Perverse, who was holding one arm twisted against his chest. Men were busy unbuckling and feeling around for their weapons. Smoke and dust filled the cabin and more sand blew whistling in through a great rent in the overhead, where rivets had popped and seams split. There seemed to be no fire. At least not yet.

"Top? Get everybody out. I'll check on the crew."

"I got things under control."

"Hustle, everybody. The perps'll be looking for us."

The aircraft had come to rest on a nose-down slant in the wadi with the tail section broken and stuck up in the air like a scorpion. Sculdiron's booming Polish accent urged everybody to "get the lead out" as the major, submachine gun slung over one shoulder, worked his way through the wreckage to the opening leading to the cockpit. He didn't have to look to know that Gloomy was right behind him. Gloomy had long assumed the boss's security to be his personal responsibility.

"Boss," he said, "every time I go anywhere with you, *something* happens."

"Luck of the Irish, I suppose."

"You didn't tell me it was all bad."

"Why do you think they call this mission Aces Wild?"

While Brandon and Gloomy cleared the opening of the forward cabin in order to get in and check out the flight crew, Top Sculdiron pried open the side door and evacuated the team. The first man out, Mad Dog, stepped out into darkness and fell six feet straight down. He let out a blue streak of curses when the second man out, Diverse Dade, landed on top of him.

"Whattaya think this is, Diverse?" Mad Dog rumbled. "A watermelon patch?"

"Can the bullshit," Top Sculdiron barked. "Get the fuck move on. You know the drill."

SOP—standing operating procedure—called for the detachment to reconsolidate at ten o'clock in the direction of last movement.

In the beam of his flashlight, Brandon found the crew chief already out of his middle seat and tending to the pilot. The cockpit had absorbed the brunt of the crash. A ledge of stone sticking out from the opposite bank of the wadi had smashed through the wind screen and into both pilots. Captain Wilbanks remained buckled in his seat, his head lolled back and his face webbed with blood.

"He's dead," the crew chief said. "Lieutenant Gardner is unconscious but still alive."

"How about you?"

"I think I'm all right."

Brandon's light played over the Night Stalker sergeant's face. He had a nasty cut on his forehead but otherwise appeared unharmed.

"Let's get out of here, then. We're going to have tangos all over us in a few minutes."

"What about Captain Wilbanks?"

"Get the other one out first."

Gardner groaned in pain as the two Deltas and the crew chief pulled him from his seat and carried him to the escape door. Brandon jumped out first, landing on his feet. He found Diverse Dade waiting for him. Together they received the unconscious man and lowered him to the ground.

Gloomy and the crew chief went back for Captain Wilbanks. Diverse accepted the body. He dragged it up the wadi and concealed it in some rock. He hurried back. Gloomy and the crew chief were already on their way to the rally point with Lieutenant Gardner. Major Kragle stood next to the smoldering aircraft, listening for the on-coming enemy or for the engine sounds of the other two Blackhawks. The howl of the increasing storm drowned out all except its own noise of wind and scouring sand.

"Is anyone left inside?" Diverse asked, standing near so he could be heard over the wind.

"All clear. Blow it so we can get out of here."

"I've already got charges set on the fuel bladders."

It was also SOP to leave nothing behind that might benefit the enemy or that could identify invaders or their nationality. The M60 fuse lighter popped.

"Fire in the hole!" Diverse said. "Thirty seconds until detonation."

The two men sprinted toward their ten-o'clock position. Blowing sand lashed at their faces. Wind carried faint voices from the direction of the downed aircraft. It sounded like the enemy was about to discover the wreck. *Good luck, assholes.*

Efficient as always, Sculdiron had established three-sixty security at the rally point and accounted for every man. Brandon and Diverse entered the perimeter on the run.

"*Everybody down!*"

They had barely thrown themselves to the ground when the helicopter exploded in a monstrous ball of flame that rattled and scorched the surrounding terrain. Concussion waves snatched Gloomy Davis's bush cap off his head. Someone at the explosion site screamed in pain and surprise. Yep, the enemy had discovered the wreck all right.

"And *that*," said Diverse with satisfaction, "is *sayonara*."

First things first: Evacuate the crash site, account for personnel—and now, get the flock out of the AO. There was no time to lose. The detachment possessed the latest model in the Motorola Saber handheld encrypted radios. Brandon wore a headset. The wires from it threaded through the lining of his SWAT jacket to a small speaker in his left collar and a microphone in his lapel. Volume and frequency controls were built into his sleeves.

Crouching to get out of the wind, he dialed in a freq and raised Venom One, the air mission leader. He provided a brief SITREP: One KIA, Captain Wilbanks; at least three WIAs—the crew chief, Sergeant Corky Sanchez, and Lieutenant Gardner, whom Doc TB reported in critical condition. The helicopter had been destroyed as per SOP. There were an unknown number of enemy in the vicinity.

He concluded with, "Request extraction ASAP?"

"Negative on your request, Viper One. We've got too much weather. We can't see shit through this blowing sand, even with our NVGs. What we can see is too rugged to sit down on in this wind. We're also running low on fuel."

"What's your suggestion, Venom One?" Brandon quickly responded, more harshly than intended.

Listening closely, he could hear the faint motor hum of the two choppers circling high above, out of effective Stinger range. The tangos had gotten lucky once; it wasn't going to happen again.

"Viper, do you have GPS?"

The global positioning system was about the size of a deck of playing cards. Brandon carried it in his cargo pocket along with maps and compass.

"Affirmative, Venom One."

"We suggest you proceed to objective. You're near it," Venom One said. *"We'll return for you just as soon as the weather lifts and we can get back."*

The core of the SpecOps creed, the essence of its culture and honor, was that no man was ever left behind under any circumstances, whether he was alive or dead. He might be wounded, cut off from his buddies, surrounded by the enemy, even KIA, but someone always came back. Captain Wilbanks would be buried at home.

"*We'll be back, Viper,*" Venom One repeated.

Until the return of the choppers, it would be a matter of survival. Detachment 2-Charlie, Operation Aces Wild, found itself alone on the desert in the middle of a fierce sandstorm and surrounded by unknown forces in unknown numbers. The glow of the burning helicopter penetrated the gritty darkness, red and festering. Excited yammering rose from the crash site as bad guys approached it.

Brandon assembled the men to explain Venom One's suggestion that they proceed to Hill 138. Although officers made final decisions in Special Operations, every man down to the lowest rank had a voice in it.

"We don't know if the package will still be there or even if he'll be alive when we reach him," Ice Man pointed out. "Even if he's there and alive, we might have to fight our way through to get him."

"We can't wait here and we can't go back," Gloomy Davis said. "Looks to me like we only have one choice— and that's to go ahead with the mission. The sonofabitches can kill us, *maybe,* but we're damned sure too tough for them to eat."

"Anything else?" Brandon asked. There wasn't. "Good. Done. Deal the aces. We have a mission to run. Doc, get the wounded ready to move ASAP."

Every plan sounded good up until boots hit the ground. And then there was always Murphy: Anything that could go wrong, *would*.

CHAPTER 30

Tampa, Florida

Seventy-two hours. General Kragle had to move fast, convinced as he was that there were connections between his "Jerry Hurst" calls warning him to resign, the resignation of General Etheridge, and General Holloman's talk of resignation. He grabbed a flight to Tampa and arrived before noon. He had to talk to them in person, *make* them talk to him. It was a place to start in unraveling whatever the hell this was all about.

The plane was taxiing in to the terminal when, having just turned his cell phone back on after landing, he received news from CENTCOM that his eldest son's helicopter had been shot down over West Sahara. At last report, Brandon's detachment was on the ground and proceeding with its mission.

Gloria rang him as he was rushing to grab a taxi. He could almost see her finger wagging underneath his nose.

"Darren, has you seen the newspapers?" she scolded.

"I have."

"What in the good Lawd's name is you gonna do about it? That be your *son* them A-rabs has caught. They done got our Cameron."

"Sugar Mama, we're taking care of it."

"You sure 'nuff better be," she snapped. "Them terror people is done kilt one of they hostages and is gonna start on the others. Darren, listen to me now. If you ever wants me to speak to you again, you go over there and you get Cameron."

She broke into great blubbering sobs. "That is my baby over there," she cried. "Darren, do *something*."

He dared not tell her about Brandon. That news on top of everything else would be more than she could handle all at once. She would never get used to the dangerous type of work in which her boys were involved.

"Brown Sugar, I'll call you later. Keep a stiff upper lip. Say hello to Raymond."

"You ain't gonna *have* no upper lip, stiff or otherwise, if something happen to my boy."

The General's POV, private vehicle, was parked in the garage at his Tampa residence, but he didn't want to take the time to retrieve it. Instead he gave the Yellow cab driver General Paul Etheridge's address in a breathless rush.

General Etheridge's house was a two-story brownstone with a view of St. Petersburg across the bay. Paul's wife, Mary, a matronly little grandmother, hugged Darren and burst into tears. Her eyes were already red from weeping.

"Mary, where's Paul?" the General asked.

"It's been a horrible last few days," Mary blurted out. "Paul just suddenly . . . Suddenly he turned into Mr. Hyde. Everything changed in just a single day. He called in his retirement from the army and took off in the car without a word. He didn't say where he was going or when he'd be back. That's the last I've heard from him."

"Do you know what made him want to retire like that?"

"It was the strangest thing. I . . . I . . ."

"Mary, was there a phone call?"

She looked up quickly. "There *was* a call. Everything *did* seem to start from there. How did you know?"

"Mary, I'm getting them too. Who was the call from?"

"He wouldn't tell me. I was in the room with him when it came. You know how Paul's lips compress whenever he's angry? They were a hard line. He just listened. He started to say something back, but I guess the other party hung up. He wouldn't tell me what it was."

Everyone had *something* in his past for which he was ashamed and wished to hide. All a blackmailer had to do was find out what and push the right buttons. For General Kragle, it was Jerry Hurst. Who or what was it for General Etheridge?

The biggest question of all remained: Why were they being targeted? There had to be a motive behind it all, a common purpose, yet the General was hard put to venture even a guess.

"Mary, are you going to be all right here alone?"

"Our son will be back shortly. He only went to the store."

General Kragle hugged her again and directed the waiting cabbie to drive him to General Ray Holloman's address in St. Petersburg. Childless and a widower for years, Holloman, commander of the Air Force Special Operations Command (AFSOC), doted on his niece Kelli. It was out of concern for her safety that Ray imposed upon the Kragles for Cameron to escort her and the other women of Reach the Children Inc. to Algeria.

Holloman commuted between Hulbert Field and his St. Petersburg residence, where he spent most weekends building miniature aircraft and translating his own copy of the Bible from the ancient Greek. General Kragle was willing to bet he had also received a "Jerry Hurst" call.

The Holloman house was much more modest than the Etheridges—a low South Florida bungalow with a red tile roof, lots of screened windows and palm and orange trees growing on the front lawn. General Kragle asked the cabbie to wait while he trotted to the door and knocked. The ring of his cell phone made him jump. Tension, he thought. The phone readout displayed Claude Thornton's name and number again. He still didn't want to talk, so he let voice mail take it.

A thin middle-aged woman with dyed-red hair answered his knock. She looked him over.

"The others has just left," she said.

"The others?"

"You are a policeman, ain't you?"

General Kragle's heart skipped a beat. "No, ma'am. I'm a friend of Ray's. I need to talk to him. Who are you?"

"I'm the new housekeep, but I'm afraid you're too late, mister. I'm just cleaning up."

The words failed to quite sink in. "Cleaning up?" he repeated, feeling like a parrot.

She looked him over again. "I guess you ain't heard. Mr. Holloman shot hisself. I found him this morning at his desk."

The news left the General temporarily speechless with shock. He sagged against the door. Ray and he had been friends for a long time. The cleaning lady's hard face softened.

"I guess if you was his friend, you might as well come on in," she said. "You look like you need to sit down. The police has done finished their investigation anyhow. Made a bigger mess and left me to clean it up. I suppose I'm out of a job anyhow. You don't need a housekeep, do you, mister? President Tyler's tax breaks for the wealthy is sending all us poor people to the poor house."

Recovering from the jolt, General Kragle walked past her and directly to Ray's study. Police crime scene tape, fingerprint powders and chalk marks littered the room. Detectives had ransacked Ray's desk and other papers, apparently looking for a suicide note. A model F-14 jet had crashed on the floor and lost a wing.

"Did he leave a note or anything?" the General asked.

"I don't think the cops found none."

A thick pool of blood and brain matter coagulated on the desktop, splattering over onto a framed photo of Ray and his niece Kelli together on the beach.

"I found him right there when I come in to clean this morning," the lanky redhead offered. "There was a pistol still in his hand."

The General had to ask, although he shouldn't expect a new cleaning lady to know. "Did he receive a telephone call? A strange one? Something different?"

"How would I know that? But . . ."

The General turned and made a gesture for her to continue.

"I guess the police overlooked it. I was in the Florida room cleaning just before you come and I found where he records his phone calls. It seems weird to me—"

"Show me, ma'am."

The Florida room was at the other end of the house. Wraparound windows looked into a small backyard enclosed in a privacy fence. Sure enough, Ray had rigged a makeshift recorder to his telephone. The General sat down and played back conversations Ray had had over the past few days. Most were routine, having to do with work, or they were private with friends and family. Several calls from the American ambassador to Algeria pertained to niece Kelli and the other missionaries. The General listened to them but learned nothing new about Cameron. Ray had also made two calls to the State Department asking what was being done about the missionaries and received the usual toe-tapping responses. Ray's voice, although concerned, certainly didn't sound suicidal.

Then someone on the recorder uttered two words: "Gerda Groner." Followed by a hard, mirthless laugh. As though that wasn't enough to identify the crackling voice as that of General Kragle's own tormentor, the caller added his signature phrase to remove all doubts: "General Holloman, we're ba-a-a-a-ack!"

The mystery caller was brief, although he seemed more loquacious, more specific, with Ray than he had previously with General Kragle.

"General Holloman, you will resign from Special Operations Command within seventy-two hours or your lovely niece and the whole world will know about Gerda Groner. Is that clear?"

Ray's voice went tight and edged. "Who are you? I don't know what you're talking about."

"You know, all right. Gerda the Groaner."

"Why are you doing this?"

The hard taunting laugh, the crackling voice. "You and all the others are following Woodrow Tyler in leading the country toward fascism even though he wouldn't understand the word fascism anyhow."

Click.

CHAPTER 31

Vietnam, 1968

From the battle noises ahead, it sounded like Colonel Bruton's command was pulling a General Custer. *Where the hell did all them Indians come from?* More battle noise from off to the east announced how the assault rifle platoon also had run into something heavy. That left Captain Darren Kragle's Mike Force on its own, without communications, without artillery or air cover, and cut off from a return route to Vinh Tho.

Darren lifted his head toward a bruised and swollen sky that squeezed a raindrop onto his forehead. Clouds promised a monsoon deluge, but it still held off. Combat soldiers normally hated rain—there would be no air cover in this weather—but today a canal-swelling, mud-making, blinding gully washer might be just the thing to conceal Captain Kragle's loyal 'Yards until they could fade away into the forest.

A shallow canal lined with high patches of reeds traversed the rice paddy, leading at an angle toward a small farmers' village that squatted in a thick grove of coconut palms about eight hundred meters away. Since VC owned the woods and jungles surrounding the rice field, the canal provided Darren's soldiers with their only covered escape route. He ordered his force into the canal, whose combined wild bamboo and elephant grass provided a screen against enemy observation and fire.

The enemy opened up as though on signal. The rattle of automatic weapons lent impetus to the organized retreat. Snapping bullets cut into bamboo and reeds like hordes of vicious, deadly insects. Bits of leaves and grass filled the air. Fire came from both sides and from the rear as the 'Yards scurried toward the village along the canal in the water between its brush-choked banks.

"They're trying to fix us in place," Captain Kragle shouted. "Hurst, keep 'em moving. *Di-di dau! Di-di.*"

Lieutenant Hurst's eyes were stretched wide from fear and alarm. "Where?" he cried.

"We can't let 'em pin us down." He pointed at the far scattered hooches in the grove of palms. "Through there. It's our only way out. Get on point and lead the way. Follow the canal around to the hooches."

"Captain, I can't—"

"God damn it, Hurst. Get up there."

He grabbed the cowering man and threw him bodily toward the front. Hurst collapsed, shaking all over. The poor bastard was virtually useless.

"God damn you, Hurst." He looked around. "Ching Hi? Ching Hi, do you see what I'm talking about?"

"Number one, *uy dai.*"

"Get up there, then. Move it."

Darren ran up and down the canal, yelling and waving and snatching 'Yards by their fighting harnesses and slinging them in the direction he wished them to go, pushing the column. Hurst scrambled off the ground and stumbled along halfway up the line where he felt most secure. Mud sucked at their boots, sapping strength, as they jogged toward where the canal curved back toward the hooches and the palms.

The dreaded *Thunk! Thunk! Thunk!* of mortar tubes joined the fray. The first rounds burst in the paddy about a hundred meters away, making explosive geysers. The enemy quickly adjusted. Geysers walked into the canal and chased the 'Yards and their two U.S. advisors.

One small group of Montagnards found the going too slow in the canal and thought to make a run for the hooches by taking the trail that followed the top of the bank. The trail detonated underneath their fleeing feet in smoke, fire, and clods of earth. Shrapnel tore short screams from the throats of the dying men. A man's trunk, minus both legs, landed at the water's edge directly in front of Hurst, causing the lieutenant to begin screaming and flailing his arms in horror. His M-16 flew into the canal. He bolted blindly for the palms. Ching Hi tried to catch him.

"Let him go!" Darren called out. "Maybe somebody'll shoot his worthless ass."

Hurst, unscathed, lay trembling and blubbering on the ground when the rest of the outfit caught up with him and reached the village. It was deserted. To Captain Kragle's dismay, he discovered the palms and village formed a sort of island surrounded by more rice paddies. He had expected a passageway through it into the forest. Even worse, the rippling flicker of many rifle shots coming from a treeline beyond the rear paddy meant the Mike Force was now surrounded on all sides. A blocking force of VC had moved in with superior numbers.

Damn it, *damn it*. He had tried to warn Bruton.

Darren ordered Ching Hi to spread the fighters into a thin three-sixty perimeter around the tiny scattering of five or six huts. It was damned accommodating of the VC to have earlier dug shallow fighting holes around the hooches in some operation of their own. As a final touch, Darren planted his only M60 machine gun to cover a likely avenue of enemy approach facing the canal by which they had arrived at this sorry destination. With luck, they should be able to hold out—providing they could unjam the radio and make contact with FSB *Savage* and its 155 howitzers.

That would require not *just* luck, but a *lot* of luck. Petrus Thuong crouched with the PRC-10 radio at the edge of the canal and desperately tried to coax it to useful life. Only a steady painful stream of whistles and squawks issued from it.

More explosions raked the edge of the palm grove as VC mortar gunners sought range and deflection, feeling for victims. Palm fronds rattled like skeletons as a fresh breeze chattered raindrops across their tops.

God, please let it rain. Hard.

"*Uy dai!* They come. They come!"

The enemy suddenly seemed to pour across the rice fields like water from a breeched dam. A solid wall of bodies clad in black. Leaping and darting, crouching, running, shouting, muzzles blasting, flopping bush hats bouncing. Bullets tore overhead, zipping and hissing and snapping. Captain Kragle lay flat on the ground and selected targets from the rushing human waves. His automatic Stoner recoiled steadily into his shoulder.

Lieutenant Hurst, unarmed, lay whimpering in a fetal position at the bottom of his fighting hole.

CHAPTER 32

Tindouf Airport

The C-130 Hercules that flew Major Dare Russell's detachment from Baghdad to Algeria approached the Tindouf Airport high and fast, then bled altitude and passed low and fast over the airstrip to check for barriers or obstacles. Old pickup trucks sat on the strip at intervals close enough to prevent even a Cessna from landing. A terrorist further dramatized the airport's closure by darting out of the terminal and spraying the sky with an automatic rifle as the huge plane roared over.

Unable to airland, Russell's detachment quickly rigged Dash-1s for a low-level parachute jump as the Hercules circled in the morning sun. The Dash-1 standard paratrooper's 'chute was more reliable and positive-opening at low altitudes than the HALO (high altitude, low opening) square canopies Delta normally used. Major Russell, a lean, blond officer with a pencil-line mustache and a terse businesslike manner, designated as the DZ a small patch of desert behind a maintenance shed at the approach end of the runway. The drop zone lay at least a thousand yards from the terminal and therefore out of effective rifle range.

"First, they separate the men from the boys," Bobby Goose Pony quipped. "Then they separate the men from the fools. Lastly, the fools jump."

The hop-and-pop from an altitude of less than eight hundred feet went off without incident. The cargo plane flew at odd angles to the runway to avoid ground fire. Eight black-clad figures tailgated it. Parachutes mushroomed in a spray and the men landed almost immediately.

The Deltas had barely rolled up the stick and collected parachutes when they detected activity at the terminal, almost as though in response to their dramatic arrival. Three armed men in white robes and headdresses dragged a small black man out of the sand-colored two-story building into the early-morning light. A stiff breeze, the edge of a sandstorm currently blasting the desert further west, whipped their robes around their legs. Major Russell and his detachment watched from the maintenance shed they had appropriated as the team's CP and tactical operations center. Team sniper Sergeant "Peedy" Moody peered through his rifle scope.

The terrorists escorted the captive onto the aircraft parking apron. The small black man's white-ringed eyes clearly reflected his fear. Two of the gunmen carried assault rifles, one with a bandoleer of shiny ammo strung across his chest Poncho Villa style. The third man was taller than the others, had a blacker beard, and wore a red-and-white keffiyeh. He brandished a pistol and looked directly at the Delta team, sneering defiantly, and jabbed the muzzle of the weapon against the black African's temple. The black man's legs gave out on him. The other two tangos had to hold him up by his arms.

"He's gonna do it, damn him," Team Sergeant Alan Bodine murmured in disbelief.

Peedy Moody settled his crosshairs on the tall man's chest, twisted the right dope in on his telescopic sight, and said, "Major, I can stop the bastard."

"Hold what you got," Major Russell said.

"Are we going to stand by and *watch* him do it?" another Delta demanded, his voice strung taut.

"That's exactly what we're going to do," Major Russell snapped. "Our mission is to rescue U.S. personnel. We might save that poor miserable wretch, but then they'd likely execute one of our own in retaliation. We think Sergeant Kragle's brother is in there, so if that man's death buys us some time, so be it. Mission comes first."

Tension built among the operators as they stared in horrified anticipation at events unfolding on the distant tarmac. They winced in unison when smoke puffed from the executioner's pistol. Smoke and a gore of blood and brains blew out the victim's opposite temple. The African flopped to the apron an instant before the sound of the pistol's report, faint and distant, reached the maintenance shed.

The three tangos turned nonchalantly and walked back to the terminal, confident that they held all the aces and that no one dared fire on them. The dead man lay face down on the tarmac. One leg twitched and then was still. The red sun shone down on him. Its heat already seemed to weigh on his body.

The shooter turned his head toward the Delta detachment, smirking, before he disappeared into the terminal.

"I would take great pleasure in wasting that bastard," Moody the sniper said.

CHAPTER 33

AMERICAN HOSTAGES HELD, ONE HOSTAGE KILLED

Algiers (CPI)—Even as the Algerian government fights for its survival, rebels associated with Amari Saichi's Salafia Jihadia have begun executing hostages at the airport in Tindouf. One unidentified man was shot in the temple early this morning as American troops watched. Rebel terrorists promise to shoot one hostage each day until their demands are met. Added to the original demands is the withdrawal of all U.S. troops encircling the Tindouf Airport.

An unknown number of hostages are being held. Salafia Jihadia released the names today of three American captives. They are identified as Kelli Rule of Tampa, Florida; Rhoda Hoffstetter of Kansas City, Missouri; and U.S. Army Chaplain Cameron Kragle of Fort Bragg, North Carolina. One American, Jean Marrs, is believed to have been killed when Salafia Jihadia attacked Sahrawi refugee camps on Algeria's border with Moroccan-held West Sahara.

The execution and the threat of further executions elicited an immediate response from Party of the People presidential candidate Senator Lowell Rutherford Harris.

"When I'm president of the United States," he said from New Hampshire, "I'm going to take care of the American people. We are not going to have one of these terrorist incidents. This could have been prevented with proper leadership, the same as 9/11 could have been prevented. I cannot even imagine four more years of this administration. We're on a road to fascism with no stop signs. The only really good news will be when we put an end to Woodrow Tyler's reckless, go-it-alone approach."

President Tyler fired back with, "Without a bitter cost in casualties, we have defeated two ruthless dictators in Afghanistan and Iraq and liberated fifty million people, only to retreat before a few thugs and assassins. We will never surrender without victory. Not on my watch we won't . . ."

CHAPTER 34

Langley, Virginia

CIA Deputy Director of Intelligence Tom Hinds, a former college halfback gone a little to pot in middle age, pushed his chair back from his desk and lit a cigarette. He offered Claude Thornton a Marlboro. Thornton declined.

"There's nothing more condescending and self-righteous than a recently divorced reformed smoker," Hinds said in his gravelly smoker's voice, blowing smoke.

"Edith left over a year ago," Thornton said. "She took my stress with her, so why should I smoke?"

The CIA spook blew more smoke, squinting his eyes at the black FBI agent. "You are indeed a rarity, my friend," he said, "an American without stress. Maybe I should consider the same option to stop smoking."

Thornton chuckled. "Works every time."

Hinds got up and walked to his seventh-floor window of CIA headquarters at Langley. He looked down on the summer green of the Potomac River Valley, as though still contemplating Thornton's question of why would the Party of the People National Committee chairman meet with a porn peddler and lobbyist on the same day the porn maker got waxed? What was the connection?

"You do realize that the CIA isn't allowed to conduct intelligence gathering within the United States?" Hinds reminded the agent. "Wasn't it J. Edgar and the FBI who gathered all the dirt on politicians?"

"J. Edgar's dead. Congressional limitations on the Surveillance Act have crippled everybody. Now we have to depend on the Culinary Institute of America."

"Limitations that were pushed through the Senate by Senator Lowell Harris who continues to serve on the Senate Select Intelligence Committee while he stumps for the presidency," Hinds said.

Thornton knew the CIA deputy director rarely engaged in idle speculation or unguarded observations. Hinds continued to gaze out the window, looking thoughtful.

"Off the record?" he asked presently.

"Isn't it always?"

Hinds nodded, returned to his desk and sat down. "Claude, there is no previous connection that we know of between NCC Gerald Espy and Charles Edward Lough. Lough seems to be a dark horse who suddenly appeared on the scene."

Thornton started to look disappointed.

"But . . ." said Hinds.

"But?"

"But there's an even more interesting marriage than that between Lough and Espy, even more interesting than boys marrying each other in San Francisco—that between Gerald Espy and Senator Harris."

Thornton raked a heavy hand across his bowling-ball head and leaned forward.

"According to a recently released KGB report to the Soviet Communist Party Central Committee in 1978," Hinds went on, "Espy sought the help of an ambitious freshman senator named Harris in establishing a relationship between the Soviet apparatus and an electronics firm owned at the time by Espy."

"What kind of relationship?" Thornton wanted to know.

"Espy's firm would supply the Soviets with key electronics guidance systems."

"And Espy got what?"

"Money. That's what makes the world go 'round. It was all illegal, of course, but what the hell? Détente and 'Can't we all just get along?' and all that."

"And Harris's motivation? The same—money?"

"Partly. It takes money to keep getting reelected. The KGB went ahead and recommended the relationship on the grounds that Harris was already connected with a trusted KGB agent in France named David Barr."

"Is Harris a commie?"

"We don't use the C word anymore. It's so un-PC."

"Socialist?"

"*Progressive* is the today term," Hinds corrected and went on. "Apparently, Espy did well in his Soviet relationship, while Harris dropped out of the picture until about 1983. In that year, Espy delivered a message from Senator Harris through David Barr to Yuri Andropov, the general secretary of the Soviet Communist Party, in which Harris expressed his concern about the anti-Soviet activities of President Ronald Reagan. The message said it was Harris's opinion that American opposition to Reagan remained weak because speeches made by the president's opponents were not well coordinated and effective, while Reagan used successful propaganda. Harris offered to 'undertake some additional steps to counter the militaristic policy of Reagan and his campaign of psychological pressure on the American population.' Espy requested Andropov meet with Harris so Harris could 'arm himself with the Soviet leader's explanation of arms control policy so he can use these later for more convincing speeches in the U.S.' This was all in the KGB reports. Harris through Espy also offered to help get Soviet views on the

major U.S. networks and suggested the Soviets invite
Walter Cronkite, Barbara Walters, and the ABC chairman
of the board to Moscow."

Thornton shook his head in amazement. "And this guy
keeps getting elected?"

"You don't have to fool all the people all the time, to
paraphrase Abe Lincoln. You only have to fool enough to
keep getting elected, which gets easier and easier to do."

"I don't understand what this has to do with Lough's
murder and the dead ragheads in Yuma," Thornton puzzled.

"You wanted connections, Claude, I'm giving you connections. The Feebies will have to figure out what it
means. Foggy Bottom can't operate in the U.S. against
American citizens, remember?"

"I'm all ears."

Hinds nodded.

"In 1940," he went on, "President Franklin Roosevelt
ordered the FBI to wiretap Nazis and communists because they were operating in the United States on behalf
of hostile foreign powers. That eventually became FISA,
the Foreign Intelligence Surveillance Act. After 9/11,
when Congress discussed legislation under the Domestic
Terror Bill to extend FISA to wiretap enemy agents and
terrorists, Gerald Espy, as National Committee chair of
the Party of the People, and Senator Harris, with the support of the ACLU, began a campaign to craft surveillance
restrictions into the bill and raise the barriers as high as
possible. Harris introduced the concept in the Foreign Intelligence Surveillance Bill that requires hard evidence
that someone is actually providing classified information
to a foreign enemy before a wiretap warrant can be obtained. Someone who *only* has a clandestine relationship
with a foreign intelligence officer and who carries out

covert influence operations for a foreign power can not be wiretapped."

"Such as anyone associated with David Barr," Thornton pursued.

Hinds shrugged. He lit a fresh cigarette off the butt of the old.

"My guess is, they're trying to protect their own asses from people like you and me nosing around in their trash," he concluded. "It does sound to me like there *is* some trash here. So Espy meets with Lough and Lough ends up taking a few through the gut. What does it mean? What does it have to do with Harris and Espy or Barr and Espy, if anything? The ball's in your court, old friend. We spooks can't touch it."

Thornton exhaled a deep breath. "This is a U.S. senator we're talking about here."

"Why should politicians have more character than the CIA, the FBI, the local cop, or anyone else? It's been my experience they have less, especially if they're ideologues who believe America is on the wrong road and it's up to them to save the world and make a difference. Harris could very well become the next president of the United States. Espy is pulling the strings to make it happen. These are ambitious people who will stop at nothing to gain power."

A scary thought. Thornton would have to mull it over and see where it fit in. He rose to take his leave.

"You got time for lunch, Claude?" Hinds asked, grinning and immediately pushing business to the side. "I think it's your turn to buy."

"I buy every time."

"Which only proves Spooks are smarter than Feebies."

"Sorry, Tom. I'll have to forego the pleasure. President

Tyler is giving a speech in Tulsa in a day or so and I want to check in with the Secret Service and advance teams."

Hinds walked him to the door. Thornton was still pondering Senator Harris's peculiar background and his possible connection to Lough when he drove out of the parking lot. He tried General Kragle's cell phone number and again received a recording. What was the General's connection to Lough?

CHAPTER 35

TERROR FIGURES RESIGN, COMMIT SUICIDE

Washington (CPI)—The War on Terror has lost at least two of its top warriors and there are rumors that others may resign shortly. General Paul Etheridge, commander of Central Command (CENTCOM), which led the war in Iraq and has headed most counterterrorist operations in the Middle East and in Southeast and Southwest Asia, unexpectedly tendered his resignation yesterday. He gave no reason for his move.

In another unexpected turn of events, General Raymond Holloman, commander of the Air Force Special Operations Command (AFSOC), apparently committed suicide at his Florida residence. Friends say he has not been despondent. He left no reason for his actions. AFSOC supplies aircraft in support of Special Operations.

Senator and presidential candidate Lowell Rutherford Harris expressed regret at General Holloman's death, but said that his suicide as well as General Etheridge's resignation likely resulted from disagreements they have reportedly had with the Tyler administration's conduct of the war. He said dissension over the war has reached top levels in the administration and within the Counterterrorism Center.

"Tyler is making America less fair, free, strong, and smart than it deserves in a dangerous world," Harris said in a prepared statement. "Tyler has a foreign policy

that is not good for America—not good for the world—
and many who work for him are beginning to recognize
that. Tyler is not a Hitler—for one thing, he's not as
smart as Adolf Hitler . . ."

CHAPTER 36

West Sahara

Instinctively, the first thing every man had grabbed when the chopper went down was his weapon. For Major Brandon Kragle, that meant his H&K G3 automatic rifle, a short accurate weapon with a retractable stock. Gloomy had Mr. Blunderbuss, a faithful friend he never let out of his sight. Ice Man Thompson, the detachment's weapons expert, stuck with the old standby, an M16-A4 with attached M203 40mm grenade launcher. In addition to pistols and combat knives, most of the others carried some version of the MP5 submachine gun, an effective weapon for CQB—close quarter battle.

Specialists lugged additional gear—Diverse Dade his bag of C-4 explosives, det cord, caps, and other "Bang-Bang" materials; Doc TB, his well-stocked medical aid bag; communications sergeant Mad Dog Carson, an AN/PRC-137 long-range radio system in a pack on his back; Ice Man and Perverse Sanchez, spare weapons parts and repair and cleaning gear. In addition, per SOP, each man carried an MRE (Meal, Ready to Eat) stuffed into his web gear fanny pack, along with extra ammo, grenades, survival supplies, and other necessaries. An operator on mission kept his equipment attached to his person from the time he stepped into whatever conveyance was delivering him until he reached safe harbor again. As a result, a team was always prepared for such an emergency as a premature insertion because of aircraft failure or shoot down.

Brandon heard enemy Jihadia around the fire glow of the downed burning helicopter only a couple of hundred meters away as he saddled up the detachment to move it out. The storm masked sound and movement. Mad Dog hoisted one end of the poncho stretcher containing the unconscious body of the copilot, Lieutenant Gardner, balanced on the other end by Doc TB. Both were large, strong men. Perverse Sanchez carried his broken arm hastily splinted and in a sling, his submachine gun in the other hand. The helicopter crew chief wore a battle dress bandage on his forehead but seemed otherwise entirely functional.

Brandon issued the word. "Move out."

"Sergeant Thompson, you take drag," the team sergeant said.

The battered little patrol set out through the howling wind and stinging sand, wearing goggles that protected their eyes but also further restricted vision. The best missions were like a three-step dance: get there, get it done, get back. Murphy could screw up even a dance.

"Situation normal—all fucked up," Mad Dog grunted as he stumbled past with his end of the copilot's stretcher.

"Will the Low Self-Esteem Support Group please go to the rear?" Gloomy Davis cracked.

Brandon took point with the GPS. Storm and darkness limited visibility to the length of one's arm. To avoid losing track of each other, members trailed so closely together that they could reach out and touch the man ahead.

A GPS was a remarkable instrument. It triangulated signals off three or more satellites to provide present location, destination, and the fastest route between. It also recorded the route of march in case backtracking became necessary. In this instance, Brandon thought, backtracking was not an option. *Failure* was not an option.

Brandon traveled the detachment slowly to accommodate carrying the wounded copilot. The glow of the burning helicopter vanished quickly to the rear. The terrain, more felt and experienced than actually seen, consisted mostly of flat desert scarred by wadis, stone hills, and occasional briar fields into which team members blindly stumbled. Why were wars always fought under the most inhospitable conditions?

Mad Dog had made a solemn vow after enduring the constant rainfall of the Philippine mission: "I ain't going to no more wars unless they're held on Miami Beach." But, of course, here he was in the column carrying not only his commo pack and weapon but also the wounded Night Stalker. These men, Brandon thought, *these men*. Where did Americans get such men?

During a rest halt to allow switching out on the stretcher, Brandon made his way to the back of the short column to listen for pursuit. He heard nothing except the wind, saw nothing other than blowing sand inches past his goggles. Without the GPS they would have been hopelessly lost. Gloomy took a knee next to him and offered to pull a stay-behind to pick off any enemy who might attempt to track them.

Brandon refused him. "They aren't going to track us in this crap. We're not getting separated. I'm not losing any more men on a mission."

The lives of his men were *entrusted* to his keeping. He violated that trust every time he lost one.

"Boss, losing them wasn't your fault."

Gloomy always seemed to read his mind. Brandon said nothing. He was getting soft. Maybe it really was time for him to take that desk job Colonel Buck offered and turn the field missions over to hard cases like Sergeant Sculdiron, who remained emotionally detached from his soldiers, the military way. Mission had to come first, always, even over the lives of soldiers. That was the way it was in Delta: Mission first, men second.

"We all knew the risks when we volunteered for this outfit," Gloomy said. "Risk comes with the territory."

But Delta was composed of small bands of brothers, the death of even one of which diminished them all. Brandon wondered when it was that he had lost his direct-action mentality and started obsessing over such things. Since he became a married man? Since Summer started talking about having a baby?

Brandon rose to his feet. Wind tugged at his bush cap and whistled, stinging, against his ears. "Sergeant Sculdiron," he called out softly. "Saddle 'em up."

"Yes, sir."

The top sergeant moved off quickly, tapped the men to their feet, making sure the column was tight and together as the march resumed. Under such weather conditions, two full opposing companies of infantry might stumble around in a two-hundred acre field for days and not find each other, or they could blunder into each other immediately. It all depended on chance, and on Murphy.

Dawn came unnoticed until it was well advanced. The sun rose, but it appeared only intermittently, blood red, through the battering waves of blowing sand. It improved visibility somewhat and allowed the detachment to make up for lost time. Brandon was surprised that they hadn't run across at least some of the fleeing Sahrawi; this desert must be overrun with them, yet they remained invisible in the storm. The wind showed no signs of letting up.

"Fu-uck," Mad Dog groused. "Why do I do this shit?"

"Because you eat it up," Diverse Dade said.

"You and Ice are gourmet cooks, right?" Mad Dog said, straining with Diverse and Gloomy Davis to get the injured copilot across a gully. "I'm hungry. Why don't you go cook us up a nice breakfast of fried chicken, grits, collard greens, and watermelon?"

"You are a racist individual, Sergeant Carson," Diverse jabbed back.

Bantering between the black man and the hulking commo sergeant had gone on like this since the day Sergeant Dade reported to Troop One, a condition that was slowly forming an unlikely but sound friendship between the two men.

"I ain't racist, Zulu," Mad Dog countered. "I just don't like black guys."

No one ever accused Sergeant Mad Dog Carson of being sensitive. Politically correct he wasn't.

Hill 138 couldn't be much of a hill, not with a "138" designation. But, still, it was probably one of the dominant terrain features in this flat rub board country. Brandon gave the detachment a break on a low ridgeline while he and Sergeant Sculdiron used binoculars to glass the countryside. They couldn't see much through the sand, but they hoped to at least discern outlines and shapes during moments of clarity between wind gusts. They had humped most of the night and into daylight without seeing another living being. Not an enemy soldier, not a Sahrawi. Not even a goat or a camel. Brandon was wondering if Aces Wild might not have been sent into a dry hole. They were a goodly distance across the border, certainly too far for a man on foot to reach, even if he was fleeing terrorists bent on slaughtering him.

Doc TB came over and squatted. He said, "Major, the copilot has internal injuries. I have him on IV meds, but he's not going to make it if we don't evacuate him soon."

Brandon dropped his binocs on a thong around his neck and looked at the young bear of a medic.

"You have to do the best you can, Doc. Mad Dog requested a weather update when he radioed in our morning report. It's clear in Algeria, but there's no telling how long the blow will continue here."

"Yes, sir. We're also going to have a problem with water. Wind and heat are sapping the men fast. One canteen of water per man won't take us much farther. I'm rationing water, if it's okay with you?"

"You're the doc."

They sat together for a minute, their backs behind a boulder and against the wind while the storm broiled around them. Sergeant Sculdiron seemed to be intensely studying an outcropping of distant rock through his binoculars.

"When's your wife due to deliver, Doc?" Brandon asked.

"In a week, maybe two." His voice grew distant. "I'm hoping I can be there."

Brandon slapped him on the back. "You will be, Doc. We'll get you home in time."

"Is that a promise, Major?"

"You got my word on it."

"Major?"

"Yeah?"

"What about you and Summer? Are you going to have a baby?"

Brandon turned away. "No," he said.

A father should not be in Special Operations. Brandon had already asked Colonel Buck to transfer Doc TB out of Delta. He would already have been gone if Aces Wild hadn't come up so unexpectedly that the Doc was the only medic currently available. Doc wasn't going to like getting booted out, but it was for his own good.

"Major, sir," Top Sculdiron interrupted. "Take a look here, sir. I think I've discovered a vehicle."

Major Kragle sprang up. He slammed his binoculars to his eyes.

"Over there, sir. Next to that peculiar-shaped rock that looks like a camel."

Brandon found the rock. Just as he glimpsed a dull blue shape beyond it—an upside-down Land Rover, it seemed—a sudden spatter of gunfire jarred his attention toward the base of a small hill. He saw nothing for a moment or two because of the sand. Then the air cleared momentarily to reveal small figures ducking and dodging among boulders on the side of the rise, shooting at people on top, who returned fire but who were obviously outnumbered and at a disadvantage.

"I think we've found 138," Brandon said. "It looks like we may be too late."

CHAPTER 37

Tindouf Airport

Using binoculars, Sergeant Cassidy Kragle pulled a sur-veillance shift from the maintenance shed at the Tindouf Airport, recording his observations on a notepad. After a suitable passage of observation, Major Russell and Top Sergeant Bodine should be able to compile a reasonable estimate of how many tangos occupied the terminal, where they were in the building, and what their habits were. It would be near suicide for either the hostage take-down team or the hostages themselves to launch a raid without first amassing all available data on the target. Suc-cess depended upon surprise, swift violence, and knowl-edge of the enemy.

No terrorists had ventured outside the terminal since that morning when they brought out the small black man and pumped a bullet through his skull. The body lay where it fell, face down on the tarmac. It seemed to grow smaller and smaller under the weight of the hot African sun. A large gray-black bird soared into Cassidy's binocu-lar view, zooming low over the body before circling back and landing next to it. Its head was almost featherless and corrugated like ripe flesh. It hop-waddled over to the body, reached down with its hooked beak and began to tug at the dead man's blood-and-brain-matter-encrusted ear.

Oh, Christ!

The young sergeant swept his vigil back to the terminal.

He didn't even want to think about the dead man. This time tomorrow, if the terrorists kept their promise, which he had no doubt they would, two corpses might be lying out there for the vultures to snack on. The next one might be American.

The Arab with the red-and-white keffiyeh, the big-nosed murdering bastard who executed the hostage, appeared to be in charge. He ran all over the terminal, upstairs and downstairs, front and back, making his rounds. Cassidy saw him pass behind an upstairs window. Underneath the heading "Red-White Headdress" on the notepad, where a number of items had already been entered, he wrote, "White, Bravo, 6, 1300."

Target buildings were coded for easy reference. Colors in the code designated specific sides: the front was "white," the rear "black," left side "red," and right "green." Each floor or level was assigned a phonetic alphabet identification beginning with "Alpha" on the ground floor, "Bravo" for the next, and so on up to the roof. All openings, whether doors or windows, were numbered left to right on respective floors. Using this system, Cassidy had noted the big-nosed leader was spotted at 1300 hours at the front of the terminal, second floor, sixth opening from the left, in this case a window. Previous watches had observed him an additional eight times during the morning. *He* would be the first target, if feasible, when the takedown began.

While Cassidy kept watch, the rest of the detachment gathered around charts, maps, and sketches spread on a tool table at the back of the building. Team Sergeant Bodine and Commo Sergeant Edwards discussed some point of tactics while Major Dare Russell talked on the PRC-137 radio. Any plan settled on would be discussed, modified, altered, and revised up until the very moment the operation began.

This operation appeared particularly challenging. To begin with, open ground surrounding the terminal building on all sides posed a major first obstacle. There wasn't a concealed approach from any direction. Windows on the lower accessible floor were made of hardened thick glass and fixed, meaning they could not be opened to gain entry. They would have to be blown or shattered. There were only four doors total into the terminal: Double side-by-side heavy metal doors at front and back, a single metal door at each end. All this made it easy for the gunmen inside to spot an assault right away and cover all entrances.

Bobby Goose Pony broke away from the rear table to relieve Cassidy on surveillance watch.

"Still hanging around, eh?" he greeted. "You must like the chow 'cause I sure don't see no booze or pussy about."

"You are one gross Indian."

"That reminds me," Goose Pony said, pulling up a bucket and sitting on it. "Cass, are you porking that little girl from Funny Platoon? Sergeant Foster?"

"Like I said—gross."

"That serious, huh?"

Cassidy put down his binoculars to make a note on the black-scarfed terrorist.

"How many do we have in there?" Goose Pony asked, diverted from his original inquiry.

"It looks like about fourteen so far. Each one of them is armed with an AK or SKS. That's a lot of firepower."

"It sounds like another al-Qaeda deal."

"There are so many others, all affiliated," Cassidy reminded him.

"I thought your brother's detachment knocked off Osama bin Laden in Afghanistan."

"Have we heard anything from Osama since then?"

"I guess we haven't."

"I rest my case."

Major Russell got off the radio and walked to the front. "Sergeant Kragle?" He sounded grim. "I've just confirmed the identities of the American hostages."

Cassidy stiffened. He knew. "Cameron's in there."

The major slowly nodded. "Chaplain Cameron Kragle and two female missionaries named Kelli Rule and Rhoda Hoffstetter. Cass, I can work you out of the operation if you'd rather?"

Although every Delta trooper practiced CQB in the House of Horrors, sometimes using live student "hostages" among the mannequin targets, the thought of having to shoot for real like that with his own brother's life at stake gave Cassidy a chill. Few Deltas ever actually had to utilize their shooting skills in an actual situation where things could get messy and wrong people mistakenly shot.

"No, sir," Cassidy said. "That's my brother in there. He'll be expecting me. Sir, the tangos keep going toward a room on the second floor. They seem to be guarding a door. I think that's where the hostages are held."

Major Russell nodded with approval. "It won't be long now," he said.

"How soon, sir?"

"It can't be today. We're simply not ready. Maybe tomorrow."

He walked off, leaving the two friends sobered by the news. They had suspected Cameron might be among the hostages; this confirmed it.

Cassidy went back to his binocs to keep his mind busy. Another vulture, like a night shadow, soared in, across, and out of view in his lenses.

CHAPTER 38

New Hampshire

Wearing tight faded jeans, hiking boots, and T-shirt, the shapely brunette was young enough and hip enough to blend, along with her partner Ed Tilborn, into the crowds that thronged the center green at Dartmouth College to hear presidential candidate and U.S. Senator Lowell Rutherford Harris rally his support base. Photojournalist Dee Anna Gencarelli and Tilborn, on assignment for Consolidated Press International (CPI), worked their way through the masses of screaming, shouting, chanting humanity. Dee Anna carried a Nikon SLR camera ready on a strap around her neck and a tape recorder on her belt. She and Ed would be covering the presidential election from now until November. They were having a splendid time of it. Ed compared it to being a combat correspondent.

"You get the quotes and interviews," Dee Anna told him. "I'll get the photos. Circulate. Keep your recorder going. This is scary stuff."

It was hijinx writ large. The crowds came to demonstrate, to create havoc, to express before the mass media their opposition to President Woodrow Tyler and the imperialists who waged Tyler's War on Terror. Dee Anna decided it must have been like this during the Vietnam War protests of the late 1960s and early 1970s. There was a shrillness to the crowd's voice, a fierce excitement that she recognized from old news video of that era. She shot up rolls of film, stuffing them into a small fanny pack.

It was the people's day to shine, what with TV cameras rolling to catch and record every nuance, phrase, antic, and tantrum. All the usual were present: PETA wearing whale suits or nothing at all and screaming against "people who murder and eat chickens," Greenies warning everybody that the sky was falling, ELF with photos of SUVs they had vandalized in Oregon, anti-NAFTAs, environmentalists waving signs recommending humankind voluntarily go extinct for the good of the planet, pro-choicers, and lesbians and transgender and gay men holding hands and displaying San Francisco marriage licenses, prancing around in feathers and lipstick and Dolly Parton costumes . . .

Dee Anna laughed. It was a circus.

A man worked the crowd dressed like a big penis wearing a condom. A score of naked women from age eighteen to eighty-one had painted their bodies with antiwar slogans and blocked traffic. No More War was about all the younger ones had room for on their backs; some of the flabby older ones could have printed names, addresses, and phone numbers of antiwar organizations on their backs and the entire Marxist *Internationale* on their butts. A congress of White Witches cast spells on Iraq's invaders and the perpetrators of the War on Terror, meaning the Tyler administration, while demonstrators chanted "Out of the office and into the streets! U.S. out of the Middle East!" or "Woodrow Tyler, Uncle Sam. Iraq will be your Vietnam."

Ed Tilborn cornered a demonstrator with his tape recorder. "Can you tell me the name of the president of the United States?" he asked.

"Man, that's easy. Woodrow Fucking Tyler, man." Grinning happily, proud that he knew the answer so easily.

"Who's the vice president?"

The grin began to fade. "Man, I don't care about that shit."

"Okay. Can you tell me this: Is Iraq in Africa, Asia, or Europe?"

A dark scowl this time. "Man, who the fuck cares? Get out of my face before I kick your ass."

"Oh, now, can't we all just get along together?"

American flags were carried upside down. Signs with slogans punched holes in the sky.

SUPPORT OUR TROOPS, BRING THEM HOME
TYLER LIES, THEY DIE
STOP WAR CRIMES IN IRAQ
HEALTH CARE, NOT WARFARE
IMPEACH WOODROW TYLER

One group formed a conga line and waved a huge sign depicting President Tyler wearing a Hitler mustache.

WANTED, the sign said, FOR DECEPTION, FRAUD, MASS MURDER; CRIMES AGAINST HUMANITY, ENVIRONMENT AND INTERNATIONAL LAW. THIS MAN IS HEAVILY ARMED, UNPREDICTABLE AND HIGHLY DANGEROUS, POSING A GRAVE THREAT TO WORLD PEACE.

Dee Anna had attended rock concerts whose audiences demonstrated less enthusiasm than when candidate Lowell Rutherford Harris finally made his way out onto a speaker's platform. The feisty, long-faced little man with the bitter taste in his mouth waved his arms, slung his fists and screamed, "Eeee-yah! Eeee-yah!"

People stomped the ground, cheered and shouted themselves hoarse. Dee Anna pushed her way near the platform to get good film of the event and today's hero. Senator Harris was ready.

"A powerful clique has control of the White House," he began, virtually shrieking into the microphone. Dee Anna captured images of spittle spray in the sensitive lenses of her Nikon. "We are being ruled—I said *ruled*—by a president who abuses the truth in exploiting the fears of the American people, a regime that thinks of other Americans who disagree with him as agents of treason. This machinery of fear is right out in the open, operating at full throttle by a despot using the War on Terror to justify the national security state and feed its economy. Terrorism is just a euphemism for what the conspiratorial far right considers to be the *real* enemy: Arabs and Muslims everywhere, African Americans and Hispanics, people of color everywhere who are being tyrannized in a racist and imperialistic enterprise. Woodrow Tyler should be investigated and charged in the World Court as an international criminal . . ."

The circus loved it. It began chanting: "President Harris! President Harris! No More War! No More War!"

Afterward, Dee Anna hurried to the fenced-in area at the rear of the stage, where a black limousine with heavily tinted opaque windows waited to whisk Senator Harris away to his next engagement. Police kept reporters back from the fence. Being small and agile, Dee Anna threw herself on hands and knees, squirmed through the security line, and reached the fence before anyone noticed. She began snapping frames.

The limousine's back door flew open to allow Senator Harris to get in. Dee Anna caught a glimpse of a strange-looking old man with wild Einstein-like hair, rimless glasses, and large glaring eyes. She was ready with her camera. She snapped a single frame before the old man covered his face and threw himself away from the door and back into the shadowed obscurity of the limousine. Harris jumped in with a scowl on his face and slammed the door.

The old man must be *somebody*, to be riding around in a limousine with the presidential candidate. Dee Anna thought he looked familiar, but she couldn't quite place him. She hoped she was quick enough on the draw to have gotten a photo of him.

CHAPTER 39

El Paso, Texas

Carlos, the errant clerk at the Cactus Motel in Yuma, knew little more than he initially revealed. However, under grilling by Agent Fred Whiteman and Lieutenant Appleton and Agent Pear, the Fruits, he had come up with a telephone number in El Paso for his boss, Youseff Balaghi, owner of the Cactus Motel and suspected of smuggling terrorists into the United States. Agent Whiteman had followed a separate lead to New York while the Fruits jumped down to El Paso. On the authority of Thornton's pickup order, they and the local FBI snatched Balaghi before he could vanish across the Mexican border.

Director Claude Thornton was in a reflective mood as the Homeland Security private Learjet streaked him toward El Paso. He had been constantly on the move for the past few days, hopping from one end of the country to the other, living on fast food and catching a few hours' sleep whenever he could. Perhaps Edith was right in divorcing him. He had been seldom at home since September 11, 2001, when the United States became a front line in the war with Jihadistan. War against the borderless nation of Islamic extremists was a messy business waged on many fronts and taking many avenues and levels, at times highly visible and therefore controversial when it took on state sponsors of terrorism such as Afghanistan and Iraq, at other times fought behind the scenes and out of sight.

He couldn't help thinking that America's greatest enemy lay within its own boundaries, in its lack of resolve to take the fight directly to Jihadistan rather than waiting for it to come to U.S. shores. That resolve continued to weaken under this election year's relentless assault on the Tyler doctrine. After more than three years on the front line in the declared war and nearly two decades before that, waging an undeclared war against terrorists in the Middle East and Egypt, Thornton was uncompromisingly convinced that Jihadia sought to undermine U.S. cultural, economic, and political influence in the world through committing acts of terror on U.S. soil against U.S. citizens. He was just as convinced that if President Tyler lost the White House in November, it meant a major victory for terrorists and a stunning defeat for America.

While still in Washington, he had been informed of CENTCOM's General Paul Etheridge's resignation and the suicide of AFSOC's General Ray Holloman. Now General Kragle was out of pocket and acting strangely in not returning his calls after the shooting at the Lincoln Memorial. Something was going on there, but Thornton couldn't seem to put his finger on exactly what.

Thornton traveled alone; a man moved faster that way.

The pilot's voice came over the intercom. "Director, we're on approach to El Paso International. About fifteen minutes."

Thornton dialed a number. Lieutenant Appleton of the Border Patrol answered. "We're waiting for you at the airport, just as happy as hogs in slop."

The Fruits met Thornton out of uniform and dressed in new off-the-rack business suits. Appleton's was too short in the cuffs and sleeves for his tall frame; Pear's hung baggy on his short legs and arms. They seemed glad to see the FBI agent again. He was just as pleased to see them. The two Border Patrol agents would do, "to ride the range with," as they might have put it.

"You have any better idea now than before on what all's in this cabbage patch?" Appleton asked.

"Not much," Thornton admitted.

As the Fruits drove him to the county jail where Balaghi was being held, Thornton filled them in on the part about Lough's being murdered in Washington, but withheld background history on the connections Lough might have had with Gerald Espy, David Barr, and Senator Harris. That was all speculation anyhow.

"That raghead Balaghi ain't said squat since we picked him up," Appleton said.

Pear handed over a folder. "But we got this anyhow," he added. "The guy had a laptop PC. I cracked the code and made copies."

"Ole buddy Pear here was the best computer hacker at Arizona State U before he got kicked out for cheating at recess," Appleton explained with pride.

"It's not legal to do," Pear added, "but I figured time was crucial and the goofy judges probably wouldn't have given us a search warrant anyhow. You don't know where you got this stuff, okay? I can't make heads nor tails out of it for meaning."

The folder contained little of immediate usefulness. There was a telephone book containing only numbers and first names, which Thornton decided to e-mail to Whiteman to check out. There were also some financial files from support-group contributors within the United States: Palestinian Islamic Jihad; Salafist Group for Call and Combat; Center For American Progressives; International Sikh Youth Federation; World Workers Party; ANSWER . . . A one-page schedule identified only with a *T* at the top provided dates and times for some event, but gave no further explanation. Thornton was disappointed that there hadn't been more.

At the county jail he flashed his credentials and was admitted to a room with cage wire dividing it. The Fruits waited for him downstairs in the sheriff's office. Youseff Balaghi, a slight, swarthy man, beardless, dressed in orange jail coveralls, was soon shown in to the other half of the room. He walked up to the wire and surveyed Thornton with a critical eye.

"I informed them from the beginning that I would speak only to someone with more authority than a bellhop," Balaghi sneered in good English. "Who are you?"

"Someone with more authority than a bellhop," Thornton replied, walking up to his side of the wire. Who did this terrorist piece of shit think he was? He controlled his temper. "I'm the man who had you arrested."

"You're black."

"I hadn't noticed. My name is Claude Thornton. I'm director of the FBI's National Domestic Preparedness Office. You can talk to me—or we can ship your butt to Guantanamo, Cuba, where you can rot with the other Jihadists for the next ten years. It's your choice, but I don't intend to play your games."

It was an old cop play, a calculated approach to throw a suspect off balance. *You can talk to me or not talk to me, I don't care. It's to your advantage to do so, not mine.*

Balaghi reddened with anger, but, to his credit, he kept his mouth shut while he mulled it over.

"Do you have the authority to make a deal?" he finally asked.

"From what I can see, you're only a contact for smugglers with very little to bargain with."

Balaghi licked his lips. They were so dry they almost crackled. Thornton smiled inwardly.

"Do you have a cigarette?" Balaghi asked, playing for time while he thought things through.

"Smoking will give you cancer."

Thornton waited. Balaghi's eyes darted.

"I know the name of the man who rented the room," he finally offered. "He is connected."

"With whom?"

"Can we bargain? I want to be freed."

"Not a chance."

"Then I do not know the name after all."

Thornton pushed his bluff. He shrugged nonchalantly as he turned and made to leave. He reached the door. He thought he might have pushed too far.

"Wait!"

The agent hesitated, but he still opened the door.

"What will you offer?" Balaghi asked.

"You won't go to Guantanamo."

Captured terrorists did not want to go to the military terrorist holding facility in Guantanamo, where they could languish for years.

"That is not enough."

Thornton did not want to appear overly accommodating. He opened the door wider.

"Will I go to a civilian court rather than a military?" Balaghi called out quickly. "None of what I tell you will be used against me?"

Thornton closed the door slowly and walked back to the wire divider, as though in deep concentration. "Let's talk then," he agreed. "But all deals are off the moment I find you're being less than forthcoming. To begin with, why should I believe you?"

A sly smile crossed Balaghi's face. "I am what you Americans call an entrepreneur, a capitalist. I am for hire and not a believer. I want to save my own ass, as you might say."

A rare breed here, the agent thought, a terrorist-for-hire who didn't believe in martyrdom and seventy-two virgins in heaven if he died in the name of Allah. Maybe he had stayed too long underground in America.

"Let's start with the name of the man who rented the room from you," Thornton said.

"His name is Barr."

The former KGB agent! Claude hid his surprise. Never let an interrogated subject know he was providing anything valuable or unknown if you wanted to keep him trying harder.

"What's his first name?" Thornton prompted

"David Barr. I think he's an American living in Paris."

"How do you know him?"

"I have worked with him before when Saddam Hussein was still in power in Iraq and dealing with the French. That is how I know he is connected."

"What was his purpose in renting the room?"

Balaghi licked his lips nervously. "I am dead if it is discovered I have talked to you."

"It's your choice," Thornton replied casually.

Balaghi licked his lips again and took a breath. "We were paid a good deal of money—"

"*Who* was paid a good deal of money?"

"Myself, of course. Salim and Ali-Salem."

"For . . . ?"

"Salim and Ali-Salem were to smuggle a bomb into the United States from Mexico. They were to bring it to the Cactus Motel where somebody else would pick it up."

"Barr?"

"I do not think so. Mr. Barr made the arrangements. I did not see him again. Whoever was to pick up the bomb did not arrive either, because something happened and Salim and Ali-Salem died in the Yuma hospital."

"What happened to the bomb?"

"I do not know. That is the truth."

"What kind of a bomb was it? Where did it come from?"

"My friends died from radioactivity, isn't that true? With the right contacts in the Middle East and in Russia and points of Asia, what you call suitcase nukes can be acquired quite readily."

Thornton pursued the point. "Were there other bombs?"

"Perhaps. There are many sleeper cells operating in the United States waiting for their time to strike. Each of us does not know about the others, but it is customary, isn't it, to have a backup plan in the event the first fails? Me, I would think that Mr. Barr would not put all his chickens in the same basket. Wouldn't you say so?"

What this meant was that a second "suitcase nuke," or even a third, had successfully been smuggled into the country. Things, as General Kragle's former housekeeper, Gloria, would say, just kept getting complicateder and complicateder.

Now for the *big* question: "How was the bomb going to be used? Where? When?"

Balaghi shrugged. He looked around for a chair. Finding none, he hooked his fingers into the cage wire and leaned against it.

"That is not my affair. I am being paid by Mr. Barr to pass it and its handlers along. I hear only that the bomb will help America get a new government. But then everything is political, is it not? I have told you everything I know, as per our bargain. You promised me a civilian trial. I also want my free attorney. That is guaranteed me, no? I cannot be convicted for renting a motel room to a guest." He laughed.

"Maybe not," Thornton agreed. "But I'm making you one promise you can take to the bank: Two days after you are acquitted, if you're acquitted, or two days after you get out of prison, if you're convicted, you'd better be out of this country. Otherwise you will be buried here on the third day. Got that?"

Thornton left the county jail an hour later, his head reeling with the implications of Balaghi's information. Almost as disturbing as the fact that suitcase nukes were floating around were the ties being revealed strand by strand between ex-KGB agent David Barr, NCC for Party of the People Gerald Espy, and Senator Harris on the one hand and, on the other hand, between the same David Barr and terrorist smugglers of weapons of mass destruction. He found it almost unbelievable that Espy and Harris were mixed up in this. Or that they could be involved in the murder of Charles Edward Lough.

Claude Thornton was never a believer in coincidence. Interconnecting trails usually had a common source or at least a common destination. Whatever was going on, he harbored a nagging feeling that time was running out.

He telephoned MacArthur Thornbrew, his boss at the National Homeland Security Agency.

"Mac, maybe we'd better raise the national threat level to at least Orange. I've just found out that we may have some suitcase nukes inside the country."

CHAPTER 40

West Sahara

Brandon gave it thirty minutes at most before the Jihadia, the Moroccans, whichever—it didn't really matter—rushed the top of Hill 138 and killed Sahrawi governor Chadli Malud. Brandon had never failed in a mission before.

Using binoculars and guided as much by the sound of rifle shots in the blowing sand as by sight, he counted more than a dozen men maneuvering against the hill. The ferocity of the attackers' fire indicated they were intent on putting an end to this matter as quickly as possible. Resistance from the top sounded light and faltering. The defenders were apparently few and might have even been short on ammunition.

A sheltered drainage running off the near side of the hill gave Brandon an idea. It cut down onto the flats and reached almost to the ridgeline the Delta detachment occupied before it shallowed and became part of the desert. Things weren't over until they were over.

"Get Gloomy," he said.

Top Sergeant Sculdiron passed the word. Gloomy Davis scuttled over, carrying Mr. Blunderbuss in its case. Brandon pointed out the distant attackers.

"Can you pick them off, Gloomy?"

The little sniper's eyes squinted behind goggles as he calculated range, winds, and the lay of the land.

"Six hundred meters," he mused. "Wind left to right at thirty knots, visibility piss poor. Boss, you're asking the impossible—but that's why we're in this outfit, right?"

"Get ready then. The rest of you, listen up."

With the exception of Doc TB, who continued to minister to the critically injured copilot, the Deltas and the Night Stalker crew chief gathered around quickly, lying on the ground with their backs to the stinging sand while Brandon explained his plan.

He pointed out the dry wash, which for the time being at least appeared free of enemy control. Brandon would take three men with him and, using the wash and the sandstorm for cover and concealment, run up the hill, find Malud and whoever else might have survived with him, and escort them back to the ridgeline, whereupon the entire detachment would "boogie out of the AO." If they worked rapidly enough and if Gloomy did his job of keeping the attackers occupied, they would be in, out, and gone before the enemy knew what was going on.

Top Sculdiron took another look. "They must have vehicles somewhere," he said. "They didn't walk all the way out here."

"I figure the blue Land Rover upside down in the ditch probably belonged to the Sahrawi," Brandon said. "This country is rugged. Vehicles have to stick to roads and trails. We won't."

"If we could get one of their vehicles . . ." Sculdiron began.

"Let's not push our luck," Brandon responded.

That seemed to satisfy the top sergeant. "However, Commander," he said, "I should take the patrol. It's army policy that a unit leader remain at the CP where he can control."

"It's also army policy for a leader to delegate," Brandon

snapped, then softened when Sculdiron's Slavic eyes narrowed to slits: "Sergeant Sculdiron, I need you here to take the detachment home if something should go wrong."

"Yes, sir."

"I need three men—hold on a minute," he added when the entire detachment attempted to volunteer, including Perverse Sanchez with his broken arm. He began pointing out his selections. "Diverse, you go with me. Mad Dog, I'll take you. Leave the radio here with Sculdiron. One more."

"Chew know I can still choot one-handed," Perverse offered.

"Fu-uck," Mad Dog countered. "Chew can't even talk one-handed."

"Sanchez, can you shoot the M203?"

"Chew know I can, Major."

"Ice, give your M-16 to Perverse and come with me. Take his weapon. Perverse, you spot for Gloomy and be ready to lay down some forty mike-mike grenades if we come running back down that wash with Indians on our asses. Gloomy, knock off as many of the bastards as you can. Keep 'em off that hill. We need the time. All right, we'll move out as soon as Gloomy goes to work."

Gloomy adjusted his goggles, jerked down the brim of his bush hat to help shelter his face, and began preparing for himself and his beautiful and deadly .300 Winchester a rest behind a pile of stones near the lip of the ridge. He took a cravat from his pocket and spread it on the rock to avoid scarring Mr. Blunderbuss's walnut finish. Then he took a prone position behind the rocks and began dialing dope into his scope. Perverse settled in next to him with a spotting scope and Ice Man's M-16 with its 40mm grenade launcher.

"Dan Rather, Jesse Jackson, and a Delta trooper were captured by cannibals," Gloomy narrated absently as he worked. Telling stories helped him prepare for the bloody business of killing men. It relaxed him, took his mind off the targets being anything other than targets.

Heated firing continued from the distant hill. Gloomy seated the rifle stock firmly into his shoulder, loaded the magazine, jacked a round into the chamber, and brought his eye to the scope lens, all the while talking rapidly to keep pace with his preparations.

"The cannibal chief, familiar with the custom of granting the condemned a last wish, asked Dan Rather if he had a last request. 'Well, I'm a Texan,' Rather said, 'so I'd like one last bowlful of hot, spicy chili.' Rather ate it and said, 'Now I can die content.'

"Jesse Jackson said, 'The thing I'm most proud of is my championing of the poor and oppressed. So before I go, I'd like to sing *We Shall Overcome* one last time.' He sang and said, 'Now I can die in peace.'

"Then it was the Delta trooper's turn to make a request—"

Gloomy stopped there after twisting his arm into the rifle sling. "Boss, I'm ready."

Brandon clapped him on his outstretched leg as encouragement and farewell. "Do it."

In his sniper's bubble now, silent and concentrating, Gloomy selected a target who opted to sprint from a lower boulder to a higher one. The figure was barely visible through the scope in the strobelike effects created by blowing sand. He looked like an animated flip card character coming and going from sight.

Mr. Blunderbuss cracked spitefully, the sound of the report immediately engulfed by the storm, muffled long before it reached its intended target.

A miss! A very near miss. The guy dived behind a rock, then immediately popped his head up to take a startled look around. He was dressed military in a gray-green Nazi-like helmet and camouflage fatigues. Gloomy wiped his goggles with his sleeve. He laid crosshairs just below the edge of the helmet, having already dialed in range and windage for point of aim/point of impact. He was still going to need a lot of luck, the way the wind was blowing.

"Chew was to the left on that one," Perverse directed, peering through the spotting scope.

Gloomy nodded, adjusted, took up trigger slack—and blasted off the distant rifleman's face. He immediately moved the scope toward his next victim.

"Keep on 'em, Gloomy!" Brandon encouraged.

He led his small patrol off the ridgeline at a low-profile run, Gloomy's rifle methodically spitting out death over their heads. They reached the desert floor and found the open mouth of the wash. The bottom was dry and filled with sand and stone, but it wasn't bad going. The sides provided some shelter from blowing sand.

Within a few minutes they were out of hearing range of Gloomy's rifle. The arroyo started uphill through boulders the size of native huts. The gale howled and whistled across the rock fields. Although the firefight on the hill grew progressively sharper and nearer, its ferocity seemed to have diminished as Gloomy's expert shooting took effect.

So far, so good. They had so far avoided enemy contact.

Brandon reduced the pace as the grade steepened. Breathing heavily from the sprint across the lowland, he crouched with the others between the wadi's narrowing walls to listen. They were near the top. An automatic rifle rattled off a burst from directly ahead. Ducking instinctively, he immediately discerned the fire was not directed at his patrol.

"That must be Malud," he concluded.

The challenge now came in making contact with the trapped Sahrawi without getting mistakenly shot in the process. Brandon was counting on Gloomy's having run the attackers to ground. Only a sporadic shot now and then rang out downhill on the patrol's right flank.

He tossed a fist-sized rock to the top of the hill to attract attention. When that failed to elicit a response, he picked up a handful of gravel and slung it. A cry of surprise. It sounded more like a child's voice than a man's.

"On the hill!" Brandon called out. "We are American soldiers! We are here to take you home!"

Silence. Then the unmistakable child's voice. English, but accented. It hadn't even reached puberty yet. "Liar! Liar! Come any more near and I will shoot you through the belly."

"Is Malud alive?" Brandon shouted. "Let him speak to me."

"Don't come no more near."

"Get Malud, damn it. Hurry."

They were wasting valuable time. A moment later a man's suspicious voice spoke from behind the uphill boulders. "How do I know you are Americans?"

"Weren't you told we were coming?"

"I had a satellite phone," Malud said. "I wasn't sure if anyone received my message before it went dead."

"All right. I'm going to stand up and show you. Don't let the kid shoot me in the belly."

He cautiously revealed himself. He stood up fully when no shots came. He spread his arms. Clearly by appearance he was not from this part of Africa. He heard the Sahrawi discussing it among themselves.

"Hurry, man," Brandon called. "There's no time for bullshitting."

Gloomy's aim couldn't keep the attackers down forever.

Malud stepped out from cover but remained low to the ground. Brandon recognized him from photos shown at the Aces Wild ops briefing: a man in his forties, bald on top, black hair draped around his ears. Normally beardless, he now looked unshaved from the past few days. He wore dress slacks and a sports shirt that appeared to have undergone recent tough wear. He carried an AK-47.

The kid trailed him out. Brandon found himself staring in astonishment at a runt who couldn't have been more than seven or eight years old. A mere tyke with bowl-cropped black hair and eyes so dark they looked black. Bare chested and barefooted, he wore only a pair of baggy cloth trousers tied around the waist with a length of rope. This brown little boy carried an AK-47 assault rifle with the authority of someone who knew how to use it. What kind of a world was it when children knew how to kill but probably couldn't read?

Malud dropped into the ditch with Brandon, followed by the kid.

"Are you truly an American?" the boy asked. "I really would have shoot you in the belly."

"I believe you," Brandon said, turning to Malud. "I'm Major Kragle, U.S. Army. There's not much time. How many do you have here?"

"Juba and me," he said, indicating the boy. "Three others. Two were killed yesterday when the Jihadia chased us across the desert and we wrecked our vehicle."

That explained the upside-down blue Land Rover.

"Can the others walk?" Brandon asked.

"One is wounded, but we can help him."

"Get them. Let's go, while there's a lull."

Malud scrabbled back uphill. Juba the kid looked around at Mad Dog and the others of the patrol. They crouched against either bank of the wash, eyes peeled for approaching danger. Juba grinned at Brandon.

"You are very tall, American," he said. "I shot one of them with this." He patted his weapon.

Brandon scowled. "Maybe you'd better let me take that."

Juba backed away. "No! You will need every man."

Brandon looked at the kid. Jesus! But he didn't try to take the rifle.

Malud returned with three other Sahrawi men, two of whom supported the third between them. He dragged one leg bandaged in strips torn off his shirt. They all looked enormously relieved.

"Follow me," Brandon said, eschewing further discussion. "Carry the kid if he can't keep up."

Brandon and Ice Man led the return downhill through the wash. Mad Dog and Diverse brought up drag while the Sahrawi folded into the center. Apparently, a group of the enemy had also discovered the wash and thought to use it as an attack route. Rescuers and rescued hadn't gone more than a hundred meters, their pace slowed by the wounded man, before they triggered an ambush. A startling crescendo of rifle and automatic weapons fire lashed out from the blinding storm on all sides. Brandon threw himself facedown in the ditch.

Murphy, you dirty sonofabitch.

CHAPTER 41

"WAR CRIMES" INTELLIGENCE MEMO LEAKED

Washington (CPI)—A secret memo leaked from the U.S. Senate Select Intelligence Committee indicates Party of the People members of the committee may have been working with the World Court to investigate the president of the United States for alleged war crimes. The committee chaired by presidential candidate Lowell Rutherford Harris apparently intended to call for an independent war crimes investigation of the Tyler administration in time to affect this year's elections. The memo also indicates members of the committee may have been feeding war crimes intelligence to the United Nations.

"Once we identify solid leads," the memo said in part, "we would attract more media coverage and have greater credibility than one in which we simply launch an independent investigation based on principled but vague notions . . . We can 'pull the trigger' on an independent investigation of the administration's complicity at any time. But we can only do so once. The best time for a war crimes investigation should coincide with charges in the UN and should probably occur just before the general elections . . ."

Under pressure from world peace organizations, the United Nations is reported to be drawing up new charges to be filed in Belgium and Switzerland against the President of the United States and all members of the U.S.

Central Command (CENTCOM) and Special Operations Command (USSOCOM), asserting that war crimes have been committed in Afghanistan and Iraq. Some members of CENTCOM, including its commander, have resigned, while the commander of the Air Force Special Operations Command (AFSOC) committed suicide.

The UN is the same body that appointed Iraq as a member of the World Disarmament Committee prior to Operation Iraqi Freedom and the capture of Saddam Hussein. It also elected Iran, North Korea, and Cuba to the World Human Rights Commission.

Senator Harris denied knowing anything about the memo.

"It must have been drafted by a low-level staffer," he said, "who gave his mistaken interpretation of events. It certainly does not reflect the committee's position in any way. We certainly would not politicize the committee at this critical time in the nation's history . . ."

CHAPTER 42

Washington, D.C.

General Kragle returned from Florida in time to learn that the President's assistant security advisor had unexpectedly resigned. That made two high-level resignations and one suicide, not counting the resignation the mysterious "Jerry Hurst" caller obviously expected the General to shortly tender. There must be others under the same pressure to leave. But what the hell was it all about?

The General had kept his room at the Washingtonian Hotel not only because the Lough murder was still under investigation but also because he suspected Washington was where this mischief originated. It was obviously political. The call on General Holloman's recorder confirmed that, with its mention of President Tyler and his supposed leading of the country toward fascism. It was here in Washington that the General must seek answers.

It angered and frustrated him that all this was occurring at a point when his sons, all three of them, were in peril half a world away. Although there was little he could do personally, he nonetheless suffered a feeling that he was letting them down again, as he had let them down so often in their lives. Gloria was the one who had always been there for them on their birthdays and other special occasions while he was away, going to wars and serving his country. He had never been much of a father.

This was a hell of a time to be suffering recriminations.

Restless in his hotel room, he telephoned Summer in North Carolina to see how she was doing. He gathered right off that she hadn't yet been informed of Brandon's helicopter going down in West Sahara. He saw no need to concern her either at this point until more concrete information came out of the AO.

"Is Brandon in Tindouf?" she asked.

"In the vicinity."

"I know you can't tell me anything else," she said, "but you will let me know if . . . Well, if . . . ?"

Her voice trailed off.

"Yes," he said.

He thought he heard her crying softly on the other end. That was so unlike this tough and resilient young lady whom Brandon often teasingly referred to as "the Ice Maiden." She normally held her emotions in check as effectively as any hardcore SpecOps soldier. She was a good mate for a soldier—independent, resourceful, strong-minded . . .

Lately, however, the General had noticed a softening, an emotionalism in her that might have been present all along but which she had managed to keep under wraps. For some reason, it made him think of Rita and how she softened and became emotional when she was pregnant. God, how he missed Rita. He had been in Vietnam both times when Brandon and Cameron were born and in Central America when she died giving birth to Cassidy.

He and Summer talked a few more minutes, each careful to avoid impressing his or her concern upon the other.

"I love you, Pops," she said before she hung up.

It caught him off guard. He and his sons after him were never ones for such sentiments.

"Yes," he said.

"It's okay," Summer said. "I know you love us too."

He hung up and took a shower while he continued to think things through and plan a counterattack against his mysterious caller. He knew how to fight conventional wars and was an expert in guerrilla and unconventional warfare as well. That kind of deceit, trickery, and cunning he could deal with because he knew *who* the enemy was and *why* he was the enemy. He hadn't much experience, however, in combating an enemy whose motives were never quite clear and who refused to come out and show himself.

He changed into loose Dockers, a blue long-sleeve button-down shirt, and soft-soled hiking boots. It was late mid-afternoon, time was running out on him, and he still had no idea where to start. He looked out the window toward the White House and Pennsylvania Avenue, blocked to traffic because of terrorist threats.

What was he going to do? he chided himself. Hang around until his seventy-two hours ran out and the "Jerry Hurst" nut called back to accuse *him* of following President Tyler in "leading the country toward fascism . . ."?

Wait a minute! Where had he heard that exact phrase before? Then he remembered. The *New York Times*.

Hotel maids learned never to trash anything in a guest's room unless it was obviously trash and in the waste receptacle. Yesterday's *Times* lay folded on the bedside table. The General tore into it. There it was. Front page above the fold. The Lowell Rutherford Harris quote: "President Tyler is a sad figure. He's not too well educated, and he's leading the country toward fascism, even though he wouldn't understand the word fascism anyhow."

He blinked. It was almost exactly the same quote left on General Holloman's recorder before he committed suicide. Of course he didn't suspect Harris of making the

call, but there *was* a connection somehow. There had to
be. He just had to find out what it was.

He ran a Nexus search in the hotel's computer room using the parameters "fascism," "Hitler," and "Lowell
Rutherford Harris." The Internet returned over three hundred hits. "Fascism" and "Hitler" appeared to be common
themes applied to Tyler in Harris's campaign. The senator's campaign Web site included a number of con-
stituency e-mails spewing such venom against Woodrow
Tyler.

"I expected this fucked-up administration to fuck up
but I didn't expect it to fuck up the whole world to the extent it has. I hate the pig-in-shit grin on Tyler's fascist face
every time he takes some more of our freedoms . . ."

"When I hear Tyler say, 'You're either with us or
against us,' it reminds me of the Nazis . . ."

Harris himself often compared Tyler to the Nazis in his
campaign speeches.

"He betrayed this country. He played on our fears. He
took America on an ill-conceived foreign adventure dangerous to our troops, an adventure preordained and planned
before 9/11 ever took place. This guy would be Hitler . . ."

"He has that messianic gleam in his eye, which is terribly tedious. Hitler had it."

The General pushed himself away from the computer.
Any wacko with a perceived grudge and a "change the
world" mission could have taken off on a crusade of his
own. But would such a wacko have the necessary resources
and contacts to target prominent War on Terror figures and
dig into their past histories? General Kragle didn't think
so. Whoever was doing this was . . . commited.

The General invited his brother Mike to an early dinner.
As managing editor of CPI, Mike had contacts, resources,

and a vast political knowledge that might prove enlightening. Thirty-five years ago, as a correspondent for CPI, he won a Pulitzer for his coverage of the Vietnam War. Since then he had published several important books and was now CEO of Consolidated Press International. He still liked to get out in the field and get ink on his fingers.

Mike was a few years older than the General, a shorter man, stockier, but with the same dark Irish looks. He grinned at the General as he made his way toward him through the diners at Pepe's. The General noticed with a wave of nostalgia that his brother was showing his age. His hair was almost white now and he walked slightly stooped. They shook hands rather formally in the detached Kragle way, ordered sandwiches, soup, and beer.

"When you called to invite me for dinner—your treat," Mike said, "it was funny that you mentioned The Committed."

"Funny how?"

Mike sipped a Corona. "CPI is about to do a piece on it. Let me ask you something first. Do you know who George Coalgate Geis is?"

The General shrugged. "Isn't he a billionaire philanthropist or something? Why?"

Mike passed a photo across the table. It showed a wild-looking man with bushy white hair staring in obvious annoyance from the backseat of a limousine. Senator Lowell Rutherford Harris was about to get into the car with him.

"George Coalgate Geis?"

"The same. A young lady photographer covering elections for CPI snapped this curious photo at a political rally in New Hampshire."

"He's obviously a Harris supporter, which also obviously means he has more money than sense."

"He's more than a supporter. He has declared that defeating President Tyler is the central focus in his life and is putting his money where his mouth is. He says he wakes up at three a.m. with fears shaking him like an alarm clock. He says Tyler gives him nightmares about Nazi slogans on walls—"

The Nazi theme. The General leaned across the table, more interested.

"This year alone," Mike continued, "Geis donated at least fifteen million dollars to major leftist groups like ACT UP, MoveOn.org, and the Center for American Progress. He has funded such causes as support for drug legalization, late-term abortion, abolishment of the death penalty, opposition to tough sentencing guidelines, and alternatives to prison incarceration. His Great Society Institute funds groups advocating higher taxes, increased government spending, restrictions of private property rights, state ownership of all means of production . . ."

"He's a Marxist, but what does that have to do with—?"

Mike held up a hand. "I'm getting there. Geis is a Czech who came to the U.S. by way of France and made his fortune. As you've already pointed out, he's a self-admitted communist. Tax forms show he has given a hundred sixty-one *million* overall to domestic and international nonprofit groups to promote socialism. He opposes all of the Tyler administration's domestic policies, from cutting taxes to privatizing social security. But he saves his greatest hatred for the President's post 9/11 foreign policy.

"He goes so far as to claim Tyler is cynically exploiting the 9/11 tragedy in order to gain U.S. world domination through a 'supremacist ideology,' that President Tyler believes only in brute force legitimized by law. He says the Tyler doctrine is a 'crude form of social Darwinism' that fosters poverty and breeds frustration, and therefore creates more terrorism. Geis is not simply somebody who has a lot of money to spread around. He wants to be seen as the man who ousts President Tyler and becomes a kind of savior of a new progressive America on its way to state socialism."

Interesting, but General Kragle still wasn't sure where all this was leading.

"Why does communism and Fellow Traveling always hold such a strange attraction for rich Ivy League types with three names, like John Stewart Service, Harry Dexter White, and William Sloan Coffin?" he wondered.

Mike nodded. "Well, it looks like George Coalgate Geis and The Committed have picked their candidate for this horse race in Lowell Rutherford Harris."

General Kragle's eyebrows shot up. "You mean—?"

Mike chuckled. "That's right. Geis *is* The Committed. It's a secret group of men—very rich men who are throwing their wealth behind defeating Woodrow Tyler in the next election. So far, Geis is the only member whose name I'm sure of. Now, why are you interested in The Committed?"

"Because Lough mentioned them when he told me the U.S. government was at stake," the General said. "He was gunned down before he could say anything else."

Mike's eyes widened. "Well, I'll be damned," he said.

CHAPTER 43

Vietnam, 1968

VC reached the canal and were jumping in, sailing off the opposite banks and landing splashing to charge the Mike Force emplacements. Captain Darren Kragle's automatic Stoner slapped steadily into his shoulder as he selected targets from among the human waves. All he saw through his sights and muzzle smoke were black shirts and green cartridge belts. Other enemy soldiers immediately replaced those who went down. Aim, squeeze the trigger, recoil . . . Aim, squeeze the trigger, recoil . . .

"Tien len! Tien len! Mau len, dong chi mau len!"
Attack! Attack! Rapidly, comrades, attack!

"You die!" Darren raged as he banged away with the Stoner. "Piss on you cocksuckers. You die!"

Twice the defenders hurled the VC back, each time when it appeared they could no longer hold. The attackers withdrew along the way they came. Some of them continued to fire while others dragged away fallen comrades by their arms or cartridge belts. Darren picked among the crouching figures, knocking them off one by one. He heard Lieutenant Hurst sobbing with terror in the bottom of his hole.

The third attack did it. VC broke through the defenders' battered perimeter, overran the little farmer village and scattered those Montagnards who were not killed. Only the rain saved them. It finally poured from the lowering clouds and fell so hard that friend or foe could hardly tell each other apart from ten paces. Fighting broke up into little pockets of violence as survivors split up into ones and twos to E & E their way through the blinding gray mists.

Darren yanked Hurst out of his hole. He couldn't just *leave* him, much as he was tempted.

"Follow me, damn you," he growled. "Stay right on my ass and keep your mouth shut."

Tears mixed with rain and ran down the lieutenant's face. He nodded vigorously, gratefully, and kept nodding.

Screened by blurring sheets of rain, surrounded by the popping of gunfire, Darren led the way to a drainage ditch that angled across the rice paddy on one side of the abandoned village. It was overgrown with reeds taller than a man's head and engorged with fresh rain runoff. The two Americans crouched in the water to gather their bearings. Rifle fire stammered from everywhere as VC hunted down stragglers and holdouts and finished them off.

Two indistinct forms appeared, stoop stalking through the gray stormlight. They and the hiding Americans spotted each other simultaneously. One of the VC fired from the hip, inaccurately, but his bullet still struck Darren's Stoner and spun it out of his hands.

Darren's hand darted for his holstered .45 Colt. The pistol came up spitting. The muzzle flashed four times. Two slugs ripped into each enemy soldier. They fell in the tall grass. One continued to flop about and gurgle. Darren climbed from the ditch, walked over and coolly finished him off with a head shot before returning to Lieutenant Hurst.

"Gooks are going to be all over this AO like fleas on a dog," he said. "Your best bet is to keep in the ditch until you get to the jungle. Stay low in the water. Float and go under if you have to. When you get clear, head toward the Ninth Division at Dong Tam."

"*My* best bet?" Hurst protested. "What about you?"

"One of us might get through in this ditch," Darren hurried on. "Two of us together don't stand a chance. There's not enough cover. I'm going to cut back through the edge of the village and see if I can follow the small canal. They won't be expecting that. We both might make it if it'll keep raining."

Hurst grabbed Darren's harness with the steel grip of an insane man. "I can't do this by myself," he shrieked. "You can't leave me like this, Captain! I'm going with you. They'll *kill me*!"

Neither would make it if they stayed in one place too long. Darren tried to shake him loose. Hurst held on desperately, sobbing and slobbering with the rain pouring down his face. While they were thus engaged, distracted, a patrol of six VC slipped up to the ditch. Before Captain Kragle could react, armed only with his pistol, the six rushed forward with ready rifles and dragged him and Hurst out of the flooded ditch.

Darren expected to be promptly executed. Instead, one of the patrol jabbered something and the others lowered their rifles. This guy apparently thought captured American GIs were better than dead ones. At least for the time being.

Clearly, American forces had run up against a lot more at Vinh Tho than they bargained on. Darren had tried to warn Colonel Bruton. Now, he and Lieutenant Jerry Hurst were being led into captivity from which neither would likely emerge alive.

"*Mau di! Mau di!* Go fast!"

Their six original captors turned them over to four others, who poked them with long spiked bayonets on the ends of Mosin-Nagant carbines, pushing and prodding, trying to make them run. Both Americans were too physically exhausted, too mentally spent, to manage more than a shambling half trot. They slipped and struggled in the mud and rain because their arms, tied behind at the wrists and elbows, prevented their balancing themselves. Each time they fell, the VC jerked them to their feet and prodded them even harder. Finally, their captors attached lengths of rope around their necks and pulled them at a faster pace.

The Americans were dragged for the rest of the day along narrow jungle paths. The rain stopped and humidity soared. They forded small streams where leeches stuck to their legs. Mosquitoes swarmed, driving them mad. Once, Hurst slipped while crossing a single-pole monkey bridge and hung by his legs upside down with his head under water. Laughing guards pulled him to safety before he drowned.

Dark descended rapidly. Thin blue moonlight threaded down through canopies of leaves. Terrain and the situation itself became more unreal in the night. They continued to walk until the moon was almost overhead and the dim glow of a lighted doorway appeared directly ahead.

An old man wearing a straw cone hat escorted them into the hooch. He indicated a spot for the prisoners to sit while the guards ate. The room smelled of wood smoke, oil from the flickering lamp, and the rotted stench of *nuoc mam,* the salty Vietnamese fish sauce that the Viets ate over rice at every meal. Unappetizing as it smelled, Darren would have gulped it down. He was famished. He hadn't eaten since yesterday. He heard Hurst's stomach roiling.

The one time they had attempted to speak to each other

on the trail was rewarded with kicks and blows. Darren simply looked at Hurst now and tried to convey confidence as best a man could sitting on a dirt floor with his hands and arms bound, surrounded by enemy who considered him an unnecessary burden. Hurst had cried off and on all day, but now looked numb and withdrawn.

The old papasan brought them water in a tin cup and held it while they drank. It was warm and tasted of the swamp, from which the old man had likely dipped it.

After the guards finished eating and drinking, they got the Americans to their feet and led them to a long, narrow sampan tied up at a canal. They threw them blindfolded into the bottom of it and began poling downstream. Darren promptly lost whatever sense of direction he had left.

Hurst came down with dysentery, a result of his own uncontrollable fears and the swamp water they drank. Lying in the bottom of the sampan, trying to keep his face out of the seep water, with Hurst lying almost on top of him, Darren heard the junior officer's guts grumbling and complaining. Eventually, the poor kid was unable to contain his excruciating cramps. He voided with a gaseous trousers-filling explosion.

The guards shouted in anger and disgust. One of them kicked Hurst in the side, which cause a further explosion. They stopped the sampan and tossed both captives overboard to wash them off. Blindfolded and bound, Darren thought they were being drowned. The guards laughed at their struggles before they pulled the helpless men back into the boat by using their legs and the ropes around their necks as leverage.

Hardly had they recovered from the first dunking than Hurst's dysentery struck again. He hyperventilated from his panicked efforts to hold it back.

"Oh, God, Captain! I'm sorry!"

Once again, the disgusted guards dumped them into the canal, leaving them in longer this time to teach them a lesson. Half drowned, they lay spent in the bottom of the long canoe. Hurst moaned and wept softly. The poor bastard; he would never make it through captivity.

To keep his mind occupied, Darren thought of Rita. Of going home to beautiful blond Rita. Then he forced her out of his mind. His future, if he *had* a future, looked bleak, and it was out of his control. He had to put everything out of his mind except one thing—survival. Survival depended on thinking of nothing beyond getting through the next hour. Then on getting through the next, and the one after that, and all the others that followed. One hour at a time.

Time soon lost all meaning. They became delirious from lack of food and water and the tropical heat. Guards gave them only one drink a day and they were fed once— some dried fish and even drier rice that they had to choke down. Hurst vomited his up, which weakened him even more.

After what seemed a very long time—days, but which neither man could accurately calculate—they were hoisted, still blindfolded, out of the sampan and into the hold of a larger boat. It stank of fish and felt slimy against Darren's cheek. Darren determined it must be a fisherman's seagoing junk because he had plenty of room to stretch out and he heard sails flapping in the wind and rigging slapping and banging.

Again, days ran together while they lay blindfolded and the boat sailed *somewhere*. They were watered and fed better than before, but Darren still felt weight melting off his tall frame. Hurst recovered somewhat because of the better food, but mentally he remained a total wreck. They could talk now, as the guards and sailors paid little attention, but conversation consisted mainly of Captain Kragle whispering while Lieutenant Hurst sobbed.

"Listen to me, Hurst. The only way you're going to make it is to get a better attitude."

"Why don't they just kill us and get it over with?"

The seas were rough at times. The boat was becalmed on other days. Darren wondered why the U.S. Navy and the U.S. Coast Guard hadn't intercepted them. Apparently, the VC were posing as fishermen and the ruse was working.

One day, they seemed to enter the mouth of a river because the junk reefed its sails in exchange for an outboard engine. Darren heard current lapping against the hull.

The next morning, the captives were hoisted onto the deck and their blindfolds removed. Bright sun stabbed painfully through Darren's eyes, unaccustomed as he was to the light. He finally opened his eyes, squinting. He was stunned at what he saw. The wide river ran through a large Vietnamese city.

"I think we're in Hanoi!" he gasped in startled realization.

The gates of hell.

CHAPTER 44

Tindouf Airport

Chaplain Cameron Kragle shifted his weight from one hip to the other and stretched his back against the wall, careful not to wake Rhoda who slept using his knee as a pillow. He had his arm around Kelli while she napped. It had gone numb, but he still couldn't bring himself to let her go. Zorgon snored quietly on the other side of Rhoda. From out of the darkened room around them came other snores, low cries, whispers, and the whimpering of children.

"Lord," Cameron murmured, "I am so small and you are so vast."

Kelli stirred against his shoulder. He felt her awake and was sure she was watching him even if she couldn't see. Somehow that awareness of her both thrilled him and made him uncomfortable.

"Do you remember one of the last things Jesus said when he was being crucified?" she asked in her husky Scarlett O'Hara voice.

" 'My God, why hast thou forsaken me?' " Cameron quoted.

"His doubts showed how truly human the son of God had become," she said. "Cameron, do you ever have doubts? Do you ever feel God has forsaken us?"

"Are you having doubts?" he answered with a question.

She readjusted her position to sit closer to him. She felt for his hand.

"It is so dark," she said. "There is such darkness."

They were silent while they held hands, fingers intertwined.

Spiritual specialists assured Cameron that all people, no matter how holy, occasionally had doubts, but that such doubts should not be confused with loss of faith in God. Even so holy a spirit as Mother Teresa admitted she had sometimes suffered from a "divine silence," a dark night of the soul.

"I am told that God lives in me," she was quoted in a biography as saying, "and yet the reality of darkness and coldness and emptiness is so great that nothing touches my soul. I want God with all the power of my soul—and yet between us there is a terrible separation. Heaven from every side is closed. I feel just that terrible pain of loss, of God not wanting me, of God not being God, of God not really existing."

Whenever Cameron experienced "dark nights of the soul," most generally late while he worked on a sermon in his Smoke Bomb Hill chapel, he replenished his soul by going outside and looking up into the starred heavens. The Hubble Space Telescope had photographed at least ten thousand separate galaxies lighting up the cosmic darkness. Light had left some of those galaxies more than thirteen *billion* years ago. The light endured. The light that God created *endured*. This light and its accompanying concepts of infinity and forever eluded mankind's comprehension. They reminded Cameron that no mortal could gaze into the infinite represented by the heavens and not believe in a "prime mover," a divine intelligence behind it all. In God and the son of God who came to earth to remind mankind of its place in the universe.

"I wonder," Kelli said, "if it's night or day. How long have I slept?"

"I don't know. They took my watch."

"I could feel you thinking even while I was sleeping. What were you pondering?"

"How to get out of this," he admitted.

"Bless your heart. What did you decide?"

He had no answer. He could not answer.

After a passage of time, she said, "Did I tell you I'm working on a Ph.D. in peace studies?"

"There is such a thing?"

"Of course. If you study war, why can't you study peace?"

He let it go. He didn't want to talk about it. They would only disagree over her politics.

"We became frustrated over merely marching against the war," she went on. "No one seemed to listen."

He squeezed her hand to shush her.

"I want to tell you, Cameron. Hear me out. Don Keefe, who was in charge of the human shields to Iraq, called the U.S. the number-one terrorist on the planet and said America was intent on global domination."

"You believed him, Kelli?" Cameron asked incredulously.

"I believe in peace and in the power of the Lord to bring peace," she continued. "So we human-shield volunteers got on two double-decker buses in London and rode to Baghdad in three weeks. I found out later that Saddam Hussein's Iraqi government was paying for everything, including housing and stocked refrigerators."

Here a little bitterness crept into her voice.

"We all felt we were acting on principle and if that meant dying, so be it. We thought that if the war started and we were killed for our principles, we would be remembered as strong antiwar protestors and really wake people up to the fact that war is wrong and to show just how far

President Tyler was willing to push this, up to killing white Westerners who were patrolling hospitals, schools, and other civilian installations. Oh, Cameron, we thought we were so very brave and noble. We told each other we were more afraid of what the Americans would do to us if they caught us than we were of Saddam Hussein."

Many Americans, especially Christians, were struggling with similar issues of violence and nonviolence, war and peace. Most, however, never felt the inclination to join forces with enemies. Cameron's father, the General, would never forgive actress Jane Fonda for traveling to North Vietnam during that war and being photographed with communist anti-aircraft guns. He would never forgive former president John Stanton, even though Stanton was dead, for being a Vietnam draft dodger and taking his cowardice with him to the White House. To the General, there were just wars, necessary wars. The War on Terror was one of them.

"It turned out," Kelli went on, "that even Saddam Hussein didn't really believe the United States would deliberately bomb hospitals, mosques, and schools. We wanted to be positioned at hospitals and orphanages, but it was made clear to us that no humanitarian sites would be made available. We were going to be forced to defend power plants and oil refineries located near military bases. What's more, Cameron, I began to see another side of things—"

She was trying to tell Cameron in her own way that reality began to slip into her idealism.

"I began to hear of hundreds of thousands of people who were executed by Saddam and buried in mass graves, of women pulled off the streets and raped at random, of men hung up by their heels and skinned alive merely because they spoke out, of . . . Oh, Cameron, I know you've heard all this. Iraqis told me in confidence that they would commit suicide if America did *not* start bombing. They said Saddam was a monster who deserved to die. I think this must have been the first time I actually confronted evil face to face. Bless his heart, Don Keefe was the first one of us to bug out."

"Evil will triumph unless good and Godly men stand up against it," Cameron said. "I don't think God wants evil to triumph."

"Then why doesn't *he* do something about it?"

"Kelli, God *is* doing something about it."

Rhoda roused long enough to turn over on her other side and mutter, "Amen."

"And now," Kelli stammered, "the last few days . . . what happened to the Sahrawi, to Jean, and now to Giemma . . . Cameron, there really *is* evil in the world."

"Yes."

Cameron dealt with evil versus good in his capacity as a chaplain ministering to warriors as well as in his personal life.

"America seems to no longer have a clear vision of our moral obligation to stand between evil and the innocent," he said. "We seem to want to define all violence as bad, even to the point of indoctrinating our children that it's wrong to defend themselves and others from attack by bullies. Look at Israel and the Palestinian terrorists. We've made morally equivalent the suicide bombing of innocent children to the targeting of a terrorist wrapped in bombs. Weakening of moral concepts only makes the world more susceptible to evil."

She seemed to no longer possess the heart to resist his arguments, not when they were locked in a dark room palpable with the presence of evil.

"Cameron, they'll be coming back for another of us soon, won't they?" she said.

It must be getting near morning again.

"This time it will be one of us. Either Zorgon or Rhoda . . ."

Something caught in her throat.

"You . . . Me . . ." she finished.

The events on the *Achille Lauro* luxury liner when it was hijacked in 1985 were typical of the modern terrorist mentality. The only person executed by the Palestinian extremists was an American, Leon Klinghoffer, because the terrorists knew that the death of an American citizen would make the most impact.

"Cameron?"

Kelli tugged his hand to her cheek and neck, clasping it hard and desperately. He felt her other palm cup the side of his face. He turned toward her and they kissed in the total darkness. A long kiss, bittersweet under the circumstances, but sweet nonetheless, and warm, and he tasted her and tasted the salt of silent tears and—

He jerked away. He had kissed Gypsy a last time like this. He couldn't bear for it to happen again.

CHAPTER 45

West Sahara

Brandon Kragle's well-trained rescue patrol hit the ground the instant it triggered the ambush, as did Malud and the Sahrawi. All except the little kid, Juba. To Brandon's astonishment, the tiny figure sprang out of the wadi like a Jack-in-the-box and charged off into the blowing sand, his assault rifle stabbing flickering ribbons of flame.

"Kid, no!" Brandon yelled. "Get back here—!"

His voice trailed off. Juba disappeared. Brandon heard his automatic rifle chattering. A man without a sense of immortality could sometimes be reckless and therefore a danger to his team and mission. Someone as young as Juba, and armed, went beyond recklessness.

Brandon slammed his fist against the sand in exasperation, faced as he was with making an immediate choice: mission or people. He saw that seven-year-old storming into battle and he knew he couldn't let him go out there alone and die. Just this one time, mission did *not* come personally first. He leaped to his feet and was already out of the wadi and running toward the sounds of Juba's rifle.

"Ice!"

To a unit like Delta, that one command was sufficient to inform Ice Man that he was now in charge. It meant *Get them out of here. Mission comes first.*

Fortunately, the ambush had been a hasty affair, initiated by ill-trained fighters from too great a distance, especially under conditions of reduced visibility, and therefore largely ineffective. Ice Man, shouting to be heard above the howl of the wind and the clash and clatter of small arms fire, began maneuvering to either shut down the ambush by attaining fire superiority and position or slip his patrol out of what was intended to be a kill zone. So far, not a single Delta or Sahrawi had been touched.

A near-miss bullet makes a pop like the snapping of a green tree branch. An entire forest seemed to be snapping branches around Brandon's head from the moment he cleared the wadi until he disappeared into the sandstorm. He chased hard toward the sound of Juba's rifle. A second rifle answered his, but it was an SKS with a sharper, slower rate of fire and could therefore be distinguished from Juba's. It sounded like the audacious brat had gotten into a duel with one of the terrorists.

Juba's rifle fire and the SKS quit suddenly. From that direction came nothing but the groaning of wind. Visibility was down to less than ten meters as the storm entered an intensified phase. Blowing, stinging sand grabbed at Brandon's clothing and threatened to shove him off his feet. It was hard to tell direction in the disorienting swirl of nature gone berserk. Brandon paused to get his bearings.

Ice Man and the others were starting to dominate the firefight with their MP5s. Brandon found it as difficult to tell the direction to the fight as it was to locate Juba. Wind seemed to distribute sound all over the landscape. He wiped off his goggles to clear them, but he still couldn't see shit—only the outlines of the nearest boulders and rock. The world seemed to close in on him from all sides, brown and entirely molecular, as though everything had been reduced into basic energy components of atoms and molecules.

Juba's weapon remained mute. The little sonofabitch must have gotten himself waxed. Brandon wasn't sure he wanted to see the body, even if he could find it. Viewing corpses of full-grown men was bad enough. How much worse it was when the cadavers were children, women, or the elderly. Still, Brandon had to make sure about Juba one way or the other. He picked his way through a boulder field as he crept in the general direction from which he last heard the boy firing.

A shadow, an indistinct form, flitted into and out of his view so swiftly that he couldn't be sure if he had seen anything at all. Every sense taut and on edge, finger on the trigger of his G3, he eased forward, pausing every few steps to listen.

Firing from the draw dwindled down to a few isolated, startled bangs. An ambush firefight never lasted long. Seconds, a minute or so at most. Brandon wasn't overly concerned. His men were veterans, the best in the world at their job. At this very moment, he suspected, Ice Man was leading Mad dog, Diverse, and the four Sahrawi free of the KZ. They were probably already chugging out across the flats toward Top Sculdiron and the rest of the detachment on the ridgeline.

That meant he was out here alone, except for some dumb kid who had likely already gotten himself killed. In these worsening conditions, he mustn't expect any further help from Gloomy Davis and Mr. Blunderbuss. Gloomy probably couldn't even see the hill.

He mustn't count on Sculdiron waiting for him either. While an operator was never left behind *permanently*, it was part of the drill that mission came first. Rescuing Malud, getting him out, *was* the mission. Sculdiron understood that.

It was up to Brandon alone to find that kid, be he dead

or alive, then rejoin the detachment and get the hell out of this hellhole.

Imagine a little kid like that fighting it out with grown men! Back in the United States, seven-year-olds were watching cartoons on TV and begging to go to Chucky Cheese's. In so many parts of the world, children never had childhoods.

Major Kragle made his way cautiously across an opening in the boulders and followed a washout around the curve of the hill, still heading in the general direction, he hoped, from which he last heard Juba.

He failed to see the Jihadia until he was almost on top of him. The guy was more than a shadow this time. He was skulking around the finger of a rockslide. Obviously, he was also searching for Juba, stalking him. He disappeared again before Brandon could draw a bead.

Brandon slipped off to his left, intending to cut the guy off when he emerged from the rockslide. Behind him, the sounds of gunfire ceased altogether. Instead, he heard the drift of approaching voices. He was about to have more company. Someone called out.

"Rashid? *Rashid*?"

That must be the gunman in the rubble. He didn't answer. A moment later, Brandon understood why. He didn't want to give himself away.

A tiny form slowly materialized out of the blown sand from farther up the hill and angled down toward the upper brow of the rockslide. Directly toward the waiting gunfighter. Juba! At least he wasn't dead. Yet. But he was about to be unless Brandon acted immediately.

Bad guys behind cutting him off from the detachment, bad guys ahead. The moment Brandon revealed himself, he knew, they would be all over him like stink on shit, as Mad Dog might indelicately put it.

But what other choice did he have? He took a deep breath and sprang at the rockslide behind which the rifleman had disappeared, yelling madly to divert the killer's attention away from the boy.

"Get down, Juba! Get down!"

Head and shoulders popped up from behind the rockslide like a startled prairie dog from its hole. Brandon, Juba, and the terrorist were all within a few paces of each other. As the kid dropped, obeying orders instantly for once in his life, Brandon closed the gap between the enemy and himself and opened fire on full auto. He kept his finger on the trigger even as he sailed off the slide above the guy's head. Flame from the muzzle actually scorched the man's beard as he went down hard with a final cry of shock and pain. Blood spurted from face and neck wounds.

Brandon kept moving. Reactive rifle fire exploded in his wake; the tangos apparently thought they were being ambushed. Bullets screamed off rocks, but there were no snapping tree branches. The Jihadia were simply shooting and shouting blindly into the storm.

Brandon scooped Juba off the ground and tucked him underneath his arm with hardly a pause. Juba kicked and yelled in protest.

"My rifle! I dropped my rifle, American!"

"Hush. I'll get you another one."

CHAPTER 46

Between El Paso and Washington, D.C.

Director Claude Thornton pondered the information he obtained from Youseff Balaghi on his Learjet flight back to Washington to meet with Secret Service advance teams concerning President Tyler's first major political speech of the Funny Season in Tulsa, trying to piece together all the scraps of intel he had garnered from various sources since the two Arabs showed up glowing in Yuma. He wrote each item in chronological order on a yellow legal pad in hopes that it might help him see more clearly and form connections.

    —Two illegal Arabs via Mexico die of radiation poisoning. Where is the WMD that killed them?
    —Unknown renter at Cactus Motel calls Lough. What is connection between Lough and NCC Gerald Espy?
    —Lough assassinated in Washington in company of General Kragle.
    —Espy, Senator Lowell Harris, and former KGB agent David Barr have longtime connections.
    —CENTCOM resigns, Tyler's assistant security advisor resigns, AFSOC commits suicide, USSOCOM won't return calls.
    —Balaghi says David Barr rented room at Cac-

*tus Motel, meaning he is behind smuggling of Arabs
and their WMD.*

   *—Balaghi insinuates terrorists are attempting to
prevent President Tyler's reelection.*

It wasn't much to go on, hardly sufficient to justify a
good suspicion. Yet, Thornton felt in his bones that he was
looking at political terrorism. Terrorists were going to detonate a suitcase nuke in an American city to influence the
upcoming elections. Why not? It was working in Spain.

All indications pointed toward Spain's ousting its current pro-American president at the last minute and going
socialist in response to the bombings of Madrid's commuter trains; the socialist candidate promised to withdraw
from alliance with the United States in the War on Terror,
exactly what terrorists anticipated. Thornton considered
how much greater an impact on the U.S. population a
WMD would have than conventional TNT, as in Madrid.
Public opinion on the war, already split nearly fifty-fifty,
might easily reflect in the polls in favor of the presidential
candidate who vowed to retreat to "Fortress Americana."

All right. So Thornton thought he knew *what* and *why*.
So what about *where, when*, and *how*?

He stayed on the phone most of the way back to Washington, D.C., attempting to shake something loose. He issued a worldwide FBI pickup order to arrest David Barr
for aiding in the smuggling of aliens. He encouraged
NEST to send Nuclear Emergency Search Teams to Arizona to see if they might come up with a clue on a WMD.
The CIA was busy in Iraq and the Middle East, but Tom
Hinds promised to put out feelers for terrorists with links
to Mexico. DIA and the National Security Agency had
massive computers out at Fort Meade that sifted through

hundreds of thousands of cellular and digital phone call waves seeking key words like *gun, bomb, assassinate* . . .

"There seems to be increased terrorist interest in Texas and the Southwest," one of the operators told Thornton.

The President's home state.

MacArthur Thornbrew, director of the National Homeland Security Agency, informed Thornton that the President was raising the national terrorist threat level from Yellow to Orange in response to increased terrorist "chatter."

"We're beefing up vigilance all through the Texas region," he said.

Thornton sighed and pressed his forehead against the cool glass of the aircraft window. He had a hollow feeling that whatever was about to happen, they weren't going to find out in time to stop it. It was like knowing on September 10, 2001, that terrorists were going to strike against the United States but not knowing their targets were the World Trade Center and the Pentagon.

Why, Thornton wondered in an odd thought, would anyone want to be president of the United States? Pressures on the president had to be ten times, a hundred times, what they were for anyone else in the country. The buck truly stopped in the Oval Office, as President Harry Truman once noted.

Since taking office, President Tyler had dealt with one crisis topped by another. In February after he was inaugurated in January, the Chinese forced down a U.S. Navy reconnaissance plane and held the crew for several nerve-wracking days; September 11 brought the terrorist attack on the Twin Towers and the Pentagon; in October, the President declared War on Terror and sent troops to Afghanistan to destroy terrorist training camps, get rid of the Taliban, and hunt down Osama bin Laden.

During the following year, he had had to deal with Palestinian suicide bombers in Israel, with Yasser Arafat and Ariel Sharon, and with the big joke of UN weapons inspectors in Saddam Hussein's Iraq. Finally, tired of the UN charade, he sent troops to Iraq to physically remove Saddam and his regime from power.

North Korea was acting up, having sold SCUD missiles to tangos in the Philippines for use against the United States. A missile aimed at New Orleans was caught just in time. Now, there were American hostages in Tindouf, genocide in Algeria, and a possible suitcase nuke about to explode in America . . .

Did it never end?

On top of everything else, various political enemies had lined up against the God-fearing man from Texas with all the fierceness and fury once reserved for Ronald Reagan. Opposition House members were trying to push through, and in secret, a proposal to greatly restrict Special Operations activities; the Senate Intelligence Committee apparently contrived with the UN to file war-crimes charges against American leaders; there was talk of independent investigations and special prosecutors and impeachment and . . . Did it also never end? The "loyal opposition" seemed to be doing everything it could to sabotage the war against terrorists and bring down the Tyler administration. A growing segment of Americans, especially the intellectual elite, even seemed to want to bring down America itself.

Attacked from within and without. No wonder the President looked to have aged so much since 9/11.

Thornton's Learjet began to drop altitude on its initial approach to Ronald Reagan International. The earth below was almost red from the sunset. Thornton dialed Della Street and informed her he was on his way to the office for another late night.

"Call Fred," she relayed.

He quickly dialed Whiteman's cell. Whiteman had followed a lead to New York.

"Get to the point, Fred. We're approaching Washington now."

"Point one: David Barr is in the United States—"

"A point we've already ascertained."

"Point two: Something called The Committed paid Barr's way from France and is apparently bankrolling him."

"I have to hang up, Fred. We're on final approach."

"I'll have a report on your desk first thing in the morning."

Thornton hung up. He made a final notation on his yellow legal pad.

—The Committed.

CHAPTER 47

WORLD WAR III RISE OF NEW FASCISM
EDITORIAL BY MIKE KRAGLE

Washington (CPI)—Military experts increasingly use the theme "World War III" to describe the U.S.-led fights and forays against Islamic extremists following the "Pearl Harbor" attack against the United States on September 11, 2001. Main battle lines zig zag from the Middle East to Africa, from Asia to as far as the Philippine jungles, from New York and New Orleans to Jakarta and Spain, from Afghanistan to Iraq and Algeria. American forces are stretched so thin that National Guard units are being activated to go to Iraq.

Battles smolder between secular governments and Islamic hardliners even where U.S. troops are not involved—in Kashmir; in Indonesia, where suicide bombings have slaughtered hundreds; in the Middle East, where Islamic militants vow to destroy Israel; in the Caucasus, where Muslims fight to bring down the government of Azerbaijan; in Sudan, Kenya, and Tanzania; in Djibouti on the Horn of Africa; in the Philippines, where Muslim extremists demand an Islamic state; in Algeria, where Salafia Jihadia terrorists/rebels slaughter hundreds of Sahrawi refugees, threaten the country's civil government, and hold American hostages; and most recently in Spain, where terrorists killed over 200 people in a spate of train bombings.

"No nation can be neutral in this struggle between civilization and chaos," President Tyler told a veterans convention.

"This third world war, I think," said MacArthur Thornbrew, director of National Homeland Security, "will last considerably longer than either World War One or World War Two."

Thornbrew and others in the Tyler administration, including the President, view the outcome of the War on Terror as being just as vital to the survival of civilization as was the defeat of Hitler's Germany during World War II. The enemy, in fact, is much the same.

Extremist Islamics who hijack airplanes, smuggle WMD and missiles into the United States, and immolate themselves in suicide bombings are soldiers of a new fascism, the goals of which are much like Hitler's—to control the world under Allah and destroy everything that gets in the way. Allah's fundamentalist representatives on earth are not merciful.

Clerical fascism is more totalitarian than European fascism under Hitler or Mussolini. Political Islam is aggressive in reaching its goals of total control. Violence is commonly used against citizens of states when Islamics prevail. Opponents are killed, imprisoned, forced to emigrate, or are bombed and terrorized if they fall outside the regime's immediate control.

Tens of thousands of people were murdered in Iran under Ayatollah Khomeini and his successors. The extent of Saddam Hussein's slaughter of his own people in Iraq is just now coming to light in the mass graves uncovered by U.S. troops. Hundreds of Sahrawi Christians are now being murdered in Algeria by Muslim fanatics attempting to take over the government and purge it of outside influences.

What most Americans refuse to realize is that the War on Terror is not a conflict between political regimes. Instead, it is a life-or-death struggle between two philosophies, between two societies, one modern and the other anti-modern. There can be no truce in a war in which one side, as it repeatedly insists, "loves death more than it loves life" and has proved itself willing to indiscriminately slaughter men, women, and children. It is a war that must be fought until one side or the other is vanquished.

What remains unclear at the present is whether the West has the resolve to meet and defeat this resurrection of the world's new fascism . . .

CHAPTER 48

West Sahara

The tall and lanky Zulu, Diverse Dade, led the band of Deltas and Sahrawi puffing up the ridge to relink with the other half of the detachment. The air blew so thick with gale-driven sand that it was almost like swimming through the earth's crust. Each group failed to see and recognize the other until they were almost on top of each other. Diverse began shouting the password: "Sheep! Sheep! Sheep!"

"All right, all right already!" Perverse Sanchez yelled back, giving the correct response: "Dip! Dip! *Dip!* We heard chew."

Mad Dog Carson threw himself on the ground to catch his breath. Ice Man immediately demanded of Sergeant Sculdiron, "Major Kragle has a Motorola. Have you had commo with him?"

"Negative."

Gloomy overheard. "Where's the boss? Where'd you leave him?" Accusingly. He *knew* he should have gone along.

"We didn't *leave* him anywhere."

"The ragheads are right on our asses," Mad Dog exclaimed.

"At ease, at ease," Top Sculdiron barked. "Sergeant Thompson, what happened?"

Ice Man told him about the boy taking off during the ambush and Brandon's going after him.

"You did right, Sergeant Thompson," Top approved. "Is one of these men our objective?"

Ice Man pointed out the balding Sahrawi. "That's Malud."

Sculdiron looked him over with his Tartar squint, like inspecting a package for delivery, nothing more. "We're going to have to move fast, fella," he said. "You have a wounded man. Tell him he'll have to keep up or we'll leave him behind. Is that clear?"

"That is very clear, Sergeant Major."

"I am not a Sergeant Major, Mr. Malud."

"My apologies, sir."

"I am also not a 'sir.' I work for a living."

He moved on, busy organizing a movement.

"Sergeant Thompson, how much time do we have?" he asked.

"We gave 'em the slip, Top. They're not going to be moving far or fast in this shit. They might not find us at all until the storm stops." He paused, then said, "Neither will Major Brandon. He left his GPS here. We wouldn't have found you if we hadn't had the dry wash to follow."

"We'll give him a half hour." He looked at his watch. "Then we're moving out. They probably have vehicles."

"Top—?" Gloomy started to protest.

"Thirty minutes, Sergeant Davis."

"Fucking ragheads," Mad Dog said. "Dirty, camel-humping, boy-porking, stinking, raggedy-ass—"

"That's race profiling, chew know that?" Perverse interrupted.

"Who else is killing us here, Spic Boy—Norwegians? Fu-uck."

Top Sculdiron coolly moved among the men, directing preparations. He turned his booming accented voice on Mad Dog.

"Sergeant Carson, I can't do anything with your damned radio except squeeze hideous screeching out of it."

"We need to stretch an antenna."

"Do it. Quick."

Mad Dog erected a directional wire antenna using Diverse and Perverse as antenna poles. Each man tied an end of the antenna to a stick, braced himself against the wind, and held the stick as far above his head as he could.

"Don't touch the wire when I'm transmitting or it'll knock your dick straight," Mad Dog warned as he hunched over his instrument to adjust and calibrate it.

Top Sculdiron continued to move efficiently about, like a motivating force. Doc TB and the Blackhawk crew chief, Sergeant Morris, were piling the last rocks on a mound. Lieutenant Gardner, the copilot, gasped his last tortured breath just as Brandon and the rescue patrol left the ridgeline. He had not regained consciousness since the crash. His death freed the detachment for greater speed of movement.

"Sergeant Blackburn?" Top said.

"We've buried the lieutenant, Top. Don't you think we should say some words over him?"

"Do it quick."

Sculdiron moved on.

"Sergeant Thompson, are you keeping a sharp eye peeled for the enemy and for Major Kragle?"

"Roger that, Top."

"Top, we got commo with Venom Nest."

Sculdiron rushed to Mad Dog, his two antenna "poles," and the PRC-137.

"I think we can move in the storm using the GPS," he

said. "We made it this far, we can make it back. Tell Venom we'll be on a heading of zero-niner-zero from this grid. Roger that?"

"That's a big ten-four, good buddy."

Sculdiron glared at him. "Tell them to extract us somewhere along the corridor when the weather clears. Tell them we have the parcel."

"Roger that," Mad Dog replied this time.

As the men prepared to depart, they kept glancing from their watches out onto the flats in the direction from which Major Kragle should appear if he was going to make it. In spite of the enlisted Delta bravado, every man, even the newcomers, already experienced a haunting sense of loss. Doc TB slapped Gloomy on the back. Gloomy and Major Kragle had been together the longest.

"He'll make it, Gloomy," Doc TB said, but his voice lacked conviction.

Gloomy dogged the Top Sergeant's footsteps. "Sergeant, I'm requesting permission to go out and find Major Kragle."

"Permission denied, Sergeant Davis."

"We have a spare GPS. The boss will need it to navigate until the storm's over. I'm not asking you to hold up movement for me. I'll join Major Kragle."

Sculdiron paused. The man really *was* as hard as woodpecker lips.

"Sergeant Davis, there are three reasons why you're not going. One, we can't even be sure he's alive. Two, you'd never find him out there anyhow. Three, I'm not risking the mission and losing another man."

"We're just going to leave him out there!"

"That's exactly what we're going to do, Sergeant. We'll be back for him after the mission is completed."

Gloomy wasn't ready to give up. "You sonofabitch! If you were out there, would you expect us to abandon you?"

"That's exactly what I would expect. Sergeant Davis, *you* can expect to be court martialed when we return, on charges of disrespect for a senior NCO."

Sculdiron's hard eyes bore into Gloomy's flinty blue ones. They seemed to soften, if only a degree.

"Sergeant Davis, what would Major Kragle do under the same circumstances?" he asked.

Gloomy Davis didn't have to answer. He turned his eyes away and focused on the swirl of sand in the direction in which Brandon had last been seen. There was no question about it. Mission came first. Brandon would have it no other way. Gloomy suppressed a sinking feeling that he would never see his commander and friend again.

"Saddle up," Top Sculdiron said. "We're moving out."

CHAPTER 49

West Sahara

Brandon sprinted blindly through the storm until rifle fire
stopped seeking his flesh and the shooters vanished somewhere behind him. Juba squirmed angrily underneath his
arm, insisting that he be placed back on his feet. Brandon
slung his G3 over his shoulder, whacked the kid a sharp
wallop on the butt, and ordered him to shut up and keep
still. That did the trick. He was an easier burden after that.

Brandon jogged for a quarter-hour, intent only on putting distance between them and their assailants. It was impossible to tell direction in blowing sand and zero
visibility. He tried to raise Sculdiron once on the Motorola, but the radio was dead and he couldn't spare the
time to check it over. By the time he paused to catch his
breath and take stock of the situation, he had absolutely
no idea where he was in relation to Detachment 2-Charlie.
He listened for gunfire, hearing nothing except the high
keening of the desert wind and the scouring sound of sand
against rock.

He put Juba down. The kid backed away and stuck out a
quivering lower lip. "You hit me," he accused.

Brandon knelt to get on an eye level with him. "We
have to get one thing straight, kid—"

"My name is Juba."

Brandon sighed. Sand clogged his nose and throat and
burned his eyes even through his goggles. Juba, without

goggles, must be almost blind. He kept covering his eyes with his hands.

"All right," he said. "Juba." He had no patience for a sulky, back-talking little boy. They were lost in the middle of the desert, in a sandstorm, with bad guys all around trying to kill them. "Juba, I'm really going to pound your scrawny little butt if you don't do exactly what I tell you from now on. If I say hop, you ask how high. Is that clear, Juba?"

He shook Juba gently by the shoulders to impress upon him the rule. The boy felt as frail as a bird.

"I asked if that is clear?"

Juba thrust out his chin. He nodded his head and answered through tightly compressed lips. "Y—yes, sir."

"Good. Now let me ask you something else. What was the idea of running off the way you did?"

"I did not run off. He was shooting at us. I was going to—"

"I know. Don't tell me. You were going to shoot him in the belly."

The boy smiled for the first time. His little face lit up. "That is right—shoot him in the belly. You believe me?"

"How could I doubt it?"

"You lost my rifle." He had to get in the last word.

"Don't worry about it. I still have mine."

Brandon looked around. He checked the Motorola and discovered why it wouldn't work. A bullet had smashed it where he carried it on his belt. He hadn't even felt the blow. So much for that.

He had a compass and a map, but had left the GPS with Top Sculdiron. A compass was practically useless until he was able to see again. Wandering around in the storm would only get them even more hopelessly lost, until they

blundered into bad guys again. The first thing they needed
was shelter.

"Juba, follow me. Stay close and keep quiet."

He set off slowly in what he hoped was a neutral direction, head bowed against the blow and leaning into the
wind. He looked back and saw the kid being buffeted
about like a twig in ocean surf. Sand blasting against his
bare chest, arms, and back had abraded it from brown to a
scalded, sore-looking red.

Brandon stopped and took off his black tunic and
army T-shirt. He gave the T-shirt to Juba and put his tunic
back on.

"Wear this," he ordered.

Juba held the T-shirt, looking at it. "I don't want nothing from nobody," he said.

"Look, kid, you don't owe me anything for it, all right?
No obligations, no strings attached. Now put it on."

"It's Juba, not 'kid.'"

"Put the shirt on and let's go."

Soon they stumbled upon a ridge of rock along a deep
but narrow wadi. Brandon explored along it until he located a sort of erosion in the bank. A large outcropping of
flat rock extended over it like a roof, making a cave about
eight feet in depth. It was dark inside and Brandon hoped
it contained no snakes. He found a stick and poked and
rattled it around the walls. When nothing ran out, he motioned the boy inside and crawled in after him. There was
ample room and it provided protection from the storm.
They couldn't be seen either unless an observer stopped,
got down on hands and knees, and looked inside. Only by
accident would anyone find it.

Juba pulled up his legs inside the too-large T-shirt and
wrapped his arms around them. There was little illumina-

tion inside the cave even after they got accustomed to the
dimness, but there was enough light for Brandon to make
out the boy's staring eyes. There was something haunting
about the sober, dispassionate way Juba looked at him.
His eyes were very old and wise for one with so few years.

"How did you learn English?" Brandon asked him.

"Hablo Espanol tambien," Juba said, then switched to
Arabic. *"Itkallim Aarabee.* I speak Spanish, Arabic, and
English. I am well talented."

"You are, at that," Brandon agreed.

"Sahrawi speak Spanish and Arabic," Juba explained.
"I am orphan boy. When American missionaries come to
the camps, I sometimes stay with them because they
feed me and give me things if I am helpful. I am most
helpful."

Brandon nodded absently. His thoughts had passed on
to take a mental inventory of their assets in preparation for
escape and evasion. With the boy, he would never be able
to overtake Sergeant Sculdiron and the detachment, providing they could slip back through the Jihadia, who must
even now be out looking for them. That meant they had a
few long, tough days ahead before helicopters flying his E
& E corridor located them.

Juba watched with curiosity as Brandon checked ammo
for both the auto rifle and his 9mm Glock pistol. He had
plenty for both, barring some kind of lengthy siege. He
then unbuckled his butt pack and arrayed items from it between his outstretched legs.

He had a sheath knife, a pocket knife, and, inside his
survival packet, a small clasp knife. The survival packet
also included a tiny signal flare and signaling mirror, wire
for making animal snares, waterproof matches, a first-aid
kit, fish hooks and line—just what he needed in the

desert—and a few other odds and ends, including an Arabic-English phrase book. *I am an American . . . I need help . . .* That sort of thing.

His mind strayed for a moment. Summer was the best phrase book he had ever employed, that first year after he met her and they worked together in Afghanistan, she as interpreter. An image of her face flashed into his mind: the emerald eyes, the wide mouth, the straight nose, and light-colored hair. He could almost smell her hair fresh after she showered, feel the smooth curve of her stomach down to the silky mass of hair . . .

He shook his head to clear it and bring his mind back to business.

He laid an MRE chocolate bar on his knee and checked his canteen. Food and water might be a problem. The canteen was less than half full. He had given the Night Stalker crewman his only MRE (Meal, Ready to Eat) and kept the chocolate bar for himself. Juba's eyes followed the candy bar and canteen as Brandon started to put them away.

"You said you would get me another rifle," Juba charged, but his eyes remained on the chocolate. "What happens when we get in trouble?"

"Kid . . . Juba, we're already in trouble. When was the last time you ate or drink?"

The boy dragged his eyes away from the chocolate with a visible effort.

"There was no time to concern ourselves with food when we were attacked in the camps," he said. "I ran deeper and deeper into the desert until Senor Malud saw me and picked me up in his car."

"You haven't eaten since then?"

"We found water, enough to keep us alive. There was no

water on the hill after the bad men chased us and made us crash our car."

Juba's lips were parched and cracked, his cheeks hollow. Brandon offered him the canteen. His hand shot out, but then he slowly withdrew it.

"I cannot take your water and food," he declined, his gaze still riveted on the chocolate. "What would you do?"

Brandon's heart went out to this kid, who would rather starve than take food from someone else. There was real character in that tiny body.

"Look, Juba. No matter what, you and I are partners until we get out of this. We share whatever we have."

"I have nothing to share. I have even taken the shirt off you."

Brandon thrust the canteen at the boy, followed by the chocolate. "Drink slowly so it doesn't make you sick," he admonished. "Eat half the chocolate. We'll need the other half later."

"I will pay it back someday. Juba never forgets his responsibilities."

"I believe that too."

Juba did as he was told—eating and drinking in controlled nibbles and sips. Brandon repacked everything. He tossed the mangled Motorola aside, keeping only the wire that threaded up his sleeves to his ear pieces and throat mike. It might come in handy later.

While his situation was not exactly hopeless, it was also far from optimum. He was lost, surrounded, short on food and water, and without communications. And, oh, yes. He had a half-starved kid with him.

CHAPTER 50

Fayetteville, North Carolina

Sergeant Margo Foster's bright red Mazda turned into the Kragle drive in the row housing addition outside the gates of Fort Bragg. The sun had barely risen. Summer Marie Kragle was still in the comfortable old robe she had taken to wearing during her pregnancy while Brandon was away. She looked out the window and frowned. Margo and she had a date to go shopping together later today, not *this* early.

Mollie Thompson, Colonel Buck's wife, got out of the passenger's side of the car. Summer's heartrate picked up. Margo was always so vivacious and chatty. This morning she looked somber and almost pale. She wore a BDU uniform. She and Mollie walked to Summer's door.

Oh, my God!

During the post-deployment meeting, Summer had listed Margo and Mollie as the ones to come to her house for support if something should happen. But where were the two officers in dress greens who normally accompanied such a delegation? She ran to the door and flung it open.

"What's happened to Brandon?" she cried.

Both women rushed to her side.

"Calm down, girlfriend," Margo said, attempting to sound upbeat. "It's not as bad as all that."

"What do you mean it's not as *bad* as all that?"

"Let's go inside, honey," Mollie suggested.

The went in and closed the door. All remained standing. Margo hugged Summer, but Summer pulled away and braced her face and her emotions.

"Tell me," she said. "I can take it."

A tear escaped one emerald eye, but she kept her head up, refusing to break down in front of other women, no matter the news.

Mollie took a deep breath. The only way to say it was just to come out with it. "Brandon is missing in action."

"Missing?" Even to her, her voice sounded shredded. "How? Where?"

"We don't have any details yet," Mollie said, "but the colonel thought you should know before you heard it from someone else. CENTCOM is in radio contact with his detachment. Brandon is not with it."

"We assume he's in Algeria," Margo added.

"You work at Delta, for God's sake!" Summer raged suddenly. "You should know."

"Even in Delta, no one has access to mission details unless he has a need to know," Margo said, batting back her own tears. "Yes, I would say Algeria. The only thing we have so far is that there was some trouble and Major Kragle got separated from the rest of the detachment."

"How long ago?"

"It's been about six hours now. The detachment broke contact with the enemy, according to its last situation report."

"Do they know what happened to Brandon? Was he hurt?"

"Honey, that's all we know," Mollie Thompson said hoarsely, herself ready to cry with the prospective new member of the Gold Star Wives Club.

Summer turned away. "He's not dead," she said.

He wasn't dead until the two officers in green came and said so.

Brandon Kragle knew how to take care of himself. The man was invincible. Hadn't he rescued her and the Korean children from the *Ibn Haldoon* in the Philippines? Hadn't he pulled her and his detachment through Afghanistan? He won a Bronze Star in Iraq. He was a professional warrior. He was good at his job. Besides, he had been "missing in action" before—and had always come through.

"My husband is not dead," Summer insisted.

"Of course not, honey . . ."

"He's *not* dead."

She turned and walked quickly to Brandon's study, where she always felt nearest him when he was away. Margo followed. Mollie collapsed on the sofa and covered her face with her hands.

Summer looked small and almost lost as she gazed around the room so filled with Brandon, all the photos on the walls and the mementos of Brandon's career in Special Forces and Delta. Her fingers traced the outline of his first beret, now bronzed on a little base. She bent over to smell one of his old combat boots on a shelf. It smelled of leather and earth and, if she closed her eyes, she could smell Brandon.

"They put Sergeant Major Shumate's mustache in the Hall of Heroes," she mused, her voice harsh with sudden bitterness. "I wonder what part of Brandon they'll put there."

"Girlfriend . . ." Margo started, rushing to embrace her.

Summer pushed her gently away. "I can take it. I'm the Ice Maiden, remember?"

She walked slowly around the room, looking at the things that meant memories to her warrior husband.

"Brandon was right all along," she said, sadness replacing the bitterness. "It isn't fair for us to have a baby. It's not fair to the baby. It's not fair to Brandon or me. A baby needs a real family, not a father who keeps going away and may never come back."

She paused at the window and stared out it, her spine stiff and her back to Margo. The lawn needed mowing, she thought. Brandon had liked to spend Saturday afternoons mowing, getting sweaty, then running inside to drag her laughing into the shower with him. Afterward, they made love, went out to dinner, maybe saw a movie or met some of the Deltas at a club or nightspot. Just like ordinary people.

Just like ordinary people . . .

"Margo, I'm not going to have this baby," she decided.

"Summer, don't give up on him. You said it yourself—he'll be all right."

"It doesn't matter whether he's all right or not. I'm still not going to have this baby."

CHAPTER 51

Washington, D.C.

Summer seemed cold and detached when General Kragle called to offer his long-distance comfort, as though she were already forcing herself to accept the inevitable.

"I *know* he'll be all right," she said, but her voice sounded weak and uncertain.

He also spoke to Gloria and endured a tearful long-distance, five-minute, finger-wagging chewing out. She concluded by saying she was getting in her car *right now* and driving to Fort Bragg to share the ordeal with Summer.

"That poor chile! Lawdy, what must she be going through! I know what that honey-chile is feeling 'cause I seen what Rita put up with when she was married to you before the Lawd done call her blessed spirit home. Darren, you get both my boys home safe, ya hear?"

One son lost in the desert and another held hostage. And there wasn't a damned thing he could do about it personally either, except offer condolences to a daughter-in-law and a surrogate mother, which he wasn't very adept at doing. Gloria and Summer would be more comfort to each other than he could ever hope to provide.

In the meantime, he had only a few hours left before "Jerry Hurst" surfaced with a splash that, in the least, would force him to resign from USSOCOM. He could sit around the hotel waiting for another call, hoping it would reveal something useful, dwelling on the plight of his sons, or he could start thinking like a cop and do something. Detectives went fishing for clues in their victims' past lives.

The only thing he knew about Lough was that he worked for Entertainment Media Enterprises. He looked up the address in the phone book and left the hotel wearing a light blue windbreaker. He drove a rented black Chrysler to a large warehouse occupied by EME behind a weed-choked vacant lot in an industrial area west of the Potomac.

A soundstage took up most of the downstairs open area of the warehouse. At the far end, floods illuminated a set made to look like an ordinary bedroom. A bed was the most vital prop in the porn business. A youngish blond woman, apparently a "starlet," lounged seductively among mussed covers, a sheet thrown carelessly over the lower half of her body. She seemed unaware or uncaring in exposing bare breasts. The General suspected she was about to show much more than that. A cameraman took warm readings of her skin with a light meter while the director and the producer loudly argued over the next scene. A male star with a towel wrapped around his waist waited in the wings, smoking a cigarette. He was a lean and hungry-looking man with long hair and earrings.

The director—General Kragle knew that because he had DIRECTOR on the front and back of his T-shirt—looked up and spotted the intruder. He was a rat-faced little man, exactly the stereotype one expected of a pornographer. He rushed over.

"No visitors are allowed in here, Bub."

The General was in no mood to be called *Bub* by some greasy-looking smut peddler.

"I'm not a visitor, pervert. Who's in charge?"

Rat Face took a step back. "You a cop? This is a legitimate, legal business and—"

"I'm here to ask questions, not answer them. I asked you once, Who's in charge?"

Rat Face wiped his sweaty forehead and pointed to a stairway. "Mr. Goebling. First door upstairs to your right, Bu—" He caught himself when the General's hard gray eyes pierced him like a pin through an insect. "—mister," he amended.

"That's better," the General approved.

A red-headed receptionist, doubtlessly a gone-to-seed former "starlet," stopped him in the outer office. Her desk plate identified her as Darling. She took his name and reported to the inner office, closing behind her the door with Goebling's name on it. She returned shortly.

"Mr. Kragle, Mr. Goebling is in a meeting right now," she apologized. "He asks if you will take a seat and wait."

The General waited. He thumbed through a *Vanity Fair,* an *Adult Entertainment* and a *Skin.* Mr. Goebling still did not appear.

"How long is this meeting going to take?" the General asked Darling.

She smiled, popped her gum and readjusted her blouse to reveal more cleavage, but she didn't answer him.

Goebling walked out thirty minutes later. He wore a five-hundred-dollar sharkskin suit, pointed wingtip shoes with white inlay, a bright yellow shirt, and a purple tie that clashed with pale blue eyes and hair bleached almost white.

"We've already talked to the police, Mr. Kragle," he said bluntly. "I have nothing else to say."

He turned to retreat into his office.

"Hold up," the General said, rising to his feet. "I have a

personal interest in this. I was with Charles Lough when he was shot."

"So I've heard," Goebling said over his shoulder.

How would he have heard that? The General's name hadn't been released to the media and police surely wouldn't have revealed such information.

Goebling closed his office door behind him. General Kragle was stunned by the abruptness. This man had kept him waiting nearly forty-five minutes merely to tell him to buzz off? Darling could have done that and saved everybody some time.

He started to barge in after the porn maker. Darling snapped to attention, phone receiver in hand.

"I'll have to call Security," she threatened.

The General sighed in frustration.

"Who dresses that guy anyhow?" he asked in a parting shot. So much for the cop approach.

He was surprised to find the blond bedroom starlet waiting in the hallway outside the door. She was chewing her nails and had a nervous look on her face. The camera didn't care about her nails anyhow. The General glanced at her and started to walk on to the stairwell.

"Wait!" the blond hissed.

He paused.

"You *are* General Kragle, aren't you?"

"How do you know that?"

"Chuck had a newspaper clipping of you. He showed it to me."

"Chuck? You mean Lough?"

She nodded. She wore a thin pull-down shift over well filled out curves. It was obvious she wore nothing underneath.

"Chuck was always good to me," she said. "We need to talk, but not like this. Follow me."

He started to fall in step with her.

"Walk behind," she directed. "Act like we're not together if we see somebody. There's another stairway at the far end."

They strolled slowly along the dimly lighted hallway, he a step behind. She talked without turning her head. He had to listen closely.

"You're here asking about Chuck, aren't you?" she asked, and went on without waiting for an answer. "I recognized you when you came in."

"Why wouldn't Goebling talk to me?"

"Mr. Goebling and Chuck were doing some business with somebody else, but I don't know who. Some men came to visit him after Chuck was shot. Real tough-looking guys. Mr. Goebling acted real scared."

"All right. So what can you tell me about Chuck?"

"I know he was going to meet you."

"He told you that?"

They spoke hurriedly in order to finish before they reached the stairway at the other end.

"Do you know why he was going to meet me?"

"He said it was probably the most decent thing he had ever done in his life. He was going to have lunch with somebody first, then he was going to call you."

"Who was he having lunch with?"

She shrugged. "He was real anxious about it. He said he and Rufus—that's Mr. Goebling—had gotten in over their heads with some people."

They were almost to the other end. She turned suddenly and thrust a scrap of paper into his hand.

"This is his mother's address in Arlington. He was acting real funny that day and asked me to give this to you if anything happened. I tried, but I didn't know how to get hold of you. Imagine what a surprise when I seen you walk in. Tall as you are, distinguished-looking, you're hard to mistake. Chuck said you'd understand once you talked to his mother."

With that final word, she returned the way they came, walking fast and not looking back, bare feet whispering on the carpet. Baffled, General Kragle took the stairway down and went out to the parking lot. He refrained from looking at the address until after he started the Chrysler and was pulling out onto the street. He turned in the direction of Arlington.

A blue Ford occupied by two white males and a swarthy-skinned Middle Easterner pulled out of an alley and followed him.

CHAPTER 52

Hanoi, 1968

American inmates of the old colonial prison of Hoa Lo in the center of Hanoi dubbed it "Hanoi Hilton." The prison was actually a series of prisons, or compounds, each of which was given an appropriate nickname, such as "New Guy Village," where POWs were first taken for interrogation, "Heartbreak Hotel," "Las Vegas," and "Camp Unity."

Captain Darren Kragle found himself thrown alone into a cell as dark, dank, knobby-walled, and filthy as an animal's den. He was naked, his clothing having been taken, covered with filth and blood, and shivering from chill, hunger, and thirst. Spiders half the size of his hand hung all around him in the semi-darkness. Ants crawled over his body. Mosquitoes fed ravenously on his blood. Gecko lizards scurried through litter consisting of human excrement from previous occupants, plaster, rotted rags, mold, and mildew. Large, hungry rats looked him over.

His "interrogation" was just beginning. It would not end for a month.

Vietnamese guards were determined to break him. Every day they beat him with leather crops and commo wire, leaving hideous welts and open, suppurating wounds. They forced his ankles into shackles and locked both legs into place using a pipe and a rope. Next, they forced his arms behind his back and tied them from above his elbows to his wrists. A guard shoved a foot against his spine to force the lacing tight enough to cut off circulation and disjoint both shoulders. Then they took another length of rope, tied one end to his bound wrists and fed the other end through a pulley in the ceiling that suspended him in excruciating agony with his feet dangling off the floor. He was left like that each day until he passed out from pain.

Guards shackled him to a heavy timber in rear cuffs and irons whenever he wasn't being "interrogated." He couldn't move. Humidity and temperature both spiked around one hundred. He developed severe heat rash. Red welts turned to blisters and blisters to boils. Boils covered every square inch of his body—underneath his arms and in his crotch, the crack of his buttocks, inside his nose and ears, on his head, arms, legs, and between his fingers and toes.

Two daily meals consisted of pumpkin or cabbage soup greased with a few small pieces of pig fat—a starvation diet. His resistance to disease and infection dropped. His intestines worked with parasites that surfaced in disgusting ways. One night he awoke with what he thought was a thick string hanging from his nose. It began to wriggle back into his nostril. Horrified, he snorted out a six-inch worm.

Eventually, he thought, the guards and interrogators would kill him. He soon understood that he could tell them *anything* and it wouldn't make any difference. Their goal was not to extract information. After so long a time in captivity, he had nothing valuable to tell them anyhow. What they wanted was to break him as a human being, to crush his will to resist. They wanted him to accept and embrace the communist philosophy.

As determined as they were to break him, he was just as determined that he would not be broken.

One day as he hung swinging in suspended agony, gagging at the stench of his own body where he had soiled himself, his skin crawling with biting, stinging pests, a guard looked in on him. Through the crack in the open door, Darren saw Lieutenant Jerry Hurst standing among Vietnamese guards in the corridor. Although dressed in gray POW garb, he appeared clean, shaved, and reasonably well fed. Certainly he wasn't being "interrogated."

Their eyes met briefly. Lieutenant Hurst averted his eyes quickly and ducked his head, as though embarrassed. He stepped out of sight.

CHAPTER 53

BILLIONAIRE PHILANTHROPIST FUNDS ANTIWAR GROUPS
BY DEE ANNA GENCARELLI AND ED TILBORN

Washington (CPI)—Records recently obtained by CPI show that billionaire philanthropist George Coalgate Geis, an avowed socialist and former member of the American Communist Party, has donated more than twenty million dollars to the World Workers Party (WWP) for the purpose of organizing antiwar demonstrations in the United States. To divert scrutiny from itself, however, and its nearly century-long association with international communism, the WWP runs demonstrations by using front organizations such as International ANSWER (Act Now to Stop War and End Racism). ANSWER puts up tables and booths at protest rallies and demonstrations where posters, books, and pamphlets are sold or handed out.

"This material is virulently anti-American," said MacArthur Thornbrew, director of Homeland Security, "and almost rabidly supports socialist and communist agendas. Much of it calls for the defeat of the United States and the replacement of the American government by Soviet-style socialism."

Martin Moore, a spokesman for WWP, said the characterization was unfair.

"In labeling us unpatriotic and anti-American," he

said, "the Tyler administration equates dissent with treason. Pro-war columnists, right-wing news organizations like FOX and CPI, and radio gas bags like Rush Limbaugh, Sean Hannity, and Michael Savage are on a campaign to demonize protestors by labeling us anti-American, communists, or apologists for terror."

One ANSWER-distributed pamphlet describes the 1992 Los Angeles riot as a "legitimate rebellion." Posters for sale bear slogans such as "Defend Iraq and North Korea Against U.S. Imperialism and Capitalist Restoration." One booth promotes "Revolutionary Literature" in front of a big red flag and photos of Che Guevara and Saddam Hussein. Other booths sell T-shirts calling President Woodrow Tyler an international terrorist and depicting him wearing a Hitler-like mustache against a Swastika background. Flags of France and the United Nations outnumber those of the United States.

There are also "Peace Candidate" tables manned by the Harris for President campaign. Literature describes Senator Lowell Rutherford Harris as "tan, relaxed, and ready" to restore "'civil' to civilization." Following a campaign event and demonstration rally in New Hampshire, Senator Harris was photographed leaving in a limousine with George Geis . . .

CHAPTER 54

West Sahara

Brandon dozed inside the cave. The sandstorm was still raging when he awoke. His mouth tasted gritty with sand. It crusted his eyebrows, lashes, and mustache. Sand was piled up a foot high at the cave's entrance. Daylight was rapidly fading. It was starting to get cool with the approach of nightfall and Juba had crawled over and snuggled next to him for warmth.

Enough illumination remained inside the shelter for Brandon to distinguish the kid's features, if incompletely. Asleep, Juba's wise and hardened little warrior's face was replaced by that of a normal seven-year-old's. The black bowl-cut of his hair fell in a straight line over his brow. His lips twitched from some dream and he let out a little sound. He looked so small and vulnerable, curled up inside the brown army T-shirt as though it were a sleeping bag. What could have happened to turn a boy so young into a savage little adult boasting of shooting someone in the belly?

It was almost full dark by the time Juba stirred a half hour later. He blinked, sat up, and pulled away from Brandon as though embarrassed.

"Did I sleep too much?" he asked. His voice rasped. "Should we go?"

"The storm hasn't let up," Brandon reassured him. He offered the canteen.

Juba shook his head. "I will wait until you drink."

"I'll drink later."

"Then I also will drink later." His voice sounded as though his throat was too dry to form words.

Brandon unscrewed the canteen plastic lid and took a small sip. Juba drank this time when it was offered. He clearly could have downed it all, as an ordinary child might have, but he took only a small drink and handed the canteen back.

"There is not much water for us to find in the desert this time of season," he explained.

Brandon nodded. Wind sniffed and huffed around the cave entrance. Sand hung suspended in the air, making breathing laborious and even painful. Brandon gave Juba a cravat to tie around his lower face as a filter. The kid's voice sounded muffled through it.

"What about you?" he asked.

"I'll use my patrol cap." Brandon held it over his nose and mouth.

Presently, Juba asked, "What should I call you?"

"My name is Brandon."

"*Senor* Brandon. *Mucho gusto a conocerle.*"

"*Equalamente,*" Brandon said, smiling.

"Do you have sons, Senor Brandon?" Juba asked.

"No."

"Daughters?"

"No again."

"I thought not."

"Why did you think not?"

"You do not seem a father," he said.

What was with this kid? As direct and straight ahead as the General.

"That's because I'm not," Brandon said for lack of anything better to say.

"A man your age should have sons," Juba said after thinking it over. "Why don't you, Senor Brandon?"

"A soldier shouldn't have children."

"A son would be proud to have a soldier as a father."

The subject made Brandon uncomfortable. He had explained it all to Summer. Why should he have to go through it again with a seven-year-old? To divert Juba, he teased, "How about you, Juba? Do you have sons?"

Juba giggled like the little boy he was. "I am too young, but one day I will have strong sons. Even if I am a soldier."

"*Touche*."

"*?Lo siento?*"

"*Nada*. Juba, what happened to your parents?"

"Do you really want me to tell you, Senor Brandon?"

"I wouldn't have asked otherwise. You said you are an orphan?"

The boy seemed to brighten with enthusiasm, as though this was one topic he enjoyed talking about.

"My parents were heroes and very brave during the Green March," he said. "Have you studied the Green March, Senor Brandon?"

"That was when the Sahrawi fled to Algeria after Morocco invaded?"

"All the Sahrawi know of my parents, Rafi and Embarka," Juba said. "Have you heard of them?"

"This is my first time in Algeria."

Juba's voice lost its enthusiasm and became disturbingly hard and sad.

"I hardly remember them," he lamented. "They were assassinated when I am but three years old. They were brave during the Green March when they were very young—and they were brave later too. Abderrazak the Paratrooper had them killed, I am told, because they were Christians and they were organizing the Sahrawi to resist

Salafia Jihadia. That is why I shoot Muslims in the belly, in honor of my father and my mother. I want to grow up to be like my father."

Enthusiasm returned as he told the story of his parents, a tale he had obviously recounted over and over both in his own mind and to anyone who would listen. It was perhaps the only thing he retained of them—a story of heroism thirty years ago.

"My father Rafi and my mother Embarka were neighbors in Leone and grew up and were in love even though they were very young," began the low child's voice, disembodied in the darkness. "My father Rafi joined the Polisario to resist the Spanish when he was but fourteen years old. He went to prison because he would not name his comrades. When he got out of prison, he was exiled and my mother went to Mauritania to look for him. She looked for him for one year before she found him.

"They returned together to the homeland and worked with the Polisario. My mother went on secret missions to deliver messages. My father was a fighter. They defeated the Spanish, but the fighting was still not over. One night the lights in Leone went out. Moroccan soldiers were in the streets and everywhere. My mother saw them moving in the city. Things were worse than when the Spanish were there. The Polisario warned my father and mother to leave.

"A car was waiting for them. They went to Umgallah and made camp in the valley, where they organized people that were fleeing. People were running away in cars and trucks and some rode bicycles or walked. The Moroccans bombed them with airplanes. My mother and father helped many people escape before the camp was bombed. My mother was injured, but my father carried her as they walked for one hundred miles until they came to the border."

The boy seemed to sink deep into silent memories, as old people sometimes did. His voice when it returned was choked and passive.

"I wish I could remember them," he said. "I try and try, but what I remember is what I am told by others."

No light entered the cave now. Wind snuffled outside. Juba scooted close to Brandon and pressed against his side. He was shivering like a brittle autumn leaf. The Sahara was one of the loneliest deserts in the world. Brandon hesitated. Then he wrapped an arm around the little old man of a child and held him close to warm him. Juba soon fell asleep again and dreamed, perhaps, of his father and mother who were heroes long ago and who would live always as heroes in the story he told of them.

CHAPTER 55

Washington, D.C.

Director Claude Thornton worked to almost midnight when he returned from El Paso and then was at his desk again before daylight. He laid out his yellow legal pad of clues, if they could be dignified with that term, and went down them step by step, finally giving up in exasperation. He seemed to be making little progress in unraveling the mystery behind the dead Muslims in Yuma, former KGB operator David Barr and his association with "The Committed," whoever the hell they were, and Barr's even more perplexing connection with NCC Gerald Espy and Senator Lowell Harris. Add to this mess the matter of a missing WMD, possibly even more than one, smuggled-in terrorists, AFSOC's suicide, the inexplicable resignations of key War on Terror figures and talk of even more resignations, and what did that give him . . . ?

A headache bigger than Texas.

How do you effectively combat such craziness, when it has tentacles that reach into so many different areas of the world? You couldn't win a war by simply running around stomping out brush fires. Sooner or later you had to strike at the main flame. But first you had to find it.

Sometimes it seemed to Thornton that he had a telephone growing from his ear like an appendage. Della Street came in early and together they worked the phones most of the morning.

"Have you be able to get Darren Kragle on the hook?" he asked her.

"I've called every few hours for the last two days, Claude. All I get is voice mail. It's like he's avoiding us. He's never done this before."

CIA deputy director Tom Hinds called. "Claude, do you remember we were talking about David Barr the last time we met and you wimped out on buying lunch?"

"Why would I forget?"

"At your age, Alzheimer's? Were you also aware that Barr was in Spain the week before the train bombings in Madrid? And that Charles Edward Lough was with him?"

"How did you find that out?"

"What do you think we do in Foggy Bottom besides sit around conspiring to create AIDS to kill gays, murder the Pope, and otherwise subvert democracy? Sources, good buddy, we have sources. Barr and Lough met in Madrid with an interesting character named Abu Dujan al-Afghani. Mean anything to you?"

It didn't, not right offhand. The FBI had a list of suspected terrorists the size of the New York telephone book. *Try memorizing that.*

"I'll fill you in," Hinds volunteered. "The afternoon of the day the trains blew up, a video was left for a London-based Arabic newspaper in a trash can near a mosque in Madrid. Let me quote from it: 'This is a statement by al-Qaeda and Salafia Jihadia spokesman in Europe, Abu Dujan al-Afghani. We declare our responsibility for what happened in Madrid exactly two and one half years after the attacks on New York and Washington. It is a response to your collaboration with the criminals Tyler and his allies. There will be more if Allah wills it.' *That* is the al-Afghani who met with David Barr and Charles Lough a week before the trains blew up."

"Barr is now somewhere in the United States," Thornton supplied. "I think he's succeeded in smuggling a WMD across the border from Mexico."

Hinds took a long, long breath. "Whew!" he said. "Could the sonofabitch be planning another Madrid in the States?"

"What else? It worked there, why wouldn't it work here?" Thornton reasoned. "Before the bombing, pre-election polls favored the existing Conservative Party in Spain to win. Now, after the bombing, the Socialist candidate promises to bring home the troops and 'mind our own business,' and it looks like he'll win today's election."

"The goddamned fools! One bombing and they're ready to throw up their hands and beg terrorists: *Please, please, please don't hurt us.* Don't they understand history? Don't they realize that the only thing accomplished by giving in to terror is even more demands and more attacks? But you're right, Claude. Who says the same thing can't happen here? Christ, half the people are ready to give up now. But where will it happen? When?"

"Those are the sixty-four-thousand-dollar questions."

"Claude, you got a big job cut out for you. We'll keep digging on our side of the street. And you wonder why I smoke."

Fred Whiteman was still in New York, after having e-mailed in a report of what he had learned so far about The Committed. It wasn't much. All he knew was that The Committed seemed to be a group of wealthy men working to elect Senator Lowell Harris as the next president of the United States. A *secret* group of wealthy men.

"I still don't have any names for The Committed, Claude," Whiteman said when he reported in. "I'm still working on it and on why whoever they are would hire somebody like David Barr. I only found out about The Committed because Lough had name-dropped it to a couple of porn bitches he and Barr were out with one night in Manhattan. He had a little bit too much to drink and he let it slip that they were 'king makers.' Anyway, everything is in the report I sent you."

"Right. Moving right along . . . ?"

"I've been checking out those telephone numbers you got from the Balaghi dude's computer in El Paso. Every one of them was a public telephone. Three were here in New York, one was a public telephone in Yuma, Arizona, and ten of the numbers, the majority of them, belonged to public phones at Quik Trip stores in Tulsa."

"Tulsa?" Claude thought out loud.

The President of the United States was scheduled to launch his campaign for reelection with a speech tomorrow at noon in Tulsa. Thornton riffled through a file open on his desk. It contained the printouts from Balaghi's computer. Telephone numbers, financial contributors, the single sheet of paper headlined by a T. Tulsa? The date under the T was tomorrow's date. And the time noted: *12:00 o'clock.*

"Fred!" Thornton interrupted him. "How soon can you meet me in Tulsa?"

"Wassup?"

"Just get there."

"I don't have a Learjet like some folks, but I'll catch the next available flight out of New York."

"I'll let you know where I'll be."

He hung up and immediately dialed MacArthur Thornbrew.

"Mac," he said immediately, eschewing formalities, "you have to stop the President from going to Tulsa."

"Are you out of your mind, Claude? He's not going to

cancel. You've been talking with the advance team reps, right? What do they say?"

"I didn't know then what I know now. I think there's going to be a terrorist attack in Tulsa."

"You *think*? President Tyler is not going to scrub his campaign and hide out in the White House just because you *think* there'll be an attack. My God, man, do you want him to lose the election? Harris will crucify him over it. Talk about *The Passion of the Christ*! We'll have F-15s patrolling the skies over Tulsa. The military is deploying surface-to-air missiles. We can protect the President."

"He doesn't have to be the target, Mac. Director, I need to keep your airplane a bit longer."

"Where are you going?"

"Where the corn grows as high as an elephant's eye."

A Madrid terrorist encore in the same city where the President was speaking would, in terrorist minds and in the minds of many Americans, demonstrate the inadequacy of the United States and its vulnerability to terror. Former KGB agent David Barr, along with The Committed and assorted Jihadia, appeared to have engineered a strategy in Spain to influence elections and topple a hard-line government. Now they were going to do the same thing here.

CHAPTER 56

WORLD TAKES SIDES ON U.S. ELECTION

Washington, D.C. (CPI)—United Nations peace groups in Belgium intend to try U.S. President Woodrow Tyler and members of his defense and homeland security teams in absentia for war crimes committed in Iraq and Afghanistan. U.S. Secretary of Defense Donald Keating said if such action went through, he would move NATO headquarters out of Brussels. President Tyler said he would also stop U.S. funding of the UN. The court action was dropped.

This is one example of the bitter division that exists not only in the U.S. during this presidential election but also throughout the world. Countries around the globe are taking sides in what may be the most partisan and brutal federal election in U.S. history between incumbent President Woodrow Tyler and challenger Senator Lowell Rutherford Harris.

Antiwar protestors all over the world have become particularly vitriolic. About 250 antiwar protests were held this week, from Spain to Egypt to the Philippines, sponsored by organizations such as ANSWER, United for Peace and Justice, and World Workers Party.

In Rome, activists decked out in rainbow-colored peace flags and chanting "Assassins!" demanded that the Italian government withdraw its troops from Iraq and cease assisting the United States in the War on Terror. European Commission president Romano Prodi said he had no doubt that the Italian Left, if elected, would end this nation's military involvement.

At the televised North American Music Awards, singer Eddie Crotch of the Jewels repeatedly smashed a Woodrow Tyler mask against the stage. Columbia University professor Roger Genova organized a "teach-in" during which he said that "American patriot" has become another term for white "supremacist."

"The only true heroes," he added, "are those who find ways to help defeat the U.S. military. If we really believe this war is criminal, then we have to believe in the defeat of the U.S. war machine."

The "Guerrilla Girls," a group of feminists dressed up in gorilla suits, threw six thousand dollars' worth of bananas (paid for by tax dollars) at a UNC-Wilmington audience in an event designed to take aim against a Tyler second term. San Francisco taiko drummers, cyclists, activists, and other protestors chanted, "End the occupation of Iraq!" and "Impeach Tyler!" The Reverend Jesse Jackson urged those attending a Chicago rally to express opposition to the war by voting against Tyler.

"It's time to fight back," he chanted. "Remember in November."

Harris, the Party of the People candidate, is seeking to capitalize on the antiwar fervor.

"I will go to the United Nations and travel to our traditional allies to affirm that the United States has rejoined the community of nations," he said. "This present administration is an embarrassment to our country in both word and deed, in its profound ignorance and arrogance. President Tyler's fascist, racist war has been revealed as mindless, needless, senseless, and reckless. By his over-reaction to 9/11, he has turned the world into a breeding ground for terrorism."

Harris's wife has been handing out campaign buttons decorated with caricatures of Tyler administration officials, each emblazoned with the slogan *ASSES OF EVIL*.

Faced with wavering allies and a divided America, President Tyler emphasized once again that "there can be no neutral ground in this struggle against terrorism." In a speech at the White House addressed to ambassadors and diplomats from 84 countries, he set down what he called an inescapable choice between standing with or against the U.S.-led anti-terror battle.

"This is not the time to say, 'Let's stop what we're doing and pull back.' It's time to redouble our efforts, not run and hide, and think it won't come and get us. There is no neutral ground, *no neutral ground*, in the fight between civilization and terror. There can be no separate peace with the terrorist enemy. Any sign of weakness or retreat simply validates terrorist violence and invites more violence for all nations . . ."

CHAPTER 57

Arlington

Mother Lough lived in an older section of the city near George Mason University. Twice on the way there, General Kragle noticed a blue Ford in his rearview mirror. It followed him onto I-66 and hung back a quarter mile or so. He took an exit on the pretense of getting fuel. The Ford exited with him and kept going. The General thought he must be getting paranoid—but just because you were paranoid didn't mean they *weren't* out to get you.

He dismissed the incident until he glanced up at his rearview again and spotted the same Ford. He tested it with a few old Delta SpecOps tricks—speeding up suddenly, then slowing down. Once he even pulled to the side of the road and lifted his hood, as though experiencing car trouble. The Ford sped up and slowed down with him. When he stopped, it sailed on past. The occupants—two white males with a Middle Easterner in the backseat—stared pointedly ahead as though having no interest in a stalled motorist. The General jotted down the plate number.

He knew he was being tailed, no doubt about it, when the Ford appeared in his rearview a third time. Now he understood why the garish peacock of a porn boss Goebling kept him cooling his heels for forty-five minutes. He wanted the time to get his goons in place. Goebling and these thugs must have something to do with gunning down Lough at the Lincoln Memorial. But if they had wanted the General dead, why didn't they take the opportunity then to put a bullet in him and leave his body next to Lough's?

He would have felt a lot better if he were packing his big Colt .45 auto from Vietnam.

He skirted downtown Arlington. Just past the intersection of I-66/State 309, with the Ford still behind him in heavy traffic, he eased into the inside speed lane. As soon as the next opportunity presented itself, he twisted the wheel suddenly to sail the Chrysler off the highway and across the center median. He cat-spun it nose to tail, not letting up on the gas, burning rubber, and plunged into traffic going the opposite direction. There was a hairy moment when a delivery van blowing its horn almost wiped him out. Wrestling the wheel, narrowly averting a collision, he darted toward the outside lanes and immediately took the next exit. The Chrysler was heavy enough not to flip from his maneuvering.

He executed a few more quick turns into a residential area just for good measure, then pulled into a driveway and waited for fifteen minutes. Good. He had caught the characters in the blue Ford by surprise and lost them.

A few minutes later, he parked in front of a two-story brownstone with a postage stamp of a lawn hugging a quiet residential street. A slow *Clunk! Clunk! Clunk!* on hardwood floors answered his knock on the door. The door cracked to reveal a wizened face as wrinkled and parched as old canvas and ringed in frizzy white hair.

"Yee-ah!" the old woman croaked in one of those Eastern accents that spoke of good breeding and a long family line.

"Mrs. Lough?"

"What do you want?" Not budging from the crack, but not widening it either.

"My name is Darren Kragle. I'd like to talk to you about your son?"

"And him not even in his grave! Why doesn't the police leave me be?"

She started to close the door in his face. He jammed a foot between it and the frame.

"Mrs. Lough, I'm not the police. I was with your son when he was murdered."

That and the foot in the door stopped her. She blinked and squinted to study the General's face.

"What did you say your name was?" she asked, concentrating.

"Darren Kragle."

She slowly repeated the name, almost letter for letter, frowning. Something seemed to dawn in her memory.

"Were you in the military?" she asked.

"I'm still in the army, ma'am."

"You were a prisoner of war in Hanoi."

The statement caught him completely off guard.

"Well, don't just stand there like a donkey," she scolded. "You're already here. You may as well come on in."

Clunk! Clunk! She moved back to open the door. She was using a four-legged walker. She leaned heavily on the top bar, her clawed hands around it making her look like an ancient sparrow perched on a branch.

"Come into the library," she invited, leading the way. *Clunk! Clunk! Clunk!*

General Kragle held his curiosity in check. The library was large and dark with light-absorbing wood and floor-to-ceiling bookcases crammed with well-used hardcovers. In a center arrangement were a sofa and a lounge rocker facing each other across a crystal-topped coffee table. The General made to help Mrs. Lough from her walker to the rocker.

"Do I appear helpless?" she resisted. "I'll see to my own needs, thank you. You may be seated."

He took the sofa and waited until she was likewise comfortable. She breathed rapidly from the exertion. She was one proud old woman.

"I would offer you tea or coffee," she apologized, "but I gave my house lady the day off. I wanted a day alone with memories of my son. Do you understand?"

"Yes, ma'am. I won't keep you. How did you know I was a prisoner of the North Vietnamese?"

"Because my husband was also a prisoner of war."

The General stiffened as old memories rushed in. Charles Edward Lough must be the *son* of . . .

"John R. Lough," he recited. "Colonel. B-52 pilot. U.S. Air Force. Serial number 3503671. We memorized each other's name and essentials so we could pass the word along about who all were in the camps if one of us managed to escape."

The old woman's eyes turned inward. Then she came back.

"Until the day he died ten years ago, my husband could itemize in alphabetical order the names of all the men who were in the camp with him. You were the young captain who led the escape? John always told stories of the escape and how brave you were. When Chuckie was just a little boy, he always wanted his dad to tell him that story. John told it to him over and over again. You were a little boy's hero, Captain Kragle."

That, the General thought, explained *why* Charles Lough might have tried to warn him that night at the Lincoln Memorial. However, it failed to explain what he was involved in that led to his murder.

"Mrs. Lough, I know this is a bad time," the General said gently, "but I need to ask some questions about your son."

She dabbed her eyes with a handkerchief twisted in her gnarled hands. The General took that as acquiescence.

"Do you have any idea who might have wanted to kill your son? And why?"

"Chuckie had no enemies," she asserted. "He was in the movie business and highly respected in the industry."

After asking only a few more questions, the General saw that she had no idea of her son's business dealings. She knew little of Chuckie's affairs, friends, or activities. Obviously, he lived a secret life of which he knew she would disapprove.

"He had a townhouse in Wheaton, so I'm afraid I didn't see him as frequently as I like," she admitted. "He was a good son though. He deposited funds in my account each month and stopped by as often as his busy schedule allowed. He kept an office upstairs."

"Would you allow me to look in the office?" It was clear she wasn't going to be much help.

"The police have already taken just about everything. But go ahead if you think it will help. I'm afraid you'll have to show yourself." She gestured toward her walker. "I don't do stairs much anymore."

The office looked to have been stripped of all papers and files—police, no doubt—and then cleaned up afterward—the "house lady," no doubt. The General wasn't sure what he was searching for. He opened file cabinets. All empty. Two sports jackets and a pair of slacks hung in the closet. He went through the pockets. Nothing, not even a paper clip.

There was a stack of books on the table: *For Whom the Bell Tolls*, *Always a Warrior*, *The Grapes of Wrath*, *One*

Shot—One Kill, Raider . . . He fanned the pages. Detectives had done a thorough job.

He sat down at the desk and rifled through its drawers. Paper clips, ballpoint pens, a bag of stale Fritos, some still photos of sex scenes . . .

Now what? He raked a big hand across his short-cropped hair and rested his elbows on the desk calendar pad. The connection between Lough, Jerry Hurst, and the "Hanoi Hilton" became clearer, but he still had no idea what it all meant. So where did he go from here?

His eyes scanned the pad idly. They froze on a single faint pencil notation on the calendar: *Committed, 8 p.m., 18732 Kirby Road.* The memo was written under today's date. Apparently, the police had overlooked it or failed to see any significance in it.

The General sprang to his feet and consulted his watch: 6:30 p.m. Surely "Committed" referred to *"The* Committed." Something was going down.

He hurried back to the library and quickly begged Mrs. Lough's leave. She nodded mutely and watched as he showed himself to the door. He paused with his hand on the knob, then walked back to the library. She still sat where he left her, staring at the handkerchief and twisting it around and around in her ruined hands.

"Mrs. Lough, I'm so sorry," he said.

"Yee-ah."

He was scooting into the driver's seat of the Chrysler when the squeal of tires startled him. The blue Ford swerved into sight from a side street and bore down on him, burning rubber. Somehow the three thugs must have figured out where he was going. Or the blond sex kitten from the bedroom scene had either set him up or been persuaded to talk.

He glimpsed a weapon extended from a rear window. A stubby Uzi or MP5. It began to chatter, its muzzle flashing bright in the calm haze before nightfall. Lough's executioners were returning to finish the job they had started at the Lincoln Memorial.

CHAPTER 58

Hanoi, 1968

After a month of daily torture, when it became obvious to even the North Vietnamese guards that the U.S. Special Forces captain would die rather than provide anything other than name, rank, and serial number, the interrogators gave up and released Captain Kragle into the general prison population. One of the reasons guards kept POWs isolated was to prevent escape attempts. Those men allowed into the general prison were either too subdued by illness, starvation, and abuse to do anything other than exist, or they were recent victims of "interrogation," so psychologically beaten up they were unable to pose a threat.

Darren could hardly walk. Both shoulders were swollen. His arms barely responded. Fingers and bones in his feet had been shattered by guards wielding rifle butts and hammers. He resembled a large dysfunctional skeleton over which had been stretched a covering of yellow parchment.

The first thing he did was start planning an escape. He knew he had to go soon, before he became like most of the other prisoners—too weak, starved, parasite-infected, and demoralized to do much beyond look up at the patch of blue sky above and dream of home and freedom. He let the guards believe his injuries were healing slowly and that he had turned passive and obedient in captivity. As long as they thought that, he avoided close scrutiny while he regained strength and planned his escape.

He formed an escape committee consisting of himself, a fighter-pilot lieutenant named Rancher Corbett, and U.S. Air Force B-52 pilot Colonel John Lough.

Corbett was about twenty-four and had been tall and lean to begin with. After having spent some time at "Alcatraz" before being transferred to the "Hilton," he was bones, a ragged scarecrow who nonetheless retained spunk and guts.

Lough was an older pilot, in his early forties, quiet and balding but possessed of a burning determination to get out and go home. He had been in the Hilton for nearly two years.

"I got a wife and a two-year-old son," he said. "I'm going back to them alive, one way or another."

The three members of the "committee" spent long hours in a corner of the exercise yard plotting while they pretended to play cards with a homemade deck. Deciding how many would go, who would go, and how they would go. Corbett wanted it to be a mass escape, insisting that the more of them who went, the better the chance that a few would make it. Darren argued that such an attempt was impractical, considering the poor health of most of the POWs. Besides, the more men who knew of the plan, the more likely it was that the guards and the camp commandant would find out and execute the ringleaders. There were POWs in the camp—collaborators and stool pigeons—who were willing to sell out their own mothers for an extra portion of rice and cabbage soup or to avoid "interrogation." Broken, pathetic, frightened creatures with all humanity starved and beaten out of them. The North Vietnamese were artists in using a prisoner's fears and insecurities against him and his fellow inmates.

The escape committee was haggling over prospects, points, and details of a breakout attempt one afternoon when Lieutenant Hurst ambled over. Conversation instantly died. While known or suspected collaborators were rarely harmed, because of feared retaliation from the guards, they were nonetheless shunned or ignored.

"Mind if I sit in for a hand?" Hurst asked, indicating the cards.

Colonel Lough looked up, lifted a brow, and said in that soft, laconic manner of his, "Why don't you go play with your buddies?"

He shifted his gaze pointedly toward the guard known as Piss hole. Piss Hole was watching. Hurst cast a beseeching look at Captain Kragle, who pretended interest in his cards. Then he shambled off and stood by the inner security wire, looking back. The poor bastard. Darren almost felt sorry for him. It must be hell going through life being so afraid all the time.

"That man is a threat to us all," Corbett said. "We have to be real careful what we let him hear."

"He suspects something," Lough worried. "Watch how he's been looking at us. Maybe we should have let him play."

"I don't want to touch a card or anything else that rat touches," Corbett said.

The committee devised a simple plan that depended on the nearby Red River reaching flood stage in early spring. The escapees would steal a boat, float it down the river under cover of darkness to the Gulf of Tonkin, where they would signal high-flying spy aircraft and wait to be picked up by helicopter or submarine. If they were unable to get a boat, they would simply use driftwood.

The three selected two others to go with them, bringing the total number to five. Airman First Class Carl Downing and army helicopter pilot Rayson Tunney were both young and in reasonably good shape, considering the environment. The selection was based, first of all, on who was most physically capable and, second, on who could be trusted to keep preparations secret. Lives depended on it.

Darren calculated they had about a month, maybe less, before monsoons flooded the river. It was already raining a few hours every day, casting even greater discomfort upon the living skeletons inside Hanoi's cold stone and wire prison. And if the rains were uncomfortable for the prisoners, they were at least inconvenient for the guards, who didn't like to get out and stomp around in a deluge looking for contraband.

Gradually, over a period of time, the five Americans secured supplies they needed, stealing everything the guards might carelessly leave lying about, constructing other things out of common available materials. They hid all their supplies in holes in the ceilings of their cells and covered them with a cardboard-like material made from lime mixed with toilet paper. Charcoal rubbed into the cardboard blended it to the color of the walls.

They made Vietnamese peasant costumes out of old prison uniform rags, including cone straw hats fashioned from grass. They made a rope ladder, hoarded a mirror for signaling, and honed a sharp edge on a table knife a guard dropped from his mess kit. They even made keys for their cells using ground-down flintstone.

The conspirators were almost ready. The moon would rise its latest of the month in three nights, ensuring full darkness in the event it did not rain and there were no clouds. They would make the attempt at midnight on that date. Tensions and anticipation rose as the time drew near.

The oldest POW in the compound had been captured in

1960, when Americans first began acting as advisors in South Vietnam. Sergeant Robin Conley had had both his ankles crushed during "interrogation." The bones knit crooked and deformed. The only way he could walk was with the assistance of a pair of sticks he had fashioned into crutches. He hobbled over to Captain Kragle and Colonel Lough and pretended to pick at a sore on his arm while he hissed in a low tone, "Piss Hole knows something."

"How do you know?" Darren asked, his heart racing.

"You're gonna break out, aren't you?" Sergeant Conley said.

"What have you heard?" Lough put in. It was difficult to remain outwardly nonchalant when their lives might be on the line.

"I overheard the snitch talking to Piss Hole," Conley said, using his eyes to signify Hurst. Hurst was watching from across the compound. "They suspect you're planning to escape. I don't think they know anything, but somebody is going in for interrogation. That's all I heard."

Darren smiled to avoid the appearance of a serious discussion. Conley gimped off.

"Now what?" Colonel Lough wondered.

"We're going tonight," Darren said. "Pass the word. Midnight."

That night, late, but before the escape attempt began, there was a commotion in a cell down the way from Darren's. Darren lay helplessly awake on his makeshift bed of dried grass and listened to guards beating on Colonel Lough and ransacking his cell. After a while, they dragged Lough away for "interrogation." The night fell silent again, except for the whimpering and occasional cry of a man having a nightmare.

The escape had to be canceled. Guards were on the alert. Darren slept not at all for the rest of the night. Few men could resist "interrogation" if the guards got serious about it. If Lough broke, the rest of the plotters could expect to be executed before another night fell.

CHAPTER 59

SPAIN ELECTIONS GO SOCIALIST

Madrid (CPI)—As polls close in Spain, Socialist Party candidate Alexandro Delgado has been elected prime minister to succeed the moderately conservative Popular Party administration of two-term prime minister Jose Aguilar. Delgado came from behind to overtake Aguilar after the Madrid bombings by promising to withdraw all Spanish troops from Iraq and to withhold Spanish involvement in the U.S.-led War on Terror.

It is the first time in modern history that the effects of terrorism have succeeded in toppling a leader. Before the Madrid bombings, it appeared as though the Socialists, trailing by more than eight points, would go down in defeat. The bombings changed everything.

"It is clear that using force is not the answer to resolving the conflict with terrorists," Delgado said in an interview.

"They chose to change their platform and to, in a sense, appease terrorists," said MacArthur Thornbrew, Director of Homeland Security, adding that terrorists may conclude that the reaction of the Spanish electorate to the bombing may be replicated in the United States during the presidential election cycle. "If we follow the new Spanish administration and we accept failure and permit victory by the terrorists, there will be no counting the number of people around the world who will suffer.

Having altered one democratic election, having induced one nation to abandon the War on Terror, why should they stop now? Why should they not now massacre Italians, Poles, Brits, and Americans?"

"The Spanish are right," said Senator Lowell Rutherford Harris, Party of the People presidential candidate. "Fighting terrorism with bombs and Tomahawk missiles isn't the way to defeat terrorism. Terrorism must be combated by the state of law. President Tyler was the one who dragged our troops into Iraq and the War on Terror, and his actions apparently have been a factor in the death of over two hundred Spaniards. When I am elected president, I will bring American troops home."

"Those who kill and use terror to bring about political change are listening," Thornbrew said.

Delgado's position on "bringing home the troops" was so well known that a Jihadist Web site posted this prediction: "The Spanish government will not stand more than two or three blows before it will be forced to withdraw. If it remains allied with the Great Satan after these blows, the victory of the Socialist Party will be all but guaranteed..."

CHAPTER 60

Tindouf Airport

The door flew open, letting in light and a refreshing release of some of the cell's built-up stench. Big Nose and his two terrorist gunmen stood haloed by the blinding morning light. It was time for a second sacrifice. Big Nose chuckled something that sounded like a predator's growl as he surveyed the cowering herd of prey trapped inside the room.

"Americans!" he called out, taking a step toward them.

Here it came. For Chaplain Cameron Kragle, it was better to die on his feet fighting than with a whimper on his knees at the mercy of evil. A plan of action formed in his mind. He would take out at least one of the two rifle thugs when they started to drag away Kelli or Rhoda, for he was sure one of them, a woman, would be the choice to make the greatest impact. If he could get his hands on the thug's weapon, he had a chance—a slim chance, but still a chance—to give a good accounting of himself. If and when he finally went down, maybe they would accept him for today's victim and leave the others alone. Surely Delta Force was working on the problem and would burst in before these killers executed a third day's sacrifice.

He pulled his legs underneath his weight and bunched his muscles so tightly he thought they would snap.

"Lord, my God, I commit myself to thine care at this hour of tribulation . . ." he murmured.

Kelli grasped his arm to restrain him. "They will kill us all if you fight," she hissed. "Better that one of us should go than all."

"Someone out there knows we're here," Rhoda put in. Her head diddle-doodled anxiously in the fresh light streaming through the open door. "We wouldn't be held and killed if nobody knew about us. They'll rescue us soon, I know it. Maybe even today. Kelli's right, Cameron. If one of us dies, it's better than all three and Zorgon."

"No! They're going to kill us one by one anyhow—"

"Americans! Shut up!" Big Nose shouted. "Prepare yourselves." That heinous chuckle again. "But not today. Not yet," he added. "They are watching, and that is good."

Was that an acknowledgement that American troops had surrounded the airport?

"They do not take our demands to heart," Big Nose continued. "But Americans are cowards and soft, and they will capitulate. Is that a good word or not—*capitulate*? By the grace of Allah, I am prepared to give your government one last chance. If, after this morning, your government has not capitulated, this will be the order of execution for following days: Tomorrow"—he pointed at Kelli. She cringed. Then he jabbed a finger in turn at Rhoda, at Zorgon, and finally at Cameron. "You," he said to Cameron with obvious relish, his fierce martyr's eyes burning, "will live to see the others die."

"You're mad." Cameron's voice sounded harsh and raspy.

Big Nose seemed unoffended. "The world is mad," he said, "but Allah will make it sane again when we have killed all the infidels."

He took a step back and barked an order at his henchmen. He pointed to the nearest Sahrawi, a young woman wearing a yellow robelike *myfla*. The armed escorts dashed forward and jerked her off the floor. She screamed. The scream turned into a long drawn-out wail of fear and sorrow as the terrorist tossed her bodily through the door into the corridor outside.

The Sahrawi set up a tremendous racket of protest. Big Nose whipped out his sidearm and fired a shot into the ceiling. The deafening report of the pistol in the confined space silenced the outburst.

Kelli tightened her grip on Cameron's arm when she felt him about to spring. She whispered desperately, "No, Cameron. No, no, no . . ."

Big Nose's black beard bristled with indignation and self-righteousness. "Fools!" he snapped. "Don't you see this is what Allah ordains? What Allah ordains is what Allah gets. *Allah akbar!*"

The terrorists breezed out on the same ill wind that brought them in, once again slamming the prison into total darkness. Allah's next offering screamed once in the corridor, after which there was silence so complete among the hostages that a child's sniffle echoed. Cameron experienced a hollow sense of guilt and failure as he and the others awaited the expected gunshot with bated breath. He felt as though he had somehow let God down by preparing to fight for his own and not for the others. He should have been more Jesus-like, have been willing to sacrifice for all mankind instead of only for those closest to him. He would ask God for forgiveness.

No one in the cell seemed to breathe for a full ten minutes.

Bam!

As quick and undramatic as that, the sound was so muted through the thick walls of the terminal building that it would have gone unnoticed, had everyone not been listening and waiting for it. A collective flinch shook the room. Kelli let out a startled sob. Rhoda wept and prayed. Zorgon remained still. Some of the Sahrawi women, long inured to suffering and sacrifice, wept quietly. For the others, there was a sigh of near relief because it was over for another day.

Hardly anyone spoke for over an hour. What was there to say after something like that? Kelli laced her fingers into Cameron's. Both were aware of the kiss that lingered between them, of its implications, and of what little time they had left to explore possibilities. Tomorrow . . . Tomorrow . . . The thought of Kelli's being taken away and shot left Cameron choked up and voiceless.

I couldn't save Gypsy either . . .

Wasn't *saving* something that God was supposed to handle? But didn't God use whatever and whomever was available to him?

Guards opened the door and placed two plastic milk jugs full of water on the floor along with an empty pail to be used as a toilet. Everyone had been going on the floor in a corner. The foul odor was near unbearable, and it wasn't going to get any better with only one pail. The water wouldn't go far in the suffocating heat, but it at least kept them alive. So far, there had been no food.

Cameron gazed thoughtfully through the dark in the direction of the door from which he had last seen light. He noticed that guards hesitated a long moment to let their eyes grow accustomed to the dimness when they first entered. The water bearers had paused. So had Big Nose and his cohorts, both times when they came. The germ of an idea began to grow in the chaplain's mind. Perhaps a moment was all he needed.

"We're not letting them take you, Kelli, or anyone else without a fight," he vowed.

"As missionaries of the Christian faith," she replied, and he thought she sounded resigned to her fate, "we must be willing to spend our lives, even risk them, to pass on the word of Christ and the living God. *Love your enemies,*" she quoted, "*and do good to them that hate you, and pray for them that persecute and calumniate you.*"

"Mad Dog Carson is the commo man on my brother's Delta Troop One," Cameron said. "He suggests a way of dealing with those who argue against retaliation on political, humanitarian, or religious grounds."

"If he's got a name like 'Mad Dog,' bless his heart, I can only imagine."

"He's actually quite a philosopher in his own rough way. He says you should start by listening politely while the other person explains how revenge is immoral and that by attacking those who attack us we're only spreading violence. Then, right in the middle of his explanation, punch him in the nose without warning."

"What a wonderful philosophy."

"He's not finished. When the person gets up off the ground, he's probably going to be angry and may even try to hit back. That's when you quickly and calmly remind him that violence only begets more violence and that he should therefore turn the other cheek and lead by example in negotiating a peaceful resolution. He'll think about it a minute and will probably agree that you are right. That's when you hit him in the nose again, only much harder. Keep repeating these steps until he finally realizes how stupid an argument he is making."

"Bless your heart, are you going to punch *me* in the nose?"

"The moral of the story is that we either strike back, *very hard*, or we'll keep getting punched in the nose. Zorgon? Zorgon, I need a weapon. I need your arm."

CHAPTER 61

SECOND HOSTAGE EXECUTED IN TINDOUF

Algiers (CPI)—The government of Algeria confirmed today that a second hostage was executed at the Tindouf Airport. The hostage was not identified, but she is not believed to be one of three Americans being held by Salafia Jihadia.

According to reports from American military officials at the scene, the victim appeared to be a Sahrawi captured when terrorists raided nearby refugee camps, slaughtering hundreds of people. Three insurgents marched the hostage out onto the airport apron at 7:21 a.m. Their demands had been turned down for the third straight day by U.S. counterterrorism authorities, whose policy it is to not negotiate with terrorists.

The woman, who looked to be in her early twenties, wore traditional native dress, including a veil. She knelt to pray in the morning sun. One of her captors then drew a pistol and shot her through the temple.

"Our primary mission is to save the American captives," explained a U.S. commander. "We could have saved her, perhaps, but we are convinced the terrorists would then have immediately killed the Americans."

The commander refused to explain any military plan to save the Americans.

The young woman collapsed on the tarmac next to the body of yesterday's victim. Both corpses remained in open sight throughout the day . . .

CHAPTER 62

West Sahara

The wind lay two hours before dawn. Sand suspended in the air slowly sifted out again and whispered back to earth. Brandon nudged Juba awake and urged him to drink and to eat the rest of the chocolate. He refused to touch it unless he shared with Brandon. Brandon took a bite and washed it down with a swig of water. So much for breakfast. He shook the canteen. It was almost empty and today already had the makings of becoming severely hot.

He wanted to make up as much time as possible before the sun rose to suck out their body moisture. He first considered finding his way back to the ORP (organizational rally point) on the ridgeline where he'd left Sergeant Sculdiron. He dismissed that idea. Sculdiron was a by-the-book military man, as was proper under these circumstances, and had undoubtedly already saddled up the detachment and struck out on his E & E corridor to be extracted. Mission came first. Besides, the last time Brandon saw bad guys, they were between him and the ridgeline, and boy, were they pissed off.

Since he was without commo and therefore possessed no means of communicating with the detachment or anyone else, his only reasonable option lay in striking out on his own E & E corridor for the Algerian border and trusting the Night Stalkers to find them. He and Juba crawled stiffly from the cave into a vast and silent desert stillness. Stars shone magnified through a foglike veil of suspended sand. Brandon knelt in front of Juba and took him by the shoulders.

"It's a long walk," he said.

"I am very strong. You will see."

"I've already seen."

"The camel gets there, Senor Brandon, by taking the first step."

Brandon smiled and nodded at the wisdom. He stood up and shot a compass azimuth for due east after factoring in the G-M angle. He pointed toward a distant rise in the earth distinguishable against the lighter sky.

"That's our first point," he said.

They set off, the tall man in black SWAT suit and Ranger patrol cap, stubby rifle slung over one shoulder, and the very small boy wearing a billowing army T-shirt that almost wiped out his tracks. Brandon slowed his pace to accommodate his companion's shorter stride.

The sun rose and spilled blood color across the broad reach of the sky. The temperature pegged one hundred degrees by 0900 and the needle continued to rise. Brandon stopped every half hour to glass the terrain for enemy signs and to let Juba rest. He half expected to find fleeing Sahrawi, but Juba and he were apparently still too far away from the border for most fugitives on foot to have reached. He didn't know yet what he would do if they came across refugees. Large groups were in much greater danger of being discovered by the enemy.

They drained the last of the water from the canteen at ten.

Two days of being trapped with Malud on the hilltop, waterless, plus another night in a cave, had taken a toll on the little boy. Although he trudged gamely along, he soon began weaving and staggering, forcing Brandon to stop and rest more often than was safe. Juba's burnt and peeling face resembled an old shoe left too long in the weather. His lips and eyelids swelled and he spoke in a painful squeak.

Brandon finally picked him up and placed him on his shoulders. His short legs dangled on either side of Brandon's neck. He struggled weakly in protest.

"Be still, Juba," Brandon scolded. "Ride. We're partners, aren't we?"

The kid weighed less than fifty pounds, but even that small amount of extra weight underneath a burning sun sapped Brandon's strength. He had had little water himself since the helicopter crashed. The desert was harsh, relentless, and unforgiving. Brandon's lips cracked and began bleeding. The brightness of the sun glaring off the flat plane of sand almost blinded him. Dizzying patterns of light played before his eyes. He scanned the sky for helicopters.

It became obvious by 1400 hours that they needed to find water in order to make it through another day. They struggled to the top of a low ridge that crisscrossed above a wasteland of wadis and dried thornbushes, hoping to find something encouraging on the other side. Instead, it was nothing but more of the same.

Brandon dropped exhausted to his knees and helped Juba dismount. The boy stumbled, his legs too wasted to hold his weight, and fell facedown on the sand. He crawled to the meager shade provided by a low outcropping of rock. He closed his eyes and began breathing in great ragged draughts of scorched air.

"Forgive me, Senor Brandon?" he begged.

There was nothing to forgive. Brandon was almost spent himself. He moved into the shade next to the boy to rest until the cool of the late afternoon. They had to travel during daylight hours in order to be more readily spotted by rescue choppers, but he had to at least consider moving at night. He sat there leaning against the rock with his legs stretched out in front of him, the automatic rifle lying across his knees.

He thought longingly of Summer, but such thoughts were too painful under the circumstances. He thought of Cameron being held hostage in Tindouf—or had Dare Russell's team rescued him by now? Cameron always prayed for his brothers whenever they were in peril. Brandon wondered if prayer did any good.

Gradually as he sat there pondering, regaining his breath and strength, letting his eyes habitually play across the horizon for danger, he became aware of a discoloration on the skyline. Rocky deserts such as this came in varying shades of browns, tans, and grays. Even vegetation was rarely ever green, tending to gray or dark. What had caught his eyes, however, was . . . *green*.

He eagerly glassed with his binocs. The top of a date palm leaped into view. The fronds were more gray and brown than green, but there *was* green. The curvature of the earth concealed any lower growing vegetation, but palms did not grow on the desert unless there was water. It had to be an oasis, a source of water and life.

Although excited at the discovery, Brandon forced himself to let Juba sleep for another couple of hours to restore his waning strength. He dozed himself, fitfully, for he didn't want to miss hearing or seeing the rescue choppers when they came. And they *would* come—of that he was certain.

At last, when the afternoon began to cool, Brandon woke the boy and pointed out the palms. Juba's eyes brightened.

"There will be water," he agreed. "There is always water where there are trees. Jesus has answered my prayer."

"You prayed?"

"Why do you think there is water? Don't you pray, Senor Brandon?" Juba's eyes widened in disbelief that people actually existed who did not pray.

"You need to meet my brother," Brandon responded gruffly. "You could quote scripture to each other. Come on. We have to go. We can rest some more when we get to the oasis."

Distance in open country could be deceiving. Purple dusk was spilling across the sky by the time they passed over a small rolling dune. Brandon, staggering with Juba on his shoulders, looked down onto a tiny lush oasis of three or four palms and some smaller growth. Everything was green. *Green*. There appeared to be a walled well in the center of what was undoubtedly a stopover and watering hole for desert nomads and their camels and goats.

The kid would have gone galloping and stumbling ahead, but Brandon restrained him, gently pushing him behind a boulder and out of sight. As eager as they were to reach the water—they could almost *smell* it—old military habits were hard to break. Brandon lay belly down on the hot sand to give the oasis a lookover before they exposed themselves.

He studied every feature with a practiced eye toward detecting anything unnatural. There wasn't much—four large palms, some thick bushes, the well walled in waist-high stone. Patches of wiry grass grew out from the well's moisture in a circle. Sand further out appeared trampled by beasts. Brandon noted several piles of camel dung. He couldn't tell if they were fresh or not. Nothing moved. Not even a bird.

He glassed the countryside around the oasis, again observing nothing suspicious, before returning his scrutiny to the oasis for one last look. It appeared safe, but he wanted to be sure before he and the kid ventured from concealment.

That was when he detected movement. An Arab stood up from behind the well and stretched. He must have been napping there all along.

"Damn!"

The Arab's all-black outfit, including his headdress, gave him a sinister look. Yawning, he walked a few steps away from the well and lifted the front of his robe to take a leak. He turned his head to talk to someone else still out of sight behind the well. That meant there were at least two, possibly more.

"Damn!"

The Arab carried an assault rifle slung across his back and wore a waist bandoleer of ammo. He was no simple nomad passing through with his camels and goats.

CHAPTER 63

Tulsa International Airport

"Tulsa Tower, this is Cessna 314."

"314, Tulsa Tower."

"Tower, I'm having engine trouble. Request landing instructions."

"Are you requesting an emergency, 314?"

"Not yet, Tower. But I need to get down."

"Roger, 314. Clearance approved. Runway one-niner-zero, winds light from southwest at five. Check with Air Service when you land. Do you require emergency assistance?"

"Negative, Tower. I think I can make it okay."

The single-engine red-and-white Cessna 180 executed a straight-in approach to the general aviation runway a half mile west of the main Tulsa International complex. The engine popped and coughed puffs of black smoke as it touched down and taxied to the Service Station hangar separated from Sheridan Avenue by a high net fence. The pilot, a clean-cut, olive-skinned man in his mid-twenties, got out of the aircraft in the late-afternoon sunshine. Teams of policemen and plainclothes federal agents descended upon him. Half began going over the airplane with radiation detectors while the others hustled him off to a room for questioning.

"What's your name? Let's see your pilot's certificate and driver's license."

"Why did you land here? What's wrong with your plane?"

"Where are you from? Where are you going?"

"Are you a U.S. citizen?"

The pilot told them his name was Jonathan J. Smith and he was from Dallas on a VFR flight to Kansas City when he began losing oil pressure. He landed because Tulsa was the nearest airport. NOTAMs warned that the airport would be shut down tomorrow because of a VIP visit, but they said nothing about today. He had read in the newspaper that President Woodrow Tyler was the VIP.

"I voted for him last time," Smith said, "and I plan to vote for him again."

He finally grew weary of the questioning. "Look," he complained, "just get my airplane repaired and I'll be out of here in an hour. There are mechanics working, right?"

A young power plant tech dressed in greasy coveralls and carrying a toolbox was summoned. He said it was quitting time for the day shift, but he agreed to take a look at the Cessna.

He pulled the cowling and tinkered with the engine, frowning and mumbling to himself. Finally, he arched his back to take the kinks out. Jonathan J. Smith, flanked by a pair of uniformed policemen, stood by, watching him. The plainclothesmen left.

"All right, dude," the mechanic said to Smith, "you got, like, a real problem with your oil pump."

"I already figured that. Can you repair it?"

The mechanic made a production of consulting his watch. "I'm supposed to be off work right now. Got a babe waiting for me, like, at the Zebra Lounge. Know what I mean?"

"Is there anybody else here?"

"I'll be back to work in the morning. But I'm, like, out of here now."

"I could pay you extra."

The mechanic hesitated. "I'd have to rebuild the pump."

"How long will it take?"

"Like midnight, two a.m."

Jonathan J. Smith slapped his forehead in frustration. "Fix it. I'll be back in the morning if I can find a decent hotel in this cow town."

"The airport is sealed off tomorrow until the afternoon," one of the policemen advised. "You won't be flying out of *here* in the morning, and you're not flying out tonight either, unless this guy can get that pump fixed before midnight."

"There's extra money if you fix it before midnight," Smith told the mechanic. "I'll call and leave a number."

He stomped off, mumbling and cursing his rotten luck. A few minutes later a taxi pulled up on Sheridan. Smith got in and left, never to be seen again in Oklahoma. The mechanic opened his toolbox and began work.

Apron lights switched on automatically with nightfall. The mechanic went into the shop hangar and brought out a second toolbox. One of the policemen asked him to open it so he could look inside.

"Okay," the policeman said after looking. "It's all right. Go ahead."

The policemen hung around the front of the hangar drinking Cokes and chatting. The mechanic removed the oil pump, worked on it, and found himself in an awkward position while trying to replace it. He had his head and arms inside the engine compartment and both hands occupied with a ruptured oil line.

"God damn it!" the policemen heard him exclaim.

"Hey, officers! Like, I'm up to my belly button in alligators here. Could one of you bring me that other toolbox, the big red one? It's sitting on the floor in there. It's got some parts I need."

A policeman lugged it out, groaning, "This thing's heavy as hell. What do you have in it?"

Fresh oil covered the mechanic's face. He appeared to be in a bind, straining.

"Could you hand me that quarter-inch socket? There." He pointed. "Thanks. You got an extra hand? Like, can you hold this for me a minute?"

The distracted policeman forgot about looking inside the third toolbox. He soon went back to drinking Cokes and chatting with his buddy.

The mechanic completed his task shortly after midnight.

"That guy's gonna, like, be pissed 'cause I couldn't get it done in time," he said. "Fuck him if he can't take a joke."

He cleaned up his tools and put them away. The third tool box, the big red one, was considerably lighter in weight than it had been before. The mechanic carried it back into the hangar himself, so the policemen didn't notice.

"Officers, I gotta start work at six anyhow," he said, "so I'm gonna, like, sack out on the sofa."

Contents previously in the red tool box were now secured inside the Cessna's engine compartment. Wires led through the firewall to the instrument panel.

CHAPTER 64

Tulsa, Oklahoma

The headlines were already smeared all over the evening papers.

SPANISH SOCIALIST LEADER DELGADO ENDORSES HARRIS

"We're aligning ourselves with Senator Lowell Harris in the American presidential elections," newly elected Spanish prime minister Alexandro Delgado said. "Our alliance will be for peace and against war, no more deaths for oil, and for a dialogue between the government of Spain, the Harris administration, and negotiations with Osama bin Laden and other insurgent leaders . . . I think Harris will win. I want Harris to win . . ."

Also in the same piece, Kim Jong II, the North Korean dictator, was said to be rebroadcasting Harris's campaign speeches on state-run radio. Cuban dictator Fidel Castro condemned President Tyler after Tyler referred to him as a "ruthless despot." Yasser Arafat, whom Harris called a "statesman" and a "role model," castigated President Tyler for standing with Israel.

Senator Harris claimed "numerous foreign leaders" were endorsing him for the presidency. "I've met foreign leaders who can't go out and say this publicly, but they look at me and say, 'You've got to win this, you've got to beat this guy. We need a new policy.' Things like that. They're right."

Fred Whiteman, who had also been reading the evening papers, shook his large head and grinned wryly when Claude Thornton picked him up at Tulsa International in a rental car.

"Suppose you were an idiot," he said. "And suppose you were a member of the Senate running for president. But I repeat myself."

Thornton and Whiteman spent the afternoon's waning daylight hours attempting to determine a potential target for the terrorist WMD, although both understood that it was almost impossible to prevent underground attacks from determined, suicidal extremists. A Madrid-like bombing timed to go off precisely at noon tomorrow when President Tyler began his speech at the Tulsa International Airport would be the shot heard 'round the world. Thornton could already hear Harris and the antiwar appeasers clamoring to make a separate peace with the terrorists. The goddamned fools.

If Thornton knew the terrorist mindset—and he did—a bomber would want to kill as many people as he could and do it in a particularly spectacular fashion to eclipse even the World Trade Center of 9/11. Problem was, there simply weren't that many prospects in Oklahoma's heartland. Although Tulsa, with less than a tenth of New York's population, sprawled across the plains to cover an area three or four times the size of New York, there were no commuter trains, subways, or other major city transportation systems other than city buses. Skyscrapers were modest, workers were not concentrated in any particular sector, and little stood out as a suitable target. About the only thing going on in town other than the President's speech was a Britney Spears concert at the downtown Civic Center, but that was tomorrow night after the President had already departed.

Breaching the Keystone Dam up the Arkansas river from Tulsa offered real potential from a terrorist's point of view. It would flood Sand Springs and Tulsa and create a disaster of monstrous proportions. Thornton persuaded the governor and the mayor to call in bomb teams to sweep the dam and to assign police and state troopers to guard it during the night and during the President's visit tomorrow.

That accomplished, the two men from the Domestic Preparedness Office looked around to see if they really were prepared. No one, Thornton thought, was ever prepared. As President Tyler often said, all a terrorist had to do was be right one time in order to score; his targets had to be right one hundred percent of the time to prevent it.

"Aren't we overlooking the primest target of all?" Whiteman mentioned.

"I've already thought of it," Thornton said.

The President would speak in an enormous American Airlines hangar on the opposite side of the main runways from the terminal complex. The hangar was rather isolated, therefore aiding in security, but at least ten thousand people were expected to cram into the building and its adjacent grounds. The President of the United States and ten thousand people . . . What a target!

Thornton called Director Thornbrew and again suggested the presidential appearance be postponed.

"If he cancels, especially after what happened in Madrid," Thornbrew said, "it's a clear signal that the terrorists are winning. President Tyler is a true cowboy, Claude. It's High Noon and Gary Cooper is going out in the street, no matter what. If he runs away, if he gives the *appearance* of running away, he loses the presidency and America loses the War on Terror. It's that clear, that black-and-white."

"And if he's assassinated . . . ?"

"God forbid. Claude, the Secret Service, the FBI, NSA, and God only knows how many others have swept the entire airport. As of midnight, the airport is completely secured and Tulsa airspace restricted. No private aircraft at all. Commercial air is being escorted in and out by fighter jets. Anti-missile missiles are in place, warplanes are patrolling the skies . . . Claude, we've done all we can, I think a *snake* couldn't breach that kind of security."

Nonetheless, Thornton still had this unsettled feeling in the pit of his stomach that they had overlooked something. As Brandon Kragle would say, it was Murphy's Law—anything that could go wrong, would. So much was at stake, so very much.

"Claude," Thornbrew reassured him, "everything is under control."

CHAPTER 65

Arlington

General Kragle's instincts, sharpened and honed by decades in training and on the battlefield, kicked in even as the gunner in the blue Ford opened fire on him. He threw himself to the pavement beside the rented Chrysler. Bullets slapped the grass behind him, ricocheted off the curb, punched holes in the side of his car. These guys hadn't bothered with silencers this time.

The Ford roared past on the street, the submachine gun still chattering viciously.

He propelled himself to his feet and away from the car, darting toward the passageway between Mrs. Lough's brownstone and the almost identical brownstone next door. "I'm getting too old for this shit . . ."

Brakes squealed as the Ford reversed itself. The gunmen were coming back to finish the job. This time they wouldn't miss.

More brake sounds behind him. The rattling chatter of additional weapons. A symphony of automatic rifles and a pistol kicking in, contrapuntal to each other. He had had firefights in Vietnam without this much shooting.

Shadows purpling into the evening air caused distortions and tricky eye patterns that made accurate shooting difficult. Otherwise, he might have been ripped to shreds. Even so, something punched him hard in the upper left arm, spun him with the impact, and slammed him to the ground. In that instant of spinning he glimpsed three men chasing across Mrs. Lough's front yard, their weapons blazing.

"We got the fucker!" somebody shouted.

Like hell you do!

Those short on combat backgrounds often let down their guard when they think they have felled their enemy. The General took advantage of that moment and disappeared between the houses. His left arm stung something fierce, but he found it still functional. He pulled himself over a six-foot-tall wooden privacy fence that enclosed Mrs. Lough's backyard. He dropped down on the other side into another backyard.

His would-be slayers bayed and shouted in pursuit. His arm felt numb from the shoulder down, but he didn't think any bones were broken, and the wound was hardly bleeding at all. Flesh wounds often sealed themselves.

The privacy fence was old and weathered. He ripped a two-by-four off it to use as a weapon and plunged into the shadows between two other houses. This was a neighborhood of older people, retirees afraid of the dark and the crime rate. Many of them were hard of hearing and kept their TVs blaring at full volume. If they heard the gunshots at all, they probably thought some neighbor had his TV *really* turned up.

General Kragle heard persons skirting to his right through a neighboring yard, running hard. It sounded like they were trying to beat him to the next block and catch him in the open when he crossed the other street. He heard the third man clambering over the privacy fence behind him.

He figured his best chance was to return to his car while the gunslingers looked for him inside the block. But first he had to get through the guy behind him. He flattened himself against the side of the house, the two-by-four gripped firmly in his big right hand. Arriving nightfall settled in to provide camouflage.

He waited, breathing hard. Damn! He was going to have to extend his daily morning run to three miles if he intended to engage in cops and killers.

The sound of the guy's footsteps slowed to a hesitant walk, as though he were leery of an ambush. The sonofabitch had good instincts. Too bad he didn't have good sense to go with them.

"Martin? Martin?" he called out in a low tentative shout.

What's the matter, asshole? Losing your guts when you're alone?

The General heard and felt him pause just around the corner of the house. Not more than five or six feet away.

"Martin?"

Be afraid, asshole. Be very afraid.

General Kragle was nearly six-five, a broad-shouldered, big-boned, muscular man in good military shape. Even at almost sixty years old, he slapped baseballs way into the outfield at the annual SpecOps picnic and baseball game.

The stalker's head and shoulders appeared. The General knocked a home run with his two-by-four bat. He felt flesh bursting and bone cracking. Blood squirted. His target dropped to the grass kicking and screaming in shock and pain.

In SpecOps, a fighter was conditioned never to let an enemy up after he was down. Permitting him to survive might be a fatal option. The General took a step forward and with deliberate aim jabbed the board viciously into the guy's throat, crushing everything all the way to the spine. That hushed him, except for the liquid rattling of his death knell.

He scooped up the man's weapon, a semi-auto 9mm Beretta. At least the guy had reasonable taste in weapons. The General climbed back over the privacy fence, sprinted across Mrs. Lough's lawn and jumped into the parked Chrysler. It occurred to him that bullets might have cracked the car's block and it wouldn't start.

It started on the first crank. He thrust the Beretta into his waistband underneath the blue windbreaker and slammed the lever to DRIVE. A few minutes later he was barreling northeast on I-66. Lough's killers might have somehow found him this time, but he felt certain he had lost them now, one of them permanently. He felt no regret. The way he saw it, the man was a killer and a thug who had the death penalty coming.

He had a hunch he would find the answers to many of his questions at tonight's meeting of The Committed. He also had a hunch that whatever was going on was much bigger than he could imagine. He started to call the cops on his cell phone but changed his mind. What were the police going to think about his showing up with another dead man? They would probably tie him up for the rest of the night when he had other plans.

He punched Claude Thornton's office number into his cell. Claude kept a twenty-four hour watch on duty at his office. Della Street answered.

"It's seven o'clock, Della," he pointed out. "Has the slave master got you working late?"

She laughed. "Isn't that a hoot? The grandson of slaves turning into a slave master. If you're looking for him, General, he's in Tulsa, Oklahoma."

"What's going on there?"

"He asked me to stand by personally near the telephone tonight and tomorrow—so I'm sleeping in the office."

"You're a dedicated public servant, Della. I need you to call the police for me. Don't tell them how you found out yet, but there's a dead guy in Arlington who probably helped kill Charles Lough. Lough's mother may also need some protection. Two more killers are driving a blue 2002 Ford."

He gave her Mrs. Lough's address and the Ford's license plate number.

"General Kragle, what's going on?"

"Damned if I know. Della, I don't have time to talk to Claude now, but have him call me on my cell."

He hung up, found some Kleenex, and wiped the spattered blood off his face. He pulled into a rest area and ripped off the tail of his sports shirt to use as a bandage for his arm wound. There. That wasn't too bad. The blood was hardly noticeable on his windbreaker unless you looked real close.

He shuddered now that the excitement was over. He remembered Jerry Hurst when he jabbed a board into *his* larynx.

CHAPTER 66

Hanoi, 1968

A man being dragged out of his cell in the middle of the night for "interrogation" always precipitated three or four days of subsequent terror while the ruthless prison staff "investigated" and weeded out the "guilty" to take out and shoot. A hush filled with tension settled over the camp. Inmates slunk sheepishly about, hoping they wouldn't be noticed, staying to themselves for fear of guilt by association. Whenever they did speak to each other, in brief snatches of passing conversation, they whispered while their eyes flitted back and forth. There was one question on everyone's mind: *Who was next?*

Captain Kragle expected the "interrogators" to come for him before the day ended—either he or one of the other conspirators. He steeled himself for the ordeal, conditioning his mind and emotions to accept "interrogation" and even death rather than squeal on his fellow POWs.

To the camp's surprise, Piss Hole and another guard hauled Colonel John Lough back to his cell in the compound in the early afternoon. Lough was only half-conscious, looking more dead than alive. Blood crusted his swollen and battered face. The guards threw him on his rancid straw pallet, kicked him in the belly, and walked out, leaving the cell door open so everyone could see him—a deterrent and a lesson to others who violated the prison's unwritten and ever-changing rules.

It was an old guard trick to let prisoners stew in their own juices over who was next before bringing down the hammer. Anyone who attempted to assist a prisoner following "interrogation" was automatically considered guilty and faced interrogation himself—often a virtual death penalty. No one dared enter Lough's cell to help him.

Lough could be heard moaning in a semi-coma, occasionally crying out from pain whenever he shifted positions. Other prisoners found an excuse to slouch past the cell while pretending disinterest. They stole a glimpse of him from the corners of their eyes, but no one dared stop or go in to check on him.

"I think he's dying," Airman Carl Downing whispered to Captain Kragle in passing.

"Do you think he told them?" Rancher Corbett worried.

"I suppose we'll soon know," Darren said.

The moaning finally ceased. Darren pretended to return to his own cell for something, passing by Lough's on the way. He glanced in. The Colonel was awake and conscious. His eyes met Darren's so intensely that the captain knew he had something urgent to pass on.

Darren, Tunney, Downing, and Rancher Corbett, the escape conspirators, set up an early-warning system against the guards and dispatched Sergeant Conley, the old POW with the broken feet and ankles, to talk to Lough. Conley occupied the cell next to Lough's. Crippled and in pain, it wasn't unusual for him to lie around his cell during the day. It was easy enough for him to talk to Lough through the wall.

The plotters and Conley later took a chance and got together for a game of Hearts in their customary corner of the yard, hoping their boldness would be interpreted by the guards as a sign that they had nothing to hide. It didn't make any difference what they did anyhow, if Lough had broken and revealed everything. They would all be shot as soon as the guards tired of playing with them.

"Colonel John didn't break," Conley said, "but he says they know something is up. Hurst is the one ratting all right, but he doesn't know much either. Colonel John says if you're going, you'd better go tonight. There may not be another opportunity."

"Maybe Lough ratted on us too and is setting us up to get caught," Corbett suggested.

Darren shook his head. "The gooks don't need to set us up," he said. "If John squealed, they would have already taken us out and shot us."

The others thought about it and agreed. Corbett fed Tunney "the Bitch," the Queen of Spades, on the next hand. Tunney threw down his cards.

"You cocksucker," he said, grinning.

"But I'm not a rat."

The deal passed to Conley. He flicked out the home-made cards, saying, "The gooks don't know it, but the Colonel has learned to understand what they're saying. So they talk right in front of him. He thinks Piss Hole is leaning on Hurst—"

"*He's* the cocksucker," Tunney interjected—

"—to give up some more names real quick or go to interrogation himself. Hurst is yellow all the way down to where his balls used to be. That's why John says you have to go tonight, because one way or the other somebody's going to get shot tomorrow. He overheard one of the interrogators tell Piss Hole to leave Hurst's cell door unlocked at night for the next week so Hurst can keep watch and go to Piss Hole if he sees something happening."

"What about Lough?" Downing asked. "Can he make it?"

Sergeant Conley shrugged and looked over his hand.

"He says you'll have to go without him. He can hardly walk."

"Damn."

They played two more hands in silence while they thought about it.

Darren said, "Boys, these are the choices: we either get shot tonight or we get shot tomorrow."

"Go," Corbett said immediately.

"Go," Tunney echoed.

Downing: "Go."

"I wisht I was able to go," Sergeant Conley said. "If you make it, will you tell 'em I'm still alive?"

"We won't forget you," Darren promised.

A few fat drops of rain announced the start of the every-afternoon monsoon deluge. Tunney quickly gathered up the deck of cards.

"You know the drill," Darren said before they split up. "It's tonight right after the midnight bed check."

"Luck," Sergeant Conley said. "You're going to need it."

Darren could not remember a night longer than this one. The rainfall was the hardest he had ever seen. It drummed and howled on the cellblock roof. He lay on his straw bed pretending to be asleep while rats and spiders scurried about and hordes of mosquitoes buzzed around his ears. His heart thumped against his ribs when he heard the midnight guard pass by, rattling the cell doors as he went, his flashlight flickering through the small barred windows on the doors.

He jumped to his feet as soon as the guard passed. It was now or never. Weeks of planning came down to the next few hours. For the escape, they had settled on a single blind place in the wall where Darren thought they could go over from the roof of an inside building and then lower themselves from the outside wall with the rope ladder. After that it became a matter of disguising themselves, reaching the river, stealing a boat, and going for a ride on the swollen fast current all the way to the Gulf of Tonkin. They had to trust in the rain and the late hour to keep most Hanoi folks off the streets.

Darren quickly dug his supplies from hiding. He donned his disguise of black PJ's and cone hat over his regular prison uniform. He was the tallest Vietnamese any commie would ever see. Hopefully, no one would get close enough to compare sizes.

He secured food rations—rice and a piece of dried fish—in a rag pouch tied around his waist underneath his shirt. Unfortunately, Lough had the homemade knife. The guards had undoubtedly seized it. Darren had found a small board about a foot long and hid it in his straw bed as a weapon. He took it with him as he unlocked his cell door with the stone key and stepped cautiously into the blackness of the mud-floored corridor that ran down the middle of the building between the cells. He had to pass Hurst's cell on his way to the open end of the corridor that opened onto the yard. He quietly tried Hurst's door. Sure enough, it was unlocked. He was sure Hurst must be watching and listening.

The square of the corridor opening was only marginally lighter than the interior of the cellblock. It was one dark night. Rain roared and splashed. Good. It would smother any sounds they made. In this storm, a guard would have to be especially alert to see black-clad figures darting across the compound and over the wall.

"Captain?" It was Corbett, his voice low and strained with fear and excitement.

"Yeah. Where's Tunney and Downing?"

"Right here."

"What about Hurst?" Corbett asked. "The bastard'll be sucking up to Piss Hole before we ever get to the wall."

Darren had already made up his mind. It was something that had to be done. "Wait for me. I'll only be a minute."

"Darren—?" Corbett's voice broke. He exhaled. "Goddamnit."

"Yeah. Goddamnit."

CHAPTER 67

West Sahara

Jihadia were scattered out all over the border region, hunting. It was open season on the despised Sahrawi. Every would-be terrorist, thief, thug, and self-described rebel from either side of the border who could lay his hands on a weapon was out gunning for a trophy. In the desert, an oasis served as a magnet, a collection point that drew both predators and prey.

Little Juba's face fell when he realized they were blocked from reaching the well by the two men below.

"We're going to have water," Brandon reassured him.

At this point, it was no longer a question of whether or not. They *had* to have water. Survival depended on it. The kid was on his last legs. He could not go farther, whether he was carried or not.

Belly down on the low hogback to the west of the oasis, Brandon continued to glass the objective. Juba lay next to him, his breathing hoarse and raspy.

The second man rose from behind the well. In the dying twilight, Brandon could barely see that he wore baggy brown pantaloons, a faded blue blouse, and a head rag. He propped his rifle against the stone well and leaned over it to drop a bucket on a rope. He retrieved it hand over hand full of life-sustaining water. He tilted the bucket up to his face and swigged directly from it. He poured the rest over his head. It sparkled like jewels in the last light of the day. His partner in black laughed at him.

"They are drinking," Juba said. The boy's tongue crackled across his dried lips.

"Shhh," Brandon cautioned. The human voice carried remarkable distances across the desert in the evening.

"How—?"

"Shhh. Let me think."

Juba edged closer to the big Delta leader. Brandon hesitated, then placed a comforting hand on the boy's back. Brandon unexpectedly promised himself that he was going to get Juba to safety if he had to shoot down every varmint between here and Spain.

Juba whispered directly into Brandon's ear, suggesting, "I could make them chase me while you run down and get some water."

"They'd catch you."

"I am very—"

"I know. You're very fast, but they'd still catch you. Let me think."

He recognized two options: force or stealth.

Two men posed little challenge for a trained and practiced Delta operator armed with an automatic rifle. He could simply shoot them down like the stray dogs they were and *take* water. That option, however, entailed certain risks. For one thing, what would Juba do if something *did* go wrong and Brandon were wounded or killed? They would kill him too.

For another thing, he couldn't be sure there were only two enemy down there. A series of low barren hills lay southeast of the oasis, parted by a valley of sorts whose mouth opened onto the watering hole. A well-worn trail leading out of it indicated heavy traffic. A dozen other men and their mounts or vehicles might easily be lurking in it.

He settled for option two. He and Juba would wait until they were asleep down there before he sneaked to the well to obtain water. That might be a while though. The Mujahideen had began gathering dried camel dung, weeds, and thornbushes to build a small cooking fire. Soon they had it going. Stars came out bright and hard, but the fire was the brightest beacon that could be seen for miles across the flats to the north and south. The aroma of roasting meat wafted to the rise where Brandon and Juba hid. Brandon's stomach growled with hunger. Juba licked his lips.

"Could we also get meat if there is any left when the pigs finish?" he pleaded.

"We'll try."

The two cooks must be exceptionally hungry. Through his binoculars, Brandon counted a dozen strips of dark, half-spoiled meat draped from a long pole over the fire, slowly blackening and draining juices that flared in the flame. Soon, he understood why the bounty. A third man materialized out of the night and squatted next to the fire. He carried what appeared to be an old M1 rifle from World War II. Brandon was correct in assuming other men were camped in the low hills. He was glad now to have settled on option two.

When the meat was done, the newcomer took off his head rag, filled it with steaks, and carried them away, disappearing.

"He is taking the meat!" Juba cried. He had eaten nothing but the chocolate for at least the past three or four days. No wonder he seemed frail enough to blow away like a leaf in the next dust devil.

"Hush. I'll buy you the biggest steak in Algeria when we get out of here."

"In a restaurant?" Juba asked in amazement.

"The best in town. It'll have tables with white linen and silverware and candles."

"I have never been in a restaurant, but the missionaries who come here tell me about them. They say music plays while you eat, that all you do is sit at the table while slaves—"

"Waiters. They aren't slaves."

"—bring food to the table. Is it like that, *verdad*?"

"Truly," Brandon said. "You'll see."

"You must tell me about such wonders," Juba said in a faraway voice. "Promise? You have been all over the world . . ."

Yeah. To kill people and break things.

"Do you think I will ever go to America?" Juba wondered. "I am told everyone can go to school in America. I do not know how to read. Do you have camels?"

"In zoos."

"What's a zoos?"

Brandon squeezed the boy's bony shoulder to silence him. Something was about to happen. The two men at the fire stood up to listen. Soon Brandon heard it too. At first he thought it was a helicopter. But then, disappointed, he recognized it as the sound of an approaching automobile.

The hum vibrating across the desert grew louder and louder until, fully five minutes later, a battered green Toyota pickup filled with armed men pulled onto the oasis and parked near the fire. Five men jumped from the bed. Two more got out of the cab. The two original happy campers spitted more meat for the guests.

Brandon's heart sank. Water remained his objective. It was just that the equation had unexpectedly tilted heavily in favor of the bad guys. It there was one thing you could always count on, it was Murphy.

CHAPTER 68

Arlington

General Kragle's brother Mike had told him The Committed was a group of very wealthy fat cats. It looked like he was right. The address where The Committed was apparently meeting on Kirby Road belonged to what could only be termed a mansion. A high brick-and-wire security fence enclosed its five acres of groomed prime real estate. Lights blazed in the three-story antebellum manor. A uniformed guard at the gate cast General Kragle's rented Chrysler a disdainful look as he drove past and took a look up the drive where outside lamps illuminated a parking lot full of Mercedes, Jaguars, and the occasional lowly Cadillac.

Pornographer Chuckie Lough failed to strike General Kragle as being the type of guest placed on the short list for such an affair. Maybe there was a servants' entrance for the hired help. Without an invitation or authorization from the head honcho, the General doubted he could even get in that way.

He drove on past the gate. People had already been shooting at him. He certainly didn't want to draw further attention to himself. There had to be another way in.

Kirby Road ran past the front of the estate. A dimly lighted street looped around one side and the back, while a city park abutted the third side. General Kragle parked the Chrysler in a residential neighborhood where a patrol cop was unlikely to see the bullet holes and start snooping around. He walked to the park where it was still early of an evening warm enough for lovers and children. Children's voices rang out high-pitched from jungle gyms and swings. A couple hand-in-hand stopped to feed swans at the duck pond. The boy and girl barely cast a glance at the General as he slipped past in the dark and made his way to the security fence.

He pulled himself over the wall and dropped down on the other side into what appeared to be an extension of the park, except the grass was better groomed and the trees shaped and pruned. He made his way toward the house lights, careful of dogs, guards, and security devices. He would really have a lot to explain to the police if he were apprehended for trespassing and breaking and entering with a bullet hole in his arm, more bullet holes in his car, and a dead man in his wake.

He reached the house without encountering anything more threatening than a bunny and a night bird. A black limousine came down the lane from the gate. General Kragle crouched behind some hedges as the headlights flashed by, glad he had chosen to wear dark clothing and soft-soled shoes.

The limousine stopped at the wide front steps and porch. Somebody dressed like a hotel doorman rushed out and opened the back door. The first man to exit was a tall Lurch-type individual decked out in a black suit and tails. The second man's face appeared regularly on CNN, the networks, and the front pages of the *New York Times*— presidential candidate and senator Lowell Rutherford Harris.

Complicateder and complicateder.

The General carefully emerged from behind the hedge and made his way to a light-framed window around the corner from the front entrance, curious about who else of note might be attending this shindig. He peeked through the window. He was in luck. The great room alone appeared larger than most ordinary houses, and it was crowded. Crystal chandeliers, glistening hardwood floors with tastefully arranged Turkish rugs, art on the walls, money in the air. A marble balustraded stairway led up out of the far end of the room.

Groups of well-coiffed and well decked out people mingled around cocktails and hors d' ouvre carts manned by servants. The General recognized a very famous and very wealthy singer and actress known for her antiwar activities, generous contributions to liberal "causes," and left-wing politicians, and her championing of the homeless, the poor, and the downtrodden. She was chatting it up with an Academy Award-winning actor who had gone to Iraq before the war to castigate President Tyler as a "warmonger." The Socialist Party presidential candidate for 1984, 1988, 1992, 1996, and 2000—General Kragle couldn't remember his name—already looked to be getting a little tipsy, while the head of the World Workers Party, an old commie from the Brezhnev days of the Soviet Union, looked like a wealthy member of the ruling class bougeoisie was decked out in a five thousand dollar suit with so much gold on his hands that he almost glittered. The General failed to identify any of the others. He didn't run in these circles. He assumed they were intellectuals of the arts, academia, the press, and politics.

Why was it that the socialist types fighting for the "common man" were always so wealthy and ostentatious?

Actions and dress singled out one small group of men who didn't quite fit in with this crowd, Chuckie Lough types who kept to themselves at the far side of the room. They wore ordinary business suits. The General couldn't get a good look at them because of all the movement and activity and his restricted view from outside the window. Something about one of them, however, seemed vaguely familiar.

A man on the other side of the window stopped to talk with a TV home fashion star recently indicted for insider trading. Even at such close quarters, the General couldn't hear a word they said. It did him no good to *see* Senator Harris hobnobbing with what he assumed to be The Committed; he had to *hear* what was going on. To do that, he had to somehow get inside. Risky business, but he had gone too far to back out now.

He slipped along the outer wall in the dark until he came to the window of a room without a light. He doubted the home alarm system was activated, since so many guests were coming and going. He tried the window, wincing at the strain on his injured arm. It was locked.

He moved around the house trying other windows. They were all locked. He returned to the first, where he removed his windbreaker, wrapped it around his hand to prevent getting cut, and tapped a lower pane until it cracked. He carefully pried out the pieces and lay them on the ground to prevent noise. Finally, he reached in, unlocked the window, raised it and crawled through.

Something else to explain to the police.

A bedroom, probably for guests. A dim nightlight glowed in a socket near the baseboard. He removed it to avoid casting shadows. He had to find a way to get close enough to hear what was going on. He cracked the door into a hallway after first listening to make sure no one was outside. He heard the buzz of conversation, the tinkle of glassware, laughter. He couldn't see or hear more unless he stepped into the hallway.

He took a deep breath and stepped out—right into the

pathway of a pair of women walking back to the gathering from the ladies' room. They emitted dainty little gasps. They were unlikely to take him for a guest, dressed as he was. He smiled, thinking fast.

"Sorry to startle you young ladies," he said. They hadn't been young in a long time. "I'm Stanley Hogben, and I was just checking up on home security."

"Oh," said one lady in a black evening dress. "Mr. Geis is always so cautious."

So this was the home of, or at least *one* of the homes of, George Coalgate Geis, the billionaire Marxist philanthropist whose fears of President Tyler's reelection kept him awake nights? Mr. Committed himself.

"He is, isn't he?" the General agreed, hiding his surprise. "Well, you young ladies enjoy your evening. I'll conduct my inspection. The little woman is holding dinner for me."

The other woman, in scarlet, boldly looked him over. "My, my, you are a fine hunk of man," she said. "Would you care to have a drink with *us* before dinner?"

He flirted with his gray eyes. "Madam, nothing would please me more. However, as you can see, I'm not appropriately dressed for the occasion. Rain check?"

He kept his left arm turned away so they wouldn't see the blood.

"Certainly, Mr—?"

"Hogbind." Or had he said Hogben? Hogbine? "Stanley. You can call me Stan."

"Okay, Stan. I may call Mr. Geis later to get your number?"

"Certainly. I'm also in the phone book."

They walked away, tittering with each other like teens rather than mature females in their fifties. They reminded him why he never remarried after Rita died.

To keep them from getting suspicious if they looked

back, which they did, he hurried along the hallway rattling doors until they turned the corner into the great room and left him alone in the hallway. He would have to trust they said nothing about the encounter to the other guests.

He discovered an enclosed emergency stairwell behind the last door in the hall. He climbed to the second floor and found that door opened onto a widow's walk. It ran open all around the top of the great room with its elevated ceiling. He was on a level with the hanging chandeliers. Ventilator louvers in the door provided a limited view of a small portion of the great room below while also allowing him to hear some conversation. He would have to settle for that, as there was no way he could get out on the walkway without being noticed, and he was unlikely to find a better site. On the positive side, no one was going to blunder into him unless there was a fire or something.

He felt like a sneak thief. It was an uncomfortable feeling. A private detective he wasn't.

He hadn't been there long, watching and listening, before a short, aging man with an Albert Einstein bush of white hair and rimless Freud-type eyeglasses walked up to a podium on a little stage conveniently placed within the General's range of sight. He tapped a spoon against his glass to command attention, an unneeded signal, since chatter immediately ceased anyhow out of deference to George Coalgate Geis.

"Ladies and gentlemen, comrades of the world community," he began, his words easily rising to the second floor. "Welcome to this meeting of The Committed, a group of progressive and socially conscious people dedicated to the one goal of universal economic and social fairness and justice—"

"*Two* goals!" a voice called out from beyond General Kragle's view.

Geis chuckled like a kindly, tolerant professor. "*Two* goals then," he amended. "But the replacing of the Tyler administration is merely a component of the other."

The room burst into sustained cheering that went on and on until Geis finally tapped his spoon against his glass. As the noise subsided, Geis said, "Good news, comrades. I would like to point out that the current odds for the presidency since the Spanish bombing are in favor of a Senator Harris ticket. In a hypothetical match-up between Woodrow Tyler and Lowell Harris, the respectable Gallup organization shows Harris leading 49 to 46 percent if the election were held today. Comrades, we are on our way to a victory in November that will be celebrated globally as a triumph for peace and for the international equality of mankind."

Again, cheering. The philanthropist beamed and nodded his head. He tapped his glass.

"When the Tyler administration first came into office and decided they would try to undo everything that President John Stanton's administration had accomplished," Geis said, "I must admit I took that personally, because I thought we had made a lot of progress in those eight years. What this current administration is attempting to do is turn back the progress of the entire twentieth century with an extreme right-wing agenda pursued on behalf of a different kind of America, while having very little to do with what we have invested in and grown over the last fifty years. Comrades, we are in accord that the goals of a progressive United States should be one of egalitarianism, of global borders, and of a single international government run by workers of the world. United, *committed*, we will accomplish our goals. Social justice will prevail!"

Geis continued when the applause died down: "Comrades, we need a nominee who can stand up to this president eye to eye, toe to toe, face to face, and make it clear that the Party of the People knows how to make this nation safer, kinder, more just, and more equitable to all."

Again the room erupted. From where he listened, General Kragle began to feel a tinge of disappointment. This appeared to be nothing more than a political rally, a fat-cat fundraiser for Lowell Rutherford Harris and the Party of the People. Where were the answers he sought? Murder and conspiracy to subvert a legitimate U.S. government? He had gone to all this effort to listen to some rich old windbag extol the benefits and glory of Stalin's dead communist society?

During the continuing applause, Geis called out loudly above the crowd, "Mr. Barr, Mr. Espy, Mr. Hunt . . . Yes, yes. There will be an executive committee meeting upstairs in the library right away. Will all of you go on up?"

He tapped his glass.

"Comrades, I would now like to introduce you to the next president of the United States—"

That was all General Kragle heard. Party of the People NCC Gerald Espy and another social dandy with a neat gray-and-black beard joined the little group of men in business suits who didn't seem to fit in. The "executive committee" filed past the old bushy-haired geezer Geis toward the marble staircase. The General had eyes only for the man whom he earlier had thought familiar. Now he was sure of it.

He paled. He gasped and almost rushed out of hiding to get a second look. It was as if he had seen the ghost of a man dead more than three and a half decades. A man, improbably but most certainly, who was none other than Lieutenant Gerald R. Hurst.

CHAPTER 69

Hanoi, 1968

Security at Hanoi Hilton had never been particularly strict. After all, the prison sat in the middle of North Vietnam's capital city. Where would a prisoner go, even if he escaped? A tall, round-eyed Caucasian stood out in Hanoi like a giant in a circus act of forty midgets cramming into a Volkswagen.

"Nobody, to my knowledge, has ever escaped," Sergeant Conley had said earlier during the day of that night's escape attempt. "The gooks shot three or four for plotting, but none ever made it."

"I'm afraid they'll shoot Colonel Lough if we go," Darren had worried.

"They'll shoot you if you don't—and shoot him anyhow."

"I'm unlocking your cell tonight before we take off. I'll leave the key for you," Darren told him. "Give us forty-five minutes. Then I want you to slip out of your cell and go to Colonel Lough's. I want him to start shouting and yelling that we've escaped. Understand? It's got to look like he's corroborating with them to catch us."

"What about Hurst?"

"I'll take care of that."

"Consider it done, Captain. I have a letter I've written to my son. Will you take it out with you?"

"I'll deliver it personally."

* * *

That night, Captain Darren Kragle took the short piece of board with him into Lieutenant Hurst's unlocked cell and did what had to be done. It was an awful thing to handle the still-warm body of a man you had just killed, especially if the man was someone you knew and had served with.

After it was done, Darren closed the door and stole in the darkness of the corridor to the lighter open end where the others waited for him. It was still raining so hard that even Noah might have entertained second thoughts about venturing forth. Darren flattened himself against the wall with Corbett, Tunney, and Downing. The tower floodlight beamed watery and refracted across the compound, moving slowly, shooting down the cellblock corridors, moving on. It took thirty-three seconds for the light to make its rotation and start all over again.

"After the next one," Darren said.

"Well?" Corbett asked.

Darren let the question pass. Hard splashing sounds of rainfall roared in his ears. The floodlight made its rounds. The beam was on its way back.

"Get ready!" he said.

The four POWs in peasant garb waited their chance. The floodlight beam swept eerily through the downpour, turning rain into curtains of shining silver ribbons. The shaft of light shot down the corridor, moved on.

"Now!"

They had thirty-three seconds to escape. Darren led the way running to the building next to the wall. An overflowing rain barrel stood next to it. He vaulted from it to the roof and reached down to assist Tunney, who then helped Corbett and Downing while Darren secured the rope ladder and threw the loose end over the wall.

They let themselves down on the other side of the wall

into a flooded, narrow street. What few lights burned in the city this late were muted and washed out. Nothing more than tiny candle flames futilely attempting to cast illumination on a turbulent world.

Depending upon his memory and information gleaned from other inmates, Darren struck out in the direction of the Red River, hurrying through the rain along Asian streets guttering shin-deep with runoff and lined by ratty little shops shuttered against the rain. The only person they encountered was a shopkeeper dashing across the street holding a tarp over his head. He didn't even glance at the strangers, probably didn't see them.

Darren began to believe they might actually make it.

It took them a half hour to reach the waterfront, good time considering their debilitated condition. They heard the rush and roar of water long before they came to it. The river was up, out of its banks, and spread back into the mangroves. In Asia, it was almost an unwritten law that peasants living near oceans and other waterways were fishermen. Fishermen owned boats. That was why they were called boat people.

They bumbled into a few ramshackle huts built next to footpaths twining through mangrove thickets. They wasted valuable time feeling around in the dark for anything that would float—a sampan, a small junk . . . They would have settled for a big log.

Where the hell were the boat people's boats?

"It's been about forty-five minutes," Corbett guessed. "They'll be searching for us."

Darren doubted they would check the flooded river right away. Nobody was crazy enough to try to escape that way.

Growing more desperate by the minute, the Americans followed the river downstream, slogging through water that sometimes reached their waists and chests. Mud sucked at their bare feet. They became entangled in mangroves and wasted even more valuable time repeatedly extricating themselves. They clung to each other for support and to avoid becoming separated in the near total darkness.

The prison announced the escape attempt with a long, shrill, drawn-out wail of its whistle that seemed to linger in the drenched night air for an eternity before it warbled and faded—then began all over again. Alerting the citizenry that the enemy was among them. Darren imagined mobs of townspeople chasing Frankenstein's monster in the passion of burning torches.

Darren blundered against a darkened shack that sat on a hummock free of the river. Feeling with his hands, he identified a makeshift pier of sorts. Tunney hissed from nearby, "Here's a boat!"

It was a short-hulled, hollowed-out log sampan big enough for three Vietnamese who weighed about one hundred pounds each. Even emaciated, each of the Americans weighed more than that. There were also four of them, and they were large framed. Darren himself was six five and weighed about one fifty.

"Will it hold us?" Corbett doubted. "Maybe we should try to find another."

They felt around for a second boat. Finally, Darren said, "There's no more time. We have to be off the river and into the gulf before daylight."

Holding onto the sampan, they pushed it through the still backwater until they felt the strong current grabbing at it and at their chests and legs. Suddenly, the boat bucked. Its prow thrust high into the air. It took off like a shot with the flood, dragging the four men off their feet. Downing yelled something as he lost his grip and vanished into water and darkness, one indistinguishable from the other.

The three survivors clung to the little craft for their lives in the wildest ride any of them would ever experience. Sweeping toward the Gulf of Tonkin and, hopefully, freedom.

CHAPTER 70

West Sahara

The last embers of the Jihadia cooking fire went out, leaving nothing but night and silence. A late-rising three-quarter moon erased the darkness and replaced it with a glow that bathed the desert in cold illumination. With the aid of moonlight and binoculars, Major Brandon Kragle counted four dark shapes sleeping around the dead fire. He looked for the others near the green Toyota pickup and among the palms. He wondered where they had gone. Back into the saddle beyond the oasis? Good enough. He shouldn't have to contend with them when he went for water.

He checked his H & K, making sure the round in the chamber was seated and that blowing sand had not gummed up the works. Juba shivered next to him.

"Are you cold?" Brandon asked his pint-size companion.

"Not if you are not, Senor Brandon," he croaked from his parched throat.

"Good boy. Here's the plan."

He pointed toward an unusual rock formation that resembled the spire and roof of a church. It was about two hundred yards away and along the E & E corridor that Blackhawks should be flying come another day.

"I want you to go to that rock and wait for me, Juba. I'll be along as soon as I get us some water."

"And food?"

"Yes, and food."

"Senor Brandon, what if you need help? I have no rifle," he said in that accusing tone he used whenever the subject came up.

"Jesus Christ, kid."

"Senor Brandon, what if—?"

Brandon touched Juba's lips with his fingertips. There must be no *what if*. The kid was going to die if Brandon failed at the well. It was that simple. Brandon took his pistol from its holster. He owed the kid at least a chance.

"Do you know how to use this?" he asked.

"Show me."

"A round is already chambered," Brandon explained. "There, see? That's the 'safe' switch. Push it like this to fire the first shot. From then on you just keep squeezing the trigger."

"Like with my rifle?"

"The same."

This kid was only seven years old and he was teaching him to kill. No. That wasn't correct. *This* kid already knew how to kill.

Brandon rose to one knee. Juba stood in front of him, the T-shirt hanging to the ground, clutching the big pistol in both hands. Rest and the cool of the night appeared to have rejuvenated him. Brandon tousled the tiny Sahrawi's hair.

"I'll meet you at the rock in about ten minutes, Juba. Scoot along now. We got work to do."

Still Juba hesitated. "Senor Brandon, do not *not* come." He flung himself into Brandon's arms and hugged the man hard around the neck. Then, without looking back, he slipped off the rise to skirt the oasis, quickly melting into a boulder field.

Touched in spite of himself by the little boy's display of affection, Brandon waited another few minutes to make sure the boy was well on his way before, rifle ready, he slipped off the crest of the hill toward the oasis.

The four date palms stood out enticingly against moonlight. Brandon quietly merged into their shadows and crouched for a two-minute listening halt. He heard only someone snoring where the fire had been earlier. Odors of cooked and burnt meat hanging in the still air reminded him of how hungry he was.

Sleep on, sweet princes.

He made his way to the well, bending low to cut down his profile. He found the bucket and rope. There was still some water in the bucket. He greedily drank most of it and splashed his face with the rest. His dried skin sucked in the moisture and he felt immediately revived.

Luck was with him when he discovered a water flask one of the Jihadia must have left at the well. It was wrapped tightly in leather and had a long sling attached to it for carrying. He drew a bucketful of water, careful not to bang the bucket against the well, and filled both the flask and his canteen. They now had water. He secured his canteen to his battle harness, slung the flask's carrying strap over one shoulder and looked around.

He smelled the cooked meat and thought of Juba's sunken cheeks, hollowed eyes, and bony ribs. The body could not continue to function without fuel; Juba required fuel. He knew he should leave well enough alone, take the water and go, but even the wildest and most wary of beasts will risk dangerous encounters if it is hungry enough. Besides, he had promised Juba food.

A whisper of sound made him drop to one knee, finger on trigger. He listened intently and scanned his surroundings with keen, probing eyes. After a few minutes when the noise wasn't repeated, he decided it must have been an errant breeze whisking through the palm fronds.

He rose and started toward the sleeping men and the fragrant grease-scented ashes of their fire, carefully feeling each step with his boot toes lest he snap a twig or loosen a pebble and wake them. They slept soundly on. Their snores grew louder as he approached.

One of them stirred in his sleep and turned over. Brandon froze and gave him time to go back to sleep before he resumed his quest. He passed so close between two sleepers that he could have knelt and cut their throats, rendered to them the notorious Kabylie Smile.

Again that whisper of sound arrested him. He heard nothing else, however, saw nothing, and the Jihadia slept on.

A few scraps of cold half-burnt meat remained on rocks around the ashes. Brandon quickly stuffed them into his pocket and looked around for more.

Crack!

The pistol shot exploded directly behind him. He combat-rolled on the ground and came up with the G3 on target and the trigger already half-squeezed.

"Senor Brandon!"

Christ! He almost shot the kid.

Juba was *here*. There was a Jihadia attempting to run away in a bent-over hobbling gait. The picture came instantly clear. Juba must have trailed after him to keep an eye on things. Those were the sounds he heard. *That kid! Couldn't he follow orders?*

Good thing he hadn't though. Brandon was so preoccupied with gathering food that he got careless and hadn't heard one of the men approach. The guy was about to lower the hammer when Brandon's tiny guardian angel winged him instead.

Pandemonium erupted as the gunshot resonated across the desert. There was no need for further stealth. The proverbial excrement had struck the proverbial oscillator. These guys were going to be all over them like stink on skunk.

Brandon sailed right over the head of one of the sleepers struggling to sit up and get his eyes open. He snatched Juba up under one arm and broke toward the east and the church spire of rock, ignoring the wounded man who was hurt and out of it anyhow.

"Senor Brandon—his rifle! He dropped it. You promised."

"You got the pistol, kid."

He started to run on past the parked Toyota before it occurred to him that the bad guys would use it to give chase. Maybe Juba and he could better utilize it. He darted to the driver's side and felt through the open window. Damn. No key. That settled that option. He dropped Juba to the ground.

"Don't move a step, kid."

He jabbed and ripped holes in both rear tires with his combat knife. Satisfied, he tossed Juba over a shoulder and held him in place with one hand as he dashed downfield past the palms.

The confused Jihadia finally spotted them and opened fire, the sudden crackle of their rifles angry and popping and incongruous on such an otherwise lovely night. Bullets sonic-cracked as they snapped past.

Brandon whirled and, one handed, sprayed the area with his automatic rifle. That should give the tangos second thoughts and slow pursuit. He and Juba reached the church spire while chaotic firing at shadows continued at the oasis. Brandon set Juba on his feet.

"I told you to meet me *here*," he scolded. "Why don't

you do what you're told? Don't you know you could have been killed?"

"He was going to shoot you, Senor Brandon," Juba protested. "I shot him in the belly."

How could Brandon sustain anger at someone who had just saved his life? His voice softened. "Here." He pushed the flask of water at Juba, who drank eagerly.

"Not so much at once," Brandon cautioned. "It'll make you sick. Here's some meat. Chew on it. I'm putting you back on my shoulders. We got to bug out of here quick."

Shouting and some more stray rifle shots echoed from the oasis. They had maybe a half hour's head start at most before the Jihadia got things unraveled and organized a chase. Revived by water and a chunk of hard meat stuffed into his cheek, Brandon started off toward the east at a slow mile-eating jog. From his perch atop Brandon's shoulders, Juba said, "We are partners, right? You and me?"

"You betch-um, Red Ryder."

"You should have got his rifle for me," Juba said.

CHAPTER 71

Tindouf Airport

Major Dare Russell prepared his Aces Wild Det 1-Charlie for takedown mission under cover of darkness and an Arabic-speaking negotiator from a U.S. Special Forces psyops team. The negotiator had been choppered in during the day to "dialogue" with the terrorists via telephone. He was simply part of a diversion, a means of occupying the attention of the nameless killer leader inside the airport terminal while troops assembled, deployed, and prepared to storm the terminal and rescue the hostages. Otherwise, negotiations were not expected to make progress, to concede, procure, or settle anything. It was U.S. policy to give hijackers, hostage takers, and terrorists nothing except a bullet. Although the policy was highly debated in the U.S., it had been proved sound again and again. Once a nation stooped to negotiating for the release of its seized citizens, well, terrorists would seize them again and again.

Major Russell's detachment ran final rehearsals and equipment checks throughout the day. An air of excitement and anticipation hung over the maintenance shop TOC. Finally the Deltas were going to do something to end this standoff and the daily executions of victims that, so far, had left two corpses rotting on the tarmac. The terrorists were expected to deposit an American captive there next. They had reiterated their "non-negotiable" demands and gave the name of the next day's sacrifice in case their demands were not met: Kelli Rule, AFSOC's niece.

"The bloody bastards will not execute another," Dare Russell promised, his pencil-thin mustache quivering with rage. "When we go in there, we go in with the intent of killing every cocksucker who so much as frowns at us. Is that clear?"

"Hoo-ya!"

While the negotiator "negotiated," troops from the 10th Mountain Division in lightly armored Hummer vehicles secreted onto the perimeter of the airport to await orders to storm the terminal in force once Delta breached its defenses and had control of the hostages. C-130 aircraft were already in the air, circling the airport high above, out of sight and hearing. Some were armed with 105mm howitzers and Gatling guns to provide cover for the rescue ship when it touched down to pick up the recovered Americans and fly them to safety.

"It'll be just like shooting CQB in the House of Horrors back at Wally World," Major Russell declared following the detachment's final briefing and rehearsal. "There's only one exception—the targets are all live action. Men, this is what we've trained for. So let's do it. People are depending on us."

"Hoo-ya!"

"All right. All you idiots fall out and get some rest," Top Sergeant Bodine bawled. "It's going to be a long night."

Goose Pony held his place as the others dispersed. "Top, sure was a lot of them idiots, wasn't there?"

Every man knew exactly what he must do. The action, swift, deadly, and thoroughly choreographed, followed a perfectly timed sequence—and it all centered on a windowless room on the second floor of the terminal at the head of the stairs. After two days of surveillance, the detachment felt confident it had pinpointed the prisoners in that room. Its single door remained under twenty-four-hour terrorist guard, terrorists were seen taking water jugs to it, and the last victim had been dragged out of it. The takedown would occur in this order:

Upon the signal for action relayed by Major Russell via Motorola handheld tactical radios, the assault Delta teams, one in front of the terminal, two in the rear, would blow the doors with breaching charges and enter. Major Russell's three-man team would engage resisters in the front passenger waiting area while the other four Deltas in two teams covered for each other in a headlong rush to get upstairs to the cell before the tangos started machine gunning hostages. The detachment sniper, Sergeant Peedy Moody, would take out the guard and prevent other tangos from rushing the room. He waited in a hide at the end of the runway, where he commanded observation of the cell door through an upper terminal window.

While this was going on, the 10th Mountain would roar down the runway in their Hummers to join the assault and neutralize remaining resistance. Other troops would clear the old pickups off the runway to allow a C-130 to land and pick up the rescued hostages.

Everything depended upon diversion and surprise.

The drama began at 0300 in the darkness before dawn, when, studies show, human beings are the groggiest. Million-kilowatt lamps suddenly flashed on to sear the terminal in brilliant light and blind its occupants. At the same time, loudspeakers began blaring the most hideous music imaginable, AC/DC screaming *Hells Bells* at the top of their amplified lungs.

The lamps and sound were turned off thirty minutes

later, when the terrorist leader got on the hook with the Special Forces negotiator and threatened to begin shooting hostages immediately, starting with the American missionaries. But that half hour had been sufficient time for Major Russell's hostage takedown detachment to get into place at strategic locations around the terminal. Major Russell and two Deltas were on the north side near the front that faced the runway. Cassidy and Goose Pony formed a team on one side of the back door while Sergeant Bodine and Commo Sergeant Edwards had the other side of the door. Lying next to the outer walls, as close as they could get to them, a team could not be seen by terrorists unless a tango came outside to look, which none had seemed inclined to do so far, or stuck his head out a window, which the tangos also seemed disinclined to do even if they could have opened the sealed windows.

The hurry part was over. Now it was wait for the signal. Major Russell had chosen to strike at dawn as that would give the tangos time to settle down again after the light and sound show. To Cassidy Kragle on the ground hugging the back outer wall with Goose Pony, it seemed daylight would never come. The longer they maintained a position, the greater their chances of being discovered.

Cassidy tried to shake the dark thought of what would happen if the takedown failed and everything went terribly wrong. How would he ever break the news to their father if Cameron were killed during the shooting? Worse yet, how would he find the courage to tell Brown Sugar Mama?

One time when they were all little kids and their father was away on an early Delta mission before he became USSOCOM, Gloria received a telephone notification from the military that he was missing in action in Iran. Tears streamed down her round black cheeks when she gathered the three sons and told them. Two tense and tearful days passed before he showed up alive but battered in Turkey.

Gloria's chastising finger worked overtime. She shook it under each boy's nose and scolded him individually and thoroughly.

"Y'all listen to me, hear? Lawdy, I ain't gonna put up with this stuff 'til it makes a old black woman of me with white hair. It be bad enough your daddy go out gallivanting and shooting at folks and getting shot back it. Y'all ain't gonna do this to me too, you understand? My boys is gonna be teachers and preachers and doctors and stuff. Listen to me now. You ain't *gonna* be soldiers. You just *ain't*."

All three turned out to be soldiers, and in Delta Force no less. Brown Sugar dyed her hair red, she said, to hide the white hair.

Daylight gradually seeped over the Tindouf Airport. Buzzards appeared and slowly circled the decaying corpses on the tarmac, eager to resume their feast. To Cassidy, the horrid birds looked fatter than they did a couple of days ago. He shuddered and turned his head away. He fingered the trigger and safety of his MP5 submachine gun. He looked at Goose Pony. Goose Pony nodded. It was almost time.

A burst of premature gunfire suddenly erupted—from *inside* the terminal. Bobby Goose Pony gasped in alarm.

"God Almighty!" he hissed. "They're killing the hostages!"

CHAPTER 72

Arlington

Lieutenant Hurst *was* dead that rainy night in the Hanoi Hilton. General Kragle had been sure of it all this time—until now. His mind continued to spin as, hiding in the emergency stairwell of the Geis mansion, looking through the louvers of the door, he watched The Committed's "executive committee" chatting casually as its members worked their way up the marble staircase to the second floor. He counted eight men, only two of whom he recognized: Gerald Espy, the national committee chairman, whom he had seen on TV; and Jerry Hurst.

He still found it hard to believe, even though seeing was believing. Hurst had aged, of course, grown a bit pot around the belly and gray of hair, but the weak chin and watery darting eyes gave him away. Hurst had somehow survived that night.

The executive committee members entered wide double doors at the far curve of the walkway. The door closed behind them. Below, in the great room, Geis finished introducing Senator Lowell Harris, who took over the podium to wild applause. These people were true believers. Geis clapped, smiled, bowed, and gracefully escaped to the marble stairs. A minute later he joined the executive committee in the library.

That was the meeting on which the General needed to eavesdrop. He was no longer interested in Harris or what he had to say. There were kings and there were king makers. The king makers were upstairs.

While Harris was bloviating and keeping the believers occupied and distracted, General Kragle took a deep breath and stepped out onto the empty walkway. There was a door on either side of the library. The General tried the first. It was another bedroom. He went in, locked the door behind him to prevent unannounced interruptions, and pressed his ear to the wall that separated him from the library. He heard the buzz of conversation but none of the words.

Damn. *Damn!*

That meant he had to try the other room. If that didn't work . . . ? But first things first.

He adjusted the Beretta 9mm underneath his windbreaker for faster access and looked out into the walkway. Harris was just warming up. Geis was talking in the library as the General passed the double doors. People listened when you spoke if you were a billionaire.

He was in luck with the second room. It was a tiny kitchenette/snack bar affair for servicing the library. A small lamp burned on a table next to the fridge, but the room was unoccupied. Better yet, a bar-top opening in the wall to allow refreshments to be passed through likewise allowed the passage of conversation. The General slipped along the wall and sat underneath the opening, his legs drawn in tight. He couldn't see the speakers, but he could hear them.

"The only reason God gave him a mouth," someone was saying, sounding disgusted, "was so he could put his foot in it. A few more remarks like the one in Alabama about rednecks voting on 'race, guns, God, and gays' and our candidate will go down in flames—"

"He's useful," Geis interrupted, regaining the floor.

"He has at least one thing in common with John Stanton. He worships power and will do anything to get and retain it. Harris is a dupe who won't ask any questions on how we give it to him either. He'll be *our* man in the White House if we don't screw it up like we did during the last election in Florida."

Brutally candid these people were, if nothing else.

A pause filled the library. Papers shuffled. The executive committee sounded ready to get down to business. So these, General Kragle pondered, were the puppeteers about whom Charles Lough had tried to warn him?

"A lot of things have happened since we last met," said Chairman Geis, "but it's a long way until Election Day. We need to talk now about what's gone wrong and what's gone right and how we are going to adjust in order to obtain ultimate victory. I would say we seem to be on track. Our candidate's numbers are up. However, we have suffered a few setbacks, such as Belgium and its failure to indict Tyler and members of his administration—"

"That's not lost yet, Mr. Geis. We're still working on it."

"Let me finish, Mr. Barr."

"Yes, sir."

"The Senate Intelligence Committee thing was a fiasco. How could Harris be so stupid as to let that memo get leaked to the press—?"

"There's an explanation."

"Mr. Barr, please? I'm going to request a full explanation on Yuma, in private—"

"We've rectified that situation, sir, and everything is again on schedule—"

A stern silence and probably an even sterner look from Geis.

"Yes, sir," Barr said.

General Kragle was unable to understand all the references, but the impact of the conversation so far left him stunned with disbelief. "Dirty tricks" in politics was one thing, but this seemed to go way beyond that, into the realm of international criminality. Charles Lough apparently hadn't exaggerated that night at the Lincoln Memorial when he warned that the United States government was at stake. This multibillionaire Geis seemed to have his fingers into manipulating events all over the world in a way that would shock even the most cynical conspiracy nut. Mr. Barr, apparently, was his engineer.

"We have also enjoyed some stunning successes," Geis went on. "The Madrid episode was absolutely brilliant, Mr. Barr. I understand now why you were so highly regarded in the KGB."

KGB? The General wasn't sure for a moment he had heard correctly. KGB, as in the old Soviet Union? The man who strived to be the next president of the United States was being manipulated by rich communists, former KGB agents and assassins? Jesus to God, what was happening to this country?

"All right, let's hear first from your project chairmen, Mr. Barr," Geis said. "Then you can summarize afterwards and brief me on details. Fair enough?"

"Who do you want to hear first, sir?"

"That's your choice, Mr. Barr."

The General heard a chair scraping back as Geis took a seat.

"Mr. Hunt, why don't you go first?" Barr suggested.

Another chair scooted back. Unbelievable. These people, these *conspirators*, were sitting around a conference table talking about taking over a government as though it were no more than a CEO's strategy meeting on better ways to sell soap or dog food.

The General recognized "Mr. Hunt" as soon as he began talking. His was the anonymous blackmail voice on the telephone, the crackling, hoarse tone that sounded as though he had been punched in the larynx. Which in fact he had been, over thirty-five years ago. Underneath the crackle came the whine from Vietnam that the General might have tagged right away if he hadn't thought Hurst dead.

"So far, we have two resignations in the Tyler administration and one suicide," Hurst reported. "I assume that even as we speak the administration is losing its USSO-COM. I tried to tell Mr. Barr that Kragle wouldn't be scared off. He should have been neutralized when Chuck Lough was dealt with. We still don't know how much Lough told Kragle before he died. But I do know Darren Kragle. He's too hardheaded to turn loose when he gets onto something."

You rotten sonofabitch.

"Mr. Barr," Geis said, "is that being handled?"

"Yes, sir. Hunt is right. Kragle was going around asking questions. But he's being taken care of as we speak. I should have reports soon."

"Good. Mr. Hunt, what other prospects do you have in the works?"

"It hasn't been easy, Mr. Geis," Hurst whined. "Gathering dirt on such people—"

"Mr. Hunt!" Barr snapped.

"Yes. I expect another member of the President's cabinet to resign within the next day or so. We're also waiting on one of the Joint Chiefs, and there's some stuff on the head of the National Domestic Preparedness Office."

They were going to blackmail Claude Thornton too!

"Mr. Espy, has this been effective?" Geis asked.

"A very successful campaign," Espy responded. "The resignations are receiving wide coverage in the media.

Talking points have gone out to the media and to high-profile supporters. They stress how President Tyler's own counterterrorism team is quitting because they are disillusioned with Iraq and the War on Terror. That resonates with a large percentage of voters. Polls indicate voters are questioning our Iraqi presence and are unsure on whether or not we should continue the War on Terror. We need to keep hammering on that issue."

"Which we shall, Mr. Espy," Geis said.

Barr designated the next speaker. "Mr. Parker."

"Yes, sir. There is an old Muslim saying that goes 'Kill by a thousand lashes.' Generously funded antiwar demonstrations are a thousand lashes against the conscience of America. They are casting doubts on this president the same as the antiwar movement did during the Vietnam War. Both President Johnson and President Nixon were brought to their knees."

"Then, by all means, we must be generous in continued support. Wouldn't you say so, Mr. Parker?"

"I would indeed, Mr. Geis."

"Mr. Cartwright, tell the committee about Europe," Barr said.

"There are many details too intricate and sensitive to discuss so openly," said Mr. Cartwright. He spoke with a French accent and obviously possessed a suspicious nature. "The United Nations is, of course, willing to accommodate in its condemnation of the Tyler administration as long as France, Germany, and Russia continue to stand up against him. Spain is now afraid of terror and is in our camp. I expect Italy to be next. All it needs is a little Madrid push. We're also putting a great deal of pressure on the British prime minister. It is unfortunate that the Belgium courts may be chickening out on a war crimes trial, but I still firmly expect the UN to issue a censure against Tyler and the United States for human rights violations in Iraq and Afghanistan."

"Mr. Espy?" Geis said.

"We have the media and supporters chattering about atrocities committed by American troops in Iraq," Espy began. "That will help promote the censure, as will the campaign to depict Tyler as a fascist bent on world domination."

"What happened with the leaked intelligence memo?"

"It wasn't hard to persuade Senator Harris to organize the Senate Intelligence Committee politically to provide fuel to the war crimes tribunal in Belgium. That was one of the reasons Belgium was even considering a war crimes trial in the first place. Somehow, one of the memos got leaked to CPI. We don't know how yet. We're working on it. Harris is starting to ask a few questions. Not that he's coming down with ethics or anything. He's just curious. I think we should continue to leave him completely out of the loop. The less he knows about anything, the better it is."

"Agreed," Barr said. "All he cares about is getting rid of this piece of shit Tyler and becoming president himself. He won't ask any questions if we can give him that. He'll do as he's told."

The longer General Kragle listened from his unseen vantage point the more it overwhelmed him. The Committed was obviously well funded, well connected, and organized like military subversives willing to use even terrorists in order to further their goals. They also appeared to be succeeding—*would* succeed unless stopped.

How could one man stop them, even if he was a general officer and the commander of the United States Special Operations Command? Everybody would think he had gone off his rocker if he started running around shouting about a clever coup to take over the American presidency. He would be dismissed as some kind of kook, a conspiracy nut attempting to besmirch the reputation of a candidate with whom he disagreed.

General Kragle hardly believed it himself.

"While you're with us, Mr. Barr," Geis was saying, "what happened in Yuma?"

Barr emitted an explosive curse. "The idiots! But we've worked it out. If it worked in Madrid, it'll work here, only bigger and better. The package is now ready for airmail delivery and—"

General Kragle's cell phone rang, cutting Barr off in mid-sentence. The General had neglected to turn off the damn thing after asking Della Street to have Claude call him. He slapped it off before it could ring again. Too late. The library next door was engulfed in a threatening silence.

CHAPTER 73

North Vietnam, 1968

The Red River flood pushed the sampan past the muddy island at its mouth and far out into the Gulf of Tonkin. For two desperate days the three Americans clung to it beneath a fierce tropical sun and even fiercer evening and nighttime monsoons. They tied themselves to the sampan using strips ripped from their clothing so they wouldn't be lost if they passed out from exhaustion. Sometimes they hallucinated as they waited for spy satellites to pick up the SOS flown from the flag Captain Kragle fashioned prior to the escape.

They thought they were still hallucinating when a helicopter hovered overhead and roped the half-dead escapees into its belly. Captain Kragle slept for three days before he awoke in a hospital in Da Nang. In the bed next to him, Sergeant Tunney had lost a leg from the knee down due to infectious gangrene that had started from a small cut. Rancher Corbett in the bed on the other side laughed, in good spirits, and then grew serious.

"Captain Kragle, we'd still be in Hanoi if it weren't for you," he said. "What you did that night took guts. It was necessary. We believe that. He would have got us all killed, and probably a lot of others as well. This is the last word either Tunney or I will ever say about the matter and it is, from our hearts: Thank you, sir."

The General never spoke of Lieutenant Jerry Hurst

again either. That didn't mean he had put Hurst out of his mind. For years afterward he had nightmares about that dark cell with the rain drumming and splashing on the roof.

Gradually, however, the awful memory faded. Sometimes he went whole days, even entire weeks, without thinking of that night and agonizing over it.

CHAPTER 74

Tindouf Airport

In Chaplain Cameron Kragle's mind, as in the minds of most Westerners, the thought that God could sanction the cold-blooded murder of innocent people was inconceivable. Yet, Hamas in Palestine sent mere *children* with explosives strapped to their bodies to blow up Jewish schoolbuses and synagogues in Allah's name, while throughout the Muslim world there was never a shortage of martyrs eager to go to paradise if they could send their enemies to hell. Some Muslims considered it holy to slay an infidel, no matter the infidel's age, no matter the manner in which he was slain.

In the deathlike stillness before dawn, Kelli and Rhoda prayed together in the darkness of the prisoner cell and held hands. None of the prisoners could be sure what time it was, but their senses told them daybreak was near and with it the demand for Allah's daily human sacrifice.

"Back home, Sister Grace published our weekly church bulletin," Kelli reminisced. "Bless her heart, she was always making these hilarious little mistakes in grammar. One of the funniest was, 'Ladies of the church have cast off clothing of every kind. They may be seen in the basement on Friday afternoon.'" She laughed sadly. "Then there was 'Miss Charlene Cooper sang *I Will Not Pass This Way Again*, giving pleasure to the congregation.'"

Her hand reached for Cameron's and their fingers clasped.

"But Sister Grace had a heart bigger than Dallas. 'Preach the Gospel at all times,' she would say. 'Use words if necessary.' Cameron, I would rather let God take me today than risk the lives of all, or to risk your soul, when the Commandments clearly state 'Thou Shalt Not Kill.' I have tried to live my life as an example of the Gospel. What kind of an example am I if I should go to heaven—or even if I should live—with the blood of others staining my soul and my spirit?"

Cameron gave her words a thoughtful pause. Then he said, "Kelli, imagine, if you will, that Caesar has thrown a bunch of Christians into the Colosseum and in a few minutes he will let out the lions. One among the Christians has a sword. What kind of man of God would he be if he did not try to defend his people against the lions?"

"Cameron, bless your heart, you don't have a sword. All you have is . . . is Zorgon's *arm*."

"I love hearing you say that—'Bless your heart.' " He found he also loved the deep Texas in her accent, the r's turned into h's, the nasal twang. He wondered if you could miss people after you were dead.

She kissed him tenderly. A last kiss for the condemned. He held no illusions about the odds of his success in fighting off the terrorists and for breaking the prisoners free. There would be one-armed Zorgon and himself against God only knew how many of *them* outside in the airport terminal. What the two of them were doing, he acknowledged, amounted to sacrificing themselves for the chance that the rest may live another hour, another day. The best he could hope for was to acquire a rifle and buy time by holding off the terrorists. Surely the men from Delta were out there around the airport by this time and would come to his assistance once the fight started.

Either way, he knew he couldn't stand by and watch while Big Nose and his killers marched Kelli out and shot her. They couldn't continue out of fear and intimidation to let madmen execute them day by day like sheep thrown to lions. The sheep were going to fight back—go down, if necessary, but they were at least going to *fight*.

They could expect no help from the other prisoners. Captured Sahrawi men had been killed during the original attack on the camps, leaving only women, children, the elderly, and the infirm as hostages. Everything, therefore, depended on surprise and swift violence. Cameron hefted his weapon—Zorgon's arm, satisfied that it would serve as well as the jaw of the ass with which Samson slew a thousand Philistines.

"I wish we could have gotten to know each other under different circumstances," Kelli lamented.

"Yes." Cameron took a deep, ragged breath and tapped Zorgon. "Are you ready, my friend? It must be getting near time for them to come."

"Chaplain Cam'ron, my arm goes with you, and the rest of my body as well. If . . . If Swelma and my son—" He choked up. He tried again. "If Swelma and my son . . . Do you think I will see them again in heaven?"

"I'm sure of it. But they may well have escaped. After this is over, my brave friend, I'll get you a new arm. And I'll buy you that chair too."

He pulled his hand free of Kelli's. She held on as long as she could. "Lord, deliver us from evil . . ." she prayed.

Cameron and Zorgon moved to the door, feeling the way with their hands. They sat with flattened backs against the wall to the side where the door opened. A preacher and a cripple against terrorists.

"When I take out the first man," Cameron whispered to Zorgon, going over the plan one last time, "you take the second before he can use his weapon. I've noticed they're careless and relaxed when they enter. They expect us to be sheep. I'll grab the man's rifle . . ."

An hour passed, then almost two. Not even a crack underneath the door admitted light to signal Cameron whether it was still night or whether day had arrived.

Perhaps something had happened. Maybe Big Nose had had a change of heart.

Not likely.

Finally, approaching footsteps on tile alerted him. He nudged Zorgon. The footsteps stopped outside the door. A key entered the lock. Cameron eased to his feet, crouching in the dark ready to spring, every muscle in his body stretched, Zorgon's fake arm drawn far back to obtain leverage.

The door opened wide. Big Nose stood backlighted. One of his riflemen stepped quickly inside even though his eyes were unaccustomed to the darkness. The other hesitated, blinking, as though suspicious. The guard stood in the passageway, leaning against the stairwell railing. For no apparent reason, he suddenly jerked as though in seizure, toppled over the railing, and fell to the floor below.

It was during that moment of terrorist surprise, indecision, and blindness that Cameron and Zorgon struck from out of the room's total silence.

Det 1-Charlie's sniper waiting in his hide six hundred meters away at the end of the runway called the first shot. Each operator carried a Motorola radio with earpieces and throat mike so he could work and communicate at the same time. Sergeant Peedy Moody's voice suddenly and urgently entered the net.

"Okay, okay, I've got movement. Coming up the stairs . . . out of sight . . . out of sight . . . I got 'em . . . approaching the door . . ."

"They're early . . . at least an hour early . . ." Major Dare Russell said, his voice taking on the same urgency. He had been within seconds of triggering the takedown raid. The strain in his voice told everyone that the terrorists had caught him by surprise. He had not expected the execution ritual to begin for at least another hour or so. "Aces, stand by . . . stand by . . . Copy? Everybody ready . . ."

Sergeant Moody: *"Three of them . . . The leader is one . . . and one guard at the door . . . They're opening the door . . ."*

"Stand by . . . Three . . . Two . . . Execute! Execute! Execute!"

"There's a struggle at the door! It's the prisoners! Jesus! I'm taking out the guard . . ."

"Go! Go! Go!"

Cameron swung Zorgon's arm with all his strength, aiming for the nearest rifleman's face. The digited rubber hand caught him across the side of his head with a crunch of busted skin and cracking bone. The guard staggered back, slamming against the wall. Cameron dropped the arm and rushed him, grabbing for the man's rifle. He used an old Delta trick of quick counter movement to wrench the weapon from the man's hands. He hopped back a step and squeezed the trigger.

It was on *safe*.

He fumbled for the little lever on the side of the AK-47.

His opponent went for his pistol. He never made it. The AK in Cameron's hands spat flame and smoke that scorched hot lead point-blank into the tango's chest and walloped him to the floor. He screamed as he went down. Someone else in the room screamed in echo.

At the same moment that Cameron took care of the first Jihadia, wiry little Zorgon hurled himself at the second rifleman. His target eluded him by springing away from Zorgon's one grasping hand. He pumped a round into the little Sahrawi. Zorgon dropped.

Cameron wheeled to face this second threat. Gunsmoke swirled around him. The man who shot Zorgon stood over the body. Big Nose had leaped back and was now behind him next to the stair railing, clawing for his sidearm. Two more terrorists were storming up the stairs to join the fight.

Like every Delta trooper, whether chaplain, medic, or PAC clerk, Cameron had practiced many sessions in the House of Horrors preparing for just such an occasion. A Delta trooper had to remain calm and professional and not miss what he aimed at. Cameron shot the second terrorist. He fell on top of Zorgon, who, although wounded, remained alive and struggling to regain his feet.

A pistol cracked at short range. The impact of the bullet into Cameron's side felt like a major leaguer hitting a home run against his ribs. The force of the blow spun him. The AK-47 flew back into the cell. Cameron went down hard, head ringing. Through blurred vision he saw Big Nose aiming his pistol to place a round where the first had gone, only much nearer the heart.

"No!" A short shriek, part in horror, part in rage.

In that slow segmented motion in which the brain breaks down action too fast otherwise for comprehension, Cameron caught glimpses of Kelli with the retrieved AK-

47 in her hands. Rushing forward, screaming at Big Nose. *Screaming.* "No! No! No!" Laying down on the trigger. Flame blossoming from the muzzle. Blazing lead into Big Nose. Thumping him until he was like a puppet on the strings of a crazed puppeteer. He shouted in surprise and pain, lurched backward and plunged over the railing, disappearing.

Kelli flung the rifle aside as though it were suddenly a despicable thing heated red hot. She threw her own body across Cameron's to shield him from the other two terrorists bearing down on them.

And then chaos broke loose in the terminal from everywhere. Explosions. Banging grenades. Rattle of automatic weapons. Thick smoke suddenly everywhere. Shouting. American voices. GI voices. It was the House of Horrors writ large and real. The two tangoes running toward the carnage at the prison door dropped simultaneously, dead in their tracks.

Kelli shattered into tears on top of Cameron, embracing him in a desperate effort to will him back to life. Rhoda shouted prayers at the top of her lungs as she dashed out and pulled Zorgon out from underneath the dead tango who had collapsed on him. The last thing Cameron heard before he lost consciousness was a familiar voice. It sounded like his brother's.

"Americans! We're Americans! We're here to take you home!"

CHAPTER 75

West Sahara

Brandon had disabled the Toyota and fortunately the Jihadia weren't equipped with camels or other transportation. Nonetheless, nearly a dozen strong, they appeared fresh and rested against a tired man and a half-starved boy. They rapidly gained ground, cutting Brandon's estimated half-hour lead down to a quarter hour by daybreak. Occasionally, one or another of the pursuers paused, lifted his rifle, and squeezed off a shot. The slug thudded into the ground or ricocheted off a rock. None came close enough to cause any concern. It wouldn't be long, however, before the bad guys closed the distance to within accurate shooting range.

It was going to be another desert scorcher, clear and bright with nothing ahead but desert and nowhere to hide. Brandon anxiously scanned the eastern horizon; no flying specks appeared against the hot red rise of the sun. Unless helicopters came, the outcome of this unequal contest wasn't hard to predict.

Man and boy slogged along at the fastest pace they could maintain. The only thing keeping the kid going was sheer willpower. He had more guts than many men Brandon had served with before Delta Force.

The sun turned from red to white hot as it inched upward. Heat devils squiggled against the horizon. Mirages appeared—clean cold water that turned into heated sand upon nearer inspection. The desert became an oven turned to slow broil, a foreign place where men were not meant to live. The fugitives emptied the flask of water by mid-morning and started on the canteen. Conserving water under these circumstances would only weaken them and hasten the end.

The Jihadia doggedly and relentlessly closed the gap. Bullets now struck near enough to pose a threat. Brandon began to think about making a last stand.

The trail funneled between two low, rocky hills. As soon as Juba and he curved around the trail's bend, out of their pursuers' sight, Brandon hurriedly rigged his last grenade into a booby trap by using the wire he had saved from the smashed Motorola. He strung the trip wire between two boulders, the most likely path the terrorists must use, and hoped they would overlook it. Juba and he waited on a rise beyond to observe the results of his handiwork.

They watched expectantly as the point man reached the boulder. He walked on through, unscathed. He hadn't seen the wire, however, for he kept going without raising the alarm. Brandon had stretched it only an inch above the ground so it blended with the sand and became hard to spot.

The second man approached. He wore dark pantaloons, a black *kaifa*, and a heavy beard. Brandon watched through binoculars as the guy stepped on the wire and froze. Ice must have shot through the poor bastard's veins when the grenade spoon *pinged* and the little dislodged hand bomb rolled off the boulder and landed at his feet. He seemed frozen in place. Only his eyes moved as they stupidly followed the track of the grenade all the way to the ground.

A burst of smoke around a core of flame. The delayed clap of the explosion reached Brandon's ears a moment later. The blast slammed the victim against the opposite rock before depositing him wrecked at its base. Sand and gravel rained down on him.

His comrades hit the dirt. After they realized what had happened, they began to jump about and shake their fists in rage, emptying magazines in the direction of their quarry.

"They are . . . How do Americans say it?" Juba observed. "Pissed off?"

"They are truly pissed off, Senor Brandon."

The grenade had its desired effect, at least for a while. Caution caused the guerrillas to slow the chase and allowed Brandon and Juba to pull ahead somewhat. However, the bandits picked up the pace once nothing else occurred and they regained courage. Again, they closed the gap.

Brandon wasn't through with them yet. Juba and he crossed the top of a gentle rise and came to a shallow wadi at the far bottom. He set up a shooting stand by using the bank of the washout as a rifle rest. The H & K G3AR was not designed for long-distance marksmanship. What he needed was Gloomy Davis and Mr. Blunderbuss. But a good shooter—and Brandon was one of the best—should be able to reach out with the stubby little rifle and tap someone at three hundred yards.

The terrain was such that the pursuers appeared piece-meal as they climbed the opposite side of the hill. First the top of a head appeared, then gradually the shoulders and trunk of the body until he came completely into sight at the crest. Brandon had chosen this particular location for its tactical advantage. If he were lucky, he might knock off one or two. The others would go to ground on the opposite side of the crest. While they tried to figure out what was going on, he and Juba could slip away and extend the gap between them.

One head appeared, bouncing in the haze of distance. Then a second head. Brandon waited, his sights already on the first man. His mouth felt like he had a dry lizard in his throat. Even as he went through his repertoire of deadly dirty tricks, he realized this contest couldn't go on much longer. Alone, he might have a chance. But with the kid . . .

He glanced at Juba. The boy had dark rings underneath his eyes. His breathing was sharp and raspy and he had stopped sweating, a dangerous sign. The kid was still game though. He lay against the wadi bank next to Brandon, ready to do anything he could.

"You should have—" he began.

"I know, I know. Gotten you a rifle—"

"Yes."

The lead target became visible up to the waist. Brandon placed his iron sights directly on the man's chest and then elevated two feet above his head to compensate for bullet drop. It was a long shot. There was little wind. He took in a half breath, held it, and stroked the trigger.

The guy froze in his tracks. Near misses only counted in horse shoes and hand grenades. Brandon was back on target by the time the rifle report echoed off the rise. He released a second round. This one caught the target and dropped him writhing to the ground. Winged but not killed.

The other man dropped out of sight. Brandon waited to see what happened next. Nothing moved on the crest other than the guy with the bullet in him. He flopped about and was obviously raising one hell of a racket. Another terrorist ran out to drag him to safety. Brandon fired at him, but missed.

Again, nothing moved.

"They must really be pissed off now, huh, Senor Brandon?"

"Let's move, runt."

It wouldn't do to tarry in one spot. The enemy would surely attempt to encircle. When Brandon chose the final battlefield, it would be on high ground with good cover and concealment. And how about a McDonald's, a Motel 6, and a detachment of Troop One Deltas?

Brandon slung Juba to his shoulders and took off. They had moved another four hundred yards, gaining both ground and time, by the time the Jihadia closed in on the wadi. Rifle fire spattered in their wake as the tangos killed the wadi. One of the bad guys popped up on the bank of the washout and pointed. The entire horde began howling and shouting and jumping about. Juba was too spent to comment about their being pissed off. Brandon had to hold onto his ankles to keep him from falling off his shoulders.

Baying like hounds, smarter now and spreading out across the terrain to avoid floundering into any more traps, the remaining pursuers gradually closed in again as the hours wore on. The closer they got, the more excited they became. They smelled blood. The prey was rapidly weakening. It wouldn't be long now.

The helicopters still didn't come.

"Maybe they have forgotten us," Juba said.

"They'll come," Brandon said.

The Jihadia pinged away with their weapons, as though competing to see which of them brought down the American and the Sahrawi kid. Brandon saved ammo for when it was most critical and could do the most damage. He tottered gamely along, a strong, determined man weakened by the unforgiving sun and Juba's weight on his shoulders. He was still a dangerous man.

And the boy? What a kid.

For the last hour Brandon had been heading toward a boulder-strewn knoll that rose in the shape of a despoiled tit from the desert floor, intent on making his defense there. The enemy was coming as the Indians had come at General Custer on the Little Big Horn. And they would show just as much mercy. While Custer's last stand had made the history books along with the Alamo and many other battles, Brandon doubted anyone would ever hear of him and a brave Sahrawi kid named Juba and their last stand.

They collapsed to take a short rest break. "I would make—" Juba croaked. His swollen, cracked lips moved, but no words came. Brandon bent near.

"I would make . . . a good son . . . for you?"

A question from an orphan who could not remember his father or what it meant to be a son.

"Juba—"

The boy's eyes closed from exhaustion and his chin fell against his chest. Brandon picked him up and carried him in his arms. Bullets whistled around his head and spurted little geysers out of the desert floor. Something tugged at his trouser leg. He looked and saw blood where a slug had gouged a thin furrow across his calf.

Men were spread out behind them and running fast, shooting as they came. Brandon called upon his remaining energy and ran toward the knoll, determined to reach it, make his stand and take as many enemy down with him as he could. His pursuers discerned his intention and increased their efforts to bring him down with withering rifle fire before he reached the natural fort.

Bullets peppered around Brandon like hail as he wound

his way up through the boulders that littered the tit. Eyes darting, he scanned the east, searching the pale hot sky for signs of the helicopters he knew would come. Nothing. Juba hung limp in his arms. Brandon gently lay him behind a large rock for protection. He gave him a sip of water from his canteen. Juba stirred and seemed to revive.

"Senor Brandon . . . give me the pistol again."

Brandon hesitated before removing the handgun from its holster and handing it over. The terrorists were going to kill both of them anyhow. Juba took it in unsteady hands. He rolled over on his belly and rested his forehead against his hands and the gun.

"Pick your targets carefully," Brandon cautioned. "Conserve ammunition."

"Will they kill us together, Senor Brandon? I don't mind to die if you are with me."

"We're not going to die, kid."

He didn't really believe it.

He shoved rock and dirt into a barricade between two boulders, then unbuckled his battle harness containing ammo pouches and placed it within reach of both himself and Juba. Next, he crawled around the top of the hill to check out approaches. The top was only about eight feet across at its widest and offered good observation down all sides. The Jihadis were going to pay a high price in blood before they took the hill.

"If I had a rifle—" Juba ventured.

Brandon eased himself behind the barricade with his weapon. He tousled Juba's hair. "Kid," he said, "you're something else."

"Something else? I do not understand."

"It means you're all right.

"You are all right too, Senor Brandon. You can call me 'kid' if you want to."

The Jihadia reached the base of the hill and spread out to start their assault on it. They were already laying down cover and prep fire. Brandon dared not show his head. He kept a hand on Juba to also keep him down, remembering how the boy had chased the ambusher on Hill 138 to shoot him in the belly. They would wait to return fire until the attackers started up through the boulders.

"Juba," Brandon said, lying flat under the sun, rifle in hand and cheek against the dirt, "I would want him to be just like you if I had a son."

Juba wasn't listening. He unexpectedly flipped onto his back and began to laugh and shout, pointing at the sky. Brandon looked up.

Two Blackhawk helicopters soared toward them out of the east, their pilots already interpreting the situation on the ground. Miniguns began to blaze. Rockets contrailed toward the attackers. General Custer never had it so good.

CHAPTER 76

Arlington

What a dumb mistake, not turning off his cell phone. General Kragle knew he was in deep *kimshi* when it rang and hushed down the executive committee meeting in George Coalgate Geis's library. He drew the Beretta from his waistband and reached the door to the walkway before a pistol popped behind him. The bullet shattered the door jamb next to his head, half-blinding one eye with flying splinters slicing with excruciating pain into his head. He twisted around in time to see from his good eye a blurred figure in the service opening taking bead on him for a finishing shot.

His years of practice with firearms served him well. He snapped off two quick rounds. The blurred figure staggered back from the opening, hit hard. He crashed over something in the library as he fell.

The executive committee members stormed out into the walkway to block his escape. The harsh banging of gunfire spawned pandemonium in the great room below—women screaming, men shouting, everyone bolting in a mob for the doors, led by politicians who couldn't afford to be caught in a situation like this with elections coming up. All the "Beautiful People" panicking and getting the hell out of Dodge.

The General also needed to get the hell out of Dodge. Only, he found himself trapped, wounded and half-blind in the kitchenette. Pain stabbed into his brain like fire pokers. He wiped his eye and came away with blood on his fingers. He was getting too old for this shit. He was a war planner these days, not a war fighter.

He slammed the door against the chaos on the walkway and locked it. Someone banged on it with his fist. Others joined in. General Kragle snapped a bullet into the molding above the door to give them second thoughts. The banging stopped. Working fast, spurred on by desperation and pain in his eyes and from the wound in his left arm, he toppled the refrigerator onto its side, spilling food and drinks across the floor. He put his back to the exposed bottom of the fridge and pushed it firmly against the door to block it. That should hold them for awhile.

The kitchenette was windowless except for the service opening into the library. He stole a quick look into the library to make sure all the committee had vacated it. It blazed with light absorbed by dark bookcases filled with leather-bound volumes and modern art abstracts framed on open wall space. In the center were a conference table and chairs. A coffeepot and coffee cups had been overturned on the table in the previous occupants' haste to evacuate the premises. Spilled coffee dribbled off the edge of the table into the upturned face of the bearded man the General had killed with two shots.

Jesus! How was he ever going to explain this one to the cops? He had already killed one other man tonight.

He hurried through the service entrance into the library and quickly bolted the double doors. As added insurance, he wedged the conference table against the doors and piled chairs and a sofa around it. He had to keep Geis's goons from getting to him, buy some time and stay alive until he could talk to the police.

They were going to have to kill him. He knew too

much. Geis could simply claim that the General was an intruder who broke into his house, which he had, shot one guest, which he did, and was brought down in return. All perfectly legal and in "self protection." No one would ever know the truth about The Committed.

General Kragle checked the Beretta. The original owner had fired it several times, in addition to the three cartridges the General expended. That left two rounds, hardly enough to hold off a determined rush. So far, confusion outside kept anyone from coming up with an assault plan.

A scraping noise from the far corner of the room! General Kragle wheeled to face the threat, gun pointed and ready for action.

"Don't shoot!" a frightened voice cried. "Please don't shoot me!"

The General batted his eyes to open his vision. He saw a man huddled on the floor, partly concealed by window drapes, palms thrown out in front of his face as though to ward off bullets. Lieutenant Jerry Hurst, true to his nature, had collapsed in fear when everyone else rushed out of the library. The General pictured him that day at Vinh Tho, trembling and blubbering on the ground, incapacitated by fear while the Mike Force made its defense at the canal.

The General walked over to him. "Mr. *Hunt*, I presume?"

Hurst cautiously dropped his hands. His lips trembled while he watched the General's every move. The little bastard was having flashbacks of his own.

He had aged badly. He still had the weak chin and watery, weak eyes, but the baby face of his youth had dissipated into decadence. He was almost bald. What hair remained was wispy and white. The ugly scar on his throat stretched from just below his chin to the knot of his red power tie. The General winced; he knew how that had gotten there.

Hurst gave him an idea. So far, it was merely the word of an intruder against one of the richest men in the world and his friends. But if the General were to elicit a confession, the police would have to listen to him. He had to work fast though. He pulled up a chair and sat in it facing the cowering man on the floor.

"There's no time for games, Hurst," he warned, waving the barrel of the gun toward the noise on the other side of the door. "I want answers and you're going to supply them."

Hurst swallowed with an effort. "Why should I talk to you at all?"

"For God and country," the General scoffed, angered, "and because you were a chickenshit who got better men than yourself killed."

"What has this country ever done for me except send me to Vietnam?"

"You're a real piece of work, do you know that, Hurst? You always were. You're a lap dog and an ass kisser, the perfect dupe for socialists and Marxists."

"I want to talk to my lawyer."

"I'm no cop, you asshole. You'll talk to me now because you're a coward—and because if you don't, this time I really will kill you." He traced the Beretta muzzle across Hurst's scar. "You know I'll do it too."

Hurst paled and licked his lips. His jaw quivered uncontrollably, as though it could hardly wait to start spitting out words. Banging and shouting outside the library doors seemed to give him momentary hope. The General turned his head and called out, "The first man who sticks his head through that door gets a bullet through it."

"We've called the police," a voice threatened.

"I'll wait for them in here."

The last thing these guys wanted was the police.

The General turned back to Hurst. "Are we ready to start now?"

Hurst stared, trembling all over.

"Good. Just for my own curiosity, what happened that night at the Hanoi Hilton after we escaped?"

"You tried to kill me," Hurst accused bitterly.

"I tried indeed."

Hurst stared wide-eyed into the muzzle of the General's pistol. He must have been an easy mark for North Vietnamese "interrogators." He probably started squealing before they ever laid a glove on him. No wonder he changed his name; the General wouldn't want anybody to know his past either if he had one as disgraceful as this pathetic little creature's.

"Colonel Lough found me," he finally volunteered. "He kept me from dying. I suppose I should be grateful for that, even if he waited an hour so you could get away before he called the guards. I tried to tell them he was in on it too, but they chose to believe him since he saved me and sounded the alarm. You could have gotten us all killed."

"How did you get mixed up with Colonel Lough's son Chuckie?"

Hurst appeared less reluctant to talk as he warmed up. "I stayed in North Vietnam after the war. Don't look at me like that. Why shouldn't I? The U.S. didn't give a fuck about me. I met David Barr in Paris. One thing led to another and I got involved in the international peace movement. The U.S. is truly an evil, imperialistic, capitalist, warmongering, fascist—"

"I get the gist. Which one is David Barr?"

Hurst indicated the dead man and cringed. "You eliminated him. You always were a cold—"

"Keep talking or we'll see just how cold. And Chuckie Lough? He was working for David Barr too?"

"Lough was about as idealistic as a beach crab," Hurst said disdainfully. "He was in it for the money. All those disgusting pornographers he works with will do anything for the right cash."

"Is Goebling the one who set me up after I left EME this afternoon?"

"Probably. I know he set Lough up after Lough argued with Gerald Espy and said he was going to you about it. Barr got a call from Goebling. Goebling found out Lough was meeting you at the Lincoln Memorial."

"This gets better and better. So Chuckie found out you were blackmailing me and knew his father and I were in the Hanoi Hilton together? He argues with Espy about it. Espy calls Barr, and Barr has him killed. Is that about it?"

"Lough heard me on the phone when I called you about Jerry Hurst. I guess he put two and two together—"

"—and found out who you really were and had an attack of conscience."

"I wouldn't call it conscience. He was a weasel."

"Why didn't they kill me too?"

"Barr didn't think you needed eliminating at that time because you were too high profile. Mr. Geis wanted to discredit the Tyler administration by making voters think everybody was bailing out on him before the election."

"You were behind the blackmail?"

"Barr was. Barr was behind everything. Him and Mr. Geis. I guess he got his orders from Mr. Geis, but we all worked for Barr."

"A cozy little nest of snakes. And when I didn't resign like I was supposed to—?"

"That, and you started snooping around. Barr had no choice but to order you neutralized."

"You mean *killed*. Are you squeamish about the word?"

"It's a cinch you aren't," Hurst shot back, looking at the dead man.

"I'm not, so keep talking," the General said when Hurst then glanced hopefully toward the doors. "The first bullet's for you if they break in, so you had better hope they don't."

The General knew he had to hurry. Everything outside the door had gone unusually quiet; they were up to something. He couldn't call the police yet either. The moment he did, Hurst would realize he wasn't going to be shot and would dumb up.

"How did Lough and you get mixed up with Geis?" the General asked, prodding with his pistol. "Through Barr?"

"You know it doesn't make any difference what I tell you?" Hurst asked. "You're never going to get out of here alive with it anyhow."

"Just keep talking."

"Barr knew Espy from way back. Mr. Geis has the money. Barr was hired to ramrod a campaign on a number of fronts to discredit Woodrow Tyler so he would lose the election."

"That included blackmail, dirty tricks and dirty politics, funded antiwar protests, murders, collaboration with terrorists . . . ?"

"You have no idea how deep this thing goes," Hurst gloated. "Capitalism is doomed. The Soviet Union failed to bring America to its knees, but where it failed we will succeed. You can't stop the fall. Nobody can stop it as it crumbles from the inside out."

"I should have made sure you were dead the first time."

"I'm just a small cog in a big and powerful movement of the people."

You couldn't argue with a True Believer.

"One more question: You blew up the Madrid trains?" the General prodded. "You're going to do the same thing in Tulsa?"

Hurst balked at that one. General Kragle thrust the pistol muzzle hard against his temple.

"I swear, that was Barr and Lough and the Muslims," Hurst responded, the words tumbling out. "I don't know what they did there, except Mr. Geis said we could always deal with the Muslims later. A lot of things are compartmentalized and we all don't have a need to know."

"I heard Barr talking about a 'package' being delivered to Tulsa. By that, did he mean a bomb?"

Hurst cast a strange look at the dead man. "I assume it is."

The General tapped him harder with the gun barrel.

"Yes, yes, damn it. All I know is it came in across the Mexican border. They're detonating it when the President begins his speech tomorrow."

"How are they detonating it?"

"I don't know. I swear I don't know for sure. Airplane, I think."

"All right, keep going. *Where* is it being detonated?"

Hurst was almost in tears as he stared into the gun barrel. "I'm going to enjoy watching them kill you," he whined.

"You'll never see it. Go on."

"I overheard Barr saying Tyler was the target."

"Why would they assassinate him after going through so much trouble to discredit him?"

Hurst swallowed. "You have to know Barr and Mr. Geis. They want to make sure he's dead and out of the picture, but they don't want him to die a martyr and become another JFK. If he's disgraced and then dies at the hands of terrorists, Mr. Geis thinks the American people will seek a new socialist leadership of peace and international equality."

"As Spain did?"

"As most of Europe will, sooner or later. America will follow."

General Kragle looked at him with stunned disbelief. "You're all crazy if you think that will stop terrorism."

"Terrorism is a secondary concern," Hurst said. "The first objective is to convert the world to socialism. That's always been the goal of Marxism."

"The end justifies the means?" the General quoted.

"Hasn't that always been the way it is?"

The General produced a yellow legal pad and a ballpoint pen from a small writing desk in the corner opposite. He handed them to Hurst.

"Write down everything you've just told me," he ordered. "Sign and date it when you finish. You have five minutes. I swear I'm going to kill you if you leave out a single thing. Start writing."

By this time Hurst was too scared not to do as he was told. The General heard people at the door as he punched two different numbers in sequence into his cell. The first number was 911.

"Police department? Yes. Copy down this address carefully: 18732 Kirby Road. Got that? There's about to be a hell of a shootout. You're going to need a lot of cops, and you're going to need 'em fast."

The second number was Claude Thornton's. It was about time he returned his old friend's calls.

"Claude, you have to stop the President," he warned. "They're going to assassinate him tomorrow when he gives his speech in Tulsa."

CHAPTER 77

Tulsa

"Darren, I can't stop the President. I've tried."

"I hate to drop this in your lap like this, Claude, but I'm in a bit of a bind at the moment."

"Where are you?"

"At a cocktail party. You might say I crashed it. George Geis. Ever hear of him?"

"You're *where*?"

"Geis's mansion. George Coalgate Geis."

"Holy smoke, General. Do you know who that man is?"

"Not only do I know *who* he is, I know *what* he is. I've got a dead man here named David Barr—"

"Barr!"

"I take it you know him."

"I have an FBI arrest warrant on him, or would have had shortly. I could have told you all this if you'd return my calls."

"I didn't know you cared. I've been busy."

"Sounds like it."

"So you know what's going on? Is that why you're in Tulsa?"

"It sounds like I'm in the dark compared to you. How is this assassination supposed to take place?"

"First I heard them talking about Yuma and Madrid. This ring any chimes?"

"Like the Mormon Tabernacle. What else?"

"A 'package' was smuggled across the Mexican border. I take it that was in Yuma?"

"Correct. Two ragheads died of radiation poisoning."

"And you didn't tell me?"

"How could I? Damn!"

"It really *is* a WMD? Nuclear?"

"It appears so. The Arabs fucked it up."

"Only one of the WMD, Claude."

"That's what we figured. Go on."

"Barr said they had worked through it. It's supposed to be bigger and better than Madrid. As far as I can determine on this end, tangos are supposed to detonate it during the President's speech—apparently by aircraft."

"Aircraft! We've got the airport shut down tighter than a nun's pussy."

"I'm just telling you what I've picked up. Incidentally, I've also got a signed confession. Uh-oh, like I said, Claude, I'm in a bit of a bind. I hear sirens coming now. You're going to have to handle this yourself. Claude, if you don't find that thing, they're going to kill the President of the United States."

Claude consulted his wristwatch. After midnight. Less than twelve hours to go.

CHAPTER 78

POLITICAL CONSPIRACY EXPOSED

Arlington (CPI)—Police this morning are attempting to sort out the facts in overnight developments that left two men dead, eight so far in custody, and the presidential campaign of Senator Lowell Rutherford Harris under a cloud. Police say they have also solved the murder of Charles Edward Lough, who was gunned down earlier this week on the steps of the Lincoln Memorial in Washington, D.C. Among those in custody so far are billionaire socialist philanthropist and political activist George Coalgate Geis and Party of the People National Committee chairman Gerald Espy.

The dead were identified as David Robert Barr, a former KGB agent with the Soviet Union and a displaced American with French citizenship, and Carl P. Shaw, an ex-con from Cleveland, Ohio. Darren E. Kragle was treated and released for a gunshot wound. Kragle is the commanding general of the United States Special Operations Command (USSOCOM).

According to detectives, police received a telephone call in reference to a pending "shootout" at Geis's suburban estate. Upon arrival, they found Kragle barricaded inside the residential library with a man identified as Gerald R. Hurst, who goes by the name of Gerry Hunt, and with the remains of David Barr. Hurst has been officially listed as "Missing in Action, Believed Dead" since the Vietnam

War. Barr and Hurst were reportedly employed by Geis and an organization known as The Committed.

In statements to police, Kragle named The Committed as an organization of wealthy socialists and Marxists formed to sabotage the reelection of President Woodrow Tyler by any means possible, including extortion and murder. Hurst reportedly signed a confession in which he implicates Geis, Barr, NCC Gerald Espy and others in the plot to unseat President Tyler. Among federal charges expected to be filed today against Geis, Hurst, Espy, and five other men are first degree murder, attempted murder, conspiracy to commit murder, extortion, conspiracy under the RICO bill, and domestic terrorism under the Patriot Defense Act. Other indictments and arrests are expected to follow as police and federal agents continue their investigation.

Earlier in the evening, Arlington police arrested two men in a vehicle after receiving an anonymous tip pertaining to another shooting. According to reports, three men attempted to gun down General Darren Kragle in front of a residence belonging to Charles Edward Lough's mother. One of the gunmen was slain in the encounter with the intended victim. Police found the body in a neighboring yard.

One of the gunmen allegedly confessed to Lough's murder and to the attempted assassination of General Kragle. He is reported to have named David Barr as the man who hired them for the job.

When contacted at his Washington, D.C. residence, presidential candidate Lowell Rutherford Harris refused comment. He later released a statement through a spokesman in which he said he had been at Geis's mansion for a fund-raising event earlier in the evening but had departed before the episode in the library. He denied any knowledge of a PAC known as The Committed. He said he was "shocked" and "dismayed" when informed of Geis's complicity in the affair.

Geis and Espy have released statements through their lawyers claiming they are innocent . . .

CHAPTER 79

Fayetteville

Gloria had hurried directly to Fayetteville to stay with Summer while Brandon was missing. She kept trying to take Summer's mind off her worries by entertaining her with amusing stories about her husband and his brothers when they were children.

"You wouldn't know it none nowadays by looking at Cassidy, he so handsome," she narrated, "but he was the ugliest baby I ever seen when he was born. He had black hair down his neck and all down his poor back. Lawdy, lamb chop, he look just like a little *monkey*. When I take him out somewhere, I cover up his face with a diaper 'cause I don't want nobody to see him. He always telling people nowadays I kept a diaper on his face 'til he started school, but that ain't the truth."

When Brown Sugar Mama chuckled or giggled and got all that flesh to going she shook all the way from her dyed-red hair to the round tips of her brown toes.

"Truth is, I only covered his face for about three months. Then he got pretty."

Gloria and Summer usually started out laughing and ended up crying in each other's arms.

"Mama, what am I going to do if Brandon doesn't—? Well, if he doesn't—?"

"Hush, chile. I been praying to Lord Jesus every night

and every morning and in-between times. I done told Jesus that He better listen to this old black woman, else He gonna have to deal with me come Judgment Day. So hush, chile, them boys is gonna be fine."

Summer wondered if she really believed it or was just trying to make her feel better.

"You gonna see, honey dumpling. He'll be back and you gonna have your little family. And when that baby done come along, all you gotta do is give him some time to accept it. Brandon'll come around, chile. I know that boy better'n he know hisself."

"I'm not sure about that, Mama. I'm just not sure if he ever will."

"Honey, you got to give him a chance."

Summer agonized over decisions about the baby during tension-filled days while the two women awaited news on the fates of the Kragle men—Chaplain Cameron held hostage at the Tindouf Airport and Brandon lost in the desert. Even the General seemed to be out of pocket, unusual for him when his sons were on a mission. Gloria suspected he was keeping a low profile because of what he knew she may well say to him for not telling her about Brandon's situation right away.

"Lawdy," she threatened, limbering up her formidable finger for the task ahead, "am I gonna give Darren Kragle a piece of my mind when I sees him again."

Summer considered herself a feminist in the sense that she was a strong, self-reliant woman who believed women should accomplish whatever their abilities and talents allowed. As she told Margo Foster, she had done all that and collected the T-shirts. Now she wanted something more out of life: family.

Trouble was, Brandon wanted *her*, not *family*.

Even if he returned this time, there might certainly be a time when he wouldn't. It wasn't fair to a baby to be born into a house like that. Brandon was right. It wasn't fair, it just wasn't fair . . . damn it.

Summer researched Planned Parenthood on the internet and learned that the organization performed over 230,000 abortions annually. Margo assured her that abortion was a simple procedure. She knew plenty of female soldiers who had had it done. Go in for an hour's counseling, make an appointment with a doctor—and, lo, problem solved. No more baby.

Summer experienced pangs of guilt, even though she knew in her mind that it was the right thing to do. She made an appointment with a counselor, telling no one what she was doing. Brown Sugar Mama would be scandalized if she learned Summer intended to *kill* Brandon's baby, her foster grandchild.

"A modern woman has control of her body," the counselor said. "We have choices now that we never had before."

She was a bleached woman in her mid-forties with hard lines in her face.

"Have you had an abortion?" Summer asked her.

"We're not here to discuss—"

"Have you?" Summer insisted.

The counselor looked away. She looked back. "Yes," she said.

"Do you have children?"

"No."

"Do you ever regret it?"

The counselor stood up. "I'm not going to answer that." But she already had. "Don't forget your doctor's appointment at nine," she said.

* * *

Summer showered and dressed without looking in the long mirror at her body. She informed Gloria she would be back later. The counselor said she might be a little sore afterwards, but nothing that would give her away to friends and family.

"Honey, is you okay?" Gloria worried, sensing something amiss.

"Mama, do you believe everything we do comes out for the better?"

" 'Course I does, dumpling."

Summer nodded thoughtfully. "I'll be home in a little while."

She was back by noon. Gloria, Margo, Mollie Thompson, Doc TB's pregnant wife, Carole, and several other Delta women burst out her front door to meet her. Summer's heart pounded with dread until she saw laughter and tears.

"We've just found out," Mollie Thompson said, rushing her words through sobs of joy. "Major Brandon's team was extracted this morning. They're all right, everyone of them, except for one minor wound and a broken arm—"

Summer couldn't wait. "What about Brandon?"

"He was picked up late this afternoon. He's okay too."

"They is on they way home," Gloria put in, literally whooping with relief. "They got Cameron out too. Brandon and Cameron is both on they way home."

She directed a broad beaming smile at Summer.

"Know what else?" she said with a wise and meaningful look in her eye. "Brandon had this little boy with him. He refuse to let that little guy out of his sight 'til he was sure he gonna be all right. Colonel Thompson say it was almost like Brandon be that little boy's *father*."

CHAPTER 80

ALGERIAN SALAFIA JIHADIA ROUTED

Algiers (CPI)—In a series of rapid developments beginning yesterday, the Algerian government with the assistance of U.S. forces repulsed the attempted takeover of this northern African nation by Salafia Jihadia insurgents. U.S. Marines supported by elements of the U.S. 10th Mountain Division relieved the nation's capital at 9:00 a.m. local. President Ahmed Ali Benflis had been under siege by radical Islamic rebels known to have ties to al-Qaeda and other terrorist groups. Rebel commander Amari Saichi, also known as Abderrazak the Paratrooper, is believed to have escaped into Morocco.

U.S. troops and loyal Algerian forces also have Salafia Jihadia on the run in the southern and western Sahara after radicals there massacred hundreds of Sahrawi living in refugee camps along the border. The Sahrawi governor-in-exile Chadli Malud, originally listed as missing and possibly killed, is reported to have been rescued somewhere in West Sahara. No details were forthcoming. Malud is scheduled to meet this week with President Benflis to discuss rebuilding the camps and affording the Sahrawi more autonomy.

American Special Forces also stormed the Tindouf Airport shortly after dawn to liberate three American missionaries and 23 Sahrawi being held as hostages by the

Islamic Jihad Black Death Squad, an affiliate of Salafia
Jihadia.

The sect's lieutenant, Abdul Qadeer Khan, threatened
to execute all the hostages unless his demands were met.
Two Sahrawi had already been gunned down on preced-
ing days. Khan and nine of his terrorists were killed in
an exchange of gunfire with rescuers. Two hostages were
wounded, including Chaplain Cameron Kragle of Fort
Bragg, North Carolina. Both are expected to recover. One
American missionary had been executed before the
hostage siege began . . .

CHAPTER 81

Tulsa

Unlike the rental truck loaded with fertilizer and diesel fuel used by Timothy McVeigh to blow up the Murrah Federal Building in Oklahoma city, unlike the ton or so of TNT terrorists detonated against the Madrid trains, a nuclear device containing enough power to bury the American Airlines hangar at Tulsa International Airport, where President Tyler was scheduled to speak, would fit inside a piece of luggage and could be delivered by an ordinary car or a single-engine aircraft. The plane didn't have to be a hijacked 767 or an Air Bus.

Preparing for a visit by the President of the United States, especially after 9/11, was a major production requiring hundreds of personnel from Secret Service, FBI, CIA, NSA, Homeland Security, and local law enforcement agencies. Squadrons of fighter jets patrolled the skies over Tulsa with orders to shoot down any aircraft that flagrantly violated restricted airspace without authorization. Anti-missile missiles and antiaircraft missiles under the same orders were set up in strategic locations all around the airport. Snipers armed with high-powered rifles sandbagged themselves in on top of the American Airlines hangar. All other hangars and terminals were shut down and placed under guard. Aircraft on the ground would remain grounded until after the President finished speaking and left. Feds and uniformed police with dogs patrolled the runways and adjacent areas. Roads into and out of the airport were either barricaded off or placed under strict access control. Ready forces of Army troops and SWAT teams of police stationed themselves for immediate response to a crisis.

FBI Agent Fred Whiteman, Claude Thornton's deputy director of Domestic Preparedness, slapped his boss on the back. "Relax, African American," he said. "This asshole is shut down so tight a gnat can't get through it."

"I'm no African American," Thornton snapped, in no mood to be joshed into better spirits. "I was born in America, not in Africa."

"Claude, it'll go fine."

"We mustn't underestimate them," Thornton said. He would not be satisfied until the President had come and gone again without anything blowing up.

"You've done everything humanly possible, Claude."

"Have I? Is it enough?"

General Kragle's surprise telephone call at midnight had confirmed what Thornton suspected all along but had considered improbable: that the President himself was the target and not a dam or some public building. With the revelation that an aircraft might be used for the WMD delivery, Thornton, Whiteman, and teams of agents spent the night searching and closing down small municipal or private airfields within a fifty-mile radius of Tulsa. Thornton's guts continued to churn, however. Open fields all over the plains around Tulsa provided excellent sites where a small airplane could land and take off.

KRMG and KVOO radio along with TV Channels 2, 6, and 8 broadcast advice to all pilots, including those of gliders and ultralites, to stay out of the air or risk being shot down. Even a hawk, buzzard, or eagle flying through restricted airspace raised blood pressures and made trigger fingers itch.

Security was indeed tight. But was it tight enough? Secret Service knew its job of protecting the President, but Thornton checked and rechecked nonetheless. He couldn't seem to settle the queasiness in his stomach.

Crowds began gathering at the airport at 10:30 a.m. Police required all vehicles to park in a field on the other side of Mingo Road from the hangar. Security searched trunks and underneath hoods and frames. No large purses or packages were allowed inside the airport area. Everyone without exception passed through metal detectors. Some people were questioned. Plainclothesmen circulated in the crowd listening for a chance remark and watching for suspicious behavior. The ever-present protestors carrying placards exhorting fellow travelers to *IMPEACH TYLER* or *END THE FASCIST WAR AND RACISM* were restrained to a single enclosed space.

After a final run-through, Thornton and Whiteman returned to the hangar, parked Thornton's rented black Buick in a lot reserved for law enforcement vehicles, and climbed to the hangar's flat roof. Using binoculars, they glassed the entire airport from the terminals opposite to the ILS lights and other navigational aids at either ends of the runways. Armed men were everywhere while fighter jets in pairs circled both high and low.

"What's that?" Whiteman asked, pointing.

A portable navigational-aids trailer ramp had been left on the median between the two main runways. An armed guard walked past it with hardly a notice. Thornton radioed Secret Service and was told someone would shortly tow it off. Before that could be accomplished, however,

Air Force One with its blue and gold markings entered the holding pattern. It landed at 11:30 a.m.

Fighters armed with air-to-air and air-to-ground missiles preceded it in landing. Other fighters followed it in. Another trio roared on overhead and circled. Thornton always experienced a particular thrill in watching the President of the United States land and knowing he was an integral part of it all. Not bad for a Mississippi boy who grew up in old sharecropper shacks.

President Woodrow Tyler was an immensely popular president in the small towns and on the farms and ranches of "fly-over country"—out between the big coastal cities where folks were traditional and still believed in conducting business with a handshake. They appreciated a man who walked tall, shot straight, said what he meant, and meant what he said. Woodrow Tyler was their kind of man, a home-grown Texan with an earthy good humor, malapropisms and all. They chuckled with him whenever he got one over on the city slickers with their pointy-toed shoes, who got their hair "styled" in a "salon" rather than cut in a barber shop. Stories reported by the eastern press designed to make him seem like an ignorant country bumpkin only endeared him further to the *real* folks of the *real* America.

There was the one about reporters and other media types following him around on his working cattle ranch in Texas while he explained the workings of cows and bulls. At Rainey Creek, one of the greenhorns asked him if the water was drinkable.

"Sure," President Tyler responded, then waited a heartbeat while the coiffed newsman cupped water into his hands, brought them to his lips, and sucked it down, whereupon the President added, "If you don't mind the taste of cow shit."

Just before Air Force One landed at Tulsa, the President got on the plane's PA system and announced to accompanying pool reporters, "Get 'em now. This is your last chance for malaprops."

Most of the more than ten thousand people who showed up at the American Airlines hangar to see him could chuckle at stories like that. To them, President Tyler was "just folks," one of the highest compliments they could pay him.

He was a punctual man too. He approached the podium at precisely noon—and the folks greeted him and kept greeting him. An outside PA system accommodated all the people unable to crowd into the hangar to see and hear him in person. His strong voice with its Texas twang rose to the hangar roof where Claude Thornton and Fred Whiteman systematically and methodically glassed the airport for threats. Instead of diminishing, Thornton's sense of foreboding only heightened as the President proceeded with his speech.

"America today is a nation called to great responsibilities," the President said. "We are rising to meet them. The American people have faced serious challenges together, and now we face a choice. We either go forward with confidence and resolve, or we turn back to the dangerous illusion that terrorists are not plotting and outlaw regimes are no threat to us. There is really only one choice. Terrorists do continue to plot against America and the civilized world. Regimes do harbor and support terrorists and could supply them with nuclear, chemical, or biological weapons. We must refuse to live in the shadow of this ultimate danger. America will never seek a permission slip

from the United Nations or a coalition of any nations to
defend the safety of our people . . ."

Movement caught Claude Thornton's eye. He focused
his binoculars on an air service station on the opposite
side of the airport next to the single runway dedicated to
general aviation. It was a good half to three quarters of a
mile away, beyond the airport's main terminal area.
Claude watched a man in mechanics overalls hurry from
the station and walk rapidly toward a red-and-white
Cessna tied down on the parking ramp. He carried a steel
plate-like contraption.

"Free nations must be willing when the last resort oc-
curs to restrain aggression and evil by force," the President continued. "To those who decry the use of force
even in the restraint of evil, I say to them that the women
of Afghanistan imprisoned in their homes and executed
in public spectacles did not reproach us for routing the
Taliban. The inhabitants of Iraq's Ba'athist hell with its
lavish palaces and its torture chambers, with its massive
statues and its mass graves, do not miss their dictator . . ."

The mechanic loosened the Cessna's tiedown ropes and
cast them away. He looked back toward the air service station. Where were the cops and federal agents who should
be stationed there? Thornton nudged Whiteman.

"Fred, take a look at this."

The President's words resounded through loudspeakers: "If large areas of the globe exist where freedom does
not flourish, they will remain places of stagnation and
anger and violence for export. As we saw in the ruins of
two towers, no distance on the map will protect our lives
and way of life. Such terrorists target the innocent, and
they kill by the thousands. And if they gain the weapons

they seek they will kill by the millions and not be finished. The greatest threat of our age is nuclear, chemical, or biological weapons in the hands of terrorists and the dictators who aid them . . ."

"He's getting in the airplane," Whiteman said tersely.

Thornton used his portable radio phone to raise the Secret Service agent in overall charge of airport presidential security. "What's going on over there?" he demanded. "No one is supposed to be in any aircraft."

"Let me call over there. I'll get right back with you."

"Start some people in that direction," Thornton suggested.

President Tyler continued in the background: "Say what you will about the communists, they did not want to martyr themselves in order to destroy us. If terrorists obtain nuclear weapons, they will destroy themselves in order to detonate bombs in our cities. What's left of the War on Terror could be nasty, brutish, and short. That is something we must therefore avoid . . ."

The Secret Service supervisor called back. "Something's wrong over there. I can't raise anybody."

The mechanic climbed inside the Cessna and shut the door. He placed the steel plate in the front window, like a shield for the pilot. The prop kicked over.

"The people have given us the duty to defend them," the President said, "and that duty sometimes requires the violent restraint of violent men. In some cases, the measured use of force is all that protects us from a chaotic world ruled by force . . ."

"What is that aircraft?" Thornton persisted. "Why wasn't it secured?"

The prop was whirring. The aircraft inched into forward motion.

"I'm checking the log . . ." Secret Service said. "It was an emergency landing at eighteen forty hours yesterday—"

"Oh, sweet Jesus!" Thornton was already running for the nearest stairway. "That's *it*! *That's* the sonofabitch right there—and he's coming!"

CHAPTER 82

Tulsa

The Cessna picked up speed, heading not toward the single north-south general aviation runway for takeoff but east across the broad parking tarmac directly toward the American Airlines hangar, its crowds of people, and the President of the United States. Claude Thornton had divined the pilot's intention even as he and Fred Whiteman raced downstairs from the hangar's roof. The little airplane didn't have to become airborne in any traditional sense in order to reach its target. All it had to do was sail high enough above the ground to clear parked police cars and security positions, cross the main runways and their medians—and crash into the hangar at any point. This game was like horseshoes or hand grenades. With a WMD aboard, all it had to do was get close.

Recriminations and repercussions of human error or oversight would have to wait until later investigation, congressional inquiries, and finger pointing. Two uniformed policemen and a federal agent lay dead in the air service station, gunned down by a silenced pistol in the hands of a "mechanic" who had spent the night sleeping on a sofa. He had been checked out and cleared by a previous security shift. That it happened paid tribute to the perseverance, ingenuity, and desperation of cult of death members who truly loved death more than they loved life. This guy was intent on becoming a martyr and going directly and immediately to heaven to claim his seventy-two virgins.

Security had been devised to keep terrorists from getting *onto* airport property once it was cleared and secured. No one had anticipated an aircraft bomb already being *in* the airport and in such close proximity to its target. Although patrolling fighter jets were immediately alerted, their chances of making a strafing run on the Cessna before it reached its destination were slim to none. Likewise with missile defenses located on the perimeter to take out intruders on the outside trying to get in, not those already on the inside.

Like the majority of men in specialty military or law enforcement callings, Claude Thornton was a hard charger with what General Darren Kragle called a direct-action mentality. He knew only one way to confront a challenge: head-on. Even as he saw the Cessna begin to move and realized what it was up to, even as he burst out of the downstairs hangar doors and dashed toward his parked Buick, he had absolutely no idea how he was going to stop the plane. All he knew was that he had to *try*.

Only military people, feds, and cops populated the parking area between the hangar and Air Force One parked on the tarmac. Spectators were consigned to the other side of the hangar. Most of the security personnel, unaware of what was happening, watched in astonishment as the big black man with the shaved head and his even heftier white partner barreled past.

Thornton hurled himself behind the wheel of the Buick and started it in the same motion. He gunned it with gas, burning strips of rubber. Whiteman clung to the passenger's door, running alongside until he got it open and threw himself inside. The door banged against his legs as he sprawled belly down on the seat, his legs still dragging.

Thornton saw the Cessna lift off the ṭarmac. It skimmed just above the deck, heading straight toward him and the hangar, gaining speed. Then he saw the portable navigational-aids ramp that had been left on the grassy median and realized the airplane would fly directly over it. The end of the ramp toward Thornton rested low against the ground to permit loading of Bobcats, SPUs, and other vehicles and equipment. The end toward the Cessna was jacked up to more than four feet to permit it to be hitched to large trucks. The agent had seen motocross motorcyclists use ramps like this one to hop high into the air like grasshoppers. There was no time like the present to give it a try.

He slammed on his brakes, banging Whiteman off the dash. Thornton put a big foot against his friend's shoulder and shoved as hard as he could. Whiteman tumbled from the car.

"You can't go on this one, partner," he said.

He fishtailed the Buick directly toward the ramp and the oncoming airplane. In the background he heard the *bark-bark* of sniper rifles. The pilot had shielded himself with a steel plate to protect against such an eventuality. Another bulletproof shield had likely been constructed around the engine compartment. You had to hand it to terrorists bent on martyrdom; they planned their operations.

There was no time for Thornton to consider what he was doing or the philosophical implications of it. He spotted his target and there was only one way to reach it. Others might later distinguish the important difference between sacrificing a life *for* others and the way the Jihadia sacrificed their lives in order to murder others. For all Thornton knew, the plane and its WMD was rigged to detonate on impact, which made any action at this juncture,

indeed life itself, a moot point. There wouldn't be anything left within a quarter mile of the hangar except a
seared wasteland.

He blanked his mind to everything except his goal. First,
he had to get up sufficient speed, every tic of it that the
Buick could muster, in order to get high enough into the air
to reach the airplane. Second, timing had to be perfect.

The Cessna and the Buick roared toward each other.
The Buick was up to eighty, pegging toward ninety, when
it reached the ramp's low end. The terrorist pilot recognized Thornton's intent at the last moment. Low altitude
prevented radical maneuvering, but he still attempted to
veer left. His wing dipped.

Thornton was already on the ramp. He had intended to
crash head-on into the low-flying aircraft. Now he saw he
was going to miss it. He whipped the wheel to the right.
That tumbled the vehicle through the air as it shot off the
ramp, rolling end over end.

The Cessna avoided a direct midair collision—but the
rear of the flying car snapped around at the last instant and
caught a wheel strut.

Thornton had no idea how long it was before he regained
consciousness. Hurting all over, he shook his head to
clear it and banged it on the ceiling. The roof of the car
had caved in to steering-wheel level. He was twisted to
one side and trapped between the back of the seat, the
ceiling, and the dash.

"He's alive," someone said.

Was he? He slowly and painfully opened his eyes. They
were matted with blood and he had the mother of all
headaches. Judging from what he could see, twisted into
the wreckage as he was, the Buick was a total wreck. It
had apparently flipped several times after landing before

it came to rest on its wheels. He heard shattered glass tinkle when he tried to move. Huge clumps of grassy sod were caught and wedged between the crumpled hood and what remained of the windshield. Smoke oozed from the engine compartment. Emergency vehicles, lights flashing, seemed to be everywhere.

Fred Whiteman wore an anxious expression as he knelt outside looking in through the crunched door. His face was scraped and bruised, injuries he apparently suffered when Thornton kicked him out of the car.

"We're getting you out, partner," Whiteman said.

Thornton groaned. "The airplane—? It didn't go off?"

"No. You hardheaded, parsimonious—"

"Fred, you know you don't know nothing about big words."

"Damn it, Claude. Doing what you did without me. I love you like a brother."

"Sorry. There ain't no honkies in my family's woodpile. What happened to the airplane?"

"Best we can tell, it was wired to be manually activated just before impact. You didn't give the perp a chance to do it. None of us would be standing here otherwise. Pieces of the airplane and the asshole driving it are scattered for two hundred yards."

"The President—?"

"He's still speaking. He'll finish in, oh, about ten minutes. You're a hero, Claude, you know that?"

"I always wanted to be a hero. Like Clint Eastwood or Denzel Washington."

"More like Amos 'n' Andy."

"White man, I'm going to kick you out of the car again as soon as I get out of this mess."

CHAPTER 83

JIHAD CONTINUES ON AMERICAN SHORES

Washington, D.C. (CPI)—Events in Arlington, Virginia, and in Tulsa, Oklahoma, among other sites in the United States, underscore the multifaceted nature of the War on Terror and how it is homegrown as well as foreign. President Woodrow Tyler has said all along that the war with Jihadistan will be long and difficult, and that it will be fought simultaneously at many points, including those in the United States.

Arlington: Police arrest members of an organization known as The Committed for acts of terror and other crimes related to an effort by avowed socialists and communists to sabotage President Woodrow Tyler's reelection campaign. The investigation continues.

Tulsa: Federal agents foil an attempted assassination against President Tyler, which has been blamed on The Committed and billionaire philanthropist and avowed communist George Coalgate Geis. Presidential candidate Senator Lowell Rutherford Harris has dropped dramatically in the polls since news media linked his name to Geis's fund-raising efforts.

Galveston: In an anti-terror investigation known as Operation Dry Dock, FBI and Coast Guard announced they have discovered nine members of the Merchant Marine with links to terrorist groups.

Virginia: Three members of the "Virginia Jihad Network" were found guilty of conspiracy after they were arrested for training with the intent of joining terrorists in Iraq to wage Jihad against the United States.

Texas: Youseff Balaghi, a Saudi Arabian nationalist, was apprehended by the FBI's Operation Ice Storm for smuggling terrorists and WMDs across the border from Mexico.

Idaho: Omar Ali-Hussein, a high-profile Muslim student at the University of Idaho is charged with conspiracy to provide material support to terrorism after federal prosecutors said he helped run Web sites urging people to contribute money to Hamas.

San Diego: An American citizen and a Pakistani national confess to drug trafficking in heroin and hashish in order to buy Stinger missiles for al-Qaeda.

Buffalo: Five Muslims are convicted for trafficking in untaxed cigarettes to raise money for Jihad.

Pennsylvania: A member of the Jammu Kashmir Liberation Front is arrested for kidnapping and murdering Indian diplomat Ravindre Mhatre in England.

Fort Leavenworth: The Army announced that Sergeant Hasan Akbar, the Muslim U.S. soldier who attacked and killed his own commanding officers in Kuwait at the start of the Iraqi War, will be court-martialled and could receive the death penalty.

Fort Carson, Colorado: A Muslim army chaplain has been charged with espionage for stealing and passing secret documents to Iraqi radical Muslims.

Boston: The Islamic Society of Massachusetts is building a new mosque, the grandest in the country. It boasts the backing of radical Sheikh Yusuf Abdullah al-Qaradawi, an Egyptian now based in Qatar, who is praised for his "reformist interpretation of Islam."

Qaradawi has praised suicide bombings against Israeli

citizens, recently exclaiming at a Muslim youth group convention in Toledo, Ohio, "We will conquer Europe; we will conquer America." In March 2003, al-Qaradawi issued a religious ruling, a fatwa, encouraging Muslim women as well as men to become suicide bombers in the name of Allah and Jihad . . .

CHAPTER 84

Collierville, Tennessee

The farm near Collierville had been in the family for nearly three hundred years, ever since a Kragle settled it during the French and Indian Wars. The main house was over a century old, kept in repair these days by live-in husband-and-wife caretakers, the Blakes. The original log cabin remained in reasonably good shape near the family burial plot. In the private cemetery among headstones dating back to the eighteenth century were buried the General's wife, Rita, the current generation's matriarch, Little Nana Kragle, who had died on 9/11 when Jihadia flew commercial airliners into the World Trade Center, and Cassidy's wife, Kathryn, killed in the anthrax poisonings following 9/11.

Nearly a hundred people collected at "the Farm" for a long summer's weekend "stand down." General Kragle called it the Gathering of the Clans. In addition to the Kragle family back to the General's father, Jordan, and his CPI brother Mike, a noisy and robust crowd from Delta Force, the FBI, the CIA, Joint Chiefs of Staff, the Border Patrol, and others created a robust beehive of activity. For the first time since 9/11, not a single man had been killed on counterterrorism missions.

"I owe you, Top," Brandon said to Troop One's First Sergeant Alik Sculdiron. Brandon gave him all the credit for taking charge of the Aces Wild mission and getting Governor Malud and the detachment safely out of West Sahara.

"Yes, sir. We're about to whip our reprobates into shape, are we not?"

"Sergeant Sculdiron—?"

"Yes, sir?"

"Welcome to the team. You'll do."

"You'll do yourself, sir." A twinkle appeared in his eyes and they squinted almost shut. "You could do with a haircut and a mustache trim, sir."

Sergeant Gloomy Davis walked up with Sergeant Perverse Sanchez, Perverse with his arm in a cast and a sling. He suffered no permanent deformities thanks to Doc TB's skills in setting his broken bone under emergency conditions after the detachment's helicopter crashed in the desert.

"Top Sculdiron," Gloomy said, deadpan, "is it true you're going into the hospital for surgery with an enlarged prostitute?"

Sculdiron glared. "That's an enlarged *prostate*."

Mad Dog Carson overheard. He was on good behavior, so he left out "Fu-uck." He growled, "From what I've seen, I wouldn't exactly call it *enlarged*. Looks like a real penis, only smaller."

And they were off again with the rough, bantering humor of rough men who had experienced action together and were likely to see more.

Brandon caught Summer around the waist as she and Margo Foster breezed by in the process of setting a long buffet outside underneath the trees. She thrust a sack of buns at him, kissed him quickly on the mouth, and drew him along after her with an admonition to get busy warming buns.

"Is that an invitation?" he teased.

"Kragle, you're insufferable."

Diverse Dade, the Zulu with the lion's tawny eyes,

tossed a pine cone and caught Perverse in the rump. Diverse and the Troop's other gourmet cook, Ice Man Thompson, were in charge of deserts and hors d' ouvres.

"Perverse and Diverse," Mad Dog rumbled. "The Dynamic Duo. Just what Delta needs—a short spic and a tall jig."

"Chew are a bigot," Perverse said. "Chew daddy wore white sheets and dressed you funny."

"Chew on this," Mad Dog invited.

"Gloomy, chew never finished telling about the Delta trooper's last request when him and Dan Rather and Jesse Jackson got captured by cannibals."

"Oh, yeah," Gloomy recalled solemnly. "So, Dan Rather wanted a bowl of hot, spicy chili. Jesse Jackson wanted to sing *We Shall Overcome*. Did I mention the Delta trooper was Top Sculdiron? So Sculdiron turns to the cannibal chief with his last request. 'Kick me in the ass,' he says. 'What?' says the chief. 'You would mock us in your last hour?' 'I'm not kidding,' Top says. 'I want you to kick me in the ass.' So the chief did. Top goes sprawling, but rolls to his knees and pulls out a 9mm pistol and shoots the chief dead. In all the confusion, he then grabs an M4 from his ruck and sprays the cannibals with gunfire, killing some and sending the others running.

"Dan Rather and Jesse Jackson are in shock. They ask Top, 'Why didn't you just shoot them? Why did you ask the chief to kick you in the ass first?'

" 'What, and have you assholes call *me* the aggressor?' Top says."

Claude Thornton's new friends the Fruits—Appleton and Pear—pushed him around in a wheelchair while he recuperated from his Tulsa injuries. General Kragle pulled a chair next to Claude's and sat down in the sun. He sighed.

"It's over," he said.

Thornton shook his head. "Darren, my old friend, this is not going to be over for a very, very long time. We're in a war the outcome of which is still in doubt. Do you realize how close The Committed came to assassinating the President of the United States and taking over the U.S. government by using terrorists and terrorist tactics?"

"I suppose," the General pondered, "that we can count Senator Lowell Rutherford Harris out for the election."

"Don't underestimate him, Darren. Don't underestimate any of them. They'll never rest until America is no longer a shining city on a hill."

General Paul Etheridge, Delta commander Colonel Buck Thompson and FBI Agent Fred Whiteman joined them on the lawn. Whiteman still bore bruises, lacerations, and a friendly grudge against Thornton for having kicked him out of the car at the airport.

"They're fine, fine Americans," General Etheridge said, looking out across the lawn at all the young Deltas grab-assing and kidding each other. Etheridge had resumed command of CENTCOM. Nothing had been said about the blackmail attempt; nothing would be said. Every man had parts of his life that should be no one else's business. "We may never see their like again," Etheridge concluded.

"I disagree, Paul," General Kragle rejoined. "Men like them always seem to spring up whenever America needs them most."

Rhoda Hoffstetter, happily diddle-doodling more than ever since God delivered her from captivity, brought Cameron his favorite drink, a Mountain Dew, and looked him over adoringly. He was still on crutches and wrapped at the midsection from wounds received at Tindouf Airport.

"Those men, the terrorists at the airport—" she said,

misreading his melancholia. "God understands that you had to . . . had to . . ."

"Kill them? I know."

"We have containers being shipped to the Sahrawi camps for the children next week," she said. "I've included Zorgon's new arm. It's the best prosthesis I could find."

"Thank you, Rhoda. I'll write a check. And the chair?"

"A platform rocker the size of Tennessee. Zorgon will own a chair of his own." She chuckled. "Providing he can keep Swelma and his son out of it. Thank God they are all right."

"He deserves it," Cameron said.

"Chaplain Cameron, I'm returning to the camps myself shortly. Will you return with me?"

That surprised Cameron, considering all she had been through. She saw the look on his face.

"Turn your face to the sun and all the shadows fall behind you," she said.

"Sorry, Rhoda. I won't be able to for a while. I'll be in physical therapy for at least a month. You might talk to Brandon. He's going back to see that kid—Juba, I think—who crossed the desert with him. He says he owes him a lot of steak dinners. Brandon is about to change his attitude toward kids. I even heard him say he'd have considered adopting Juba if Juba hadn't chosen to stay with the Sahrawi. Juba said that was where he belonged. He sounds like an extraordinary young gentleman."

"From what I've seen, Chaplain, the Kragles are all extraordinary gentlemen."

"Are you really going back, Rhoda?"

"If I have the answer to man's salvation, what sort of human being would I be not to share it? It's what Jean would have done if she were alive. The war against hate and extremism must be fought not only by Special Forces but also by proselytes for Christ."

"You sound like Kelli," Cameron said, his blue eyes turning inward.

"What have you heard from her?"

"You knew her Uncle Ray committed suicide? Another casualty in the War on Terror. Kelli wrote that she needed some time for spiritual soul searching after . . . well, you know. After she had to shoot Abdul what's-his-name with the big nose. He was a cold-blooded murderer, but . . . I know what she's going through. I've been there."

"Will you see her again, Chaplain?"

Cameron looked far away. He was thinking of a woman from long ago named Gypsy Iryani whom he had not been able to bring back. He brought back Kelli.

"I hope so," he replied after a thoughtful pause. "If it's God's will," he added.

Uncle Mike was all over the place shooting pictures to document the event for family posterity. Brown Sugar Mama was so filled with love and happiness at having her family back together that she hugged everyone who got within her reach. She cornered Cassidy.

"Is you hearing whistles and bells?" she asked him.

"What *are* you talking about, Brown Sugar?"

She winked and tilted her head toward Margo, who was busy with Summer and Mollie Thompson, bringing more food out of the house. This many men could put away a lot of victuals. Cassidy laughed.

"Maybe a whistle or two," he admitted.

"Lawdy, Margo is so pretty and nice. The only way you could do better, honey chile," and she laughed uproariously, "is if she be a black lady."

Margo whispered to Summer when they paused to catch their breath. "Did you do it?"

Summer knew exactly what her friend was talking about. "I had a choice," she said. She laughed aloud and looked radiant. "In another month or so, girlfriend, I am going to be *so* fat. Fatter than Carole Blackburn, and her husband has to help her out of a car."

A commotion erupted. The loveable bear of a medic Doc TB raced across the lawn toward the main house, shouting, "Call an ambulance! Call an ambulance! My baby's having a wife!"

The baby wasn't about to wait for an ambulance. Sergeant Sculdiron brought up his car, a sensible four-door Chevrolet. Doc TB, his wife, and Mad Dog all piled into it for a quick run to the nearest hospital. The others prepared to follow right away. This baby was going to have the most unusual reception into this world that any baby had ever had—almost an entire Delta Force Troop plus counterterrorism people all the way up to CENT-COM, USSOCOM, and the FBI.

Brandon watched Top Sculdiron speed off with his cargo.

"Maybe it wouldn't be that bad to have a son," he pondered, thinking of Juba.

Summer looked at him, threaded both arms around his waist, and stood on tiptoes in order to reach his lips.

"Kragle," she said mysteriously, "have I got news for you."